THE FATES WE TAME

IRON OUTLAWS MOTORCYCLE CLUB
BOOK 8

S. COLE

Published By: Kadelo Group Ltd.
Edited by: Manu Shadow Velasco
Cover design by: Letitia Hasser at RBA Design
Photographer: Wander Aguiar

E-book ISBN: 978-1-7395788-8-6

Paperback ISBN: 978-1-7395788-9-3

To You
For loving my Outlaws the way you have.
Thanks to you, these men and these books have changed my life.

NOTE TO READERS

<u>Content Warnings</u>

As with any motorcycle club (MC) romance, the typical themes apply: language, violence, use of misogynistic language.

But within this book, there are some specific themes that may not be for all:

Arranged marriage

Masochism (it's hot, trust me!)

Pregnancy (very minimal mentions of secondary characters only)

PROLOGUE

There's something wrong. I keep trying to open my eyes, but I can't.

The temperature is changing.

Barometric pressure pushes against my body. My heart pumps sluggishly; my blood feels like molasses.

Voices come and go. I can't latch on to them long enough to figure out who they are.

Some undetermined period of time ago, someone touched me. I felt cold, like water on my face, but I wasn't drowning.

I feel too hot. Like I'm in a desert.

There's a flicker of memory. Limbs spread everywhere. Screams.

A bomb blast.

I need to respond. Why can't I wake up?

Need to stay awake until morning.

Things always feel better in the morning.

I fade; the darkness keeping me under rolls back over me like a storm. I lose my grip on the present.

The world is bright beyond my eyelids when I swim to the surface of consciousness again.

"...cerebral blood flow... metabolic dysfunction... outcome unknown until..."

Her voice is soft. I want to hold on to it, but I can't. I'm sucked back under, like a surfer tumbling in the waves.

Darkness comes again.

This time when I breach the surface, I can hear him. The voice has been here before. This time it's clear. Clear as day.

"So, anyway, Ari wants a bike. I said no. Next thing I know, Niro has extended Self-Defense Sundays to include training for how to get away on a motorbike, should they ever need to. Now every old lady is learning to ride and wants a fucking bike, Switch. So, you need to come back because if those girls hurt themselves riding machines that weigh ten times more than they do, I'm gonna kill Niro for putting the idea in their fucking heads."

I understand the words, but I don't.

"Anyway, you also need to come back because I owe you a lot of money from our bet. You were right. I was wrong. Ari is mine, and perfect. She wears my property patch now, and I'm waiting for you to give me shit about being a dumbass when I was trying to fight it. You need to go spend it on some tricked-out bike I can be grumpy about because I practically bought it for you."

The bed I'm in jostles.

Fuck me.

Internally, I scream.

I don't know why I can't force my way through this.

I try to make a sound, but nothing comes.

I concentrate.

Just a single limb. A digit.

Why does everything feel overwhelming? I'm choking silently. I focus on the finger.

It lifts from the bed. Just an inch.

Then it falls back to the sheet.

Why is my throat on fire?

I raise my finger again.

Tap.

Tap.

I'm choking. Drowning.

I ache to reach for my throat.

Tap.

Tap.

"Switch. Fuck. Switch! I'll get a nurse. Wait... Help, my friend..."

The words fade. I don't hear the rest.

Tap.

Tap.

I focus on my eyes. A millimeter open. The light is too bright.

Noises flood in. Beeping monitors. Then something swishing.

Tap.

Tap.

I open my eyes wider and see an ugly fluorescent light above me.

I can move my arm. First at the wrist, then the elbow. It's slow.

Jerky.

What the fuck?

My heart races; equipment beeps.

There's a flurry of activity around my bed. Excitement. I can feel it.

"Switch. You're back, motherfucker," the man says. He

squeezes my hand hard. Phone to his ear. "King," he says. "Switch is awake."

I steal my hand back and reach for my throat.

"Theo? Can you hear me, Theo?" It's an older woman in a white coat. "I need you to stop fighting while we remove your intubation."

The man takes my hand. "Here, hold on to me. Will this hurt him?"

I glance over to the woman, who shakes her head. "It's uncomfortable." She's peeling tape from around my face. "This is just like ripping off a Band-Aid, Theo. We'll have the tube out in a second."

I begin to fight on the bed. The man looms over me. "I've got him. Just do it."

"Theo," the nurse says, holding her palm to my forehead. "Theo." When she says the name a second time, it sinks in that she must be talking to me. I stop and look up at her.

Kind eyes, the color of walnuts.

"I'm going to need you to cough if you can as I try to pull this out. Okay?"

I nod.

"On the count of three," she says, and I do as she instructed. A long tube is ripped out of my throat through my mouth.

"There you go," she says, wiping away drool with a cloth.

I feel wrecked as I wheeze and gasp and suck in air.

The pressure against my chest releases, and I look around. The man who held me down kisses my cheek. "Welcome back, Switch. The rest of the brothers are on their way."

He talks like he knows me, but I force five words through my shredded vocal cords.

"Who...the fuck...are you?"

1

SWITCH

There may be a plush beige sofa, equally beige and plush carpet, and drapes that shimmer in the early-afternoon sunlight, but nothing changes the fact this is technically a hospital and I'm still technically fucked.

Not much better off than I was when I woke up in the hospital three weeks ago, which is why the club found this state-of-the-art, bougie-as-fuck rehab center. Vex, who is apparently my best friend, found the place. My dad said King, the club president, agreed to pay for everything. But this place is too rich for me. I don't fit in. Can't get a beer or a smoke except what members of the club are sneaking in for me.

"I asked how you feel about your friends rallying for you like this."

I look up at the woman asking the question.

Dr. Katarina Polunin's thick brown hair is pulled up in a weird braid that seems to loop around her head twice. Big gold earrings hang from her ears as she peers at me over her glasses.

Sitting back in the comfortable chair, I think about what I want to say. "It's...complicated. I'm..." Words don't come quickly. I have to think deeply about what I want to say sometimes before I can grab hold of fragments of it.

Dr. Polunin waits.

"Grateful," I finally blurt out. "Grateful."

"But?" she asks.

"It's overwhelming. They keep sending me..." I wave my phone as if that explains everything.

"They are in regular communication?"

I nod. "Photos. Videos. Lots of..." Fuck, the word escapes me again. "You know..." I gesture, typing with my thumbs on my phone. "Just tell me the fucking word."

"Messages?"

"Yeah, messages. And I'm struggling to remember what they tell me. I had a whole conversation with Spark, who I remember from before."

Before has become synonymous with any time occurring a decade or more ago.

The past ten years have disappeared.

"Even the most well-intentioned friends can hinder progress by constantly trying to force your memory to return by asking you about it. What did Spark tell you?"

I put my phone down, rest my elbows on my knees, and tug my hands through my hair. "I don't know. I remember he was...here, but I can't remember shit of what he said."

"You have two types of amnesia, Theo. The first is the more commonly known and understood. You've lost a portion of your past. The second is rarer and less known about. Anterograde memory is our ability to turn day-to-day events into memory. For example, I go on vacation, and I'm able to come home and tell my friends what I did each day. You have clear symptoms of anterograde amnesia because you can't recall what happened yesterday."

"How do I fix it?" I ask.

Dr. Polunin smiles softly. "Let's back up a little. You have two types of memory. Non-declarative memory. This is the part of your memory that has enabled you to shower and get dressed and would probably allow you to jump on your motorcycle and ride without having to relearn what all the switches and levers do."

The thought of my bike gathering dust almost chokes me. I spent five weeks in hospital and have been here just a few days. Winter's coming. Leaves swirling in the wind outside are a reminder that snow'll soon make biking that much harder.

"It's sometimes called procedural memory," she continues. "Because it mostly applies to tasks that are repetitive."

"That part I can do. I tied..." Fuck, what's the word for the things on my feet? "Sneakers... Then wondered why I can remember how to do that, but not remember what my house looks like."

"That's declarative memory. Recollection of facts or specific events, usually unique. And within that, you have episodic memory and semantic memory. Episodic is more autobiographical, like my example of remembering what happened on vacation. Semantic memory is more factual. As you said, you remember you own a house...but you just can't remember where it is or what it looks like."

I sit back in the chair and straighten my jeans. "How do I fix it?"

Dr. Polunin puts down her pen. "You are an incredible human being, Theo. I've read your records. In fact, I'd go as far as to say you are a miracle. Given the severity of your injury, I think it's a marvel you are not only alive but communicating with me like this in my office. You have speech and mobility."

"Yeah, but words." I leave it there.

She nods. "I know you have some challenges with retrieving the right words right now. But with your injuries, I'm shocked you even have that."

"Not enough," I manage.

"You are very early in your traumatic brain injury journey. *Very* early. It's unreasonable to expect faster progress with a TBI. This could be a multi-year journey."

"Years?" I don't want years. I want my fucking life back. One that comes without blinding headaches and nausea. One that gives me my skills back as a medic. I barely remember my first year out of basic medic training, let alone everything I learned since. "My parents won't go home... Every day. Here. Waiting. Mom is...exhausted."

"The brain is our most misunderstood organ. A heart is mechanical. It beats. Blood pumps. But the brain is still a mystery in many ways. You are in the absolute best place in the country to increase your chances of recovery. Do everything the staff asks of you. Make it your life's work to attend every physio and rehab appointment. Speak to the therapist to work your way through these emotional issues. Keep your stress levels low by following all the programs we have in place for you. You need to give your brain every possible chance of recovery. You're in safe hands, Theo. I promise you."

"Want to be...normal...me...again."

"I understand that. But you have to understand, there is no guarantee you will be who you were again. There is no guarantee you won't be either. Some people come through TBIs and are exactly the same. Most people don't lose language capacity because it's a neural pathway skill versus something memory based. But otherwise, there are huge differences. You are about as lucky as they come."

There is a knock on the door.

"My reminder that I have other clients outside, Theo. But as your primary care doctor, I will see you three times a week to review progress."

I nod and stand. "I appreciate it, Doc."

"It's Doctor Polunin. And thank you."

"Whatever you say, Doc." And I smile at her.

She shakes her head. "There is one last thing you could do for me."

My hand is on the door handle to leave. "What's that?"

"It would be very useful if one of your friends could fill in the blanks of what actually happened to you that night."

"I came off my bike. Likely a hit-and-run."

Dr. Polunin runs her tongue over her top teeth. "We rarely see clients like you, Theo. But I promise you won't be treated any differently because of your...affiliations. I looked carefully at your records. I looked at the images. I looked at the explanation of how you were found. The photograph of your helmet and bike. The statement from your"—she looks down at a piece of paper—"president."

"And?" I say.

"The description of how you were found, which side you were lying on, does not match the damage on your helmet."

My stomach drops. I've been told but struggle to recall what really happened. My head aches as I try to remember what King told me. Club business, maybe? That I was a hero. That comes in a lot of messages. Was my crash staged to make it look like a hit-and-run? That might have been it. But the details blur, like I'm travelling at two hundred miles an hour and my memories are standing at the side of the road as I whizz by.

Dr. Polunin raises her hands in the universal symbol of surrender. "Theo. I don't care. I don't care what you did. My only concern is to give you the absolute best treatment I can. I want you to recover from your brain injury every bit as much as you do. I will not cease until I figure out every possible form of therapy that will help. But it starts with the foundation that I know exactly how your brain was injured so I don't overlook something that could be vital later."

I've been around the club long enough, even in my limited memory, that I know we never talk about club business outside the club. And while every single part of me believes there is sincerity in what Dr. Polunin says, I couldn't risk telling her, even if I knew.

I tip my chin at the laptop on her desk. "It's all in your files, Doc. Happened like they said."

"You're putting a lot of faith in your friends."

"They're my brothers. That's what we do."

"I will see you on Thursday, Theo."

I head back to my room and pick up my swim shorts. I'm not allowed to lift weights. Too much strain. Everything has to be gentle. But I sure as fuck need to get my heart rate up. I strip and look at myself in the mirror, comparing what I see to the images I've been sent of myself from the past year. My messy dark blonde hair is longer on top and shorter on the sides. It was shaved on one side for surgery, and I just evened it out, so I have the fixings of a fauxhawk growing back. There are pinkish-red scars, still healing, where my skin was peeled back so my skull could be plated back together. I'm a little softer around the middle than before. Time in a hospital bed will do that to you.

Mom told me I always worked out. Apparently, I'd bang on about how it was good for my mental health. Even when

I was deployed, I worked out every day. I'm going to believe my past self and do what I can to use exercise to get better.

I'm covered in tattoos. Some I remember getting, like the four-leaf clover on my thigh I got in Mexico. Some I've figured out their importance, like Iron Outlaws and biker tattoos. Others, I have no idea. There are a set of initials on my shoulder, a date on my arm, and a poor quality tat of a fish blowing a kiss on my hip. Without context and history, they mean nothing to me.

I pull on my shorts and head to the rehab center's large pool on the ground floor. Its restful blue and white tiles and piped-in ocean sounds make it feel more like a spa. A lifeguard stands watching. I suppose the risk of drowning is high when you could black out in the water.

This place is wild. Depending on the severity of your injury, you can walk around the place like it's a fucking cruise ship. All-you-can-eat buffet. Pool. Massages, mandatory and optional. But in between, there are scheduled therapies and treatments, like speech pathology. Makes me feel sick that rich fuckers get all this and everyone outside these walls relies on an utterly broken health care model.

And yet, here I am. Using it anyway. Because why would I turn down the best medical treatment money can buy?

There are chaise lounges around the outside, but no one is sitting on them. On one are two towels and a black eye patch. A woman is in the pool, obviously a strong swimmer. She has that natural technique, where her head is in the water for a stroke, then turns away to suck in air on the next.

I grab a towel from the rack and put it on a lounger of my own. My body aches and pulls as I struggle to lift my T-shirt off. My left arm and hand don't work properly, but I don't want to think about that now.

As I turn to walk to the pool steps, the woman is

climbing out. She's in a utilitarian black one-piece, short but curvy as fuck. Thick thighs, solid ass, and snatched waist. It takes her a minute and the use of a railing to stand. Her gait is unsteady as she limps to her sun lounger. As I lift my gaze, the scars begin. Over her arm, her shoulder. She lifts one of the towels to her face, then looks around as she lowers it.

"Shit," she says as she spots me, immediately dropping the towel and scrambling for the eye patch. She snaps it on over her wet hair, but it's too late. I already saw the scar that crosses her cheek, which I'm guessing is the reason she has no eye.

Bizarrely, it doesn't faze me at all. Must be my medic training I don't remember. "Hey, it's okay," I say.

She runs her thumb beneath the patch, then turns to face me. "Don't want to scare anyone when I don't have my prosthetic eye in, but I find swimming in it aggravates me."

"Former army...medic," I reassure her.

She smiles. "Another patient said I could be Captain Jack Sparrow for Halloween in a couple of days."

I remember that movie coming out. Went to watch it with King. "Pretty sure he didn't have an..." I can't think of the word for her black eye thing, even though I had it a minute ago.

"Eye patch," she provides.

"Yes. You're more sparrow the bird than Sparrow the pirate."

She has a pretty smile and healthy rack. The funny thing is, I don't remember most of the sex I've had in my life, but the idea of fucking her tits comes to me.

"More sparrow the bird than pirate. I like it. I'm Sophia," she says, bundling herself up into a towel.

"Theo," I say. Everyone at the club calls me *Switch*, and I remember enough about club life that it's the biggest compliment, bond, and acceptance a man could wish for. But that feels like a life I'm not ready to claim yet because it fills the years I don't remember.

And I can't remember how I got the name, which seems pivotal to feeling comfortable using it.

"Let me guess. A construction accident."

I step into the water, because the way she keeps running her tongue over her lower lip is giving me a boner. The first organic, non-morning wood I've had since the accident. "Bike wreck."

"Ouch. Mine was a car. Until I apparently thought it could fly like an airplane and went airborne. At least, so I've been told." She chuckles at that. "Anyway, enjoy your swim, Theo," she says, and I watch as she leaves in the direction of the changing room.

I guess everyone here has their own story.

Her body's a mess, and she likes to overshare.

But she's a pretty one.

And as I step down into the pool, I find I want to know more about her.

2

SOPHIA

My driver's license tells me who I am.

Sophia Chiara Viscuso. Born twenty-five years ago.

It shows me what I looked like before...

It's the only thing in the world I trust. It was returned to me by the police in a plastic bag with the only other thing they found in my car: a shattered phone.

Apparently, it was with me the day I went through the windshield of a car. A car that isn't even mine, which I was apparently driving erratically. Without a seat belt.

Before I swerved off the road and hit a tree.

My license is how the people who helped me on the scene knew who I was.

The mirror reminds me that I no longer look like the woman on my license. She's a stranger to me even though some things remain the same, like my long dark hair, minus the regrowth at the back of my neck. I know my prosthetic eye is necessary. I've been told all the reasons why. But I'm struggling to accept the changes to my physical appearance.

I couldn't bring myself to tell Theo the full story. I'm not sure why, because I'm usually an open book.

My family has been amazingly patient. Even when I asked them to see proof that we were actually family. My mother used it as an opportunity to pull out my baby books and tell me everything from the beginning, right down to how many stitches she needed post-labor. I saw pictures of a little girl in frilly dresses and knits. School photographs with bad haircuts. School plays with hideous costumes. A cap-and-gown graduation. A twenty-first birthday party with my *famiglia*. Eating a large dish of *pasta con le sarde*. Celebrating Stragusto in Trapani with my broader family and hunkered down at home celebrating the feast of Saint Agatha of Sicily.

My brothers were typical brothers, I guess. They told me stories involving escaped frogs and bloodied noses and my first date with a neighborhood boy they terrified. They showed me pictures of private air travel and concerts and, in the more recent pictures, lots of champagne.

We're obviously close.

They call me *Puparu*. It means *puppeteer*. It's a nickname I was given by my father for pulling my brothers' strings to get them to do as I said.

But when they showed me the photographs at the start of this journey five months ago, I had this weird feeling that I was looking at someone else's life.

Certainly, I was there in the images, but I wasn't.

I have no memory of any of it.

And I didn't have a real connection to any of them beyond them telling me I was loved, which felt...awkward. My initial feelings toward them were that of any stranger I saw on the street. In the months since, thanks to their efforts, I've learned to love them in my own way. They've been fierce advocates for my recovery. I worked for my father, but he won't let me even think of trying to find a way to work yet. Instead, he pays for everything.

Despite living in the rehab unit, I've visited my luxury apartment a handful of times and been to my parents' house to spend time there in the past month as my independence has grown. I'm not a hostage here, but there is safety in having on-call support at night. Of having easy access to various therapies. And of having some kind of space from the overwhelming worry my family has for me.

Plus, the other places feel...foreign. There is evidence of me in both places. Photographs. Clothes that fit me. But in other ways, neither place reflects me. I didn't like either of the books I took from my bookshelves, ones my youngest brother assured me were my favorite. And the clothes are all too...much. Too expensive, too restricting, too impractical.

All I want now is softness against my skin. Clothes that hide my scars and don't hinder my movements in any way.

I feel guilty for all of it. My therapist says it's normal to harbor the feelings I do. Their generosity overwhelms me. They pay for everything. For the care here. For my apartment because I have no work. They've bought me a new phone, new laptop, and new clothes.

And yet, I may need them to help me find a new place to live. Somewhere that will give me a new start. Maybe on a lower floor, so if the elevator ever breaks down, I don't have to walk up eleven flights of stairs.

I'm early for my session, but I no longer want to be in my room. I debate going to the roof to get some steps in on the track up there, but I find myself heading in the direction of the lobby.

"Morning, Angelique," I say when I pass the administration station on my floor of the three-story building.

"Morning, Sophia. Where are you off to?"

"Group speech therapy. Where already-damaged brains go to die from boredom." Then I laugh. Too hard for what I said. It's the one thing I can't control. You could tell me I have a month left to live and I'd likely howl. Famine? I'd laugh. Two-week-old baby thrown from the top of a twenty-floor building?

I laugh at the thought of it, even though, intellectually, I know it's not funny.

Angelique shakes her head.

I close my eyes and take three deep breaths. My strategies are breathe, adjust, think.

BAT for short.

The breath helps me calm. Adjusting helps me change my posture. I hunch my shoulders when I laugh. Thinking means to take a moment and process whether my response is appropriate.

"You're gonna be out of here soon," Angelique says. "Not sure the rest of the world is ready for you yet."

I catch a glimpse of my reflection in the glass behind Angelique. My eye patch is a black outline on my face. "Not sure I'm ready for the rest of the world."

As I pass through the lobby of the center, I see my father sign in. Next to him is a tray with two take-out cups and a folded paper bag.

"Sophia," he says when he sees me. As always, he's dressed in a suit. This one is a charcoal pinstripe that fits too snugly around the middle.

He kisses each of my cheeks and then puts his palm to my face. "You look tired. You getting enough rest?"

I smile. He says that every time he sees me. "I'm fine."

He hands me the bag. "I only got ten minutes, but want to eat with me?"

"I'm early for my session so your timing is perfect." We find a spot to sit, and I open the bag. "Cannolo Siciliano? At this time in the morning?"

Papà laughs. "Fried dough and ricotta. It's practically a grilled cheese sandwich."

"Not sure that would hold up in front of a judge."

"Freshly made by Tommaso Buscetta's mamà. The *granita di caffè* is from a Sip of Sicily, your favorite. Eat. Just don't tell your mamà I ate them too."

He winks and take some out of the bag when I offer it to him.

"Busy day?" I ask.

He shrugs. "Your brother Leo has been sniffing around Little Mikey's girl. He's gonna get his balls shot off before he even grows into them. Gonna have a word with him to stay on the right side of the Aglieris."

I almost choke on my coffee. "What about work?"

"Got a meeting with Alessio at ten. We pushed ahead with the purchase of that land adjacent to the docks you suggested. Tough negotiation, but they came down in price just like you said they would."

I wish I could remember the land and the deal he's talking about. "You know, I can help. I mean, maybe not as much as I used to. But if I could get access to my old work files, who knows, it might—"

"Soph. You gotta just focus on this. A time will come for work. You don't need to worry about money. We got you. Plus, it means you're free when I need a partner in crime to eat cannoli with in the morning. You remember anything yet?"

He always asks. I wish he wouldn't. There is nothing quite like feeling you're letting your father down every day.

I shake my head. "Not yet. You'll be the first to know if I do."

We finish our pastries and coffee with some small talk about being out of here by Thanksgiving, and I hug him when he leaves.

It's odd. He loves me way more than I currently love him because he's a man I've known for less than twenty weeks.

Alessio, at thirty-three, is my eldest brother. He's so smart and thoughtful. Luca and Leonardo, the twins, are thirty. Luca is intense. Leo is easier going. Shit, I have two more, and I can't remember their names. My short-term memory isn't firing on all cylinders today. I pull out my phone to remind myself.

Marco and Enzo.

Marco is twenty-eight and down in Atlantic City, so I don't see him as often. Enzo is twenty-six and is in Sicily. He came straight over when I was first injured but has had to go back to return to work. We've video chatted since, but it's a little stilted and awkward.

I don't remember any of them. Not a single memory, even the days immediately after I came out of the coma. It's all a blur.

None of them know why I was in the car either.

All I have is what I know of them now. They're all older than me. I'm the baby.

Friends came to visit in the beginning, but over time, I've become an obligation. I'm lucky if I see more than a couple of friends a month now. Instead, my friends are here. Dr. Polunin. Raheel, my massage therapist. Lori, who pushes me to my physical limits. Patients who have come and gone.

We're an unusual collection of misfits unified by one thing: the rehabilitation of the brain.

When I reach the group room, several people are sitting

around the table. There's Jamie. He arrived two weeks ago after three months in the hospital because he smashed up his car too. I'm slightly envious that he remembers his accident. He'd owned the supercar his father had bought him for his twenty-first birthday for approximately seven hours when he spun out on the highway. The paralysis affects both legs and his lower torso, and he's still in the raging anger phase we all go through. I wave, and he tips his chin.

Belle-Odette is a New York maven who tripped over the leads of her five Chihuahuas. The pavement and her skull had a disagreement when she landed, and she now finds it impossible to remember anything new. There's a fifty-fifty chance she'll remember my name today, but she can tell you everything about her dogs, which get brought over here in a black town car three times a week to see her.

I was the same as her when I was brought here after being discharged from the hospital. In the early stages of emergence from a coma, most people have issues writing new memories. Which is really tough if you can't remember any part of your life before, like I can't.

"Morning, Sophia." Erin, the language pathologist, points to a seat next to the only man who doesn't look like he belongs here.

"Morning, Theo," I say, recalling his name from our conversation by the pool two days ago. I saw him in the dining area yesterday with two people I'm guessing were his parents.

He glances up at me, his gaze...speculative. "Morning, Sparrow."

I suppose I shouldn't feel quite so melty that I have a nickname. It's probably because it's a genuine interaction I remember and the fact his face is so damn gruff and attractive, he belongs on one of those fancy cologne ads.

Theo is unlike any other man I know, which, let's face it, is not an extensive list, seeing I only have my family and the men here as reference. But he has the powerful combination of size and self-assurance.

It certainly helps that he's got sharp cheekbones that cast shadows.

I don't know what he does for work. I don't know why he has all the tattoos up his arms and over his back. He scares almost everyone else here with his presence. No one sits on either side of him, as if keeping their distance.

But I like his eyes. Maybe it's the fact he still has two of them.

I chuckle at my inner dialogue.

"Should we break out of here and go on a road trip to Vegas to see if our brain injuries turned either of us into a card shark?" I ask him.

He huffs a laugh but continues to look at the table in front of him. "Not sure that's how it works."

"Sophia, not everyone uses humor as a coping mechanism," Erin says. "You know this. Perhaps try to consider other people's feelings and read the room."

"Sorry," I say, not entirely sorry at all. A girl's gotta do what a girl's gotta do to figure out how to move on with her life with no discernible—or memorable—skills and mobility issues. If humor is it, then so be it.

A travel mug with a handle sits to his left side. He hasn't told me why he's here, but I can see he has trouble with his left arm as he reaches for it and uses it. The cup shakes, and he transfers it to his right hand.

"Ready for another riveting installment of regurgitating last week's news?" I ask.

He glances my way. "Can't...wait."

Oh, and he still spaces his words out, as if the next word

hasn't appeared in his mind yet. My issue was I'd just skip words all together. It wasn't that I couldn't find them. I just didn't know they existed or that grammatically I needed to use them.

"Okay," Erin says. "Let's make a start. As a reminder, this session is about helping you all with general communication in social settings. Pick any news article from the piles scattered around the table. I want you to read one, and then I want you to pick out the key facts of the article. Then we're going to work on sharing those details with the group."

Belle-Odette stands suddenly.

"Can you sit down please, Belle?" Erin asks.

"The dogs. Feeding with..." The next few words are mumbled.

"The dogs are at home with Gerald," Erin explains patiently.

I know some people have life-changing revelations about their career after something like this. You hear about the rehabbed woman who changes careers and retrains to help people just like her once she's healed, but I wouldn't do this job for all the money in the world.

It's chaos and requires vast amounts of patience.

Belle-Odette looks confused. "But... dogs they..."

"I walked them...and fed them," Theo says. "The little brown one was"—he closes his eyes tight for a second—"happy as...fuck to see me."

I snap my head to look at him, but he's just looking straight at Belle-Odette, who puts her hand to her heart. "Oh, thank you. Coco and I...went shopping yesterday." She smiles, then sits.

Confabulation. That's another thing you learn here. There's a version of amnesia where you just talk bullshit. You can completely rewrite what you think happened yesterday. Belle-Odette is always here. There is no way she went shopping with Coco, but I bet she'd pass a polygraph test if you asked her if she did.

"Get started on your news article," Erin says, and comes over to our table. "Theo," she says. "Thank you for trying to help, but it doesn't help Belle-Odette if we lie to her. It's important for her to know what's really happening in her life."

"Maybe, Doc. But to what...end? She's got clear difficulty determining...fuck me..." He breathes like we've all been taught.

I breathe with him out of habit. A part of me wants to put my hand on his back and reassure him we're used to waiting long periods for someone to speak here.

"Reality." The word comes out on a sharp snap of breath. "She's not in her home. Her dogs..." He rubs his right hand on his chest. "Give her peace, yeah?"

"Valid point, Theo," Erin concedes.

"That was really nice of you," I say, finally.

Theo shrugs. He reaches for his coffee again, but his shaking seems worse. His fingers brush the handle, and it tips over. Thankfully, it's in a cup with a lid, so it doesn't immediately spill everywhere, but I jump from my seat and launch myself across the table to catch it before it rolls out of reach.

"Parkour," I shout, even as my hip nails the hardwood edge, making me wince.

Theo shakes his head. But I see the slight twitch at the corner of his mouth. "Sit down...before...hurt."

Belle-Odette gives us a retelling of...something. I'm not sure. But we all sit riveted because she's trying so hard.

Tears sting my eyes because I remember being her when I first arrived. With a missing eye, a scarred face, not knowing anyone, trusting even fewer. The world felt, and still does, like a dangerous place.

My team has been making really strong suggestions that I'm ready to leave, but outside this building is a terrifying world I'm unfamiliar with. Leaving, as a concept, scares me.

Theo gives us a rundown of a Nets versus Knicks game. He holds his composure right to the end, even when he struggles to find the language he needs. When he's done, he skims the article like a pebble across water. I watch as it glides off the table and lands near Belle-Odette's feet.

We finish the session after I repeat the details of a play review by a major theatre critic. "In conclusion, the revival of *Chekhov's Seagull* inevitably fell flat," I say.

I manage not to laugh, but only because I breathe the heck out of the ending. I can feel the giggling vibrations in my chest though.

"You want to grab lunch together?" I ask Theo as we prepare to leave. It's always a logistical challenge. Wheelchairs, walkers, and people unsteady on their feet like me. There are porters and carers who arrive to help people move to their next session. "I've seen you looking sad and mopey all by your lonesome in the cafeteria."

Theo glances my way. "Perhaps I just like my own... company."

"Or perhaps you haven't made any friends yet?"

"Or I"—he winces—"don't like...talking now."

"Fair. But I can fill the silence. My small talk is one of my greatest strengths. Ask anyone."

He rubs his hands across his face, then glances at his watch. "You ...hitting on me, Sparrow?"

"God, no." I laugh. "To hit on someone is way above my pay grade. You're speaking to someone who can't even remember ever going on a date. Don't make me eat alone just because you're in a bad mood. I don't have massage therapy for another ninety minutes."

"Fine."

We walk to the restaurant in silence. While the paintings and window dressings and flowers are fancy, the easy-to-clean tables are industrial, and the setting is sterile. Eating with unstable limbs can be messy. Some people choose to eat in their rooms with their carers. I did for the first month I was here. After a while, the embarrassment I felt at being seen eating in public came second to feeling trapped in my room.

There are all kinds of special seats depending on needs, but Theo leads us to a table by the window without asking me where I want to sit.

A man who takes charge.

I secretly like it.

He takes a second to pull out my chair before sitting in his own.

"So, tell me more about what happened to you," I insist.

Because now that I have his attention, it's suddenly imperative I know more about him.

3

———

SWITCH

I don't know why I said yes to eating lunch with Sophia. The only thing on my mind is to get the fuck out of here at the earliest possible moment. My focus is on my physio, regaining my strength, and figuring out how to string two words together properly.

And trying not to question why my mom looks so tired, only to be met with instant dismissals that the bed in my house isn't comfortable. That she's gotten so used to the warm weather in Florida that the damp Jersey fall air is no good for her lungs and she's under the weather.

I'm not buying any of it.

So, I think, maybe, that I took one look at Sophia with her long dark hair and pretty lips and thought perhaps I just wanted to be around someone who understood for a change. That I could escape the sympathetic glances.

"We could always start with the basics. Spastic hand paralysis or flaccid paralysis?" Sophia asks, glancing down at my hand.

Not exactly the understanding I was looking for. I slide

my hand off the table and rest it in my lap. "That's a pretty... forward question."

"I'll tell you mine if you tell me yours." She laughs, and it's a pretty sound.

I shake my head as the food I ordered at breakfast this morning appears in front of me without my having to ask. I pick up the fork and firmly press the tines into my finger until they leave a row of four tiny yet imperfect divots.

The sharp pain of them centers me.

"Mine was spastic," she says, flexing her fingers in front of her.

She has no idea how reassuring hearing that is as she uses her napkin and holds a water glass like it's a crystal ball. "I see orthotic devices, mobilization exercises, and grip and pinch strengthening in your future."

"Funny. How long did...it take?"

"My hand? Four months, but I'm going home soon, not that I remember home."

"Amnesia?" I ask.

Sophia nods.

"I've lost about a decade," I say. "I remember enlisting but nothing beyond basic training. I remember some of my brothers, but not all of them. Some of them look so different to the last time I remember them. I don't remember any of their old ladies except one because I knew Gwen when we were kids."

"It sucks, doesn't it?" Sophia pauses for a moment and looks out of the window. "All of mine is gone. Every single memory. I don't even remember my family. It's like living in this other world where you once existed but don't anymore. Or like someone set you down as a blank canvas in the world."

There's a wistfulness. She comes across as so funny and

confident and irreverent, but I think back to seeing her panic when I saw her missing eye.

Then I pause for a minute. I remember something that actually happened from two days ago. Maybe that's progress.

Neither of us eats our food.

"I'm sorry, Sparrow," I say.

She shrugs and smiles like it doesn't matter. But the smile doesn't touch the corner of her eye. "We can only move forward."

"Aren't you angry about it?" I ask.

The mask slips. "Furious," she says, her voice a strangled whisper. "Some days I think if I let the rage out, I'd blow all the windows out of this room." Then she sniffs, straightens a crease in her sweater, and sits up straighter. "Still, we've got our breathing exercises to get us through, right?"

The words are laced with sarcasm that matches my own feelings on the subject.

I pick up the water glass and watch the liquid slosh inside. "I can't ride my bike."

My body has been too broken, my vision too blurred, my hand too shaky to get on my bike, even though I can remember how to do it.

"That really sucks. I'm sorry it's stopped you from doing something you clearly loved. My parents want me to move home and live with them, and while I can't remember living with them when I was younger, or living alone since, I'm certain it's a recipe for disaster."

She laughs at this, and I can see the tug of war in her features. It's as if her laughter is uncontrolled, even as she looks sad from our conversation.

"Bat," she mutters. "Just bat."

"Bat?" I ask.

"Breathe, adjust, think," she says. She closes her eyes, breathes, rolls her shoulders back, and then settles.

When she opens her eyes, she's composed again.

"Clever trick."

She circles her finger around the room. "That's why we pay this place the big bucks. Well, mainly we pay them the big bucks because we're in a five-star hospital with views over Central Park and caviar on the menu, but you know what I mean."

"That's a fair assessment."

"It's pretty privileged to scoff at the fact I have access to the fanciest health care, but it can't fix everything. I laugh at the most inappropriate topics. I still struggle with figurative things and have trouble remembering anything new. I forgot two of my brothers' names just this morning and had to check on my Notes app."

She picks up her fork and starts to eat, so I follow her lead.

I'm sure the food is perfectly seasoned, but everything has tasted like cardboard since the...

I struggle to think the word *accident*.

I force myself to try to remember the details I couldn't recall yesterday. What did King and Halo tell me about the accident? The lie is I was out on my bike and was the victim of a hit-and-run. My president found me on the side of the road.

But what was the truth? Halo and his old lady think I'm a fucking hero. Something to do with her. Saving her from something. Stepping in the way of something meant for Halo. I can sense darkness. A warm summer night maybe.

A baby?

Fuck. Who has a baby?

"Spastic," I say finally. "I struggle to bend my fingers...hurts to squeeze."

She puts her cutlery down and reaches for my hand. I've got no idea why I offer it to her, palm up. Within a second, she's somehow maneuvered her hands to either side of mine and is stretching my palm, opening it up. Then her thumbs begin to work on the muscles that feel as though they are in a permanent state of spasm.

I can barely hold back a groan.

Perhaps I should feel bad that her lunch is going cold, but I can't bring myself to remind her to eat. I close my eyes and let her do whatever this fucking sorcery is.

For the second time since the accident, my cock perks up and takes notice. Both boners have been because of Sophia. Sensory deprivation is a thing when you're in medical care. The only people who touch you are generally doing something to you. Poking you with needles, cutting parts of your body open, changing dressings. Even bed baths, the most intimate of things, feel cold because there is a high level of embarrassment, and mine were always done by a male nurse called Jude.

The touch of a woman is...

My mind drifts. For a moment, I try to pretend I'm anywhere other than here. On the bank of a lake. A beach. Even the clubhouse. But this bothers me because I don't know which room is mine now, and in my daydream, my dad is still there in his cut that proclaims him to be road captain, even though I know he and Mom retired to Florida. Wait, was he wearing a cut when he came by on...?

I can't remember what day he came before today. I can't remember if he was wearing a cut then or not. I remember jack fucking shit.

I open my eyes in frustration. Sophia is focused on my palm.

"You've been here too long if you know how to do that," a man says.

"Learned from the best, Raheel." Sophia glances to the man walking by the table. "Raheel is my physical massage therapist. Has been since I first arrived. He's amazing."

Raheel grins at Sophia, but it's the kind of smile that says he's proud of his patient. Not anything more.

Which...why the fuck do I care if it's anything more or not?

"That's very kind of you, Sophia. I hear you're considering leaving us soon."

"Everybody thinks I'm ready," she says, but there's a wariness in her tone.

Her four-word answer tells me everything I need to know. That she's not ready. But my guess from the way she is around me, and the way she spoke in our session, is that her reluctance has nothing to do with her physical capabilities.

"You'll crush it," Raheel says.

"Of course," she says, too brightly.

He falls for it.

And through it all, she keeps massaging my palm, and I'm too much of a selfish dick to stop her.

A young woman appears behind Raheel. "Your guests are here, Theo. I've put them in the main visitors' room."

I slide my hand from Sophia's. "Thanks for lunch, but I have to go."

We both look at my barely touched plate, but she smiles. "Anytime. Let me know if you want a rain check. Or another hand massage. I'm good at them."

"Maybe, Sparrow." I stand and push my chair out behind me.

The main visitors' room is large, with multiple different seating areas. It's plush, but at the same time, you can tell there is accommodation for mobility devices and different needs. King, Vex, and Halo look utterly out of place amongst the sea of beige furnishings and piped-in elevator music.

The other people seated in the guest area keep a wide berth from them.

"Switch." Halo stands, the first to see me. His eye is bruised, his knuckles raw, like he's just been in a fight. "You're looking good."

The use of my road name chafes. "Wish I could say the same for you."

I smile because they are expecting me to, and suddenly I realize Sophia and I have that in common. We're both saying what we're supposed to. I'm *supposed* to be happy to see my friends when the truth is infinitely more complex.

King stands and hugs me, but he winces and returns his right arm to its place in front of his body, as if it's in an invisible sling. "How are you feeling?" he asks.

"Like I need...a ride."

"Man, that sucks. Can only imagine," Vex says as he hugs me. "Must be utterly frustrating."

They all take a seat on the fancy sofa and chairs. Vex has come see me most. He seems to understand more than the others that this is going to be a long game. And that trite get well wishes barely scratch the surface of how I'm truly feeling. He doesn't bombard me about the past but waits until I ask specific questions.

I've been told by multiple people that he was my best friend before, and I'm starting to see why.

I look down at my hand, which actually feels some temporary relief from the stiffness and cramping I felt earlier. It still aches, but it's not as acute.

"What the hell happened to you all?" I ask.

King glances at Halo, Vex, then back to me. "Some trouble on a run last night. We sorted it though. How's the physio going?"

I don't like the way he changes the topic, so I shake my head. "Same shit as...last time we talked." Although, in fairness, I don't one hundred percent remember that conversation. Just a vague memory of King's presence. My medical team assures me this is all quite normal for a traumatic brain injury. Allegedly, I should be thrilled that I am as *compos mentis* as I am.

Instead, I feel disassociated from my life, who I am, what's important to me. My memories and aspirations and goals in life are a decade old. I look in the mirror and the person I am bears no resemblance to the person I last remember seeing there.

Lost my shit with my psychologist when I mentioned that my image catches me off guard every time I see myself, and then he insisted on digging in to it with me, which I really didn't want to do.

I have more ink, more muscle, and more lines around my eyes now. I hope to fuck it's because I laughed a lot in the last decade.

"Anything coming back to you?" Halo asks.

I fucking hate that question. Well-meaning as my brothers are, it's usually their first question. I shake my head. "That's why I didn't recognize you when I"—I search for the words—"woke up. The hair. The...beard." Because in my head, the last time I saw Halo, he was on leave from the Navy SEALs. He had a buzz cut, was clean-shaven. The long-haired, bearded man was so unfamiliar.

And King was still a mischievous teen, hanging out with Clutch and me in the garage and the clubhouse yard before

Vex had even joined. They hadn't even gotten their road names back then, and it's taking me a minute to remember them. Every now and then I need to double-check their cuts to remind me.

"How's Rae and...?" I seek Halo's old lady's name, but it floats away from me.

"Ari," Halo reminds me.

"Yeah, Ari."

Halo grins. "Too fucking good for me. Here, she sent you these, just like last week." He hands me a container that has a bunch of cookies and protein balls and oat bars.

More food. I'm gonna gain fifty pounds while I'm in here.

"You aren't allowed to bring food in," says a woman seated nearby. She's clearly waiting for someone, as she has a handful of expensive-looking gift bags in front of her.

"At twenty-five grand a week, we'll bring in whatever the fuck we want," King says.

He's changed from my last memory of him. He has the confidence of his father, Camelot. Sure and steady. Unyielding. We used to watch our fathers when they were the patched-in members, and we were simply teens who couldn't fucking wait to live the life. I remember how King used to shadow his dad. Listening. Watching. Learning.

It looks like it paid off.

I wonder if I've become the kind of man I aspired to be back then.

"Where'd the club get the money to...?" I swirl my hand in the air. "You know. This."

Vex leans forward, moving a little closer. "We got it when I was able to—"

"We have the funds. That's all you need to worry about," King says.

"Sorry," Vex says, as if he'd forgotten something important King had told him. Then he gives me a knowing look, like it's paining him to not tell me the truth.

I glance at Halo, then King. Neither of them looks straight at me.

"What the hell is going on?" I ask.

King rubs a hand over his jaw. "Just a precaution."

"A precaution for what?" I ask.

"It's probably best we don't share club business with you...for now. While your head's...fucked. It gives you options."

"What do you mean it gives...what you said?" My vision begins to waver. A sharp ache begins at my temple. It happens multiple times a day.

I need painkillers. I need an ice pack. I need a dark room and quiet.

King turns squarely to face me. "You could leave the Outlaws. Get your ink lasered, and you are free to go. You don't remember shit about this club and what we have or haven't done. You could go down to Florida with your folks. I'd sign off on it."

Leave the Outlaws?

My heart thuds. Being in the club was the most important thing I wanted when I was old enough to even know what being an Outlaw meant. I'm certain nothing has changed, seeing I was injured on club business.

My blood pressure escalates.

The wavering in my vision gets worse.

"No. I might not know who...I am. But I know I'm...a fucking Outlaw."

And as the last word spills from my lips, the world goes dark.

4

SOPHIA

It's two days later when I see Theo again in the physio room. He's lying on his stomach, lifting a tennis ball over a small cone as sweat pours down his forehead. He's wearing a black tank top and athletic shorts, and I can see the muscles in his shoulders ripple with exertion. His hand shakes, and I will it, and him, to make another pass of the ball.

When he knocks the cone over, he tosses the ball, and I see his lips form the word *fuck*.

I heard from Jamie that Theo had passed out in the area we greet guests. Said he went down like a stone and that one of his biker friends caught him before getting help.

He said they all wore leather vests that said they were members of the Iron Outlaws. Of course, I searched the internet for them. A handful of documents from the Department of Alcohol, Tobacco, and Firearms said they were a motorcycle gang. Once I knew, I hurried to my room to process the information.

Like I did when I searched myself online to see if I left any footprint and found out my father is allegedly Mafia, a

Cosa Nostra man of honor. I've researched what that means, and learned the word *Mafia* originated in Sicily but probably has Arabic roots.

I then watched every Mafia movie I could find.

I'm not sure I like being part of this family, but the images my family has shared show the complete opposite.

A luxury lifestyle. Parties with red lipstick. And I always have a glass of champagne in my hand.

My mom showed me our text messages. We clearly loved each other.

I was given a new phone by my father when I moved here, as my old one was damaged in the crash. The contacts were empty of everyone except my immediate family, but it began to fill up a little as people came to visit. Seemingly, I had no social media accounts. Alessio told me it was against our father's rules for our safety.

But I've become friends with every single person who has passed through these doors. I've built a life within these walls that feels safe, and I'm tempted to feign a fainting fit just so I can stay another month.

I've also thought about checking myself out and going to rebuild my life where no one knows me and has no expectations of me. But with no understanding of my own independent wealth nor access to any of it, I don't know where to start.

"Okay," Lori says. "I need one more circuit of the course."

"You're a cruel master." I wipe the sweat from my brow.

Lori chuckles. "So I've been told. You've gotten this far. I'm not going to let you bail now. Let's go, Sophia."

The circuit is designed to test my weaknesses. It includes steps and ramps, all with safety bars in case I need them. But the whole idea is that I don't use them. I walk towards the first low box I have to step up onto and then off.

"Lead with your left foot," Lori reminds me.

I take a breath, build up to it, then lean to my right a little so I can maneuver my foot high enough to clear the step. Instead, I kick the box slightly.

"Try it again, Sophia," Lori encourages.

"In my brain, it felt like I cleared it."

"Perception and balance can all change. With only one eye, your brain is grappling with depth perception issues. Try it again. You nearly had it."

I do as she says, and with a Herculean push, I manage to get my left foot up, swiftly followed by my right. My arms raise automatically to try and create some balance on top of the box.

"And down with your left foot too."

I look at Lori. "I'm taking a minute to celebrate the tiny miracle that is getting up here before I face the death-defying feat of getting off it."

Lori claps and cheers for about two seconds. "There you go. We celebrated. Step down."

I do as she says, but I pick up a little momentum and stumble forward a few steps. "Guess my line-dancing days are over," I say.

"You line-danced?" Lori asks.

I shrug. "No idea. My brain was restored to factory settings, remember?"

"Funny," Lori says. "Now the ramp."

I complete the whole circuit with some version of all the usual issues I'm currently working on. Walking up a steep ramp burns my legs, and I feel like I have to drag my leg the last few inches. My knees continue to turn in a little, but it's nowhere near as bad as it was at the beginning. There is progress. I can see it. Even better, I can feel it.

For a moment, I almost believe that I can get my life back to normal.

Theo finishes his session the same time as me. His hoodie is slung over one shoulder as he sips from a water bottle. Tattoos cover most of his body; I notice the words *fear none* are tattooed across his knuckles.

He has some unusual markings over his pecs. They aren't tattoos, but they are deliberate patterns of raised red lines, like scars.

"Good session?" I ask as we reach the exit at the same time.

"Depends how you define good," he says. "Feel...weak. Hold this, please." He hands me his water bottle while he tugs his hoodie awkwardly over his head, then takes it back. "Thanks."

As I walk alongside him, my limp feels a little more pronounced. It leaves me feeling a little...ashamed. Even though I know he just struggled to move a tennis ball. I feel like I want to be *her* around him. The woman I once was.

My therapist would be mad at me. I once told her I needed to get better so my family could move on with the rest of their lives. She told me that my rehabilitation and recovery isn't about them. That I need to rehabilitate for myself. That I need to accept and love myself.

As I am.

And if they thought less of me because of my injuries, then that wasn't the unconditional love and support I deserved.

"I don't know what it is about some sessions, but it just feels like you've had the crap beaten out of you when you leave," I say.

"How do you know what getting...getting...getting the crap beaten out of you feels like?"

"Fair point. I can imagine. And it can't be worse than Lori shunting me around her obstacle course."

Theo chuckles.

"Are you going to movie night tonight?" I ask. Once a week, they set up a large screen in the visitors' room, and we can all go watch it.

"I'd rather poke my own eye out," he says.

His choice of phrase stings, but I tap my eye patch. "Zero out of ten. Would not recommend."

"Ah, fuck, Sparrow. That was...insensitive."

"Better than dancing on eggshells and pretending you don't see I'm missing an eye."

He places his large hands on my shoulders, then dips his head a little so our eyes...eye...whatever, meet. "I see you, I see your eye patch, and I'm sorry I was an insensitive jerk."

Time stands still for a moment. Even though he smells a little sweaty from physio, his proximity is enough to create butterflies in my stomach.

"It's fine," I say, trying to brush it off.

"It's not. But you're kind, trying to make me feel...less of an ass. Does your physio hurt?"

I shake my head. It's hard to concentrate on his questions when he's so up in my personal space. "Not really. I mean, my muscles burn, and my joints can ache, but I like to think of it as the price of getting better. I couldn't walk when I first got here, so I see the value of progress."

"I'm gonna have to try and adopt that attitude, because I'm not gonna lie, mine fucking hurt and I sucked at it."

I place my hand on top of his on my shoulder. "It'll get easier. I mean, it might not hurt less, but when you can do something next week that you couldn't do this week you find purpose in it."

"Sophia." I jump at my name, then recognize the speaker.

Theo drops his hands from my body as I turn to face the footsteps approaching us.

I miss the warmth of him immediately.

"Theo, these are my brothers, Luca and Leonardo."

Thankfully, Luca has shorter hair, and that's how I tell them apart. In the first month or two after the accident, I literally remembered them as Luca Cropped and Leonardo Long. Everything else about them is the same. The same dark hair color, eyes the same shade of dark chocolate, aquiline noses. They're the same height; my guess is a little over six feet, but they are shorter than Theo is. I think he's about a foot taller than me because I'm...

Shit. I don't remember how tall I am.

It's uncomfortable, but they all shake hands.

"See you later at the movie?" I say to Theo.

"Not likely, Sparrow," he says.

"Sparrow?" Leonardo asks as Theo heads to the elevator.

I roll my eyes. "A nickname."

Leonardo watches Theo until the elevator door closes. "Not sure I like a guy with that much ink having a nickname for you. What do you know about him?"

"Nothing. He arrived a few days ago. I crossed paths with him a couple of times." I don't know why I feel compelled to minimize the details. Probably some muscle memory throwback to older brothers being older brothers.

"Stay away from guys like that, Soph," Luca says.

"I'll choose my own friends. Let's go to the guest area." It dawns on me that everyone else greets their friends and family in the visitors' room. I'm not sure why my brothers always seem to meet me wherever they please.

"Can we talk in your room?" Leo asks.

I can't explain the discomfort I feel at the request. I don't know the cause, other than this feels like a conversation that doesn't belong in my personal space.

"I spend too much time in there as it is. Let's go sit out in the garden."

"It's November," Luca says. "And raining."

I glance at the window. "Shit."

Leonardo looks at Luca. "Fine, the visitors' room."

When we get there, we take a seat. "We need to talk about where you are living when you come home," Luca says.

"I'm keen to live on my own."

"That's not safe," Leonardo says.

"I haven't blacked out in three months. I'm fine. I'll wear a safety bracelet or something. I know my apartment isn't ideal, given the floor I live on, but I can make it work for now if—"

"Dad moved all your stuff out and cancelled your rent last week," Luca admits.

"Oh my God. He was just here and didn't say anything beyond me moving in with him and Mamà for a month as I readjust to leaving here. Their place is so much closer to here than mine is, so I thought it made sense as an outpatient. He can't just do that. I'm a grown woman."

"Who hasn't been paying rent for the better part of this year," Leonardo adds.

"So why did he wait until I'm getting ready to leave before cancelling my lease?" On my last visit, I'd taken photographs. I'd been trying to relearn where everything was so that being there wouldn't feel like sleeping in someone else's home.

My brothers glance at each other, but I don't know what the look means.

"Maybe he thought keeping it this long would be motivation to get well," Luca says.

Emotions crash over me. The loss of autonomy. Others making decisions for me. The loss of a home I can't remember, but given how I feel about my room here, that it's my private sanctuary, I would likely be devastated about it in any other scenario.

"He was never going to let me live alone?"

Leonardo shakes his head. "Not yet. The apartment would have been impossible. If the elevator broke, there would be no way you could make it up all those flights of stairs."

"You've always listened to his advice," Luca says.

"But that's the thing," I say, my heart thumping in my chest. "He didn't give me advice. He took my home away from me without talking to me about it."

"It's for the best," Leonardo says.

"I decide what's for the best for me. I'm an adult. Papà had no right getting rid of my place. Where are all my things?"

"Papà put them in storage. That's why we're here," Luca says. "We know our parents want you to live with them when you get out, but we're going to Sicily on business for six months. Over the winter. Instead of staying with them here in the cold, come with us. Some winter sun. Milder weather. The new family property you acquired there has a guest house. It was one of the reasons you said we should buy it. You can stay in it, but then you'll be close enough to the two of us if you need us."

I can't bring the property to mind, but I can imagine the feeling of the sun warming my bones. For the briefest moment, I'm mentally packing a bag and leaving with them.

"But my things... I need to start figuring out what the rest of my life is going to look like. And, I need to stay here so I can have outpatient access."

Leonardo takes my hand. "I know the rental place where all your things are. We'll take you there and you can check everything is safe and secure. We're a wealthy and well-connected family, Sophia. We'll fly on the private jet. We'll find you outpatient care. It'll be safe. We'll be on our way before our parents realize you're gone."

"We know how overbearing our parents can be." Luca smooths a crease in his pants. "Just come with us, Soph. I promise we'll take care of you." They both look so sincere.

And hopeful.

"I'll think about it. That's the best I can say."

Because I feel like I just had the rug pulled out from beneath me.

And despite the obvious reason, that I've lost my apartment, I feel like there's something else going on that they aren't saying.

5

SWITCH

I take a draw on my cigarette and feel like a thirteen-year-old sneaking smokes from the pack my dad always left by his keys. My first ever drag on one happened down the side of the clubhouse when my father's back was turned.

As I stand in the rain, hidden by the dumpster around the back of the rehabilitation unit, trying to smoke one of the cigarettes King left behind, I feel like I'm doing something illicit all over again.

I was a dick to Sophia.

Unintentionally, maybe.

But I heard that hurt in her voice again. The hurt other people keep missing.

I feel so shitty about it, I'm even contemplating going to the goddamn movie night to make up for it.

Didn't like the look of her brothers. Can't explain what it was beyond the fact they both looked like they had sticks up their asses. Fancy suits, fancier shoes. Not a fucking wrinkle on either of them.

Could see the way they looked me up and down before

deciding I was a piece of shit. There are few moments I wish I had my cut on, but that was one of them. Fuckers wouldn't look twice at me if they knew who I really was.

But for Sophia's sake, I kept my reaction to myself and came out here for a cigarette instead.

My phone vibrates, and I take it out of my back pocket.

There's a picture.

Niro: *Got some of the wedding photographs of me and Cat back.*

I still can't get over how Niro looks now. How his scar has healed over time. But he's smiling. He's wearing his cut over a white shirt and dress denim. Catalina wears white trousers and vest. The woman's got muscle in those arms.

There's another photograph of Catalina in a white leather cut. It fits her like a glove. Even the patches are white with black writing. Not sure I've ever seen a white wedding cut before.

Clutch tried to explain to me how Cat kidnapped Niro and then saved him from himself and how the club created a special role for her. I still don't have an opinion on that, although I apparently voted in favor.

There's a third photograph of them, really fucking happy, standing in the sunshine in a town square. There's a little girl in a white dress with colorful flowers in her hair, and she's looking up at them, smiling.

Comments start to flood in beneath.

Vex. Clutch. King. Halo.

Saint, whom I don't remember, makes some comment about Bates having shaved. So, I guess the man stood next to Niro is Bates, which means the woman must be…shit…I was told her name.

A flower, maybe.

Now I'm confused. I sort of know who they are but don't. It's hard to explain what the void of a decade feels like.

But I feel it in this photograph.

I type some suitable message, then finish my cigarette.

As I'm stubbing it out, I notice my sneaker is undone, so I bend down to tie it.

"That was too easy," a man says with that New York Italian lilt.

"You think she bought it?" I can see their shoes beneath the car next to me.

I have no idea what makes me think of staying crouched, but there's a voice down inside me saying I should do just that.

It feels imperative.

Instinct, maybe.

"We can work on her over the next few days."

I'm being a fucking idiot. God knows why I'm crouched here. I hear car doors slam, and I stand. From my position by the dumpster, I see it was Sophia's brothers.

That was too easy.

You think she bought it?

"None of your business," I mutter to myself.

I try convincing myself of that as I walk all the way back into the center.

"Irv," I say, tipping my forehead at the security guard. He's eating some of the cookie surplus I dropped off earlier.

"Won't be the first to sneak out for a cigarette," he says. "But I suggest you change that hoodie so the bigwigs don't smell the smoke and know you broke the rules. You do that, and I won't tell anyone you went out the fire door."

I grin at him. "Thanks for the tip."

As I hit the stairs, my eye starts to twitch and go blurry.

When this happened the other day, I passed out, and in self-preservation, I climb to the first flat surface and sit down.

My heart races, kinda like last time. The pulsing in my temple feels like blood is forcing its way through the eye of a needle.

What was it Sophia said earlier?

BAT.

Breathe. I do that. Slowly and deeply.

Adjust. I lean my head back against the glass panel.

Think.

It will pass if you calm. Let the panic go. You're already on the floor if you do.

Everything is still racing. Pulse, heart, thoughts.

Calm.

I slow my breathing, placing my hand on my chest and abdomen so I can feel my body move. Things are flickering behind my eyelids, and a metallic taste floods my mouth.

"Are you okay?"

I open one eye and see Sophia hurrying to me as best she can, her limp more pronounced as she does. Around her eye is red, as if she's been crying.

"Don't run," I warn. The last thing I need is for her to hurt herself as she tries to reach me. Shakily, I hold out my hand toward her. To catch her or to slow her down or because I need a fucking hand to hold right now, I'm not sure.

That was too easy.

You think she bought it?

Through the darkness, the words come back to my mind.

"Do you need me to get someone?" she asks. She places her hand on the chrome rail above the glass and slowly lowers herself to the floor. It's difficult for her, and I can't immediately think of how to help her.

Once she's down, she wiggles around until she is sitting with her back to the glass too. "What happened?"

"Dizzy. Sick. My eyesight blurred."

My body is shaking. Whether it's adrenaline or something more, I don't know. I feel like I'm gonna puke, and I swear sweat is collecting on my brow and above my lip.

"Here," she says, reaching for my arm. She tugs me until I'm resting my head on her denim-clad thigh, and I don't fight it.

"Just breathe through it." She runs her fingers through my hair, scooping it back off my forehead. I focus on the sensation of her nails against my scalp.

"Harder," I encourage, hoping the sharp bite of pain grounds me.

She does as I ask. Her nails pressing harder, but not as hard as I would like it.

It's enough.

Her thigh is soft and warm to my cheek.

"Can someone come to corridor two, quickly?" I hear her say. I don't know who she says it to. "It might not feel like it right now, Theo. But I promise you it gets better."

We sit in silence. One stroke of her nails, breath in. Another stroke of her nails, breath out. I feel her abdomen move at the same pace. We're breathing together, slowing everything down.

My head pounds less.

I place my arm over her thighs and hold on to her like she's an anchor that can stop me drifting away.

"Theo, it's Dr. Sharma. Can you sit up and open your eyes for me?"

When I open them, a doctor is crouched in front of me.

With Sophia's help, I sit up and am rewarded with a light being shined into my eyes.

"It's exactly...same as." I wince.

"It's the same as what happened in the visitors' room?" Dr. Sharma asks.

I nod.

Fuck me.

This can't be the rest of my life.

"Just stay where you are, Theo. I'm going to take you for a scan. I'm sure it's just the normal pressure from the swelling you've had to the brain. But let's be certain. Don't move while I get you a wheelchair."

I try to push up. "No. I don't want... I can walk."

Both Sophia and Dr. Sharma try to stop me. "Don't risk it," Sophia says. "Trust me, you'll only do more damage if you fall."

I hate the feeling of weakness. I don't know exactly who I was before this happened, but I know I wasn't weak. My body, my cut, and my earlier memories tell me that.

But I can't explain all that to the two women looking at me.

Not when I feel so sick, like I'm gonna vomit if I so much as breathe.

Panic trickles through me. What if I'm not getting better? What if I'm actually getting worse?

"Fine," I say, placing my head back on Sophia's lap. It felt...safer...there. Like nothing could touch me and all dangers would pass.

Sophia leans forward and places her lips next to my ear. "I know right now you're having a mental battle with yourself. You want to believe Sharma's words, but you also think something is very wrong. Stop thinking about either, Theo.

Find the happiest memory you still have left and cling to it for now."

I try to find a memory. My dad's face when I got my prospect cut. A road trip we took to Baja the summer Clutch turned eighteen. But the one I settle on is my mom hanging laundry outside on a sunny day. The sky is fucking blue. The sheets, white. I have a beer in my hand, and I'm sitting shirtless on a chair in the backyard. Mom laughs at the story I'm telling her.

And it's fucking peace.

The kind of youthful delusion that I'm invincible.

My heart rate slows.

"Better," Sophia says quietly.

Staying focused on the positive memories helps as I'm wheeled to the CT scan.

I hate it. Hate confined spaces. I hate being prodded. I hate all of this.

I don't want my head shoved in another machine.

"You need to let go of my hand," Sophia says. "I'm not allowed to stay with you."

I drop it like a hot potato. Hadn't even realized I was clinging to her like some kid who didn't want to go to class on his first day of school.

"I'm fine. Thanks."

But as I'm transferred onto the medical bed, I realize I'm not.

Sophia and Dr. Sharma leave the room while the radiographer sets up what he needs.

Closing my eyes, I try to relax, but it's impossible.

"Hey." Sophia's voice comes through the speakers. "I just looked up shocking facts about motorcycles, and it said the first Harley only went forty miles an hour. Is that true?"

I huff. "How am I supposed to know?"

"You're the biker, right?"

With my eyes closed, the blurriness goes away. "Just because I'm a biker doesn't mean...fuck...not everything bikes."

"Do you think you'll still ride after this?" she asks.

I think about the rides I can remember. "First thing I'll do when I get out of here."

"Why is it so important to you?"

I imagine I'm on my bike. "Sunshine. Wind in your... face. It's the...last...true freedom."

I hear Sophia sigh. "Sounds amazing."

"Clubhouse. Asbury Park. Find me. I'll...take you."

Bet she'd look fucking cute in leather.

She talks to me all the way through the scan until the radiographer takes over. And even then, it's not for long.

I let the sound of Sophia's voice override the fear I'm feeling.

That I'm never getting on my bike again.

6

SOPHIA

Stairs continue to be my nemesis. But I take them every opportunity I get, per my physical therapist's instructions. She has some motivational quote from Aristotle about how we are what we repeatedly do or something.

I get the general idea.

Voices get louder and louder as I reach the bottom of the stairs, and I glance through the glass sliding doors into the reception area. Beyond it, I see bikes. Lots and lots of bikes.

Dawn, the manager of the facility, is in a heated discussion with Irv. "There are at least thirty people in there. It's only four guests per person, max." Her words are aggressively whispered.

Irv puts his hands up. "Better to let them in and do what they do on good terms than try to keep them all out," I overhear him say.

"I would never have accepted him as a patient if I'd known he was a—Sophia," she says, her face changing as if she hadn't been about to bad-mouth Theo.

Irv glances up at me. "Probably best to avoid the visitors'

room right now," he says. "It's Theo's birthday and he's got company."

I wish he'd mentioned it when our paths crossed in physio yesterday. Not that I could do much, but I could have perhaps ordered him a cake or gotten someone to bring a card.

"I'm on my way to the pool," I say.

"Let me walk you there," Irv says.

"It's okay, I'm good." And curious.

The door is open, the volume getting louder. And holy sex on legs. There are lots of men in leather. And girls. Well, women. And some have cuts that say things like *Property of Saint*.

If I didn't know Theo was in that room, I think I'd be scared of them all.

Two men stand just by the door but are facing into the room, so they don't see me. One has wide shoulders and hair that is part braid, part undercut. The other has shorter hair. Both wear leather vests that say *Iron Outlaws* on them.

"You think the Mafia has the edge over the Irish?" the one with shorter hair asks.

The one with longer hair flexes the fingers on his right hand, then forms a fist before repeating the motion. "Last night would say so. Cillian isn't going to go down without a fight though. It's rare for the five families to come together like this."

I feel a little sick at the thought. Is my father and the Sicilian Cosa Nostra part of this? I wonder if knowing the truth would make me more or less fearful than I am right now.

"Hey," says a pretty woman with pale skin and kind eyes. "Did you need something from in here?"

I shake my head. "No. It's fine. I just wanted to wish Theo happy birthday, but I can do it later."

"Oh, come in. We brought him cake. I'm Rae."

My hip and leg ache, and the movement and warmth of the pool help. "I should go get on with my swim. It's—"

"King," she says to the devilishly handsome, if a tad sinister, man standing next to her. "Tell Switch to get over here."

King nails me with brilliant blue eyes that contrast to his tan skin, then walks away.

"Honestly, it's better if I—"

She grabs my arm before I finish. "Red velvet or chocolate sponge with vanilla cream?"

It's ten in the morning, and I can already see there are at least five bottles of alcohol open. But there are bikes outside. I hope they aren't planning on driving anywhere soon.

Or maybe they're planning on staying here all day. I can't imagine what Dawn would say about that.

Theo appears before me, and he's wearing a leather vest like the others that says *Switch* on it. I can't quite put my finger on what it is, but he looks uncomfortable.

"You shouldn't be in here, Sparrow."

I feel myself shrink inside. I know I shouldn't be. "I'm sorry. I just...well...happy birthday."

"Sparrow, huh?" The man next to us wears a name badge that says *Clutch*. "You been through the wars too, kid?" he asks.

"Not so much a war as a duel between me and my car versus a tree. The tree won."

Clutch laughs at that. "I like you," he says.

"I very much prefer that to the alternative." I turn to look at Theo. "I'm sorry for showing up uninvited. It was rude."

"It's okay," Rae says. "We brought plenty of food. Stay

and have some. Theo told us how strict they are about nutrition. One day of treats won't hurt."

I want to stay with my whole heart. I want to talk with people who aren't my family. It's the closest I've ever been to a party that I can remember. There's a vibration to the energy.

I don't think I've ever seen a collection of such goddamn perfect women either. They're all different shapes and sizes, but they all have one thing in common.

They're all pretty.

Someone jostles me from behind. Two bikers.

It's an accident, but I can't take that much weight on my left side, and I feel my leg collapse as I crumple to the floor. Fear spirals through me, the move happening in slow motion. Flailing out my hands, I reach for something to brace my fall. Theo rushes forward to try and grab me. A slow shout from Rae.

The absolute silence when I hit the corner of a side table before falling to the ground with an ungainly thud and a cry of pain.

Tears sting my eyes.

There's a muttered curse.

I just want to die. Or at least crawl away and hide under a rock or something.

"Fuck," Theo barks, shoving his way through the crowd before leaning forward to pick me up. He takes a step, then another. I feel his arms shaking as sweat pops on his brow.

I worry about the stress of pressure on his brain.

"I can walk," I whisper.

"Shut up, Soph." He grunts with exertion.

I'm heavy. He's weakened by his accident. But somehow, he manages to get me to the sofa, where he lays me down gently. He shakes his head, winces, and then rubs his brow.

"Are you hurt?" he asks. "Do you need me to get one of the doctors?"

I shake my head. "If you could find my pride, that might help. I think it rolled under the bookshelves over there somewhere." I try to smile, to fake that I'm fine while my body shakes.

"Don't," he says.

His eyes are focused on me. It's a cliché to say it's as if there is no one else in the room. But for a hot moment, I understand why a person might think that.

It's like there's a protective bubble around us. I suppose that's what this place is for us. A safe space to find out who we're going to be without outside interference.

"Don't what?" I ask.

"Pretend. Make light of this. I'm going to ask you once more and I want an honest answer. Are you hurt, Sophia?"

"Man, I'm so sorry." A tall man, whose patch says he is called Saint, leans over the back of the sofa. "I didn't mean to knock you down."

Theo's head snaps towards him. "I'm gonna kick your ass in ten minutes. Give her some fucking space."

Saint raises his hands as he moves away.

Fast anger should probably be a red flag or something. But to know a man would fight for me and over me is... exciting.

And just like that, I'm aroused.

Which is wild.

It's not the first time it's happened. And it won't be the first time I've gone back to my room and slid my fingers between my legs. But all thoughts of sex have been put second to actual recovery and life.

There's also something in Theo's demeanor that changed in that moment. Like he was drawing on muscle memory. I can't really explain it. But I saw a flicker of the man he could have been before his accident. A man who would fit in with this group of people. He was utterly competent. Unafraid. Commanding.

Even the timbre of his voice changed, the notes of it dropping lower in register.

"It hurt," I whisper. "And I'm a little embarrassed, maybe. That I couldn't rebalance myself. That your friends, a room full of strangers, saw me fall. That you might...think less of me."

"You forget that I clung to you like a life raft in the hallway when I...collapsed. The only people in this room that understand what we're going through is you and me."

Theo brushes my hair back off my face and attempts to remove hair that's stuck in the elastic of my eye patch. He lifts it slightly, and I place my hand over it to stop him.

"It doesn't bother me, Soph. Just let me."

The urge to trust him battles with my need to be seen as who I was before. I wish he could see me without all the scars. The woman in the photographs my family has shown me.

I bet she was unafraid of what the mirror showed.

I watch his face for reactions. But not only do I see nothing but genuine care, he uses his hands to shield my face as he does so.

"Done," he says, lowering my eye patch so gently that I barely feel it.

"I was on my way to the pool. Do you know where my towel ended up?" I try to sit, but Theo places his hand gently on my neck, his thumb stroking me in a way that makes me shiver.

He leans close, our faces inches apart. "Stay and have cake with me."

"It's very early in the morning for so much sugar." His body is pressed against mine. I know there are other people in the room, and from the silence, I can only assume they are all listening to us intently, but I can't bring myself to look away from Theo and check.

"We both nearly died, Soph. I think that makes it perfectly..." He shakes his head. "Fucking words. Makes it perfectly acceptable to live like we mean it from now on. Eat. The. Cake."

"Fine," I say, but the word is a little breathier than I intended.

Theo grins, then bites down on his lower lip. "Think I'm going to have fun corrupting you," he says.

"I look forward to it," I say without thinking.

His eyes narrow. Then he stands and helps me to my feet but doesn't let go of my hand. "Brothers," he says loudly. "This is Sophia. She"—he pauses for a moment—"makes this place bearable."

There are words of welcome, and eventually the chatter returns to the levels it was at before I arrived.

I touch his temple. "How are you feeling?"

He shrugs. "Headache lasted until about two this morning. Feel hungover, to be fair."

"What's hungover?"

"You don't know?"

"Amnesia, remember? I don't remember things I've done. So, it takes it coming up in conversation. I didn't know what pets were. Dr. Sharma kept talking about Micah being up all night, and I thought she had a child, but it turned out it's a rather noisy pug."

Theo chuckles at that. "A hangover is where you drink too much alcohol, and about twelve hours later, your body pays you back. Your head hurts, sometimes you're sick."

"You poison yourself?"

"How can you know what poison is but not know what a hangover is?"

"True crime mysteries have become my friend. But it sounds like that's what a hangover is. A poisoning."

He looks over at the bottles on the table. "When you put it like that, it does sound a bit reckless."

"How do you remember?"

"Because I've only lost the past decade, and I got into a whole lot of trouble before that."

I glance at all the leather cuts in the room. "I can believe it."

Saint reappears. "Meant no disrespect, Switch," he says. "And sorry again, Sophia. Just me and Spark fooling around and didn't see you behind us. You okay?"

"It's okay. I'm good."

He offers me his hand. "I'm Saint. Or Ryker. Use whatever makes you more comfortable."

I shake his hand. "Nice to meet you."

A young woman, younger than he is, tucks herself under his arm. "And I'm Briar. Actually, Rose, but I'd really prefer it if you called me 'Briar.'"

"I'm Sophia. Would love a cool second name. It feels like a secret identity."

"Stick around long enough, and someone will give you one," says a cute blonde with a baby bump and service dog.

"I'm Spark," says the man standing next to her. "This is my old lady, Iris."

The term *old lady* rankles me a little, and I don't know why. But from the way he looks at her as he speaks, I can see he adores her.

Slowly but surely, I'm introduced to everyone.

"This is Vex," Theo says. "My best friend."

"Too right," Vex says with a wide smile. "If you want to know any secrets about him, I can tell you."

"That feels like an unfair advantage given I won't know if they're true or not," Theo says.

Vex laughs loudly. "That sounds like even more fun."

"It's really nice to meet you, Vex. I've seen the two of you together before. You came to eat with Theo one night, but you weren't wearing this." I gesture to his cut.

Vex brushes a hand over his patches. "Rare I'm without it, but it needed a repair."

"Maybe you can convince Theo to join movie night once a week."

Theo glances at me, his eyes soft and kind, and shakes his head. "Still a nope."

"I'll make a social joiner out of you yet," I say.

Vex shakes his head. "You won't make his stubborn ass do anything he doesn't want to. I've tried to get him to game with me, but the guy won't even pick up a controller."

"Asshole," Theo mutters with humor before turning to the final woman near us. "This is Catalina. Recently married to Niro."

"Congratulations." I shake Catalina's hand as Niro turns around, and I'm taken by his scar that almost mirrors mine. Except he still has his eye.

His brow furrows as he studies me. I'm sure it's only seconds, but it feels like minutes as he follows the line on my face, likely having thoughts that match my own.

"As a general rule, I don't like people," he says, shaking my hand. "But you, I'm gonna make an exception for."

"Can I...?" I reach my hand toward his face. "I know it's rude, but...mine feels so...Will it always...?"

Niro takes my hand and leads it the rest of the way to his

scar and runs my fingers along it. "You feel yours if you press your tongue against your cheek?"

I nod.

"Yeah, that doesn't go away. But eventually it won't hurt... just tugs a little when you yawn and shit."

His feels smoother, less hard, less hot.

"You got pretty lips, sweetheart," he says. "You got lucky it missed 'em." He reaches for Catalina's hand and brings it to his lips before kissing it. "About five percent of my mouth feels nothing when I do that, and it sucks."

Catalina smiles. "Good thing the remaining ninety-five percent is so proficient."

Niro glances at Catalina, and I can feel the love they have for each other. "Only with you, babe."

I turn to Theo. This morning might have got off to a rocky start, but I decide that in this moment, I'm choosing to enjoy my life. "You mentioned something about cake. I feel like today calls for some."

Theo playfully taps the end of my nose. "Good. Let's get you a slice."

"I hope you face fairer weather in the future, Sophia," Niro says.

And I smile because I do too.

7

SWITCH

"So, who's the girl?" my mom asks before I've even sat down the following day. "And why didn't you introduce us before we left when the others arrived?"

"What girl?" I ask.

She waves her hand as if waving away my bullshit. Always could see through me and my brothers.

Dad laughs. He's wearing a vintage *Rolling Stones* T-shirt, jeans, and his biker boots, even though he's no longer officially affiliated with the club.

Mischief sparkles in Mom's eyes, even as tiredness keeps them bruised. Dad always said her eyes were the reason he was able to keep his dick in his pants, unlike a lot of the other bikers in his generation. Camelot, Uther's dad, drove his old lady to leave, even though he'd tell anyone who'd listen he still loved her. And both Cue Ball and Wrinkle were part of the old-school belief that old ladies and club girls should be equally sampled.

But my dad? He set the bar for what it meant to fall utterly in love with one woman and keep it that way. Mom says it's unconditional love between them. But I remember Dad telling me when I was around thirteen years old that it was unconditional support. He knew down to his soul that Mom had his back and encouraged him to be exactly who he wanted to be.

"The girls got back to the clubhouse in such a flurry yesterday, all full of how you were looking out for a young woman called Sophia."

"And the old ladies are a bunch of gossips who have nothing better to talk about," I say, taking the plastic container of treats my mom offers.

"How is she?" Mom asks. "I heard she fell or was knocked down or something."

"She's fine. Common hazard in this place." I pop the lid on the container. Mom's made me my favorites. White chocolate chip oatmeal cookies. I lift one out and take a bite.

Dad reaches over and steals one too. "What does Sophia do?"

"Nothing right now. She has no memory at all of her studies or what she did. Apparently, she was in real estate before her accident."

"Geez," Mom says. "Can you imagine? It's more than the ability to remember. You lose your connection to everyone and everything. At least you remember us. Your family. Your brothers. It would kill me if I thought you didn't remember me. Poor thing. Is she close to her family?"

I'm not sure how to address it. Even less sure that I want to get into it with my parents. "They come visit her quite often."

"I'm guessing she's a pretty little thing," Dad says.

I try to bite back a smile at the thought of her by stuffing my mouth with one of Mom's cookies.

"I saw that flicker of a smile," Mom says.

"Don't be getting ideas," I warn.

Mom purses her lips as she studies me. "You just turned thirty, and I'm not getting any younger waiting for grandkids."

I almost choke on the cookie. "Mom, you have three grandkids. Your other sons have already started."

She leans back in her seat. "So?"

Dad pats Mom's thigh. I grew up in a touchy-feely family. Not in a weird way. Just, we show affection for each other. "Your mom won't be happy until there's a houseful. Keeps telling me I need to install two sets of bunk beds in the back bedroom so we can fit 'em all."

"Well, don't build 'em because of me. And Sophia is here for the same reason as I am. We just..."

I find it hard to dismiss Sophia like I was about to.

And a wild idea pops into my head. The two of us, married. Visiting my parents. I'm going to have to speak to the doctor to see if the pain meds I take can cause hallucinations because marrying *anyone* right now feels like a bad idea.

"Leave the boy alone," Dad says, as if he didn't just hear Mom say I'm thirty.

"You and I both know it's a tradition for the men in your family to fall hard and fast," Mom says to him. "How long did it take you to ask me to marry you? Four days?"

Dad huffs. "Took you three months to say yes though."

Mom chuckles and looks back at me. "And your grandad proposed to your gran after sixteen days. Your brother said he'd fallen in love with Ziana by the end of their first class of their first semester together."

"Okay, I get the idea," I say, humorously exasperated by Mom's efforts. "Reavis men fall fast and hard, but I swear this is not one of those times."

Except...

"And I think you should tell him," Dad says finally.

"Tell me what?"

Mom looks at Dad, and I swear tears start to swim in both their eyes. The mood changes suddenly, and I don't like it.

"What the fuck is going on?"

"Me and your mom need to head back to Florida for a bit. We need to check on the house. Pick up some of our colder weather clothes." He squeezes her leg.

"And I need surgery before I start chemo," she says.

"What? No. Why?" *Why?* I fucking know why. "Mom? Are you okay? No. You're not okay."

My heart pounds as my mom gets up and comes to sit next to me on the sofa. As soon as she does, I wrap her in my arms so tight, I swear I hear her back crack.

"It's alright, Teddy Bear," she says, using the nickname she gave me as a child. Embarrassing to admit she told me it was because I gave the best hugs, like a teddy bear, but now I want to give her as many fucking hugs as she needs.

Tears sting my eyes. "Fuck, Mom. What happened?"

She puts her palms on my chest and pushes gently. "Just before King called to tell us about the accident, I got some test results back that I have pancreatic cancer. King said the club would pay for me to have private treatment. So, I need to go back for that."

She's already onto logistics while I'm still processing that she has a disease that kills indiscriminately. I can't fight it for her. I can't ride with my club to battle it. I can't protect her from it. It's my mom facing the odds.

Perhaps logistics are her way of coping with this conversation, and that's the most important thing right now. I can process later.

"Then you shouldn't...be here. Go. Fuck...treatment. Words, shit." When I'm stressed, I find it even harder to find the right words. "Whatever it is... I'll come. Leave here."

Mom shakes her head. "I won't go if you threaten to follow. I need to know you're here. Getting the best treatment. I wanted to be right by your side while you go through this." A tear falls over her lashes, and it breaks my fucking heart.

My dad looks utterly devastated.

"You've been hiding it...from me."

Dad huffs. "Mom insisted. I figured she deserves to have her say at the moment."

She looks over at him and smiles. "Who knew it would take cancer for you to listen to me?"

"Don't joke," I say. My head is spinning with more questions and an overwhelming frustration that verbalizing them all will be a fucking nightmare. Instead, I hug my mom again.

If I'd paid more attention, I would have realized how thin and frail she felt in my arms.

"Mom. You've always been...my rock. I'm thankful you were here. If there's...a problem, I... I'll call. And I'll stay...if that's what you want."

"It's what I need, Teddy. I don't want to go. A mom's place is by her children's side when they need her. I'd hate for you to leave the best place for you so I can be in the best place for me."

Dad nods. "I've been trying to persuade her to leave for the past week."

"Then you should go. Come back at Christmas, maybe."

Mom tears up. "But I don't want to leave my baby when he's—"

"I'm hardly a baby. And I'm doing...fine. Please, Mom.

It's...been great seeing you both, and..." Fucking words. I need this to be smooth. I need to convince her to do what's best for her. I'll survive this. I need her to survive what she's facing too. I take a deep breath and try to calm myself. "I'm grateful. You moved into my...house to look after it for me and make the hour drive to come see me all the time. But... you should—" I gesture away with my hand because I can't think of the word. "You need to go."

Mom studies my face the way she always did when I was a kid. She could tell when I was lying from fifty feet.

Whatever she sees there reassures her. "Okay. Fine. But maybe do me a favor, just in case. Hurry up and marry her and make me grandbabies so I can see it."

Dad shakes his head. "You're going to be here to see it, whenever it happens. Refuse to believe anything different, woman."

We talk a little more about Mom's treatment. What it will take. Her options.

And I tell her about Sophia. What I know, at least. Do I oversell it a little? Maybe. But I feel like it's the little piece of happiness Mom is looking for. And when they finally leave, I'm exhausted and desperate for a cigarette.

How can it be fair that my mom has cancer when I've lost the last decade of memories with her? What are the chances I won't be able to make any more with her? The thought pierces my heart and strips me bare.

I take the cookies to my room and pick up my packet and lighter.

I'm almost at the rear exit when I hear a voice behind me.

"Trying to escape?" Sophia asks.

The sight of her eases the tight band around my chest.

"No. Because I'm a grown-up who does whatever the fuck he wants."

She cocks her head to one side. "Looks like sneaking to me."

"I need a cigarette. I'm going outside to smoke one. Coming?"

She nods gleefully. "Yes."

I'm not sure what makes me take her hand and lead her through the corridors, out of a rear exit I found my second week here, and to my secret smoking spot. But it's a comfort to the turmoil I feel in my gut.

"Can I try one?" she asks as I tip one out of the packet and light it.

"No."

She looks up at me. "Why the hell not?"

"Because they're bad for you."

"Perhaps I already smoked. For all you know, I might have one of those superlong cigarette holders and smoke while drinking brandy."

"Happy to give you different experiences, Sparrow, but wrecking your lungs is not one of them." The gravel of the path crunches beneath our feet as we walk.

"Why do you smoke then? I thought you were a medic."

I shrug. "Just always been something I've done."

She tucks her hands in the sleeves of her sweater, then folds her arms across her chest. It's cold, even by early-November standards.

"I think you should stop," she says.

"I think you don't get a say in what I do."

"Then I think *you* don't get a say in what *I* do, and you should just hand one over." The way she challenges me makes me think of Mom, and something snaps in my chest.

We reach my spot. Before breakfast, Irv had whispered

that he'd found two outdoors chairs and put them just in front of the screens that hide the dumpsters near the parking lot. Guess I owe him some more cookies.

When we sit, Sophia puts out her hand. "At least let me take a drag. I saw a movie the other night, and it sort of suggested that smoking behind the school was a rebellious thing to do. I feel like smoking behind the brain-trauma rehab has the same vibe."

I can't help but laugh and hand her my cigarette.

"Any tips before I do this?" she asks.

"Fuck knows. Maybe suck on it but don't inhale first. See if you like the taste in your mouth. Then inhale second. It's gonna burn either way because these are not starter cigarettes."

"Okay. No inhale. Then inhale." She takes a couple of deep breaths. Tentatively, she places the cigarette to her lips and purses her lips around it. Her cheeks hollow, and then she moves the cigarette away, holding her breath for a second, before she blows smoke into the air.

"You're cute," I say as I watch her.

"Do I look cool doing it?" she asks.

"Wish I could say you did, Sparrow."

She laughs at that. "Okay, round two. The inhale."

"Keep it small."

Sophia blows out a breath, then tries to inhale. Immediately, she begins coughing and spluttering. In between, she sticks out her tongue and looks like she's going to gag. Her eye waters. Then she sneaks a finger to wipe beneath her eye patch. I guess eyelids surrounding prosthetic eyes still water.

Laughing, I take the cigarette from her and rub circles on her back. "Easy, Sparrow. Breathe through your nose."

"I'm trying, but I think...I just burned out...my windpipe."

I take a draw on my cigarette while she composes herself.

"That was gross," she says. "How can you suck that into your lungs?"

"Pretty certain they've adapted at this point."

She leans back in her chair and lifts her face to the weak fall sun. "You should bring me a blanket."

"Or next time you should bring a coat."

"We could ask Irv for a fire pit. I bet he'd find one."

I agree. "He probably would. But I'm pretty certain the smell of something burning would send people looking for us, Sparrow."

"Oh, wait. I said yesterday to Saint and Briar that I wish I had a cool nickname, and I do. Sparrow."

"Don't read too much into it," I say. Yet I can't help but crack a smile.

"You know what's wild?" she asks.

"What's that?"

"I have this yearning to go run through a forest. I mean, I've read about them, and seen them in movies. But I have no idea whether forests are as cool as they look." She repositions her foot by lifting her knee with her hands. "Might be a while before I can run through them. Maybe more of a leisurely stroll. A saunter, maybe."

"You don't strike me as a forest girl. Did your family tell you if you ever went camping? Hiking?"

She shakes her head. "I was more a champagne and parties kinda girl, apparently."

I glance at her. "Now that I can see."

"Strange thing is that the idea of a party is my worst nightmare now. Did Dr. Polunin give you the whole spiel about the Welsh woman who woke up with an American accent?"

I nod. "She did." Along with a whole list of ways in which people were never the same person again after a coma or amnesia.

Sophia leans back on the chair and tilts her face to the sun. "I think I'm a forest girl now."

"Maybe I'll take you when we're both out of here. Don't like the idea of you getting lost."

She smiles softly. "I think that would be a really lovely idea."

We sit in silence beyond the occasional car coming and going from the parking lot. The gutsy roar of a sports car gets louder and parks on the other side of our fence screen. Two doors open and close with a slam.

"Don't you feel even a bit bad for her? Sophia's been through a lot," a man says.

Sophia tilts her head in the direction of the speaker. It must be one of her brothers.

"She'll forgive us eventually," another says.

"That's what Alessio said this morning. But she doesn't know her own mind."

There are lines on her forehead as she listens. And I remember the conversation I heard before I had trouble with the stairs. My head hurts like someone just drove an icepick into it.

"Remember our family code. *La mia famiglia prima di tutto*. We all win once she's married. Even her."

Sophia lurches to stand, but I grab her and press my finger to my lips.

The other huffs. "It's a marriage of convenience to strengthen the family. Would you want to be married to someone fifteen years older than you?"

"He's a billionaire. You know how she likes to spend money."

"How she *liked* to spend money. She's not the same as she was, and she's still not going to forgive us."

There's a pause, then the beep and click of the car doors being locked. "Then at least we'll know we're secure. Don Consolo is the *capo famiglia*. By Soph marrying his son, no one will be able to touch us."

"He called her 'damaged goods,' Luca, for fuck's sake."

"And Dad's made some bad business decisions in the past year. It's only Alessio working behind the scenes that has us holding on by a thread. It's a fair trade to align our families and have Alessio take over some of Don Consolo's holdings here."

Something in my gut flips. Sophia looks at me, terror etched in her features.

The sharp crunch of their footsteps and their voices trail away, just as the first tear spills over her lashes and runs down her cheek.

"I..." She flounders for what to say next, and I stand before tugging her into my arms.

"Stop crying," I say firmly.

She looks up at me like I'm heartless. "Did you not hear my brothers?"

I drag my thumbs beneath her eyes, skirting beneath her eye patch like I'd seen her do earlier. "Yes. I heard them. And every single thing we do next could inform them of what we know. So, the first thing is to dry your tears. You're going to need to act."

"What do I do?" she says. "Did they try to make me marry some guy and I tried to run? Is that why I was in that car?"

"It sounds like it, but we can't assume anything yet. Let's

just get through their visit. Under no circumstances go anywhere other than the visitors' area. Make up an excuse. Your hip hurts too badly to climb the stairs, the cleaning staff is in your room, anything. I'm going to keep an eye on you; you might not see me. But trust me, I'll be there, Soph."

"They told me they were going to take me to Sicily with them. They made it sound like they were doing me a favor. Like it was a holiday. They were going to give me to a man. What if—?"

"Soph," I say, cutting her off. "Focus. Tell them you've been outside. You slipped on the wet pavement and hurt your hip, which made you cry. You're fine, but you don't want to walk. We need to listen. Learn everything. Ask as many questions as you feel like you can. Go, and trust me."

We hurry back into the building, and I try to take my own advice. We can process what it all means when we've dealt with her brothers' visit. But one thing is clear: her family is connected.

I take her hand as we walk, trying to reassure her she's not on her own in this.

I'm not sure where the fierce protective urge to look after her is coming from. Guess I'll process that later too.

Along with the way her hand fits so perfectly in mine.

When we get inside, I stop and place my hands on her biceps. "Go ahead. I'll be watching, Sparrow. They will not be able to do anything to you. I promise."

I thought when my memories came back, it would be like a switch. One day I would remember nothing; the next, everything. But the truth is, my memories are like a developing Polaroid picture.

Some things are just more in focus...more instinctual.

Like setting up a perimeter to secure Sophia. Or why I even feel like I need to set up a perimeter at all. I know Irv has the front, and if I alerted him, I know he'd react quickly and lock the front door.

I close the fire door behind me that leads to the pool corridor. There's a small nook with glass walls that faces out onto the gardens. There are tall plants flanking the entrance to it, and I tuck myself behind one of them. I can see Sophia limp toward her brothers.

When they reach her, they gesture upstairs, but she stands her ground and leads them into the visitors' area.

"Good girl," I mutter quietly.

"Is everything okay, Theo?" When I turn, Dr. Polunin eyes me carefully.

I glance down the corridor. I really don't want to take my eyes off the door opening to the family room.

"I'm fine."

"I saw the record of your incident in the hallway. Are you feeling better?"

"I'm fine," I repeat impatiently.

"Theo. Do you know where you are?" She speaks softly, but I can see the concern in her eyes. She probably thinks I'm in the middle of a mental health episode.

"I was in the military. My day job, which I hope to return to, is personal security." It's a lie, but on the fly, it's a good one. "Just running through some drills. Thinking through the building, escape routes, how to find cover versus concealment."

"Do you see any enemy combatants?" she asks.

I glance down the hallway to where Sophia's brothers are attempting to marry her off to some guy in Sicily, which was frightening enough that she likely took off in a car at full speed.

"Don't worry, Doc. I'm not in the middle of some kind of psychotic break or brain injury-related delusion. I know there is no one here who shouldn't be. And I'm definitely aware I'm not under attack. Just playing a bit of a game with myself to relieve the boredom."

She studies me for an extra second. "Do you realize you spoke freely then? You didn't have to search for words?"

I hadn't.

But now she pointed it out... "You think that's progress?"

"Most definitely. Your brain is recovering every day. There is a chance that the enhanced activity, despite the headaches and dizziness, may bring with it further improvement."

"From your lips to God's ears, Doc."

"It's doctor."

"I know."

8

———

SOPHIA

"**A**re you excited for Sicily?" Leonardo asks.

I feel like I'm sitting on the other side of gauzy fabric. My brothers are there, but the fabric hides them. They are speaking words, but the fabric is muffling them.

Nothing feels real, and every word they speak feels loaded.

But I try to smile. "Sunshine sounds great. Guessing I won't be slipping on cold, damp tiles." I rub my hip for effect. I did as Theo said. They tried to steer me up the stairs, even though I limped towards them.

Instead, I redirected us to the family room, and I swear I could see the relief on Leonardo's face as we found it empty.

Luca leans forward and rests his elbows on his knees. "How do you feel about perhaps leaving a little earlier?"

"I would need to speak to my medical team to make the adjustments," I say.

"Why don't you let me take care of that for you?" Leonardo asks.

I just realized the trauma unit must have some kind of

power of attorney or guardianship agreement or something with my family that they are allowed to be so involved in making these life-changing decisions for me.

If my family members are what the media paints them to be, they are powerful, conniving, and have reach. *Foolish* doesn't even begin to cover how I feel. They've pretended to love, care, and nurture me. Now they plan to marry me to a stranger whether I want to or not. It must be why I crashed the car. I don't know the circumstances that led up to this, but I must have been frantic.

Was I trying to escape? To flee?

The first thing I'm going to do when they leave is fix who has control of what affects me. And I need to prepare for threats of removal of support. If they are willing to marry me off for the sake of the family enterprise, I can only imagine what they will do to try and control me.

"When were you thinking?" I ask. It's hard to focus on the conversation, and I'm sure they must sense something is off.

Leonardo looks at Luca, then back to me. "Tomorrow."

"Tomorrow?" That gives me no time at all. A part of me just wants to say no, that I don't want to go anymore. But if the plan is to get me to marry an absolute stranger, they'll find a different way to do it, even if I say no.

Suddenly, my two brothers feel even more like strangers than they did when I first woke up.

Worse, they feel like my enemies. "Tomorrow is too soon. I haven't even packed my things."

"That's okay," Luca says. "We can pay someone here. You can buy all new things. I've had credit cards with your name on them made. You can buy whatever you want when we get there, my treat."

"The buying isn't what bothers me. I'm not willing to fly

anywhere without clear and solid rehab plans. I've worked too hard to let it slip now." I also want to rage. Who thinks it's okay to drag me away from the care providers I've grown to trust? Who thinks it's a good idea to take a person with amnesia away from every bit of familiarity that might help them access memories?

Why the hell would I want to go? Was I always such a pushover that I'd just do what they say? I'd hate to think that I was.

"A few days without therapy won't make or break your recovery," Luca says. "We'll have everything set up for you. You don't have to worry about a thing. We'll look after you, I promise."

"I don't even know if I can fly after a brain injury like mine. I'll have to check in with Dr. Polunin. And then there's travel insurance? Health insurance?"

Both of them look at me. "Such a worrier," Leonardo says.

"I'm sorry. I don't think I feel comfortable leaving without a plan. Sicily sounds lovely, but I might be better off staying here. Or leave in a week or two so I have time to ask if the center has any recommendations for a private clinic there and we can arrange for liaison and transfer of files."

Luca smiles, but there is a sharp edge to it. "You forget who we are, Sophia. Money can move mountains. We can move quickly but still have the plans you require. Give us twenty-four hours."

The sincerity in his face scares me most. He's lying, and if I didn't know better, I'd believe he was telling me the truth.

I was only just getting my arms around this new world I live in, and now the very foundation I built it all on, my family, is crumbling.

Loneliness bites me.

Then reality settles over me. I'm the daughter of a crime family. I'm probably dragging Theo into something he doesn't need to be dragged in to. But I need his help.

More importantly, I think I'm going to need his club's help if they come for me.

"My image no longer matches my passport photograph." Like my license that has become my talisman. An anchor of who I really was.

Leonardo chuckles. "We're an important Sicilian family. And we're taking a private jet. You'll have no trouble getting into Sicily. From there, you can apply for a new passport before we travel home."

Luca gives Leonardo a brief glance, and I can almost read between the lines. He's saying too much.

I swallow three, four times to fight the tears that are threatening.

Tension crackles between us. I wonder if it's as obvious to them as it is to me that something is off here.

"That sounds good. I should probably figure out how to apply makeup before I have my photograph taken." I touch my eye patch, and Leonardo looks at me sympathetically.

"You're still lovely, Soph," he says.

"Yes, but do I leave my prosthetic eye out or put it in? Do you know the rules? And if it's out, do I still put mascara on the lids?"

Luca grimaces. "Enough, Sophia."

Leonardo laughs.

I can't bring myself to do anything. It's taking too much effort to talk as if I didn't just overhear them in the parking lot talking about effectively trafficking me to another country for the good of our family.

After the crash, I barely knew anything about my life,

but my family was the one thing I assumed I could trust. Now, I know I can't, and I remember what Theo said when we were outside.

We need to listen. Learn everything. Ask as many questions as you feel like you can.

"So, where in Sicily are we going?"

"We're going to land in Palermo and stay there for a few days," Leo says. "We have business there, so you can shop and sightsee."

"And after?"

"To our place just outside Trapani," Luca replies. "The point is to get you some sun, some fresh, clean, salty air. You need a vacation, even if it's from recovery."

I smile again because I'm supposed to. This is all too much. I start to feel sick, can feel my palms growing sweaty.

"You know, I think the fall winded me a little," I say. "I feel like I'd be better seeing one of the physical therapists to make sure I didn't do anything a little more serious. I'll message you later. Okay?"

"Of course," Leonardo says, standing before kissing both my cheeks. "We can be ready when you are."

Luca studies me for a moment. The professional liar can obviously see I'm lying too. But I can't change that.

"Be well," Luca says.

I watch the two of them head toward the exit. Their silhouettes match. Tailored suits and lean frames. The sharp click of their highly polished dress shoes on the parquet floor keeps the same beat. They are strangers.

"Sophia."

I jump at my name and turn, unable to ease my heart rate even as I take Theo in. He's such a contrast to the men who just left. Rough but honest. Tattooed and dressed in a frayed hoodie.

The relief I feel at the sight of him is immeasurable.

"I'm going to run to the back to see if I can overhear them say anything else," Theo continues. He hands me a key card. "Go to my room and wait for me there. I doubt they'd be so foolish, but if they suspect anything, they may act. You know how pissed Dawn was two days ago about the party, but she did nothing about it out of fear."

He tells me the room number, then disappears down the hallway.

Tears sting my eyes.

I don't feel safe anymore, even here, my second home for all this time. My whole body hurts; my head spins. Following Theo's instructions, I go to his room. It makes sense to hide here. My brothers know my room number, my hallway, the staff, my physio, what treatment rooms I typically use. I bet Leo could ask for a key card from Dawn, and she'd give him one.

At this, the tears fall. I swipe them away viciously. I don't have time for self-pity. I need to feel safe first. Then I can allow myself the luxury of wondering what the hell is happening to my life.

I step carefully up to Theo's room and open the door. The room is plush like mine, but where I have done things to make my room homey, Theo has few personal effects. A book sits on the bedside table, a biography of a decorated military veteran. A laptop sits on his desk.

A part of me wants to pry, to learn more about the man I'm trusting.

I look up, and the mirror is right there in front of me. I snap my eye patch over my head and force myself to stare at my reflection. It's not going to get easier.

I suddenly understand what my therapist has been saying about self-acceptance. I take in the indentation where the elastic presses against my skin. The scaly red line where the bottom of the patch rubs no matter how much petroleum jelly I put on my cheek. The red eye socket and the eyelid with eyelashes.

My prosthetic eye with its fake iris designed to match my original eye, yet it doesn't.

I lie down on Theo's bed and curl up tight. His pillow smells of him. Musky and soft. Panic washes over me in waves. I need a plan to make money. A job, of sorts. And I need a place to live that is safe and secure, which effectively rules out any of my friends. I have to assume my family will know them.

And I need to figure it out quickly.

But it's so overwhelming.

I don't think I can do this on my own.

And as I breathe, as I try to calm myself before I throw up, all I can see is Theo.

9

SWITCH

I'm not sure how I know how to do this. To hide, and yet keep targets in my sight. To use shadows for cover and the buildings to my advantage. I'm hoping it's one of the forms of memory I tap into automatically.

The corridor brings me out to the rear of the parking lot, allowing me to beat Sophia's brothers to their car by a fraction of a second.

I peer through a narrow gap in the fence. Her brothers turn the corner. Of course they are fucking twins so I can't tell one from the other beyond the color of their ties and haircuts.

A memory flickers. One I can't quite hold on to. But it features Saint and a tall building.

Sniper, maybe.

It's like a badly tuned television, and I squint. Am I thinking of him because a sniper on these two men would be handy right now? And what makes me think I'm physically in danger?

It must be my memory returning, because Saint arrived

during the ten-year window I'm missing. But I don't have time to celebrate that right now.

"You going to Mamà's for dinner tonight, Luca?"

"I wasn't going to, but I will. We need to speak to Papà." Luca's voice is a fraction deeper than his brother's. His pace of speech, slower. Less excitable.

"About what?"

"It's bothering me. The urgency. He told us to convince her to go without mentioning the wedding. To get her there so we could persuade her to go through with it. But why couldn't it wait? She knows something is wrong."

Shit. I saw the stricken look on her face before I sent her in there. Luca must have noticed it too.

The footsteps stop. "How can she? She remembers nothing."

There's a pause. "I don't know. But she does. She could always read us."

"Are you saying she has her memory back?"

A hand slams the top of the car. "I don't know. But something was definitely off. We need to get her out of here. Tomorrow. Before she has the time to make other plans."

Thoughts begin to run riot in my head. How could they take her? Where could I hide her? How do I stop it?

"You're being paranoid, Luca."

"And you're too laid-back, *Leo.* Dad wants this solved. He thinks it's the answer to the family's prayers."

"We've done everything he asked. We've cut off most of her friends, so they won't ask questions about why she's gone. She has no finances in her own name anymore, so she'll be stuck in Sicily. She doesn't even have an apartment. And there isn't a hotel in any country she can check into without a credit card or without us knowing. And none of it feels good."

"I wish we knew what caused her to drive so erratically like that. It makes no sense. And I don't know why Papà is orchestrating all this deceit when we could just have an honest conversation with her."

Leo huffs. "Papà doesn't want to give her the opportunity to say no. He's worried that the person she is now won't be amenable. But a blood commitment was made and must be honored. It's the only way without Papà facing disgrace."

"It's not enough."

Both car doors slam, and soon I hear the wheels turn in the gravel.

Once the sound disappears into the distance, I go as quickly as I can back to my room. My shoulder aches, my arm physically hurts, and I feel a level of breathlessness that I'm uncomfortable with.

I hear Halo's voice in my head call me a toddler for some reason. But I can't place the situation nor context. The words are in jest, and people around us laugh.

By the time I make it to the room, sweat has beaded on my forehead. But for the first time in weeks, my first thought is not for myself.

It's for Sophia.

When I step inside, I find her asleep on the bed. Her eyes are red from crying. Her hair is mussed. She must have been running her hands through it. I can only imagine her sitting here trying to process her grief.

I feel it for her.

It's hard to explain amnesia to anyone who hasn't had it. People just want to resume their friendship with you. But you can't remember the first thing about them. Imagine how it would feel if a complete and utter stranger walked up to you on the street and began discussing your personal thoughts and feelings with you.

That's our world.

But the concern in Luca's voice troubles me.

He's correct in his assumptions. Sophia does know.

And he wants her out of here.

Tomorrow.

I'm not sure what would happen if she refused. There's a guard on the parking lot gate. But one bullet would solve that problem. And while Irv is a good watchdog, he's already seen his best years. The security here is to prevent patients from hurting themselves by wandering out of the facility.

It would be absolutely no deterrent to someone who wanted to get inside.

Especially if that person was armed.

Which means I need to get her out of here first.

Sitting on the edge of the bed, I watch her for a minute. Her lips are lush and pink and slightly open. Long eyelashes rest against her cheeks. Her skin is smooth until it reaches her scars.

It would be too easy to be bold and tell her the scars don't mean anything to me. That I don't see them. Because I can see them, and they do mean something. They mean there was a point in her life when whatever she was fleeing was more important than her own safety. It shows that when she sets her mind to something, like her recovery, she gives it everything so she can live and function and not let it break her.

Wait. She's not wearing her eye patch. I look around for it and see it sitting on the small desk beneath the mirror.

Courage is an incredible thing. It's a well that needs refilling at the end of every day. And somehow Sophia has managed to do that.

The more I study her in the quiet of my room, the more I realize she's growing on me. She helped me when I needed it most. She's trying to be positive when you can see the whirlwind happening inside her.

And perhaps, more than that, I want to be the one to help her now when she most needs it.

Placing my hand on her knee, I shake her gently. She awakes with a start and then places her hand to her chest.

"Theo," she says quietly. "You scared me."

"I'm sorry. Didn't mean to, Sparrow. But we need to talk."

She places her hands on the bed and adjusts her posture so she's sitting straight. "Did you hear anything more?"

"Not much more than we already heard."

"You promise?" she asks.

"I'm never going to lie to you. Your brother, the one with the shorter hair..."

"Luca?"

"Yeah, Luca. He suspects something. He doesn't know exactly what. He wondered if your memory was coming back. But he said something about how you could always read the two of them. The guy you were promised to marry is rich and has connections that would help your family. They're worried you won't go through with it now because of your memory loss."

Sophia sighs and looks down. "They're right. I barely know what I'm doing with my life. Adjusting to this is enough. I don't want to marry a complete stranger in another country away from everything I know."

I take her hands. "Your father is furious about the delay. He needs the marriage to go ahead because it will give strength to the family and responsibilities to one of your brothers. Alessio. So, they want to get you out of here tomorrow before you have the chance to act on your suspicions."

She looks up at me. "I've got nowhere to go. I don't have

my bank details. My phone was smashed in the wreck, but they got me a new one without all my old details. I've been so foolish and trusting. I've let people set up online accounts for me that I'm sure use their credit cards. I was told my wallet was lost, Papà thought someone might have stolen it, so I let him cancel all my cards. I never asked where the replacement ones were. I've been hiding from my life in here, and now I have no options. They have me right where they want me. Trapped."

The waver of fear in her voice tears through me.

"You aren't foolish. And you're supposed to be able to trust the people you think love you. But you are right in that it's exactly what they've done. They talked about how they've deliberately cut off your friends, finances, and home. They know you can't hide without money. My guess is, at best, they want you amenable to marriage with a wealthy older man. At worst, they can use it to force you."

"What would happen if I went to the police?" she asks.

The word *police* makes the hairs on the back of my neck stand up. I see a snapshot. A group of old ladies sitting on the curb. A row of bikes. The police talking to us. But the fragments are gone before I can hold on to them.

"They haven't done anything…illegal yet. In fact, I'm sure they could make a good show of how they have done everything for you since you were injured. Worse, they might even be able to say the brain injury is making you see shit that isn't even there."

Her jaw opens. "Oh, God, they wouldn't."

I take a breath. "If we go too far down a conspiracy rabbit hole, we might never get back out. But I think it's enough that we know they want to take you from the country to marry someone. And you don't want to go under those circumstances, right?"

"I don't," she admits. "What do I do, Theo?"

I squeeze her knee gently. "Let's play it out. They're going to come and get you out of here tomorrow. I don't know exactly what that means. It could be as simple as them coming to pick you up because they think you have agreed to go with them, or deciding not to pay for your treatment anymore, in which case I guess you get evicted from your room. Or it could mean with force. Your brothers are obviously connected. I'm guessing Cosa Nostra, seeing as you are Sicilian."

How else could you be wealthy enough to fly a human being from one country to another without proper identification?

It dawns on me that I don't know what the club's relationship with the Cosa Nostra is today. King is deliberately keeping the current status of the club from me. If it's precarious, they may not help Sophia at all. Worse, they might even try to use her. I try to think back to my early days with the club, but like all prospects, we got told shit. But I do remember the docks were controlled by the Mafia on the New York side.

She leans forward, and her long dark hair falls over her face. It's cool where it touches my hand, and I can't help but stroke it. It's so soft. Like she is.

When she looks up at me, she looks stricken. "I searched online. About my family. There are news reports that suggest my father is a made man. They've never mentioned it. Not directly. You think they'll take me from here whether I want to go or not?"

I take hold of her hand. "I don't know what they're capable of. And I don't know what lengths they'll go to so they can keep whatever promise or contract they've made for you."

She takes a deep breath and looks up at me, fear etched into her features. "I hate to ask, but...can you help me?"

I sigh and squeeze her fingers. They are slender between mine. Pretty nails with a nude polish on them. "I'll do whatever I can. I don't know how helpful my club will be if they know who you are, though."

"Bikers and Cosa Nostra don't get along?"

I shake my head. "Never did. Doubt that's changed in the past ten years."

"So, what do I do?"

"Marry me." The words are out of my mouth before I have time to process them.

"What?" Sophia asks.

A plan formulates in my head. It's messy. Full of plot holes. But I think it could work. And, while it's reckless, marrying Sophia is something I can give my mom. The knowledge that this girl she heard about could be my everything. We can stay together long enough for Mom to get through her treatment, and then if she gets well...

When she gets well...

I can't think of that right now. In this moment, I have to think of Sophia.

"The biggest problem is that your family wants to marry you off to someone. They can't do that if you are already married."

I cup the side of her neck, allowing my thumb to stroke her jaw, and she leans into it like a pussy cat. "Thank you, but I can't let you do that."

"Why not?"

She shrugs, her expression exasperated. "For a million reasons."

"Name one."

"Fine. You don't just marry strangers."

"Apparently that's something your family *does* do."

Her mouth opens and closes for a minute. "That may be fair, but obviously the reason I am here is because I don't."

I recall some fact from high school. "Some countries have arranged marriages between strangers."

Sophia sighs. "Okay. You don't just marry someone so they can avoid having to marry someone else."

"That's fair. I'm not suggesting...for life. Twelve months, maybe. A contract." I drop my hand from her jaw and take hold of her wrist. My fingers fit around it easily. "Stop your family getting it annulled by...claiming you made this decision recklessly and without your full faculties. I doubt my club will help us if you are connected to the Cosa Nostra or Mafia. But they'll have to if you're my old lady. My wife."

Her eyes flare at the word *wife*.

"They'll know it's fake."

I shake my head. "They might think it's fake, but they won't know for sure. Especially if we act like it isn't."

"Why would you do this?"

I look over at the eye patch sitting on the desk again. Something deep inside me stirs at the idea of being noble. Of having purpose that's greater than the pieces of me. "I can't explain it to you, Soph, but I know it's the answer. It solves your problem. And my mom...she's got cancer, going through treatment, terrified she's not gonna live long enough to see all her kids settled and happy. It'll give her a boost to know I'm married to a nice girl."

Sophia looks humorously puzzled. "I'm a *nice girl*?"

"Obviously. But everything about this feels like the man I used to be before all this happened. Maybe in doing this, I put the pieces of me back together."

Sophia sighs. "I feel like it would be disingenuous to say yes."

"Remind me what that word means."

"Sort of insincere because I benefit more than you do. And they are never going to believe us. They saw us at your party."

I rub my hand along my jaw. "And what did they see, Soph? You came in, and I introduced you to each of my friends. They saw the way I looked after you. I nearly kicked Saint's ass for knocking you over. Is it that much of a leap to believe we feel something for each other? That perhaps we were hiding our real feelings but couldn't wait any longer. That maybe we're carpe diem-ing life after trauma because happiness and life can disappear in the blink of an eye. Could you make it believable?"

"You want me to pretend it's real?"

"It's the only way."

"Seems that's not fair for you either. You have to know I have a crush on you."

A crush. The word is so sweet. Takes me back to high school.

I smile softly, then run my thumb over her thick lower lip. "Well, that should make faking our marriage a little easier, then. Shouldn't it?"

"Don't tease me," she says, her voice wavering.

"Like, what if I kissed you now, so you could be ready to fake it later?"

"I said don't tease me."

"Who said I'm teasing? Was that a yes or no, Sophia?"

Her mouth opens, and when she looks up at me and sees my smile, she nods. I lean forward and brush my lips over hers. Softly, at first. In case this wasn't what she was thinking.

"Do that again," she whispers, and I oblige.

Our mouths open, and my tongue meets hers. I feel her

sigh against me as my body starts to respond to the fact I have a woman in my arms after all this time.

She's warm, soft, and utterly delicious.

I want more of her.

But gently, I pull away because time isn't on our side.

Her cheeks are pink, her eyes wide. "I'm looking forward to some more of those fake kisses later. But now we have to do something more important. We need to get out of here. Today."

10

SOPHIA

"Theo, this all feels a bit...wild," I say, even as my heart beats traitorously for another of those kisses.

"Best plans...often are," Theo says, standing up before pressing a kiss that feels like heaven and protection to my forehead. He ruthlessly shoves his laptop, book, and a handful of his clothes and things from the bathroom into a backpack. "We need to travel light. We'll go to your room so you can pack a bag while I make a couple of calls."

He takes off his hoodie, puts his leather cut on, then puts his hoodie back over the top.

It takes us a few minutes to walk the hallways to my room. It's not odd for someone to be carrying a bag. I often carry one when I go to the pool so I can use the large showers and facilities down there.

I let us into my room and start to think about practicalities. If I can't take all my clothes, I need to be smart about what I do take.

"Wow, you really made your room look nice and homey."

Theo strokes my lower back as he puts his bag down. The action sends a little shiver down my spine.

"It makes a difference to my mood."

I look at the comfortable armchair I had delivered. The burnt orange pillows and throw add a pop of color. The plush cream rug I added next to my bed.

"You've got an eye for it. Now go pack." He then pulls out his phone. "Niro," he says. "I need help."

I should probably change clothes into something more durable, warmer clothes for travel.

"Get us out of here," Theo continues. "You and Cat. One bike, one truck but with the cover over the back. Some padding in the truck bed if you can for Soph to lie on." There's a pause, and I look up at Theo, who smiles softly. "Yeah, we're busting out of the joint."

I hear a *yee-haw* so loud, Theo has to move the phone away from his ear momentarily.

I rush to the bathroom but stumble in my haste. "Careful, Sparrow," Theo says. "ETA sixty minutes. We have time."

He returns to his conversation with Niro, asking him to grab some medication on the way, and I close the bathroom door. Placing my hands on the vanity, I study myself in the mirror. My cheeks are pale, even paler against the black eye patch I replaced before we left Theo's room.

Am I leaving one danger for another?

Am I being reckless?

Will this start a war?

I'm about to run with a man whose last name I don't know, even though I know his club and my family could be at odds.

The world starts to spin a little, so I sit down on the floor and lean back against the cupboard while I catch my breath. I catch my shoulder on the knob and gasp.

The door pushes open. "Soph, are—shit. Text me when you get here," he says, then ends his call. "Hey, are you okay?" Theo asks.

I shake my head.

"What's going on?" He crouches next to me and runs a hand on my thigh.

"Am I being foolish for trusting you? Are you being foolish for trusting me?"

He's so very attractive up close. There's a ring of amber around his hazel pupils, and his skin is flawless. He moves the outer dial on his watch several clicks, then sits down opposite, his back to the wall, and stretches out his legs like we have all the time in the world.

"I bulldozed you, huh?" he says. "Pushed you into running?"

I think carefully about how I answer. While I am having second thoughts about our current plan, I don't want there to be no plan. That feels even worse. "Not exactly. We need to do something. It's just...I don't even know your last name, Theo."

He reaches for the bathroom door, closing it so it's just the two of us in the small space. It's intimate, but not intimidating. "My full name is a mouthful of former presidents. Theodore Ulysses Reavis. Dad decided a kid should be able to explain their name. Theodore because Roosevelt and..." He winces and rubs his temple. "Fucking memory. Something to do with a coal strike, maybe? And Ulysses Grant because he signed the bill to approve the Brooklyn Bridge. Random, I know. What's your full name?"

"Sophia Chiara Viscuso. I can't tell you why I'm named that because I don't remember, although I'm sure Mamà must have explained when I first woke up. I hope I have a story at least half as interesting as yours." I glance up at the closed door. "Don't we need to go?"

Theo shakes his head. "We're good. I'm thirty years old. How old are you?"

"My driver's license says I'm twenty-five."

He places a hand on my ankle and squeezes it gently. "What else do you need to know? I'll tell you as much as I can remember."

"That doesn't seem fair to you when I can't remember anything you might ask me."

"So? Hit me."

"If I go with you, will I be able to leave if I want to?"

Theo raises an eyebrow. "I don't know how much the rules have changed in the clubhouse, but my memories of it don't include holding women against their will. Oh, wait, no. I think King took Rae as a hostage. Someone told me that, I'm sure."

"Rae. As in, 'Property of King'?"

Theo runs a hand over his stubbled jaw. "Yeah, the very same. Fuck, can't remember all the details. There was a reason. Something about Shakespeare's kings. But aside from that, I don't think we take people hostage unless they really deserve it."

"That's a lot to process."

Theo winces. "Probably shouldn't have led with those details."

I can't help but laugh. It's the nervous kind. "What do you think your club will do when they find out who I am?"

"Won't matter if you're my wife, and I promise I'd protect you. But if you're really worried, I can help you in other ways. I could give you a thousand bucks and a ride somewhere, and you can get a job that pays cash so you can hide from your family. I don't want to force myself on you as a solution to this. I may want to please my mom, but not at your expense."

I run my finger along a seam between the floor tiles. It would probably be better to take his offer of a ride and some cash. But what kind of work could I do? I remember nothing. And physically, I can't do a job that will require me to stand all day.

But can I make myself go with him and beholden to him?

"Are you sure this is a fair deal for both of us?"

"My gut tells me this is the right thing to do. And I'm having to listen to my gut a whole lot more because I truly believe it knows better than my brain right now. Plus, I get to contribute in a small way to how Mom feels as she heads into treatment. Yesterday she was nagging my dad about building bunk beds for all the grandkids she wants."

"I hope providing those grandkids isn't part of this deal."

Theo chuckles at that. "No. But we'll need to stay married. For a year. Mom will be well again, and the club will believe it was real by then." He's silent for a moment and picks at a thread on the bottom of his hoodie. "And I get a chance to know you better, Sparrow."

When he looks up, there's a soft smile on his usually grumpy and stern face that shows me for all his gruffness, there's a kind man beneath.

"Which do you prefer? Theo or Switch?"

"They feel like two different people right now. Guess I'm Theo working my way back to being Switch. He's a man I don't remember, but he achieved goals I remember making when I was younger. But the guy sitting here in your bathroom...whatever he's called...he's kinda waiting to hear whether getting to know him a little better would be something you're willing to do."

I take a steadying breath. "I've been hurt enough recently, Theo. Please don't hurt me any more than you have to."

At that, he shifts clumsily, his left arm not as strong as his right, and moves to sit next to me before tugging me onto his lap.

"One day, I'm going to be strong enough to do that a little more smoothly," he jokes.

I place my head on his shoulder and look up at him. "I didn't notice."

He lowers his lips to mine, and my whole body vibrates in reaction to it. I've seen kisses in movies, but I don't remember actually having any before today. The kisses in his room were too quick, but this one... I sigh as I sink into him, gripping the ties of his hoodie. His arms tighten around me as he pulls me close. Nothing is rushed nor hurried.

Simply two people making out.

"Fuck, you taste good," he says. "Makes me wonder what the rest of you tastes like."

I can't wait for him to do that either. I swear my panties are now a soggy mess. "If you're waiting for an invitation..."

"As amazing an invitation as that is, you still have to pack. Then we have to go get married."

I run my fingers along his jaw. His scruff is long enough to be soft. "Are you sure you want to take me on, Theo? There's stuff I still need. Physio. I can try to find a work-from-home job. Maybe something administrational. I don't know how long that will—"

His lips cut me off. This time, he groans. I can feel his

cock getting hard beneath me. "Need to stop kissing you, or we aren't going anywhere."

"I was trying to tell you something serious."

He looks at me earnestly. "I know, and that was my answer. We'll get a physio to come to the house every day. They can see us both, one after the other, or together."

"How will we pay for that?"

He tucks my hair behind my ear. "I have money. My club has even more. We're good."

"This is truly wild. But okay."

Theo smiles. "Good. Though I think we should carry out all important conversations in the future in a chair that we can both get up from."

It takes a moment and significant wobbling for us both to get up. It's reassuring that he has his own limitations too. Not that I want him to be hurt, but so that we can be ourselves. I'm fed up with fully able-bodied people telling me I'm doing great.

What I really want is occasionally someone to say, *That looks fucking painful, are you okay, babe?* Or, *You know what, don't give me three more reps because I can tell you just did your best and that's enough for now.*

Theo touches my cheek gently. "I'll keep you safe until you're ready to go it alone, Sparrow. I promise."

11

SWITCH

"Why are we doing this?" Niro asks when he meets me at the back of the center's parking lot and I tell him our plan.

I glance over to where Catalina is settling Sophia into the truck bed. I picked this spot because there is no camera coverage in this part of the parking lot. It's quite possibly overkill. But I didn't feel like testing out the other ways we could have done this, like attempting to walk straight out the front door.

My worry was the reach of her family and how quick the center's security might have been to attempt to restrain us. I didn't like the idea of being forced to hurt Irv.

I was concerned that they would call her family and tell them she was leaving with me.

We need a head start to make this work.

So, we left letters in our respective rooms saying we were leaving, just so they don't think I kidnapped her. They're brief. That we needed out of here, it's voluntary, and we'll contact the center soon. And Sophia will message her family once we're married.

"It's not up for debate. I just need to get out of here," I say, glancing up at the building to make sure nobody is paying us any mind.

"You can't remember the past ten years, but this is *not* like you. On a scale of one to me on the impulsive spectrum, you were a hardcore two."

I turn to face him. "Like you said, I don't know who that man was, but I can only be the man I am now. And the man I am now needs to do this."

The loud roar of a sports car's engine alerts us of its entry into the parking lot, and I immediately recognize it. It's followed by a black Bentley. They're held up at the barrier at the entrance.

"Soph, stay down." I turn to Cat and Niro. "That's her brothers. We need to cover her quickly."

"I'm scared," Sophia whispers.

"Trust me, Sparrow," I say as Niro hands me one of his weapons out of her sight.

"You need to duck too," Niro says, shoving me down behind the truck. "I'll handle the talking."

He slams the tailgate of the truck up just as the car pulls up three spaces away from us. I see the tires from my hiding place. I don't know who I'm praying to, but I pray anyway that they have no reason to walk around this direction.

Cat and Niro are proudly wearing their cuts as they tug the cover over the back of the truck. Catalina has to step around me, but she never looks down at me. When she's done, she pulls the weapon from her holster and points it at the ground so Sophia's brothers can't see it.

The weapon Niro thrust at me feels solid in my hand. I know I've held one before and often. My ink tells me I've killed more than one man. For the club or during my military service, I'm not certain.

And I realize this must be one of those procedural memory things because I remember every single step in firing this baby.

Shiny black dress shoes hit the asphalt. "You're in the wrong state, brothers," the person says, and I immediately recognize the voice as Luca.

"My old lady's mom is in here," Niro says. "You really going to pull some turf war over a rehab unit visit? Poor bitch is tied up in knots over her mom as it is, you pricks."

I lie down, making it easier to shoot someone's legs out if I need to.

They've come for Sophia. I know it.

We're going to have a five-minute advantage, at best, if they go straight to her room. Someone would have to let them in.

"We see you Outlaws do anything other than come here, visit, then leave, there'll be consequences."

I'm certain that's Leo.

"Okay, well, unless you want to get your dicks out so we can compare lengths, I suggest the two of you fuck off where you were going because we've got somewhere we need to be," Niro says, and I roll my eyes. Although, a whisper of a memory trickles through me, of him saying something in the clubhouse that got King angry but made everyone laugh.

Maybe it'll come to me before Niro gets us all killed with his mouth.

"Fuck you," Luca says.

"I'd rather fuck her, but happy to top you anytime, sweetheart."

I cover my mouth to hide the snort. Catalina looks down at me for a second, then looks back to the Sicilians.

"Leave it, Luca," I hear Leo say.

Their footsteps fade away in the gravel.

"Wait," Catalina says quietly. She puts her hand out to stop me and squints in the direction of the center's entrance. "Now. Quick."

Niro drops the tailgate, and I climb inside before he shuts it with a slam.

I hear Niro's engine roar to life, and then the truck rumbles beneath us. It's dark, with only small freckles of light making it through the cover.

I'm glad Niro put a mattress in the back, but I'm not going to ask where he got it from because...well...it's Niro.

"I guess I just learned I'm claustrophobic," Sophia says to me over the rumble of the engine and the traffic on the street.

"We'll be out of here in five minutes, I promise. Just take a deep breath, Sparrow."

"Are you sure this is safe?" Sophia asks.

There's worry in her voice, and I slide my hand along the mattress to find hers. "It's only for a few minutes. Once we're clear of here, they'll pull over, and we'll get out."

Her fingers tighten around mine, and I rub the back of her hand with my thumb.

This could be overkill. I hear the security guard saying a few words to Niro.

And then we move.

It's uncomfortable as the truck bounces over potholes in the road. The few minutes feel like an age as I hear Sophia's small gasps of panic. When we finally stop, Catalina rips the cover from over us.

Her face is lined with anger. "You want to tell me why we're kidnapping a fucking Italian mob princess?"

"Sicilian," Sophia offers. "I mean, it's technically part of Italy, but I consider myself Sicilian."

"Does it look like she's talking to you?" Niro says. "You seem to want to get my good friend who doesn't know any fucking better right now killed."

Sophia shrinks back.

"Steady, Niro. You're talking out of concern for me, which I appreciate, but I'm not gonna take you talking to Sophia like that."

"He's right, though," Catalina says. "They were the Sicilian serpents. Two brothers who helped with the cleanup of smaller gangs in New York as part of the Viscuso vendetta. It put them at odds with Cillian and his Irish mob."

"Who is Cillian?" I ask. "Wait. Never mind. I have to go. Thank you for lending me your truck."

I make a move to take the keys from Catalina, but Niro blocks me and takes them from Cat. "Dude. I can't let you just ride off knowing who you are fucking with."

"Then just move out of my way. I love Sophia," I lie. "Now you know why I need to give her my legal protections to make sure she remains mine." I look back down the road we just traveled. "It's not going to take them long to realize Sophia isn't there anymore. And they plan to transport her to Sicily to marry some old mobster's son back home for the sake of the family." My sarcasm is heavy on the last two words. "I can't let them do that."

"Then come back to the clubhouse. We'll follow you. Just...don't do anything rash."

Another memory. Cue Ball yelling at Niro for fucking something up. He was young. His hair longer.

"I can't. Please. Just give me the keys."

"We're following you. Wherever you go. So, you might as well tell me."

"Fine. We're going to DC."

Catalina folds her arms. "Why?"

"Because you can marry the same day there."

Niro turns his gaze to Sophia, and I put my arm around her, pulling her close. She's a little unsteady on her feet.

"What the fuck are you roping him into?"

I tuck Sophia beneath my arm. I'll process why she feels so good there some other time, but something about all this feels inexplicably right.

I shake my head. "This is all my idea. They can't marry her off if she's already married."

"So?" Niro asks.

"Please. Niro. I can't risk waking up one morning in that fucking rehab to find she's been taken from me. I need the fucking keys."

Catalina frowns. "We can't let them do this. King will lose his shit."

Niro glances at the two of us as Sophia wraps her arms around my middle. Whatever he sees convinces him. "Babe, I fell in love with you the moment you pistol-whipped me."

She rolls her eyes, but there's a hint of a smile. "You did not."

Niro grins. "I did. We gotta help 'em do it. I'm a big believer in true love these days. Plus, it's been a while since I pissed King off."

She sighs. "Fine. But I'm gonna tell him you made me do this as the ranking officer."

Niro hands me the keys and the pain relief medication I asked him to grab. "This is fucked up. But if you're going, you're not going alone. Cat will ride with me on my bike, and we'll keep an eye out in case we're followed. And Sophia should probably drive. Or Cat."

I release Sophia and tug him to me. "Thank you. I

always get signs before shit happens in my head. I promise I'll drive slowly and pull over at the first inkling."

Niro tugs a hand through his hair. "This might just eclipse all the wild shit I've done."

"One last thing," I say. "Promise you'll keep it to yourself. Who she is."

Niro frowns. "Don't make me start lying for you."

"I'm not asking you to lie. Just...if no one asks. Don't tell them, yeah?"

"This has 'bad idea' written all over it," Catalina says.

Niro throws an arm over her shoulder. "Fine. Don't make me regret it though."

Sophia's cheeks turn a delicious shade of pink when she asks if I'll help her get in the truck. Despite the imminent danger, I take the opportunity to help her and steal another kiss.

Part of it is for show...to get Niro and Cat to buy into this fake relationship. Part of it is for myself, testing the waters of whether I'm just selling the schtick or I am dipping my toes into something that's starting to feel real.

We navigate our way out of New York and cross the river into Jersey. I already feel better on our own turf. It's sunny and cool, but the seasons have turned, and I feel like I missed it.

"We don't have to do this," Sophia says finally. "Just getting me out of there for the time being is enough."

I head southwest on the 95.

But as we pass the Twin Rivers on-ramp an hour later, I see chrome.

Lots of it.

"Fuck," I mutter.

Sophia looks in the side mirror.

Mixed emotions hit me as the Iron Outlaws, in official

formation, pour onto the road behind us. Niro drops back into his position, and King takes up the lead in the front with Clutch to his left.

Cat or Niro must have called them.

King salutes me, then focuses on the ride.

"Are they mad?" Sophia asks.

"Don't know what they are, Sparrow. But we'll be in DC before we find out what they have to say."

"I don't want you to get in trouble with your club because of me." She reaches her hand across the console and places it on my thigh. I place my palm on top of her hand. It's warm to the touch. I'm not sure who initiates sliding our fingers together, only that someone does.

And that Sophia doesn't mention the slight tremor in my hand I can't seem to control.

I'm relying on old knowledge and the hope that nothing has changed with the loyalty among brothers in the club.

I pray they'll have my back, but as I rub my thumb over Sophia's knuckles, I know I'll do this on my own if I have to.

12

SOPHIA

A group of people steps ahead of us. The woman is wearing a pretty ivory cocktail dress and carrying a little posy of flowers. I don't know how I imagined my wedding was going to go before, but I'm pretty sure I wasn't wearing hiking boots, jeans, and a gray sweater.

I look over to the road, where Niro's truck and all the chrome-and-steel motorbikes are lined up beneath a No Parking sign. Two younger men wearing cuts that say *Prospect* on the back stand by them. I pity the person who tries to get the men to move.

And I try to ignore the argument happening to my right.

"You can't marry a woman you barely know," King says. "This isn't you. You need to give yourself time to reconsider. Plus, your mom will kill you for getting married without her here, and then she'll kill me for not stopping you."

It's heartwarming the way these grown men are still scared of their moms.

"I know Sophia," Theo says. "Look. I almost lost my life. My chance of a future was nearly taken away from me." He glances in my direction, and I almost believe the honesty in his eyes when he looks at me. Like I'm more than a damsel in need of saving and something worth treasuring instead. "It does something to a man. Makes him reevaluate what's important. Sophia's my future, and I'm not prepared to waste a day of it."

His words make me weak.

My phone rings and I glance down at it.

My papà.

I almost answer it on autopilot.

My heart sinks. Given my brothers arrived at the center at the same moment I left, it's taken him four hours to call. It's also odd that the center hasn't attempted to call before now. Nor my mamà.

"Listen," Theo says finally. "I get it. You guys all care for me. But letting Sophia go isn't something I want. I just need you to be happy for us."

"Fuck me," Bates says. "Vi was just telling me about the latest book she's writing, and it had an insta-love trope. Like, where the guy falls first and falls hardest."

Theo reaches out his hand for me, and I make my way over to him as best as I can. My body aches right now. The more than four hours sitting in the truck didn't do me any favors. I feel like a pretzel on a good day.

King tugs a hand through his hair. "You know this is fucked up, right?"

Theo smiles. "From the stories you all told me while I was in the hospital and since I got out, it sounds like fucked up is really business as usual for us."

Vex slaps Theo on the shoulder. "Sounds about right."

Theo looks to King. "Brother, I'm doing this anyway."

"Explain it to me. Why Sophia?"

Theo shakes his head. "I'm a grown man, King. I don't need to explain my relationships to you. But what I will say is this: Sophia is loyal. Courageous. Funny. She's been an anchor when I felt like I was disappearing. Sat there and looked up shit about bikes to calm me when they were shoving me through scan after scan."

King shakes his head. "That can all be true, but you don't have to marry her to continue that."

Theo shocks me by releasing my hand and taking a step into King's space. King doesn't even flinch, but Theo seems to grow in stature and composure. "Again. I don't have to explain this to you. If you don't call a vote and sanction me marrying Sophia and making her my old lady, I'm still walking into that courthouse and marrying her."

I move toward Theo but Vex stops me. "It's okay," he says in hushed tones. "I've got him covered but let him handle this."

Halo and Spark step up on either side of King. They sense the tension like I do.

"Fine," King says, finally. "Marry her." He looks directly at me. "As far as I'm concerned, you haven't proved why you should be an old lady of the club. You figure out how to do that, and we'll take a vote."

"I'll look after him," I say. But I realize how pathetic it sounds. How on earth will I do that? I can't support him financially. Definitely not physically. Maybe emotional support is all I have, but I have no previous skills to draw on to help.

"We know you will." It's Niro who squeezes my shoulder. "I've got your back."

King eyes Niro. "Once upon a time, that wouldn't have been a ringing endorsement."

Niro shrugs. "Once upon a time, you were the asshole who thought kidnapping a brother's sister was a good idea."

King's glare eases for a moment, and I see the flicker of a smile as his shoulders relax.

"For fuck's sake, you drove the van," King says.

Niro chuckles. "Oh, yeah. Forgot about that."

King turns to me. "You happy with this, Sophia?"

A small nagging voice tells me I should share with King exactly who I am. It feels as though I am putting Theo, Cat, and Niro in harm's way. But if I do, I'm in trouble. "I am."

King offers Theo his hand. "Then congratulations, brother."

He shakes it, and the two of them hug.

"Come on, let's go register," Theo says, taking my hand eventually.

"Wait," Catalina says. "She can't get married in hiking boots. What size are you? I'll grab you something while you register."

"Oh, no," I say. "It's fine, it's—"

"Tell her," Theo says, and I find myself answering before Theo leads us around the corner.

"Your club members don't like me very much, do they?"

He looks down at me. "I remember hanging around the club as a kid. The brothers, my dad, and some of the other guys' dads, they were so close-knit that you couldn't have driven a nail between them. Their old ladies were all friends. I'm guessing that's what we all have now. They're just looking out for me."

The left side of my body aches, when my left foot hits the floor, it hurts. "Can we slow down, please?"

"Shit. Sorry, Sparrow. You want to sit for a minute?" He points to an industrial blue bench in the corridor.

"No. It's okay. But I need the steps to be a little shorter and not feel like I have to jog to keep up with your long legs."

Just before the registration office, I pull on Theo's hand to stop him. "Last chance," I say. "It's easy for me to do this. I have everything to gain and nothing to lose. You can leave me here. I'll find a shelter. Give them a fake name. Build a new life for myself doing...something."

He puts his finger to his lips and moves us away from the door. "Can't let them hear you...talking like that or they'll get suspicious one of us is...forcing the other. Last time I'm gonna say it, and you're going to listen, Sparrow. We're getting married because it works for both of us. I get to do something that'll make Mom happy and because looking after you is going to give me a purpose I couldn't find for myself. Can't explain it better than that. I was fucking aimless. Have been since I woke up in that...fucking hospital. Then you stepped out of that pool like a movie heroine."

I scoff. "Hardly. How many movie heroines have you seen with a severe limp, poor leg mobility, nerve damage, and a scar down their face?"

His gaze turns stern for a moment. "Stop talking about yourself like that."

"It's true. Look at how many villains are physically imperfect. So many movies I've watched in the past few months deliberately use it to imply nefarious behavior. The 'facial scars equal villain' trope is ableist, but it happens for a reason. People see us as lesser or a representation of evil."

"And I can't control my words."

"Perhaps you haven't noticed, but it has seemed better since we decided to run until just now."

He closes his eyes for a second and breathes.

"I'm sure Doc would have an opinion on why that is," he says finally. "But anyway, I have issues with my arms and grip. On any given day, I'm one...heartbeat away from a debilitating headache. Memories are flickering on and off, but I have no idea if they're real or not. Next time I hear you put yourself down, I'm going to take you over my knee and...spank your ass."

An ache starts in my chest, even as my whole core clenches. I can't possibly admit that sounds...delicious.

Theo reaches out and touches my cheek. His smile is all-knowing. Like he just read my thoughts. "We got off topic." He takes another deep breath. "You give me something to aim for, Sparrow."

"Wait. Did you say your memories are flickering?"

He shrugs. "I don't know if that's the right word for what's happening, but occasionally I get the ghost of an idea of why I know something. I see images out of context. Of my brothers. Of things in the past."

"Is that why you keep getting the headaches, do you think? Because your brain is healing?"

"That's what Doc thinks."

"Then you should still be there so they can help you."

King and Clutch appear at the bottom of the corridor, and Theo's thumb grazes my lips. "I'd rather get married. Plus, we need to make this real so they believe us, and that's way more fun than physiotherapy."

I study him for a moment. This handsome man who is about to become my legally fake husband. Then nod. "Okay."

He kisses me softly, his touch reassuring. "This good?" he asks.

"Very. It's not a hardship kissing you."

"The crush, huh?" Theo teases.

"A very minor one that I'm sure would have gone away the next time you annoyed me."

He slips his arm around my waist, holding our bodies

closer. It's a strain to look straight up at him; I've never been quite so aware of our height difference.

"Eventually I'm gonna kiss you when we have a little more time and nobody chasing us."

"Do you think they are?"

Theo shrugs. "I don't know, but I'll feel better once we're married."

Registering takes us about an hour. There's a line, then paperwork. My biggest fear, that they wouldn't accept my license, is quickly put to rest. We choose the self-officiating option, so we don't have to wait a moment longer than we need to.

By the time we make it back to the rest of the Outlaws and tell them what is happening, there are already bags and boxes.

"Are you okay?" Catalina asks as she follows me into the bathroom to change.

"Today has been a lot."

She hangs the bag over the cubicle door, then takes both my hands. "Close your eyes for a minute. Take a deep breath or two."

I do as she says. I flex my toes in my shoes and deliberately plant them down again to ground myself. When I open my eyes, I feel a little steadier.

"King asked me to double-check you are here because you want to be."

"I am. I...it's just..." I blow out a breath. "It's complicated."

Catalina nods. "Iris has this thing she always says. It's hard to be in this life because it's always the women who get hurt."

I run my fingertip over my scar and eye patch. "I can attest to that."

"Here." Catalina offers me a garment bag and a shoe box. "Start getting changed. Was your family really going to marry you to a stranger?"

I step into a cubicle and do as Cat says. "We overheard my brothers discussing it. I have no idea why. Honestly, I don't even remember my family. So, who they are, what they do, and how they do it are a mystery to me. But they seemed to suggest it was some big 'bringing two families together' kind of thing."

The dress is red. A beautiful, stunning deep red. With thin straps and a corseted top and tea-length full skirt, it's a piece of art.

And it will show most of my scars.

I don't know much, but I'm pretty certain a bride should feel beautiful on her wedding day, and I already feel brittle at the idea that I'm getting ready in a government building's bathroom.

"Fucking men," Catalina says. "And they wonder why we pick the bear."

I slip out of my clothes. "The bear?"

"It's a thing. Would you rather be stuck alone in the woods with a man or a bear? And women always pick the bear. You know, like, at least everyone would believe you if a bear attacked you. Or, if you were attacked by a bear, no one would ask you what you were wearing. Only men would come up with the idea of marrying off a female family member to secure power."

She's right. A bear wouldn't give a shit who I married.

With resolve, I pull on the dress and shoes, stuff my clothes and boots into the garment bag, and step out.

"You look hot," Cat says. "When I left the house with Niro, I didn't know we'd be doing wedding chic, but you can borrow my comb, my lipstick, and any jewelry I'm wearing.

And I'm sorry. I was an ass, thinking only about the club, earlier. There are times I'm more like the men than I am proud of or want to admit."

I put the things I'm carrying on a length of counter near the sinks. "I don't have any strong female friendships that I can remember, but I'm open to making new ones. Apology accepted."

Catalina hugs me. "Good. Because I really want to fix that hair of yours before you go marry your fiancé."

I laugh at that. "Like I said, it's been a rough day."

13

SWITCH

Saint marries us.

He's the closest thing we ever had to a real preacher, apparently, but I stand there with Sophia, who looks real fucking pretty in the dress Catalina brought for her. It's red. Catalina told me it was red wool and silk shantung, though I have no fucking clue what that is. It has thin straps and a fitted bodice that hugs her perfectly, then flares out over her hips.

She's wearing a cute pair of ballet slippers in nude with a little strap. I'm glad Cat or Niro saw the mobility issues she had and bought her something she's comfortable in.

When Catalina had taken her to the courthouse bathroom to get ready, King produced two rings, one a magnificent diamond, and told me that with the dress, I owed the club twenty-five thousand dollars.

Then my brothers burst out laughing, saying it served me right for marrying a woman I barely know.

The wild thing is, I feel like I do know her, even as I realize how ridiculous that sounds.

No one could look better in that Dior dress than Sophia. Especially when she smiles up at me. I like her eyes on me. I like the way she's so much smaller than me.

And when she first walked back out into the hallway, her hair in a pretty knot thing and red lipstick on her lips, she could have knocked me on my ass.

"I, Theo, take you, Sophia, to be my wife," I say, following Saint's lead.

In a moment of quick thinking, when Saint asked for our full names for the service, Sophia jumped in and suggested we didn't want anything so formal. Otherwise, the club would have immediately known who she was.

I'm holding Sophia's hands. Dressed in my cut with a clean white shirt Niro picked up for me while shopping for Sophia. I don't know how I know it but wearing my cut for this feels right. At some point in the future, I'm going to remember my life with the club or make a new one. And it will matter. I can't even explain how I know this either.

Because Sophia and I need each other.

We fit.

In this room, at this moment, given who I now am, Sophia is the one who knows me best.

The ring is somehow a perfect fit and looks so incredible on her finger, I don't give a fuck how much it cost.

Wish I could have waited for Mom to be here so she could see this, but I can't wait to make her day and deal with the fake fury she'll put me through first before she smiles and tells me I made her year. Then she'll either cry or ask for ovulation dates, the way she's banging on about grandkids.

Kids?

Fuck me.

I focus back on how Sophia's hand feels in mine. She confided in me as we walked into the room Clutch secured for us that the dress revealed more of her scars than she was comfortable with.

So, I kissed 'em, right there in front of my brothers. I mean, if you can't kiss your wife and be comfortable with it, why bother?

Finally, Saint slides his phone back in his pocket. "Don't need that anymore because we all know what happens next. You may now kiss your bride."

I slide my hand around Sophia's neck and kiss her with more heat than I have before as the other Outlaws clap mutedly.

My tongue brushes hers, and she moans softly.

The brothers are uncertain, I know. They can't decide if this is a good thing or a bad thing. Or whether it is going to bring harm to the club, even though they can't yet see the underlying threat because I haven't made it clear.

At some point, I'll have to tell them the truth. And they are going to be furious.

But for now, I savor the feel of Sophia's body pressed against mine, the way I have to bend to kiss her.

Then my brothers respond in very different ways. Niro is the first to his feet. He slaps my back and kisses Sophia on the cheek, right over her scar. "Congratulations, you two. You ever need relationship advice, I'm right here."

This makes me laugh, and I realize I like this version of Niro so much better than the angry kid who arrived all those years ago.

"Envy you, brother," Bates says as he congratulates us. "I'd marry Vi today in a heartbeat, but she wants to wait until she's not pregnant to tie the knot."

"Seeing how much you like knocking her up, that's a narrow window," Vex says.

"If you've found even half the happiness Iris and I have, you two will do okay," Spark says.

Clutch steps up and says a few encouraging words, hoping we'll be as happy as he is with Gwen.

Halo kisses Sophia's cheek, then hugs me. "Don't know if you remember but you bet me ten grand that I would end up with Ari. Was gonna pretend I forgot about it, but I'll transfer it today. Call it my wedding present."

I laugh. "I'll take the cash. But you still owe me a wedding present."

"Thanks for officially making me the last man standing," Vex jokes.

Halo throws an arm over his shoulder. "That's because you haven't felt the fucking miracle of going home to a soft bed, a softer woman, and a pussy that's thoroughly branded as yours."

Clutch laughs. "True story."

Vex hugs me, then hugs Sophia. "I'm happy for you both. Look forward to seeing more of the two of you."

King comes over last. "I feel like there's more to this than you're telling us, Switch. But Rae would hand me my ass if I didn't wish you both well. So, he is the half part of a blessed man, left to be finished by such as she; and she a fair divided excellence, whose fullness of perfection lies in him."

The conversation goes quiet around us, and I raise an eyebrow.

King shrugs. "Shakespeare."

"How the fuck do you know that?" I ask.

"Rae, obviously," Clutch says. "You forgot the whole 'she fucked with him using Shakespeare's kings as analogies' bullshit."

He's right. I had forgotten. Add it to the list of things I've been told but somehow can't keep in my head. "Now I remember. But how do you know that quote?" I ask.

Niro puts his hand in the air as if he's a school kid waiting for the teacher to choose him. "Pick me. Pick me. I know the answer to this one."

King laughs. I notice the two of them are more in sync than they ever used to be. I wonder what changed over the years, but it's almost like an older brother with his sometimes-annoying younger sibling. "Go ahead."

"I did it as a his-and-hers tattoo on the two of them," Niro says.

King rolls up his sleeve, and there in two sharp lines of black ink on the inside of his forearm, it says, *He is the half part of a blessed man, left to be finished by such as she.*

"Rae's got the other half across her hip."

"That's so romantic," Sophia says.

"Come in and I'll do you some ink," Niro says. "Call it my wedding present."

"Does it hurt?" Sophia asks.

I can't help but laugh. "Depends on where you get it, Sparrow."

"Fuck my life. He's already given her a pet name," Vex says. "I'm surrounded by chicks and sparrows and duchesses and little ones."

Once the paperwork is registered, we're officially married. In the eyes of the law and my brothers.

Once we climb into Niro's truck, Sophia turns her phone back on, and it blows up with an explosion of messages and phone calls.

"I don't want to talk to any of them, but I don't want them to go to the police or something to issue a missing person report," she says.

"So, send them a message. Take a photograph of your wedding ring. Tell them it's done and that you aren't coming back to them. Tell them you know what they planned. Or say nothing at all. The police come looking and we'll tell 'em how fucking happy we are, right? I'll call the center and we'll let them know we left, you can reassure them there is no duress, and that we'll be back to figure out outpatient treatment or something. Fuck, I'll pay our team to come visit us in Asbury Park."

Sophia shakes her head and looks down at the marriage certificate in her lap. "The center won't do that."

"Eyes on me," I say. And I wait until she does before I say, "Good girl. They will for enough money."

I reach for Sophia's hand and link our fingers in a way that leaves her ring on full display. "Take the picture, Sparrow."

She smiles and then does as I say.

"We have a family group chat. I'll put it in there. They're going to lose their shit."

I turn in my seat and cup her cheek. "You see all those men waiting for us to pull out of our parking spot?"

She looks out to where King and the others are lined up behind us, waiting for us to go. "Yeah?"

"They've got our backs. No one is going to take my wife."

Sophia smiles. "I like the way you say that."

"Say what?"

"'My wife.' Like it means something."

I run my knuckle down her cheek. "Because it does mean something. I've never had a wife before. Might be kind of fun to try and make her fall in love with me."

"You keep saying things like that and it might happen. And then where would we be?"

I release her fingers and turn on the truck as I think

about her question. Then the answer comes to me. "Happily married. That's where we'd be."

I wait as Sophia types her message, then turns off her phone.

"You good, Sparrow?"

"Yeah, I'm good."

When we pull into the clubhouse lot hours later, familiarity slides through me. It's the same, but not. There have been many changes to the exterior in the past decade. But the nostalgia wraps me in a blanket labelled *home*.

I park the truck and study the building. The Iron Outlaws logo sits on the wall, illuminated by three spotlights. There are already bikes parked, but there is a space reserved for the eight riders who came to join me today.

We're obviously a close unit of senior officers.

I only wish I knew how to step back into this group and be a medic again.

I'm not even sure what my value is to the club right now, besides being a physically subpar warm body.

Sophia is asleep next to me, exhausted after a long and physically arduous day. She's lost her family, gained a husband, left the facility that has been her safety for months —and she's still living with the daily complexities of her injuries.

I place my palm on her knee and shake her gently. "Sophia, sweetheart."

She gasps quietly, then yawns and looks around. "Where are we?"

"The Iron Outlaws clubhouse in Asbury Park like we talked about."

"Is this where you live?" she asks. I can't decide if there is disappointment in her tone.

"No. I have a house about ten minutes away from here, but I'm..."

Sophia places her palm on my thigh and rubs gently. "You're not ready to go home and be a part of the debris of your past yet."

It's not a question.

It's a statement of understanding.

"Something like that, Sparrow. Let's get you inside."

Niro grabs our bags from the back seat of the truck before I've even released my seat belt.

"I'm starved," I say. "Want me to order some food when we get in?"

"Please. I'm so hungry." Sophia turns on her phone and looks at it. "Oh shit."

While she's been sleeping, it looks like her family has gotten busy messaging their responses to her photograph.

"How bad is it?" I ask.

"It's like you said. They're playing the brain-injury card. That I'm confused. Making bad decisions. Being easily manipulated. That if I come home, they'll find me a lawyer to file an annulment. Or they'll come get me. They're making me sound like I'm mentally incapacitated." She slams her phone onto the dash of the truck. "I'm not incapable, Theo. I might be many things. A bit broken. A bit physically unsteady. A bit scarred. But there is nothing wrong with my acuity."

"I know. Let's go get some food, sleep on it, and handle everything else in the morning."

When we step into the clubhouse, I'm greeted by applause and good wishes from all the other members. But like Sophia, I'm tired.

Halo and Vex are at the bar. "You want something?" Vex asks.

"Can you run a check on Sophia's phone to make sure there are no trackers on it then bring it back to her?"

"Sure thing." He holds out his hand and Sophia places her phone on his palm.

"You really think my family would do that?" she asks.

Vex gestures around the bar. "These guys have trackers on their phones, their bikes, their old ladies. Whatever we need to do to be safe. I'm sure your family is the same."

He glances my way. It's an unspoken question. Do I want our trackers on her phone? I nod subtly. Too many women in this club have ended up on the wrong side of our enemies.

"You two lovebirds want a drink?" Halo asks as I watch Vex stride away.

"Hate to ask, but do I have a room? I kinda assumed I did as an officer of the club, but I don't remember which one it is."

I can't describe the look Halo gives me. Compassion for sure. But shock, as it really sinks in just what happened to me. He blows out a breath. "Fuck, man. Again, I'm so fucking sorry. All this...you saved Ari's life. But it's a fucking huge price you paid."

It's clear the club is expecting some kind of alcoholic binge. "Just...help me out. Can you get me and Soph to our room? Get us some food. Neither of us has the energy for anything more than that."

Halo nods. "I gotcha."

We walk down the corridor, and as we go, Halo tells me who is where. There's new hardwood instead of the old dark tile that got sticky when it was humid outside.

He opens the door to my room, but it's clear before I step inside that we can't really stay there. It's not that it's a total mess; it's not. The bed is made. It's not a complete disaster.

But it's dusty.

Smells stale.

I don't recognize the bedding, but the pictures tacked to the wall suggest I enjoyed the past decade. Many are of me and Vex. We're camping, drinking, and biking.

I think of Sophia's comment about the forest and how she'd like to see it in person. Once the urgency and danger of all this is over, I'll take her. Perhaps we'll find out if a champagne party girl can enjoy a sleeping bag and stars.

A bottle of Jack, two silver dice, and a pack of playing cards sit on a dresser. I remember the taste of whiskey; I don't know what card game I played.

Not the place I wanted to spend my first night with Sophia. It's too much. A rushed wedding, then one bed in a clubhouse. I should have taken her to a hotel or something.

But I wanted the wall of protection the clubhouse provides us.

"I got an idea," Halo says as if he understands what I'm thinking. "Come with me. This used to be Dad's room before he passed. We're renovating each room in the clubhouse one at a time. Dad's is nearly finished."

He opens a door three down on the opposite side of the hallway.

It's clean. The walls are painted a fresh cream, the trim a navy blue. A new mattress, still wrapped in plastic, sits on the bed. There are unopened boxes and packages around the room. Bedding. Pillows. Towels. "Use 'em," Halo says. "I'll get you some food. Pizza good? You want drinks?"

I look to Sophia.

"Pizza's good. Coke or some water please."

"We got any champagne?" I ask. "We should at least toast ourselves."

"The old ladies' drink of choice when they do book

club," Halo says. "Sure we've got a bottle kicking around. Let me check."

The door clicks shut after he leaves.

Silence settles between the two of us, and I reach for Sophia, pulling her to me. "So, what do we do now?" she asks.

14

SOPHIA

"We start making ourselves at home," Theo says.

"We do?" There's a pinch of uncertainty in my voice. I hate that it's there, but everything suddenly feels overwhelming.

"Look at me, Sparrow." There's a certain command in Theo's tone, and I can't help responding to it, even as I'm sure he'll see straight through how I'm feeling.

In the quiet of the room, I do as he says.

He tugs me closer, and I feel his cock harden against my belly.

"Guess I like it when women do as I say," he says with a grin. He reaches for the pins in my hair and removes them one by one and then removes the elastic holding it all together.

"I'm reasonably certain I won't always do as you say."

"I'll take my chances. But to answer your question, yes, we start to make ourselves at home. Because a home is where we are. It's not a specific set of bricks and mortar or things. It's us. So, this is home tonight. We're gonna make this bed. And while we do, you're gonna think about whether you're okay sharing it with me tonight. And we're going to ask questions to get to know each other. We'll do whatever physio we should be doing. And we're gonna eat. And maybe Halo will find that bottle of champagne and we'll have a glass to toast getting married. And we'll shower and fall into bed. And tomorrow we get to wake up married and figure out what the fuck we do next."

He's a hot box, his body warm against mine. I place my head against his chest. It's so sturdy and reassuring, and it's a precious feeling. "You make it sound so easy."

"It's as easy as we make it."

"I really want to help set things up, but I don't think I can stand for much longer."

Theo kisses me softly. "Then let me fix that." He grabs a chair and places me on it. "You sit here."

He rips the plastic cover off the mattress and quickly finds the right sheets.

"If you pass me the pillows and pillowcases, I can be making those up."

Between us we make steady work preparing the bed.

"What's your favorite color?" Theo asks.

"Still deciding," I say. "There were some beautiful peonies on Dr. Polunin's desk. Like a deep, deep pink. I liked those. But I also like the color of the tiles around the pool."

"The turquoise?"

"Yeah. Those. And then I watched a documentary on the Amazon rainforest. That deep green was so beautiful. What about you?"

"Used to be navy blue. Now I'm thinking it's red."

His eyes rove over my dress, and I feel heat hitting my cheeks. "Sweet talker."

Theo winks at me. "Swear I never even thought about

the color until I saw you in it. You look real fucking pretty today, Sparrow."

I slide my eye patch off and reveal my prosthetic eye. I figure if I can't sit here as myself in front of my pretend husband who is starting to feel more real every moment, then I shouldn't even be here.

"You okay?" he asks.

I stuff a pillow into the soft case. "The elastic on the band feels like it gets tighter and tighter as the day goes on. It gives me a headache eventually."

"Then don't wear it. Not around me. Or in our home. Or even outside with everyone else. Niro doesn't give a fuck about what everyone else thinks."

I shake my head. "You may think that because of the confident way he deals with life, but I will guarantee he does care. Favorite movie?"

"Hmm. I watched an older movie while I was in the hospital. *The Shawshank Redemption*. Great actors. Great plot. I really liked it. You?"

"You'll laugh."

Theo stops where he's stuffing a duvet into the corner of its cover. "You got me intrigued. Tell me."

"I started watching all these Christmas romance movies that were streaming."

"We only just hit fall," Theo says with a chuckle.

"Why can't Christmas be year round? In my favorite one, this woman's husband tells her he wants a divorce and leaves her the day their son leaves for college. So, she goes off on safari and ends up working at an elephant sanctuary and hooks up with a hot pilot who flies these small planes. I want to go see the world, Theo. Can we go sometime?"

"You ask me with that look on your face and that wistful tone to your voice and I'd move heaven or hell to make it happen." He holds my gaze for a moment and doesn't make me feel pathetic for wanting something I could never afford given I have no job prospects and my family will likely cut me off.

We work in silence. Theo hands me a small pocketknife and passes me boxes and packages. He doesn't assume I can't help or that I'm too weak. Just that I need to accommodate the pain of standing.

Our things get unpacked and put away. Clothes get hung. Toiletries are placed in the bathroom. I place my smashed phone and driver's license in the drawer next to the bed. For some reason, the police had kept both, and an officer came to the rehab center to return them.

Theo disappears for a moment to his room and returns with some clothes. He places one of his T-shirts on a pillow.

"For you to sleep in," he says.

"Thank you," I say as I open another box and find a lamp.

Theo chuckles. "You're welcome. I know this isn't as plush as the rooms at the center, but it's ours, and that makes it a million times better. Can't wait to fall into bed."

A knock at the door makes me jump, and Halo appears, holding a stack of pizza boxes. "Got you some pies from the pizza place down the street. Remembered your usual order, Switch. No clue what you like, sweetheart, so I got you what I usually get for Ari. But I'm sure Switch'll share."

"Smells so good," I say as he places it on the desk.

Another man I haven't met brings the drinks in and leaves without a word. The patch on his back says *Prospect*.

"You finding everything?" Halo asks.

"It's like Christmas undoing all the boxes," I say.

He smiles at me. "I'll be back with some glasses. Otherwise, are you two good?"

"We are." Theo places his hand on my shoulder. "Was everyone okay with us just hanging here tonight?"

"Yeah," Halo says. "A mix of concern though. You two have been through the wars of late."

"We're good. Better to have a safe place to land."

Halo raises an eyebrow. "Safe?"

Theo barely blinks. "Soft. I meant soft. Words get muddled."

"Yeah, well," Halo says finally. "Clutch might have told Gwen you got married. So be prepared and rest up. You're getting a party tomorrow night whether you want one or not. I told 'em you might prefer an afternoon thing. So Catalina said you should hang your dress up properly and not let Theo ruin it tonight, if you catch her drift."

I feel the heat rise in my cheeks as I look down at the floor.

Halo laughs, a loud guffaw. "Aww, little ones who get embarrassed are my favorites. Let me go get you those glasses, then I'm off home to my own little ones."

The door closes behind him. "Halo has kids?"

"He calls his old lady, Ari, 'little one.' And they have a daughter...her name?" He sighs. "Can't remember. Don't ask to see pictures. When he used to come see me at the hospital, he would show me all the pictures he'd taken. Lola! That's her name. Lola eating grass, Lola breathing, Lola being an utterly normal baby doing normal baby shit while he's talking about it like she just performed a...what's the word for those magic tricks Jesus did?"

"Miracle." I stroke his arm. I can tell he's getting tired. His words and memory are more taxing. "I wonder what it must feel like to grow up with a parent who thinks of you so highly as opposed to my dad, who seems to think I'm a pawn in a chess game. Which...shit...should I reply to all those messages?"

"Only you can decide. I'll support you. But for what it's worth, I think a message telling them you're safe and happy would be more than they deserve. However, it might bring some calm, even if it's just for tonight."

"Do you think they all knew? Like, is my mamà aware? All of my brothers?" I ask. My mind starts to fill with questions. "Were they all just waiting for me to get better? Counting down the days?"

Theo crouches in front of me. "Those questions and their answers won't bring you any peace tonight."

I look at Theo, taking in the way the bristles of his scruff grow across his cheek. He has such long eyelashes. And he feels like something...someone...I can hold on to. "I feel lost, Theo."

"I know, Sparrow. But I'm right here."

Theo kisses me, another of those whisper-soft kisses that make me melt.

"I feel like I'm fumbling my way through how the fuck to comfort my wife because I don't know what makes you feel better in situations like this," he says, sliding his hands into my hair.

"What do you want to do?" I ask. My voice has a breathy quality to it that I'm unused to.

"My body is urging me to do more than just kiss you, but I need to remember that you're practically a virgin. Zero memory of sex. I have no idea if physical comfort is what you need right now."

This time when he kisses me, he ruthlessly seeks my tongue with his and I sigh as I tumble into what we're doing. Theo stands and tugs me to my feet.

His arms tighten around me and his fingers have just

reached the zipper of my dress when my stomach rumbles embarrassingly loudly and I remember we've barely eaten since breakfast this morning.

Theo groans and then smiles at me. "Shouldn't be undressing you while you're hungry. That's definitely not taking care of you. Let's eat," he says and leads me to the pizza boxes.

We open them and look at the toppings. "Guess you really like meat?" I say as we take in the pizza loaded with pepperoni, bacon, and sausage. The receipt on the box says it's a meat lovers with double the toppings.

"We're about to find out why," Theo says.

The other pizza is a little heavier on the veggies. Chicken with peppers, mushrooms, tomatoes, and onions. "Which do you want to try?"

"I'm going in with the meat," Theo says.

I tear him a piece and put it on the paper plate.

"Thanks, Sparrow."

I tear a piece of the same and return to my seat as Theo sits on the end of the bed. It's steaming hot, and I blow on it before I take a bite. I made the mistake of not doing so early during my time at the center.

Alessio had snuck in some stuffed-crust pizza because I'd seen it on television in a movie. I bit straight into it, just as Alessio had started to warn me that I'd burn my mouth, but the damage was done. Large blisters appeared on the roof of my mouth.

As my oldest brother, he was the one I felt closest to. His gestures always seemed genuine. Kind. Thoughtful. A whisper teases my consciousness that I'm going to miss him most of all.

There's a knock on the door, and Halo returns with two champagne flutes and two regular glasses, followed by Vex.

I swallow my pizza. "Thank you."

"Pleasure. How's the food?" he asks.

"Sinful."

Halo rubs the top of my head. "Better than all that fancy shit you were eating in rehab?"

"So much better," Theo says.

"Good. I'm out. Quite a few of the guys have gone home. See you two in the morning." He offers Theo a key. "Key to the room."

"Thanks."

Vex offers Sophia her phone. "There were two trackers on it. An in-phone service where you share location, and a bit of buried code. Both are gone. But I have replaced it with some tracking of my own."

I don't know how I feel about that, but then again, I would want Theo to know where I am if my family got to me. "Thank you. That makes me feel safer."

Vex tips his head in acknowledgement once. "See you two in the morning."

And with short goodbyes, we're on our own again.

"Want to try the other pizza?" I ask Theo.

He shakes his head. "I'm not fucking with perfection. I had good taste in pizza."

I laugh. "I'm going to try it. That might be too much meat for me to digest before bedtime."

The idea of bedtime begins to move from a conceptual nightly routine to the very real idea that I'm about to get into bed with my husband.

My husband.

Theo stands and grabs the champagne bottle. He unwraps it with ease and pops the cork.

"You made that look easy," I say.

"I'm so intrigued by this separation of knowledge. You

know, autobiographical memory versus procedural memory. It's really interesting to see where things fall. Or to decide whether you did a thing because it was just common sense. Like opening the champagne." He grabs a glass and pours it, tilting the glass slightly. "Did I open it with ease because it's procedural memory? Or did I look at the wrapper and know all the shit covering and in the top of the bottle had to go?"

"I'd say it was the former, because you did some things that wouldn't be my first guess. Like the way you knew to ease the cork out of the top, that you thought to point it away from the flat-screen TV or my face, and you angled the glass as you poured."

Theo laughs at that. "There are plenty of things I could think of doing to your face, but firing a cork into it is not one of them."

He offers me the champagne glass and pours one for himself before crouching in front of me. "Here's to us," he says, tapping the rim of his glass to mine. "So far, having a wife is pretty fucking cool."

"Having a husband isn't too weird either."

Theo grins at that. "I'll take not being too weird."

"You know what I mean. I like it. Having a husband."

"Good. Now finish your food."

15

———

SWITCH

With a belly full of food and a couple of glasses of champagne in my alcohol-parched system, I'm chill as fuck.

The center was great for my rehabilitation, but probably not my sleep and stress levels.

This quiet is good.

Sophia is still in her chair. My feet are on the floor, but I've flopped back on the bed. My left hand aches like a bitch, and I find myself opening my fingers wide, then curling them into a fist.

The bed sinks next to me as Sophia sits and reaches for my hand. "Let me."

She does that thing she did in the center. Stretching my palm, then digging her thumbs in to release the tense muscles. I close my eyes as she works her magic. I feel the warmth of her thigh pressed against mine, and the soft scent of her swirls around me.

I woke up this morning a bachelor. I ended it with a wife.

I hope there's never a time I regret this decision, but right now, it feels pretty special.

"You okay, Sparrow?"

"Mm-hmm."

She flexes my fingers, runs her knuckles up my wrist and forearm. Everything is tight when she starts, but loose before she moves on.

"We should get some oil."

"First thing in the morning," I say. "Just, for the love of God, don't stop now."

Somewhere in the process, I must have fallen asleep because I wake to the brush of Sophia's lips against mine. It's the first time she's taken the lead to kiss me, and I like it.

I cup my hand around the back of her neck and hold her firmly to me. My cock hardens quickly, even though I'm exhausted.

"Come shower with me," I mumble against her lips. "I'll hold you, Sparrow. Won't let you fall."

I can see a hint of nervousness, but no fear. Her cheeks flush. With embarrassment or need, I can't tell yet.

"Okay," she says softly, and I let out a breath of relief.

I stroke my knuckle along her olive-toned skin, taking in her wide eyes, and the slight gap between her two front teeth. The most minor of imperfections is endearing.

"We don't have to do anything more intimate than washing each other," I say. "I wasn't trying to rush us along. I just...I need to take care of you."

"Aren't we supposed to consummate our marriage?"

I huff. "I suppose if we were in medieval England and thought the church or some shit was going to come after us and stone us to death if we didn't, it might matter."

Her brow wrinkles. "They did that?"

"You're relying on high school facts coming out of my

mangled head. Might be fact. Might be total confabulation like Belle-Odette."

Sophia smiles softly, and I run my thumb over her lower lip. It's plump, pink, and soft. Not sure what it is about this woman, but she sucks me into her orbit. She can't even show me who she really is because even she doesn't know, and I still find myself fascinated by her.

She's a survivor.

She's still standing.

I'm in awe of her.

She stands and turns, lifting her hair away from the zipper of her dress. "Don't forget Catalina says I have to hang it and not let you ruin it."

"You're sure?" I ask. My voice sounds like I've been on a three-day bender including way too much whiskey.

"I trust you," Sophia says.

I know she's my fake wife, but I feel like she might take my heart anyway.

My fingers are clumsy as fuck when I grip her hips and pull her back between my legs.

I've stitched a man, threaded a needle, and I can't figure out how to do this simple task. Now is not the time to over-think it, but I wonder if I'll ever be able to do any of that again.

My fingers struggle to pinch and grip the zipper, but we don't rush. I take in the way the ends of her hair flutter slightly. How smooth her skin feels beneath my knuckle as I drag the zipper down her back.

I've got no idea how long it's been since I fucked a woman, but my guess is it's been even longer since I made love to one. Just sitting here with Sophia in front of me feels more special than that.

When her zipper is lowered, I turn her around and look

up at her. Her pretty eye is on me. She releases her hair, and it falls in a dark waterfall.

I slide my fingertips along the smooth skin of her collarbones, but as I'm just about to push the straps off her shoulders, she stops me.

"It's not pretty...you know. The scars and things. I don't want you to...don't look too closely."

I don't know how to express to her just how much it doesn't matter to me in words I think she'll believe. I have to believe she won't think less of me if the movement on my left side never returns to normal.

"We're both a bit broken, Soph. Let me see the broken parts of you, and I'll share the broken bits of me with you too. Maybe our broken pieces will fit."

"Jesus, Theo," she says, swiping beneath her eyes with her fingertips. "Stop. Unless you want me a bawling mess."

"I'll settle for crying out my name."

She hiccups and laughs. "Kiss me, already," she says.

I settle my palms either side of her neck, my thumbs brushing her jawline, and do as she instructs.

I could happily waste a lifetime or two kissing Sophia Viscuso. She's a fast study for someone who confessed they don't really remember kissing. And I need to remember that I'm effectively holding a virgin in my arms. She doesn't remember what this feels like, how much it is possible to share with another person. She can't remember the first lick, suck, or slide. Or the feel of skin against skin.

Her tongue is gentle against mine, a tentative exploration, and for a moment I let her lead.

But there is a moment when her tits press against my chest.

When my cock is trapped between the two of us.

That instinct takes over.

I ache for her.

This time, she doesn't object when I slip the straps off her shoulders. We wiggle the dress to the ground, but I keep my eyes on her face. Not because I don't want to look at her body.

I do.

But because I acknowledge that she's insecure about the way she looks right now. My hope is that, over time, I can convince her to see herself the way I do.

With confident fingers that belie their physical limitations, I pop the clasp on her bra and let it drop to the floor.

I brush over the rippled skin and the smooth scars. The ridges affect me but not in the way Sophia worries. They tell me what a warrior she is. Worry floods me. We need to understand the truth of what happened to her that day. We need to know the long-term implications for her health. We need to know how to work within her limitations to continue to build her strength.

The *we* in all that doesn't scare me.

I press my lips to the side of her neck, taking in the scent of her. Sophia tips her head, and I trace the line to her ear, where I gently bite her lobe.

She shivers against me, and I grin. "Like it?" I ask.

"Love it," she replies.

Her answer gives me hope. "I want to try everything with you, Soph. I want us to learn together what we both like. I'll respect your boundaries, but let's explore."

"I'm as excited as I am nervous," she replies. "But, yes. I want to explore things with you too."

Quickly, I strip the rest of my clothes. Sophia helps. But I'm impatient.

I grab two of the new towels and lead us to the bathroom before turning on the shower. It's large with a big showerhead, and when I turn it on, steaming-hot water splashes onto pale gray tiles.

"You first," I say, nudging Sophia beneath the water.

She tips her head back and closes her eyes as water drenches her hair and body. And what a fucking body it is. Heavy tits with nipples that lean brown rather than pink. A narrow waist. But thick thighs and an ass you can grab on to.

She's got a whole lot of hair down there, hiding what I want to see.

As she turns a little beneath the spray, I see her scars. They're vicious red swaths across her body, even after all this time, which tells me just how bad they were when they happened.

"I'm lucky you're even here," I whisper.

Sophia steps out of the spray a little. "Sorry, did you say something?"

I shake my head. "Not a thing." I empty some of her shampoo onto my palm and wash her hair gently.

Bathing together in the soft light of the bathroom is an intimacy money can't buy. As she rinses her hair, bubbles and water sluice down her body, between the valley of her breasts. I follow it with my fingertips.

Sophia gasps as she experiences my touch as if it's her first time. I don't want to be a jealous guy, yet there is something innately primal about being someone's first. I don't care who came first, but I want to be the only one she remembers. I press my mouth to those lush lips of hers and pull her close. The first feel of her skin against mine is like a balm to my soul.

I wrap my arms around her, my hands gliding up her back and fisting her wet hair.

"We go too fast, or I do something you don't like, you tell me," I say.

She nods her agreement. There's a heady mix of arousal, nerves, and trust in her eyes. Tentatively, her hands reach out and slip around my waist.

This first round is going to be over way too soon. My sex-starved body responds immediately. My cock going from interested to harder than a steel pillar in about two seconds.

Sophia glances down between the two of us. "I understood the basics, but..."

Gone are the nerves, replaced with all-too-human hunger.

She reaches between us and runs a single fingertip along the side of my cock. When it twitches in response, she giggles, the sound bouncing off the tiled walls. I can't help but smile in spite of the way she's making me feel.

"Put your palm around it," I instruct.

When she does, I suck in a breath and look up at the ceiling, the image of my cock in her hand burned into my brain.

This is a really bad idea. A memory of my dad telling me to always be a biker on the streets and a gentleman in the sheets flickers. We were drinking beer at a club barbecue. He was looking over at Mom and smiling.

But I know what he means, and letting Sophia jerk me off while I just stand there isn't that.

"It's soft but hard," Sophia says.

I take her hand and press a kiss to her palm. "I want to touch you. You okay with that?"

"I'd like that."

Carefully, I get to know her body. Over the curve of her breast, brushing across her peaked nipple. Down the soft plane of her stomach, past a cute little innie belly button, and through drenched curls of hair.

Sophia opens her legs a little wider for me, and I dip

between her thighs, stroking her pussy. She bucks against me almost immediately. I repeat the action. A gentle caress.

Color hits her cheeks as her eyelids flutter closed.

I kiss the tip of her nose, then her lips as I apply a little pressure, easing the tip of my finger into her.

She's wet, warm, and squeezes my finger.

When I withdraw, I circle the hard nub of her clit.

"Theo," she gasps.

"You want me to stop?" I whisper huskily against her ear.

She shakes her head. "If you stop, I might have to kill you."

I chuckle but continue. Alternating between her clit and her pussy, I add another finger, stretching her wide.

"Faster," she encourages. I love that she's so uninhibited in this moment with me. She feels safe enough to ask for what she needs.

I do as she asks, and I'm so into it, I might fucking come just watching her, but then she cries out.

And it's not a cry of orgasm. Her fingernails dig into my shoulder, creating a heavenly glitch between pleasure and pain. "My balance. My leg."

I stop what I'm doing immediately and offer her my arms to grip onto. She tries to shake out her left side, but it's difficult. I lead her to the seat at the back of the shower and help her sit.

"You okay? What can I do?" I ask. The room is steamy and warm enough that we don't get cold.

She shakes her head but looks down at the floor. "Sorry I ruined the mood."

There's hurt and embarrassment and sadness in her tone. So, I crouch in front of her. "Hey. Look at me, Sparrow."

Sophia does as I say. "Sorry."

"No. We don't say sorry for needing to accommodate ourselves. I should have checked if you were okay. I know you were tired. You ever feel unsteady or unstable, just tell me you need to move before it becomes pain."

She bites down on her lower lip. "I was enjoying it though. I didn't want it to stop."

"Those are words to warm my heart." I slip my hands to her knees and slide them ever so gently apart. "Anything hurts, you just tell me, and we'll adjust."

She nods and lets me spread her legs. Her pussy is right there, almost at eye level, and it's a thing of fucking beauty. The ledge is at the perfect height for me to lean forward and lazily lick her clit. I can't help but think whoever designed this shower stall had that in mind.

Dirty fucker, and my new best friend.

Sophia's hands slide into my wet hair and she tugs hard as I lap at her.

She likes it.

So do I.

I alter her position on the bench so her pussy is tilted up towards me, and I dip my tongue inside her. Her hips roll as she seeks to find what she wants.

Don't know what my preferences in women were before, but I find I love the way Sophia joins in. The way she seeks what feels good.

And even though she doesn't remember what an orgasm at the hands of another person feels like, she's chasing it anyway.

I add a finger, then another. Thrusting them in and out of her. Then something else takes over. I scissor my fingers open and closed. I rub hard at the rippled surface deep inside Sophia, and she cries out as fluid rushes from her.

It's so fucking hot.

But Sophia screeches to a halt. "Did I just pee?"

I shake my head. "No, sweetheart. That was squirting. I'll explain the difference later, but I love that you felt everything we're doing so intensely."

I lower my mouth to her pussy and start bringing her up all over again. Sucking on her clit, then laving it. Alternating as I dip my fingers in and out of her.

"Theo," she gasps as her orgasm starts to build. Her fingers return to my hair, tugging on it as she rides my face with abandon.

I love the sting of her nails scratching my scalp.

Her cry echoes around the shower as she comes loudly.

"Oh, God," she gasps, her breath catching.

And I feel like a fucking man again.

Like I just did something special. Something only I can do.

Sophia's thighs shake as I pull my fingers from her. Her gaze follows as I dip them into my mouth to taste her. It's an automatic gesture, and I hope to fuck it's procedural memory leading the way.

With her eyes closed, she slumps back against the shower wall. "So, your mouth isn't just good for talking," she says finally.

I chuckle at that, even though my cock aches. I stroke it as I observe her post-orgasmic glow. "My mouth can do lots of things if you'll let it."

She leans forward and places her hand over mine. "Let me help you with that."

"We might have had enough excitement for tonight. You can go get in bed, and I'll take care of this in the shower."

"Stand, please," she says.

I cup her chin firmly. "Only because you asked nicely."

"You're going to need to guide me, Theo," she says.

I stand between her legs and place my hands on the wall of the shower behind her.

"Lick me. Suck me. Grip me and stroke me. Any of those four things and we'll be golden, Sparrow."

Sophia leans forward and licks the underside of my cock, and my eyes roll back in my head. I take a deep breath and look down to find her looking up at me.

It's a pretty spectacular view.

Her eyes are wide open, her cheeks flushed. And her mouth... Fuck, the way her tongue strokes along the veiny underside of my cock is better than any porn I watched.

I want to video that mouth and play it back.

I want to be able to see what the two of us look like together.

I want mirrors.

But more, I want the feel of her lips wrapped around my cock. "Suck me, Sparrow. Wanna see you take me deep."

Grabbing my cock, I angle it so it's in line with her mouth. And Sophia wraps me in those thick, lush lips of hers.

"Fuck," I hiss. "Feels so good."

Her hand grips the length she can't swallow, and I thrust gently back and forth, unable to control the movement of my hips.

She's so warm and wet. I close my eyes so I can't see her. Because the visual is gonna make me come way faster than I want to.

I want to savor this for a moment.

I want to remember who I am. Who I was?

I want to be Switch for a hot second.

Her saliva coats my cock, easing the slide of her palm. The sensations intensify. It's no use pretending I can last tonight when she already has me on a knife's edge.

"Watching you come got me all riled. Watching you suck my cock has me close." My breath is coming faster, punctuating my words. "You don't want me to come in your mouth, you better take me out now."

Sophia looks up, and while her mouth is occupied, I can see the making of a smile.

That one staggeringly beautiful look is enough to send an orgasm hammering down my spine, through my balls. I come hard. She can't swallow fast enough.

My cum seeps out of the corner of her mouth, dribbling down her chin.

It's hot as fuck.

Dizziness hits, and I palm the shower wall to keep my balance. My left arm shakes, trying to take my weight.

"Sparrow," I say breathlessly, before placing a kiss on the top of her head.

16

SOPHIA

Voices outside the window rouse me from sleep, and it takes me a moment to remember where I am.

The Iron Outlaws clubhouse.

A newly decorated room.

With my husband.

My thumb goes to touch the beautiful ring on my ring finger. It's solid. Has substance.

A reminder I'm a married woman.

Because my family tried to marry me off to a family ally. For what? Power? Security? Oh, God…money?

"It's okay, babe," Theo mumbles behind me, half asleep. "It's just King and Niro."

He tightens his hold on me, pulling my back to his chest, and I relax into his arms. He thinks it was the voices outside that bothered me. I'm not going to correct him.

His lips brush my neck briefly, but then he falls back to sleep. Sunlight edges in through the gaps in the curtains. And now that my brain is firing up for the day, I can't get back to sleep.

I slip from beneath Theo's grip and make my way to the bathroom. I blush when I see the bench seat of the shower.

The way Theo made me feel was...sexual. Beautiful. The whole thing intimate and way less embarrassing than I had imagined sex to be. I feel relieved.

Happy.

And ravenously hungry.

For food *and* Theo.

I want to know what full penetrative sex feels like. I watched a raunchy show set in the Regency period, so I have the basic mechanics down, but I want to experience it with Theo.

I do what I need to do, then pull on some clothes. Theo barely stirs, and I let him sleep. As we climbed into bed last night, he started struggling for words again, and then a headache hit him hard. He took some of the pills Niro had given him and finally found sleep.

Quietly, I leave the room and find my way to the kitchen.

A little girl sits on the counter while Niro makes pancakes in a large skillet.

"You hungry?" she asks. "'Cause Uncle Colton makes the best pancakes in the whole world."

Niro turns around and spots me. He waves a spatula at the seats tugged under the counter. "Take a seat. I'll make you some."

"If it's not too much trouble, that would be great."

"I'm Avery, and my dad is the enforcer of the club, which means he's the biggest and strongest."

"Hey, Avery. I'm Sophia. And I met your dad already."

"And he is definitely not the biggest and strongest in the club," Niro says with a chuckle. "He's not bigger than Spark or Halo."

Avery's eyes narrow. "Yes. But he's the fiercest."

Niro dabs a bit of pancake batter on the tip of Avery's nose. "He's probably the best at jump rope, how about that?"

Avery chuckles as she wipes it away and turns to me. "My daddy is the best at jump rope, he can cross his arms over and everything."

"That does sound like he's very good. So, your daddy is the best at jump rope, and Uncle Colton is the best at pancakes. What are you best at?"

Dramatically, she taps her finger against her lip and looks at the ceiling.

"She's best at talking. Or maybe being annoying," Niro says with a grin.

"Hey," she says. "I was going to say I'm best at being your best friend."

Niro's whole face softens. "Yeah, kiddo. You're definitely best at that." He scoops three pancakes off the griddle and hands them to Avery. "You know what to do."

She hurries to the table and then takes toppings from three different bowls. Blueberries. Chocolate chips. And sprinkles. Then she smothers the pile in syrup.

I wince at how sweet that must all taste. "All the basic food groups, huh?"

"The food we eat at mine and Uncle Colton's sleepover club stays in sleepover club," Avery says. "Mommy and Daddy will never know, will they, Uncle Colton?"

"Nope. Not a word from me. And Sophia can only be in our club if she agrees to the rules."

I put my hands in the air. "I agree to the rules."

Niro watches Avery until she's sitting with her plate and begins to eat. "Same again?" he says, tipping his chin towards Avery's plate.

"Yes, please. I might skip the candy toppings though."

"Spoilsport." Niro carefully pours three ladles of batter onto the skillet. "Sleep well?" he asks.

"Better than I have in a while."

He looks up at me for a second. "That's the power of freedom."

"What do you mean?"

He shrugs as he watches the little bubbles pop in the pancake mixture. "You and Switch, you've both been cooped up in that rehab unit, Switch without his bike, and you without whatever it is you used to do and be. Then you found out you were meant to be married off to some guy, and that's probably why you had your accident."

I look around to make sure no one else can overhear. Avery is too engrossed in her food to pay Niro's softly spoken words any mind.

"Don't worry," Niro says. "The clubhouse is slow to get moving in the morning. I was outside with King a few minutes ago because he needed to work on his bike in the garage, but that's it."

My relief must be palpable.

"Listen, I'm on your side. I'm one of the few who will be once it comes out why you're here and why you married Switch. But that's where I was going with the power of freedom. You gaining your freedom means my brother has lost his."

His words hit me hard. "There's truth to that."

Niro nods as he flips the pancakes. "And as his friend, and as perhaps the only person here who fully understands what *you're* going through, I want to hear your reasons for letting him give that up for you."

"I wish I had a better answer than I do. He's a handsome,

capable man with a kind heart, otherwise I wouldn't be sitting here. And I'm just a—"

"Fuck. Don't look at me like that. You say you're nothing, and I'm gonna punch you in the face." Niro raises his voice.

"Uncle Colton," Avery snaps. Tears fill her eyes. "Don't be mean to our new friend."

He takes a deep breath. His lips move, silently counting up to five, then back down again. "Sorry, Ave. Didn't mean it like it sounded. It's just Sophia was about to tell me that she was less."

"Less than what, Uncle Colton?"

"Less than the rest of us," he says.

"Oh no," Avery says, jumping up from her seat. She throws her arms around me. "Daddy says hugs solve everything."

Like Avery, tears sting my eyes. "Your daddy might be right." I hold her close for a second. "I got it. You know what you're best at?"

"What?"

"Making someone feel better. And hugs. You're really good at those."

Avery smiles. "I am. You have a scar like Uncle Colton."

I touch it with my fingertips. "I do."

"It makes you unique and special like Uncle Colton is."

The softly spoken words squeeze my heart.

She looks at Niro who winks at her then tips his head towards her seat.

"Go sit down," he says. "I'll make you some more when I've made Sophia's."

Avery skips back to her seat, her tears staved off by the thought of more high-octane pancake toppings.

"Niro," I say quietly. "You're right to ask. I have no income that I'm aware of. I have no career that I can draw on. And I have no past that I can remember. I stand here in these clothes that I don't remember choosing. I don't know where I go from here."

Niro slips my pancakes on my plate. "I know what it's like to remember every minute of my past, and sometimes I wish I couldn't. I remember watching my sister be murdered. I'm not sure remembering is always better. But you've been offered the gift of a do-over. Everything is a blank page. You don't like your hair, cut it. You don't like those clothes, hop online, get ideas, and shop. You want to be a fucking architect, sign up for online classes, go to college. Just...I know what it is to stay stuck. I was stuck for a decade." He glances over my shoulder briefly. "Don't do that. Move, Sophia. Be. Show us what Switch gets out of this, not for us or for Switch, but for you. You're free now, so do something fucking useful with it."

Arms slip around my waist that aren't Avery's. They're firm and strong and covered in ink. Lips brush my neck, and I sink back against Theo.

Switch.

"You can be anything you want, but you don't need to be anything other than who you are for me." Then he stands and places his hands on either side of me, gripping the counter. "Watch what you say to her, brother."

Niro pours three more pancakes onto the griddle. "As I said to Sophia, I'm on your side. Which means you need to figure out how the fuck you convince everyone that the two of you fell in love so fast before you ask them to get involved in a war no one is going to want. King doesn't think we should tell you everything because it would all be out of context. With no memory, none of it would make sense, but this"—he gestures between the two of us—"directly impacts what we have going on."

Theo's breath is warm against the side of my face, but there's a heady strength that comes from feeling him protect me.

"Then tell me," he says. "I have flashes of memory. Of you not giving a fuck about the rules. So, break them now."

"Go eat your pancakes with Avery," Niro tells me.

"No, if this involves me or my family, I have a right to know."

Niro gestures to the table. "Go sit. You want to live this life with my brother, then you need to learn some shit isn't for your ears, even if it directly affects you."

"But—"

"Do as he says, Sparrow."

I bite down the urge to tell them both where to shove it. Theo married me. The bikers are letting me stay in the clubhouse. But when it's just Theo and me, we're going to have a conversation about how he doesn't get to dismiss me like that.

I grab my plate, then walk to the table and sit down with Avery.

"Are they doing boy talk?" Avery asks.

"What, sweetheart?"

"Boy talk. It's what Mommy calls it when they go off to talk about serious things."

I smile at that. "Yes. It's boy talk. But sometimes I think they should make it everyone talk, not boy talk."

Avery nods seriously. "I overheard Mommy tell Daddy that she's a fembi-nist and that I will be a fembi-nist too when I'm big. And that Daddy needs to get with the fembi-nist program."

I bite on my tongue to stop the chuckle. "And how did he take that?"

"Daddy walked over to her, and they smooched for ages.

It was gross. And then Daddy asked Mommy whether her fembi-nist self liked his hands on her."

"Well, I'd like to think I'm a feminist too. I think that's why it bothers me they went off to talk without me."

And wait. Why am I telling a kid who can't even be six my boy problems?

I top my pancakes with fruit and a little syrup, then take a bite. "Oh my God. These are good."

Avery grins. "Told you Uncle Colton makes the best pancakes."

He does. They're light and fluffy and the perfect amount of sugar. Not even a tiny bit soggy. Cooked to perfection.

"He really does," I say with a mouth full of food.

We eat the rest of our food in companionable silence.

Periodically, I glance over to Theo and Niro, who are deep in conversation as Niro continues to make pancakes. I wish I knew what they were talking about. Theo's brow is furrowed as Niro explains something.

I see Theo mutter the f-bomb and run his hand over his scar. He glances my way, but the smile he offers me doesn't quite reach his eyes.

When I'm finished with my plate, I take it to the sink to rinse it and wash my hands. Uncertain of what to do next, I pause. But Theo reaches for my hand and tugs me to him.

"I'm gonna go out on my bike. Maybe just a short ride. Wanna come with me?" Theo asks.

Niro glances at Theo's left arm. "You sure you're good to ride?"

"Guess there's only one way to find out. What to come?" Theo asks me.

I think about Niro's words.

Everything is a blank page... I know what it is to stay stuck... Don't do that. Move, Sophia. Be. Show us what Switch gets out of this, not for us or for Switch, but for you. You're free now, so do something fucking useful with it.

I know I need to talk to him about what just happened. But I also need to take Niro's advice.

"I'd love that."

Theo grins. "But first we have a call to make."

It takes us five minutes to set the call up in our room, but as Theo's phone rings, I'm nervous. "You should have let me do something nicer with my hair," I say.

"Your hair looks great."

"It looks like I slept with damp hair, which I did."

"She's gonna love you," he says, before kissing me firmly.

"Hey, Teddy Bear. Whoa. Okay."

Theo grins and looks at his phone. "Hey, Mom."

"This must be the girl," she says, putting her hand on her heart. I immediately see the similarities. They have the same kind eyes and smile.

"Yeah. Mom, this is Sophia. Sophia, this is my mom, Clare."

"It's so nice to meet you," I say.

"Well, it's even nicer to meet you. Wait, hang on." She leans back in her chair. "Jason, get your butt in here." She looks back at the screen. "Your dad's coming."

I place my hand on Theo's thigh and squeeze hard. He glances at me and winks.

"Thought you didn't need to leave for the hospital for another ten minutes," a man says off camera.

"No." She gestures him over. "Theo's got a girlfriend. Come meet her."

Theo grins as his father comes into view. "She's not my girlfriend. She's my wife."

Both their mouths open. Then Clare raises both hands in celebration. "I *knew* it. When those girls came back to the clubhouse telling me how cute the two of you were together, I knew. It was a Spidey sense."

Jason shakes his head. "You did not know."

"Oh, shush. I knew. It's a mom's second sense. I could tell you were happy, Teddy Bear."

I glance up at Theo. "Teddy Bear, huh?"

He furrows his brows. "You ever call me that and I'll divorce you. Bad enough she still does."

"Why did you get married so damn fast? You couldn't wait a few weeks? Wait, am I gonna be a grandma too?"

"God, no. No babies. At least not yet," Theo says.

"She wouldn't have minded," Jason says. "Was just building those bunk beds in the back room she keeps going on about. Congratulations, Son. Sophia."

"Tell me all the things," Clare says. "How did you propose? Is there a ring?"

Theo opens his mouth to speak, but then doesn't. I don't know if it's because he can't think of the words, but I suddenly sense that lying to his mom isn't as easy as lying to his brothers.

"It happened at lunch," I say, stepping in. "Which I suppose doesn't sound all that romantic. But we spend time with each other every day. And we support each other through it. And you can't go through things like that without getting close to the other person. So, we were eating our food, talking about what it would look like when we left. You found it hard at first to say you couldn't live without me, right?"

Theo looks at me, his face ripe with its own kind of emotion. "It's not the kind of thing you just blurt out."

I keep my eyes focused on him, but out of shot, I press the tips of my nails into his denim-clad thigh. He seems to encourage me to press them into him harder when we have sex, and I wonder if it will help center him. "It started with where our first date outside would be." I feel awful lying to my new mother-in-law, but this was Theo's end of the deal. His mom got to see him happy while she battled cancer. I can pull this off. "You said we should go to a bike rally."

Theo glances down at my fingers and then closes his eyes for a second as he sighs.

"Oh, Theo," Clare said. "You can do better than that."

"Pretty sure a bike rally is where you conceived Theo," Jason says. "You want those grandbabies, it's not a bad idea."

I laugh as Clare blushes.

"You said we should go see the world. That you wanted to go on safari," Theo replies, brushing his thumb over my lower lip. "I said you keep looking at me like that, and I'd take you anywhere."

"You said you'd move heaven and earth to make it happen."

Clare puts her hand back on her heart. "Oh, Theo. Is there a ring?"

"There is." I hold my finger towards the camera on the phone. "No wedding band yet because the whole marriage part was spontaneous."

"Then maybe you'll let me and your dad pay for those, seeing we would have paid for the wedding. And when I'm better and not immunocompromised, you'll let us throw you a big party."

Theo coughs and finds his voice again. "We'd love that, Mom."

"And I can't wait to meet your parents, Sophia. I'm sorry we can't talk longer, but I can't miss my chemo appointment. We're happy for you. Really, truly happy for you. And if you're half as happy and half as lucky as we've been, then life is going to be something really special for the two of you."

When we hang up the phone, Theo sighs as he slips it into his pocket. "Do your physio while I go get the bike."

"I'm sorry that was tough. I could tell it was—"

"I'll be back within the hour."

And with that, he leaves me staring at the empty spot the phone sat.

17

SWITCH

Niro pulls his truck up at my house, and I get out. I was handed a bag of belongings after the wreck. My keys included.

It's a great-looking house with cream siding and navy-blue trim. Set back in a lot of land surrounded by trees, it's isolated, yet close to the clubhouse. There are details everywhere that I'm not sure I chose.

There's a cobbled pathway to the front door that I'm not sure is going to work for Sophia's limitations when it comes to walking. The surface would be a little unsteady underfoot.

There are two large planters outside the front door that I'm a hundred percent sure .my mom placed there for reasons I can't explain.

It was good to talk with her and see her so happy as she headed to her chemo session. But man, it was fucking hard lying to her.

I'm glad Sophia jumped in with the story of how I proposed, because I was drawing a blank. I thought making

Mom happy would be easy. But I wasn't prepared for how deceitful it would feel, actually lying to her.

In hindsight, abandoning Sophia like that wasn't smart nor fair. But I needed some time to get my head straight again and stepping inside my house isn't going to help that.

I just want my bike out of the garage Niro assures me I keep them in.

I look at the key chain and try to decipher which key unlocks the garage. After a few failed attempts, I'm finally in.

There are four bikes in the garage.

"There's a key safe on the wall over there," Niro says. "I looked after your bikes one summer you went to Florida for a month to visit your folks. The code is your mom's birthday. I suggest changing that to Sophia's birthday."

I roll my eyes. "Fuck you."

He laughs loudly. "Do you even know when her birthday is?"

I don't. "Again. Fuck you. She's twenty-five." It doesn't answer his question, but it shows I know at least one thing about her.

"One last question. You need lessons on how to be a husband, or you remember enough of how to treat a woman?" Niro asks.

This time I laugh. I remember this is what club life is about. Hanging with your brothers. Laughing about shit. Feeling a part of something.

"I remember."

"Thank fuck because while I would totally have done it, I wasn't up to teaching you the birds and the bees all over again."

"You know I only lost the last ten years, right? I didn't get a frontal lobotomy or anything."

I enter the code. There are keys there. But there's also a Glock, bullets, and cash. Good to know. But I focus on the key fobs. With the electronic ignition, it takes a minute to figure out which fob goes with which bike.

"The three-wheeler is your dad's," Niro says. "He leaves it here to use when they come visit. Might be a safer bet for today given your arm is still fucked and you want to take Sophia out with you. I can go home and get my three-wheeler and take Avery out on mine."

I want to argue. I've been craving my own bike. But Niro is right. I need to make sure I accommodate Sophia. I want her to be comfortable, and I don't want her to worry about being able to hold on. There is a proper second seat on Dad's bike with a back rest. She can get comfortable knowing the bike is totally stable.

I sit on the bike and start the electronic ignition. Dad's bike rumbles beneath me. The sound is so utterly familiar. The throaty roar rumbles through the garage, bouncing off the concrete walls.

On autopilot, I back it out of the garage and turn it around on the drive.

"Helmet," Niro calls out, pulling one off the shelf. "And take your mom's for Sophia."

I grip the handlebars, and the vibrations rattle through my fingers.

I close my eyes and sit here.

Fuck. It's been a journey to get here.

I'm proud of how far I've come.

It's cold but sunny. There's a breeze on my face.

"You coming in your jeans right now, or do you want to take these helmets from me?" Niro asks.

I open my eyes and take the helmet. "Putting this on feels a bit like closing the gate after the horse has bolted."

"Put it this way, your brain is only lightly scrambled. Another smash and you could end up with custard. So, let's go with the helmet until we're sure you're as capable as you ever were on a bike."

I don't want to admit he's right, but I put it on.

He tucks the spare in the hard case on the back of the bike. "I'll lock up your garage and meet you back at the clubhouse in fifteen when I've got my bike. You remember the way?"

"I got it."

"Good. Drive safe."

And I set off, but as soon as I pull out of the driveway, I speed up. I want the feel of air pressure hitting my chest. I want the pummel of it against the exposed part of my face.

God, I missed this. The road stretches out in front of me, and I open the bike up further. My reflexes are quick. My grip on my left hand is a little looser than my right. Thankfully, my front brakes are on my right, and my rear brakes are controlled by my foot.

I can feel the stress get blown away. I have no idea what state my mental health was in before the incident, but I've got to believe being out on my bike will speed up my recovery.

The ride in Niro's truck was a good refresher on the directions, and it appears that I must have a fairly good sense of location as not only do I remember it, but there is a sense of familiarity to it.

When I pull into the clubhouse, I'm smiling, but that smile turns into a grin when I see Sophia standing outside the clubhouse with Catalina, who has obviously loaned Sophia a set of leathers.

"You need to get your wife some protective clothing of her own, Switch."

"Why would I when she looks so good in yours?" I jump off the bike and remove my helmet. "Hey, Sparrow."

"I'll leave you guys to it," Catalina says.

"You look hot as fuck in these," I say, running my finger down her zipped-up front. She's curvier than Catalina, so the leather hugs her tightly. She's shorter too, so the pants are rolled up near the top of her hiking boots.

"They're too small."

"Not from where I'm standing." I place my knuckle beneath her chin and kiss her softly.

"We need to talk," she says. "You dismissed me in the kitchen and then left me after the call with your mom."

"I know."

"That's not how we do things. I've just learned I don't know anything about my own family. I can't be in a relationship, even one mostly for appearances, with someone who won't tell me who they really are. I want you to talk to me. Include me."

"I know. I'm sorry. We will talk. But humor me, Sparrow. I just sat on my bike for the first time in what feels like forever. I pulled up, and you're standing here looking like a snack I want to eat in those leathers. And we're about to go for a ride with my friend. Can we just enjoy this, and then talk later? I can't do serious right now."

I tug her to me and kiss her with more feeling. Perhaps too much, given the way Clutch whistles when he sees us across the lot. I put a finger up behind Sophia's back in his general direction.

"Okay. But only because you kissed me like that. And that I have your word we can talk later because I don't like being dismissed, Theo."

I pull her lower lip down with my thumb and kiss her

again. "I know, Sparrow. And I promise. We can talk all you need later."

"Sophia, I'm coming with you," a little voice cries, and then Avery barrels from around the back of the clubhouse. She's wearing a full set of little leathers and carrying a sparkly pink helmet.

Bates walks behind her. "I said don't run in the lot, Ave."

"Look what mine says. Look. Look." She spins around.

It says *Property of Daddy*, and beneath it, a second patch says *And Uncle Colton*.

"I love it," Sophia says. "You are very lucky that your daddy and Uncle Colton have your back."

"I bet Uncle Switch has yours. He had Auntie Ari and Lola's."

I glance at Bates, who shakes his head subtly. "What do you know about that, pumpkin?"

"I heard Auntie Gwen tell Mommy that Auntie Ari and Lola are alive because Uncle Switch was so brave."

Bates rolls his eyes. "Love our old ladies to death, but they're freaking gossips." He picks Avery up, and I have the spark of a memory: Vi telling him to put Avery down, and him saying he was making up for lost time. That's it. They were apart for a while.

"You only found you had a daughter this year," I say.

"Yeah. So?" Bates says. Then his eyes widen. "You just remembered that?"

"Memories are flickering like a fucking candle. Can't remember everything. But some things are coming back to me."

Bates puts Avery to the ground and pulls me into a hug. It's unexpected and really fucking hard. Bates is a rock-solid guy. "We missed you, brother. Not just you being around, but your presence. It's good for the club to have you as the voice of reason."

I hug him back because I guess this is something we do, but also, because it feels good.

The roar of a bike causes us to pull apart.

Niro arrives on a bright pink three-wheel Harley.

"What the fuck?" I say.

Bates laughs. "Got it for Avery. She said she wanted a Cinderella carriage. So, he bought a pink Harley, just for when the two of them are doing shit together."

"You trust him with your kid on his bike?"

"You only remember the old Niro." Bates smiles. "He's the best fucking friend I ever had. I'd trust him with my life."

"Permission to come aboard?" Avery yells up at him.

"Permission granted," Niro says and offers her his arm like they've done this a million times. He hoists her up behind him into the pillion seat and straps her in. "You two ready?" he asks us.

"Ready. You want to get on, Sparrow?"

She walks towards it. "I'm not sure how I'm going to get my leg over the seat."

I bend to pick her up, thinking that's the easiest way to get her on the bike. But then something strikes me. An echo from medical training maybe.

"Hey. I was just about to pick you up and put you on the bike. But it dawned on me. That may feel infantilizing to you. And maybe what you need is to figure out how to get on alone."

She touches my face. "That's really thoughtful of you. Can you help me figure out a safe way to get on by myself, and if it doesn't work, you can lift me on?"

"Of course. Let's try the other side because it'll probably be easier for you to get your right leg over the bike."

So, we figure out a way. I show her where the footrests are and where she can place her hands to take her weight. I'm inspired by her perseverance to do it on her own.

When she finally sits, Avery cheers, and I hand Sophia the helmet from the back of the bike.

I hop on in front of her. "Ready?"

"Yes," she says, excitement sparkling in her eyes, and I suddenly have the urge to fuck her on the bike.

I mean, I have the urge to fuck her, period. Took a lot to stop things last night after we got each other off in the shower. But as soon as we hit the bedroom, I could feel a headache coming on.

Yet now... I feel like I could move heaven and earth if I needed to.

"Down the shore, slow and steady?" Niro shouts and I nod.

I massage Sophia's calf, and she squeezes my shoulder. Shit, we need connected helmets so we can talk to each other.

We pull out of the lot in a mini convoy. Bates falls in behind us on his bike. I had no idea he was going to join us. When he pulls alongside Niro, Avery stretches out her arm to try and reach him, and I'm kinda envious of the family Bates has found.

Reminds me a little of how Mom and Dad were.

Family first.

Maybe I'm on that path because nothing about this is feeling fake.

Today, I get to ride with my wife.

And it doesn't get more fucking glorious than that.

18

SOPHIA

"I loved it," I say to Theo when we get back to the clubhouse two hours later.

He pulls me to him. "You did?"

"It felt so liberating. Plus, the water, the gulls. Those salty fries. It felt like a full vacation instead of two hours."

I was nervous about the ride. Maybe it was because I'm now living with the after-effects of one wreck already. A motorbike seemed even more dangerous. But I'd been relieved when Theo had arrived on a three-wheeler. It felt stable. I wasn't required to lean or cling to him for dear life.

Although holding on to Theo was never a bad thing.

Theo kisses me and I melt into it. I like the man I married. More, I could see myself catching feelings for this man.

Like real ones, where you love the other person.

He bites my lip, and I can feel myself getting wet.

Again.

It seems I'm easily turned on. The view of his back from my seat on the bike? Hot.

The vibration of the bike between my legs? Hot.

The way he pushed and pulled the levers with his fingers? Hot.

The way he'd reach behind him and squeeze my calf? The hottest of all.

Even watching the way he was with little Avery. I'm not sure what my views were on children before today, but I'm solely in the camp of *let's have lots of them.*

When we step into the clubhouse, we're greeted with a flurry of activity. There are balloons and banners. Gwen is instructing Clutch to move tables.

Saint and Spark are hanging streamers from the ceiling.

"Hey, pretty boy, get your fucking hands off Ari and blow up some more balloons," Vex shouts from up a ladder.

I look over to the bar. The girl I assume is Ari is seated on it, and Halo is standing between her legs, kissing her in a way that I swear will lead to those kids I was just thinking about.

"You can't be here," Briar says. "We're setting up for your wedding reception."

"You don't have to go to all this trouble," I say. Guilt ripples through me at the thought they would do all this for us, when the marriage is one of convenience.

Iris unfolds a large white paper cloth that she drapes over a long table. "Gives us a reason to have a party. We love throwing them. So, the two of you need to get out of here until we can finish it."

Rae bounces a baby, about twelve months old, on her hip. "Don't interrupt Briar and Iris when they get on a roll. They've got a giant charcuterie table to build."

I look to Theo, who grins.

"Guess we should do as they say." He leans his head close to my ear. "Plus, I got a way we can kill time."

Heat rises in my cheeks, but I let him take my hand and lead me back to our room. He stops by his old room and opens a couple of drawers before he finds what he was looking for in his bathroom.

A box of condoms.

"No pressure to use 'em," he says. "But in case I'm in any way unclear, I'd really fucking like to."

I feel a heady combination of embarrassment and lust. I find it hard to admit what I want, but he's being honest with me, so I offer him the same honesty in return. "I hope you have plenty."

Theo grins at that. "I got the best fucking wife."

"Who is still a little bit mad at you. Even though we just had an amazing ride."

"I know, but can we go straight to the make up sex now and have the fight later? Because you on the back of my bike was something else."

"You promise?"

"I do. We're doing everything else backward, so why not the way we fight?"

As soon as we get to our room, Theo slams the door shut and pushes my back against the wall. His lips hit mine with an urgency he hasn't shown me before.

It's heady.

Powerful.

And I want so much more of it.

"You got any idea how much having you on the back of my bike turned me on?" Theo asks.

"If it's the same as how much I was turned on by sitting on it, then yes, Theo, I do."

He grins and unzips the leather jacket. I strip off his cut, and he takes it from me to lay it carefully over the back of the chair. But when he returns to me, it's as a hungry man.

Buttons hit the floor. From his denim shirt or my blouse, I don't know.

I find I don't care.

Not when Theo's hand slips over my breast and squeezes it hard before slipping into the cup of my bra.

My breath catches in my throat.

His lips trace lines over my face, along my shoulder, up my neck.

He licks and bites and I follow his lead, nipping the skin of his shoulder. Theo groans as I do.

He drops to his knees in front of me and removes the rest of my clothing until I'm standing naked in front of him.

"I'm picking you up and walking you to the bed because it's fucking hot, and I want to feel you against me. Not because you need help."

"Right now, you could do anything you want and I would probably let you."

Theo is still wearing his jeans, and the denim of his fly brushes against my sensitive clit. It feels good, and I roll my hips against him.

"Fuck, I love that you're eager, Sparrow."

He lowers me to the bed, and we land in a clumsy pile. "That went smoother in my head," he says.

It hits me that I'm not the only one still reconciling with who I am now, so I stroke my fingers through his hair. "I thought it was romantic."

He kisses me. "Same rules as last night. We do what feels good until it doesn't. We should have a safe word."

"Sparrow?" I suggest.

He kisses me again, softly. "No. Because there's a chance I might say it when I'm balls deep in you, and stopping would be the last thing on my mind."

"What about 'Harley'? You took me on my first ride on one today."

"Fine. Harley," he says. "You say that, and we stop."

"Permanently?"

He shakes his head. "Depends why we stopped. If you got a cramp or need to change position, then we continue once you're comfortable. But if you've had enough, we're done."

"What if you've had enough?"

He runs his fingertips between the valley of my breasts. "Pretty certain that's an impossibility right now." His lips follow his fingers, and I press my head back against the mattress.

Theo stands suddenly, his hand reaching for the button of his jeans. "Wiggle up the bed a little more. I want you dead center so I've got room to work."

I follow his instructions without any embarrassment, even as I mentally debate removing my eye patch. But something holds me back. This moment is overwhelming already.

"You're beautiful, Sophia."

It's almost like he could read my mind, could hear the worries I had.

He slips out of his boots and socks, then removes his jeans and boxer briefs. "You're like one of those Italian sculptures," I say.

He looks down and runs a hand over his abs. "Feeling a bit soft right now to be honest."

"What would you say to me if I said that to you?"

He glances down my body, then crawls onto the bed. "I'd tell you that your body is perfect."

He licks the tip of a nipple, then sucks it into his mouth.

It makes me gasp. "Then give yourself the same grace, Theo. I'll like every version of you as you recover."

I don't know why I say that. In fact, I almost start to backpedal until...

"I like the sound of that, Sparrow."

His lips trail down my stomach, leaving kisses, occasionally nibbling or biting. And with a few shuffles and tugs, he lines us up so that his face gets my pussy, and his cock is in front of me.

When his tongue strokes my clit, it's different to the previous evening. Maybe it's the angle. Maybe it's because I feel less nervous and can relax into it. But my breath comes out on a long sigh.

His cock twitches in front of me. It's not quite at the right angle for me to suck on it properly, but I can lick it. He opens his legs a little, and I see his balls. I have no idea whether it's cool to suck on them too, but I want to.

So, I do.

"Fuck, Soph." The words come out on a grunt.

I think he likes it.

And then I lose all thought for a second as he sucks my clit into his mouth.

Theo rolls us so he's on his back, and I'm now hovering above him. "Sit on my face, Soph," he says. "I want to fucking suffocate eating you out."

My thighs shake as I hover an inch above his face.

"I said sit, Soph."

He slaps my ass cheek, and I immediately sit.

His fingertips dig into the top of my thighs, holding me in place. At first, I'm uncertain of what to do, and over-thinking gets in the way of me enjoying this moment. Then Theo's hand is on my lower back, pushing me forward.

This must open my pussy to him, but also…

I suck the tip of his cock into my mouth, the taste salty and musky. I feel Theo's abs tense beneath my stomach, and for a moment, he groans, the warm air hitting my most sensitive places.

Then he starts with his tongue and fingers.

And I stand no chance.

I try to concentrate on what I'm doing to him with my mouth and hand.

I can feel a mild cramp in my thigh.

But I'm so close to coming.

I remember his words. That we move. We adjust. So, I kneel up and do what he says. I ride his face while I seek the place where it feels best.

"Oh, God, Theo," I say. I place my hands on his hip bones and hold on as my orgasm floods through me in one rushing wave.

I lose all sense of who I am as blood courses through my body.

Breath comes fast and furious.

The world spins.

Theo places a wet kiss on both my butt cheeks. "Up you get," he says.

I flop rather ungracefully to the side of him. And Theo reaches for the condom box. He's focused as he rips a packet and pulls one on.

"There's gonna be time for a million and one positions, but for our first time, I really want to see your face." He settles between my legs, guiding his cock to my opening. "You ready, wife?" There's a glint in his eyes.

"Ready, husband."

His lips meet mine as he nudges forward.

I don't know what I was expecting it to feel like, but the firm nudging of Theo and the slickness of my pussy granting him entrance is...bliss.

And a shock that something so thick could fit where he is sliding it.

Theo's lips drop to my neck. "Fuck," he curses. "You're already choking my cock."

"Is that a good thing?" I ask.

He lifts up, his eyes intense as they study mine. "Very."

I suck in a breath as he nudges deeper.

Theo's eyes stay on mine. The intimacy in this moment is utterly breathtaking.

I want to say more, to express how I feel, but the words to describe it escape me.

I've never felt so connected to another human being.

Even as I sit in the aftershocks of my first orgasm, I feel a second one building.

Theo withdraws a little, then coils his hips, driving deeper inside this time. I raise a knee until it's up by Theo's hip. He grabs it, holding it higher, holding me more open to him.

With three more thrusts and a grunt, Theo seats himself all the way inside me. It feels so deep, and I feel so stretched, I'm glad there isn't even more of him because I wouldn't be able to take it all.

"Jesus, Sparrow," he says. "This feels so fucking good. Can't get enough of you." He pulls out and then thrusts deep again. "Just want to stay like this forever," he says.

His lips meet mine, and this time, he begins a slow and steady pace.

"Next, I'm gonna fuck you hard. From behind, probably. Then I want you on your side. I'm gonna fuck you in every conceivable position until you can't face another orgasm."

His words take me even higher. "I like it when you talk like that."

"You like when I talk about fucking you? About how wet and tight you fucking are. How you're hugging my cock so fucking hard, it's taking all I've got to not come deep inside you."

I nod and wrap my arms tightly around him. Something makes me draw my nails along his back, and Theo drops his head.

"You want me to last, you're gonna need to stop."

"Who said I wanted you to last?"

Theo chuckles. "Good point. But I want another orgasm from you before I do. Where does it feel best?"

I reach my hand between us, knowing Theo will struggle to balance, and circle my clit like I've done alone in my room.

"Is this okay?" I ask.

Theo bites my earlobe. "Fucking hot. Help me get you there."

His strokes speed up. Sweat dots his brow. But his eyes remain on mine, and mine on his.

"I want to feel you cream around my cock this time, not in my mouth. Want to feel you squeeze me even tighter."

I shift my hips a little, changing the angle for us both.

Theo closes his eyes tightly. "Aww, fuck. Soph. I'm so close it fucking hurts."

And it's those words, undone as they are, that push me over the edge.

"Theo," I gasp.

His eyes open, and his face goes taut as he comes with me. His thrusts lose their rhythm, his strokes their depth. I can feel him pulse inside me.

He groans, the sound reverberating through my chest.

"Sophia," he says, before collapsing on top of me.

I wrap my arms around him, holding him close as we catch our breath.

And wonder if I'm being foolish for hoping the rest of our lives will feel just like this.

"I'm sorry I ignored you when I left to go get the bike," Theo says. "Lying to my mom rattled me more than I thought it would. And I was angry about it. I worried if I stayed or you came with me, I'd be angry at you for it instead of me. So I went with Niro, then rode back here to clear my head. Reconciled myself with why I was doing it. Made my peace. But I'm sorry I abandoned you instead of just telling you why I needed some space."

I sigh. "Trust you to give me a good answer before I've been able to shout at you."

He glances down at me. "You still can if it will clear the air and make you feel better."

Theo reaches between us and pulls out of me. The move makes me shiver. Then he rolls onto his back but tugs me to him. I place my head over his pec and listen to the steady bass of his heartbeat as it slows. "No. That was a good explanation and apology. What about the kitchen?"

"Club's the club. I doubt you knew everything about your father's enterprise. The club's the same way. I can't tell you everything. But I promise I'll tell you what I can, and I'll make sure nothing ever blows back on you."

"I don't want to be ignored, Theo. I don't want to be dismissed. I want to be your equal. I think that really matters to me. I was going to be married off to some guy, who never even made the effort to come see me while I was in hospital, for the sake of family power dynamics. I was an asset going to be traded. I don't think I can live as someone inconsequential in your life."

Theo rolls me onto my back so he can look at me. "By virtue of the fact you are my wife, you'll never be inconsequential to me. And for the club to believe you're really, truly my wife, you're going to have to play the part of an old lady. We're both having to stretch who we are right now. You just need to decide if you can do it."

19

———

SWITCH

I should have taken my wife shopping this morning instead of driving her around on my bike and fucking her senseless in my room at the clubhouse. If I had, she'd be comfortable in what she's wearing instead of feeling self-conscious in the red dress I married her in.

She shouldn't be standing in here at the party my club is throwing for us, constantly fiddling with the straps of the dress to cover the worst of her scars or tugging at the hem.

Even though she looks pretty as a fucking picture as she talks to Rae and Ari.

She's keeping her distance. I know I gave her a lot to think about, so I'm respecting that.

"She's still right where you left her," King tells me as we lean our backs on the bar.

"Just making sure she's comfortable. It's a big adjustment."

Rock music blasts. Everyone is here: Prospects. Hangarounds.

King chuckles. "She's fine. We couldn't keep your dad

away from the clubhouse while he was back. Think he's missing the life."

"You think you'll be an Outlaw forever?" I ask King.

He eyes me carefully. "The code says we're Outlaws forever. There isn't a choice."

"I mean, Dad got out."

"On grounds of moving somewhere we don't have a chapter and four decades of incredible service to the club. Smart man only having one Outlaw tattoo. Lasering it off wasn't too painful." King studies me carefully. "Why? You thinking of leaving us?"

I shake my head. "Nah. I'm just wondering what life looks like when we're sixty. There was this whole older generation we looked up to when we were kids. Like that summer you were dating Sarah Shellis and we went to Sturgis with them. Your dad was this larger-than-life legend. Cue Ball was his infallible vice president. Now a whole new generation is in charge."

"It's how it's meant to be." King knocks back a large swig of his beer. "It's wild you remember Sarah Shellis's name but can't remember which clubhouse room is yours."

"Truth. What's with you and Niro now? It's like the two of you are brothers. The last I remember, you guys rubbed each other the wrong way."

King looks over to where Niro has his arm around Iris's shoulders. The two of them are teasing Spark, from the angry look on his face, while they laugh.

"It's fair to say we've come to terms."

A prospect rushes into the clubhouse. "Prez. You got a problem. Vincenzo Viscuso is outside with a shit ton of his snake house, armed to the teeth. Says he needs to speak to a mouthy Outlaw with a fucking scar." He looks over to Niro.

"Fuck." The word is out of my mouth and my eyes on Sophia before I can stop myself.

"You take one step towards your wife before telling me what you know about this, and I'll drop you where you stand."

"Prez. The Italians?" The prospect seems edgy. Nervous. Scared.

Maybe he should be. But Outlaws never show fear. So, he's fucked. Doesn't know he just earned a high-speed ticket out of the prospect program.

"They're fucking Sicilians. And they can wait," King says.

"But they didn't seem too willing to—"

He's stopped by the appearance of King's SIG pointing straight at him.

"I said they can wait. Go out and tell them we're discussing their request." He looks at me, then yells, "Church. Now."

There are groans.

Confused mutterings.

But I ignore them all and make my way to Sophia. I need to tell her what's happening before King tells me I can't.

"What's going on?" she asks.

"Your dad is standing outside our clubhouse, demanding to speak with Niro."

Her mouth opens. "What? My father is here? How?"

I take her hand. "Don't say anything unless directly asked. Let me lead. Trust me to know what's best for us. So far, he's only asked to speak to Niro."

Her fingers tighten around mine, and something about her drawing strength from me makes me feel like a giant. There's a galvanizing, of sorts. Of the person I used to be and who I am. A better man with all the wisdom I've learned along the way. Even if I don't remember it all.

"I can leave with him," she says. "I don't want you or the club to get into trouble or get hurt."

I pause and kiss her. Don't give a shit who sees it. Don't give a fuck if the whole club is waiting for me in church. "To be true and loyal. For better or worse. I'm not letting you leave with them."

Sophia looks up at me, a vulnerability etched in her features. "Then please keep me away from them. I'll run anywhere with you."

I nod, and we walk to the door to church together. "The windows are glass. Sit right here so I can see you at all times. Do not move. Don't let anybody tell you to. The only safe place is where I can see you."

"I promise I won't move," she says, and I lift her onto one of the long tables that sit outside.

I kiss the end of her nose. "Don't get any ideas about being a hero, either, Soph. If you run to them, I'll be forced to hurt people to get you back. We clear?"

As I say the words, I feel a settling in my own skin. I can't explain it.

As I enter, King is talking to Niro, who is sitting back in his chair without a care in the world. "You wanna tell me why there are Sicilians outside the door asking to speak to you?"

Niro shrugs. "Saw them at the rehab center. The twins. They were visiting someone. We were visiting someone. They said I could fuck them."

Catalina huffs. "They said, 'Fuck you.'"

"Same thing," Niro says.

"Did you kill any of them?" King asks.

Niro screws up his face in disgust. "What kind of question is that?"

Spark places his elbows on the table. "You forgotten how many people you killed for no reason in the past?"

Niro pulls his phone out of his cut pocket and pretends to flip through it for something. "Thirty-eight who fucking deserved it. Nineteen who were dubious. Only one I think probably was innocent, but who knows. He could have grown up to be the next Hitler and I did the world a favor." Then he puts his phone down.

Halo hides his grin behind his hand.

"So why are they here asking for you?" Clutch asks.

Niro pauses for a second. I sense his conflict. He wants to be loyal to the club, but he also made a promise to me.

And given Sophia's father is outside the door, the truth is going to be revealed real soon.

King notices I've joined them. "This better not be about your fucking wife."

"My wife is Sophia Viscuso, Vincenzo's youngest daughter."

"Fuck me," King curses.

Saint rubs a hand over his jaw. "Is that why you insisted on keeping things informal at the wedding? Why you only used first names?"

I nod. "It was."

King forms a tight fist, then releases it. "So, this is just an internal family thing? Wait, why did he ask for Niro and not you or his daughter?"

"I asked Niro to help break us out of the center when we realized her father intended to marry her to the head of another family in Sicily, and given how I felt about her and she felt about me, we weren't prepared to let that happen," I say. "We overheard her brothers, the twins, discussing it. They were making plans to transport her via private jet to Sicily."

"You can't chase your wife all the way to Italy." King's volume increases with every word.

"I'll chase her to the ends of the goddamn earth if I have to." The words don't feel like a lie. They don't feel like an act. Now that trouble is at our door, that someone wants to take Sophia from me, I'm faced with the knowledge that I'll die to stop them.

King shakes his head. "We aren't getting involved with the fucking Cosa Nostra, Switch. Not for you nor the woman you barely know outside. If your fucking bitch brought trouble to our door, she needs to fix it herself," King says.

My hand automatically closes into a fist, but I rein in my temper. "Don't speak about my wife like that." I look around the room, and then I find my voice. "I'm guessing that at some point over the past ten years, I've earned the patch of medic. I'm guessing I've kept some of you alive either by my own hands or until we could get you to a hospital. Clutch?"

Clutch nods. "Bunch of times. Got shot when they came after Gwen, and you patched me up."

"Saved my fucking life when I came off my bike trying to get to Catalina," Niro says.

Vex sits, his arms folded. "Saved me twice. Thank you, brother."

I look at King. "And you?"

He folds his arms across his chest. "Stitched me up too many times to remember, but you saved my life when the fucking Brotherhood broke into my house and shot me."

Halo stands. "You saved Ari and Lola's life, and that's how we all ended up here."

"Well, then. I'm calling in those tickets. If I ever saved your life or the life of someone you loved and you said you'd pay me back one day, I'm claiming it now. I need Sophia. Can't fucking explain it. Feel like she's been put in my path to bring me back here. Seeing Catalina, Rae, and Saint here gives me faith that the club knows how to have a brother's back, even when the circumstances make no sense."

I glance over to Sophia outside the room. She's facing me, biting the side of her thumb, something I know she does when she's nervous.

"I've got your back," Halo says. "Without question."

"So do I," Niro says.

"We vote when I say we're fucking ready," King says. "There are real consequences. The five families might hate each other, but they hate the rest of us even more. We don't need even more heat."

Vex stands. "I'm going to stand with Switch too. Brothers first, before all things. Plus, it's really gonna piss the Sicilians off. I feel like that's a bonus."

Saint stands and looks at King. "Brother," he says. "We know a thing or two about finding love where you shouldn't."

"Don't fucking start with that shit," King says.

Saint smiles softly. "Hatred stirs up strife, but love covers all sins."

"Spark?" King says.

"As a brother, I get it. Switch has stitched me up a fair few times and came on the raid to get Iris back. But as sergeant at arms, I can't justify us getting into it with the Sicilians over pussy."

I stare at Spark for a moment, wanting to hate him for what he just said. But the truth is, I get it. "You call my wife 'pussy' again and there won't be enough men is this room to stop me from getting to you."

He holds his hands up in the sign of surrender. "Poor choice of words, but you get the idea."

"Let me go out and talk with them," Niro says. "They're

gonna ask if we saw her. We say no. They're likely going to demand to search the property, and we'll tell them to go fuck themselves with barbwire."

"I'm gonna take a vote, just so this can go down in history as the most collectively dumbass decision we ever made."

"Wait," I say. "Can we do a vote before that?"

King rolls his eyes. "What the fuck can you possibly want more than the club agreeing to stand with you on this?"

"I want you to do it because she's my old lady."

Clutch shakes his head. "Dude. You've known the bitch for like, half a heartbeat. You've married her, let it be enough."

A memory comes, but it's sharp around the edges. I wince at the ache that comes with it. "You were sneaking in and out of Camelot's room when *your* bitch was in there. You thought I didn't see you, but I put two and two together and kept it to myself. Did you let it be enough?"

"Fuck you talking about Gwen like that."

"So, you can refer to Sophia as a bitch, but you can't take it when I call Gwen one? Fuck you."

An arm comes around me. Halo's.

I hadn't realized I'd leaned across the table to Clutch.

I shake Halo off and stand up straight.

For the first time, I look out of the window into the bar and see all the old ladies and prospects watching us.

"Sophia already hurts because of her injuries. Don't make her hurt even more because you don't want her."

"Brother," Bates says. He's been quiet this whole time. "It's not that we don't want her. She's a lovely woman. But we don't know what she's done. Fuck, she could even be a plant for all you know. Bit convenient you overheard her brothers plotting some nasty shit and then you end up married to her. You gotta give us time to believe it."

"You know what, given her father is outside, clearly trying to track her down, even though she has told her family repeatedly that she is okay, I don't got fucking time, Bates. I already feel like I was on the outside because of the shit going on with my head. You know, because I got my brains knocked halfway across Jersey trying to protect someone else's old lady and kid. So, fuck you all. Fuck you all for not knowing me well enough to have my back fully." I look to King. "Your dad is one of the last real things...I remember. Camelot...would ..." Words are escaping me again. I'm too wound up to manage my reactions. "He'd be fucking pissed...we're even...debating this. I'll go. Talk to her father alone. And then I'll be out of here after dark. I'll send you pictures of my...club ink removed within six months."

I walk toward the door, but Spark and Bates beat me to it. "Cool your heels, brother," Spark says.

Of course, the sergeant at arms and his enforcer would try to stop me.

My eyes meet Sophia's. I can see the fear in them. For me. For her. For what's outside the clubhouse. She stands, but I tip my chin back to the table, encouraging her to sit.

Iris and Briar are standing with her.

Bates nudges me back to my chair. "Sit the fuck down, Switch, before I'm forced to knock you down."

I shake my head. "Not sure I belong there anymore, Miles."

The use of his first name seems to have an overwhelming effect on everyone in the room.

"This is bullshit," Vex says. "No one who has sat at this table for so many years should feel unwelcome at it."

"It's not a fucking simple thing, though," Spark says. "No

one is rejecting Switch. But we can't just invite a war with the fucking Cosa Nostra. They got fucking captains and armies. Their bench depth way exceeds ours."

King slaps his hand on the table. "Fine. We vote. Do we stand with Switch and Sophia?"

"Easy yes." Halo nods in my direction, but the word feels so loaded.

"No," Spark and Bates say at the same time.

"Too much trouble for the club," Spark says. "Sorry."

Vex nods. "Yes. We stand for each other over everything, or we don't stand for anything at all."

"I know what it means to be on the wrong side of something threatening," Saint says. "Yes."

Clutch squeezes King's shoulder. "Listen. It's a fight we were already in. We know they've been battling Cillian up at the docks. It's only a matter of time before they come for the New Jersey side too. Does this up the stakes a bit? Sure. But it's not like we weren't on their radar, given they've been on ours for months."

I take a breath. Then another. I stand because I can't stay seated any longer. Bates moves beside me again. And while I'm not about to storm out of here again, I shrug his hand off me.

Spark sighs. "Valid point. Change of vote. Yes."

"What Spark said," Bates says. "Yes."

Niro throws his arm over Catalina's shoulder. "We've always been a yes."

She nods. "We have. But I can answer for myself. Yes."

"Then we go out as one," King says. "Yes?"

I should be happy. I should feel a sense of relief.

But it feels like the club's uncertainty, their lack of immediacy in supporting me, just did more damage than my accident ever did.

20

SOPHIA

When I see Bates attempt to stop Theo from leaving a second time, I'm up on my feet and headed to the door before a prospect appears out of nowhere and blocks me. Only, he grabs my arm, knocking me off-balance. I stumble and jar my hip into the corner of the table, which sends pain shooting down my leg before I fall to the floor.

When the door to church opens, Theo sees me on the ground and storms over to me.

"What the hell happened?" he says.

"It was an accident," the prospect says. "When Bates and Spark stopped you leaving, she tried to get to you."

Theo cocks his fist by his shoulder, then sends the prospect flying to the ground with a single punch. His head hits the wood floor with a thud.

"You ever touch my fucking wife again, I'll kill you. Get the fuck out of here." He turns to me. The speed with which he morphs from feral to caring is staggering. "You okay, Sparrow?"

He reaches for me and assists me to my feet, not letting

go until he knows I've found my center of gravity again. I hate that people are watching me. I wish they'd all turn away and pretend they were doing something else.

"Just caught me off guard is all." I minimize how I'm feeling because I can see how concerned Theo is. "I can't seem to rebalance myself when I take a knock. Are you okay?" I look over to where some of the brotherhood are watching us.

"You and I are going to talk to your...family, and then...I don't know. Maybe we're leaving."

I hear the edge to his voice, the struggle for words. "They didn't vote in our favor?"

He glances back at the brothers who are standing behind him. "They did. But it shouldn't have been so fucking hard to convince them to have our back."

I look at my husband, at all the beautiful wedding decorations, and feel...hurt.

I can't explain why I feel so happy being married to a near stranger, but I wish the world could see that I am. Including my family outside and Theo's family in the clubhouse.

"We can figure it out together. But I'll go where you go."

He cups my cheeks. "You sure?"

I nod. "Are we safe?"

Theo turns to Niro. "Are the gates locked?"

Niro nods.

"Yes, we're secure. Unless they shoot at us, but let's face it, it's you they want back."

He takes my hand and leads me to the door, but I stop and turn to the rest of the club. "I don't deserve your help. You're right. You don't know who I am. But Theo deserves better than whatever this is. You should be ashamed that when one of your brothers needed you, when he asked you for your help, you held a contentious vote."

"Sparrow," Theo says.

I look up at him. "It's true. I don't need to know every-thing you did in the last ten years to know that you'll have done whatever was required for the club. You've done the same for me and you barely know me."

The expression on his face softens. "Sweet that you'd defend me in a clubhouse full of bikers. But I don't need you to speak for me."

I smile up at him. "I know you don't. But I'm going to do it anyway."

He smiles at that. "Want to introduce me to your dad?"

I blow out a breath. "Not really."

He brushes his thumb along my cheek, then kisses me. "You and me against the world, Sparrow," he whispers.

In return, I nod and squeeze his fingers.

The club falls in behind us, but even without them, I'd feel capable of addressing my family with Theo by my side.

Wind whips leaves up as we step into the lot. My father stands by the gate, wrapped in a long, opened overcoat and an immaculate pinstripe suit. I have no childhood memories to fall back on. Only my opinions of him since I first gained consciousness to a larger-than-life stranger at the side of my bed. He'd seemed kind. But now all I see is hardened features and mean narrowed eyes that don't hold an ounce of compassion.

Alessio stands to his right, his dark curls lifting in the breeze. While his arms remain by his sides, he lifts his palm gently, as if he is warning me to tread softly. Leo and Luca stand to Papà's left. Leo bounces on his toes while Luca stands still as a statue.

"Papà," I say. "There's no reason to be here."

But my father doesn't even address me. He looks past me and Theo.

"I want my daughter back, King," he says.

"Papà. I'm right here. And I'm not coming with you." But I might as well be invisible for all the attention he pays me.

King crosses his arms but looks utterly unruffled. "And we're not in the mood to be handing her over to you so you can traffic her to marry some old mobster back in the old country."

"What happens to my family has nothing to do with you." He passes a piece of paper through the locked gates of the compound. King steps forward and takes it. He reads it, then hands it to me.

The words begin to blur with tears, but before it becomes too hard to read, I catch words like *conservator agreement. Legal guardian. Unable to make decisions. Brain damage.*

"They can't make me go with them, can they?" I ask Theo.

"We'll figure it out." But Theo doesn't look at me as he speaks. His gaze remains focused on Luca and Leo.

"You expect that letter to mean anything to me?" King says.

"It means my daughter is incapable of making decisions for herself. It means your man has taken advantage of a woman, my daughter, because she can't make good choices. You hand her over, and we'll leave here and consider this situation resolved."

King laughs. "Pretty sure the earbashing she just gave us suggests she's more than capable of making decisions for herself, right, Sophia?"

I step forward, fighting the tears that threaten. "I know everything."

"You know nothing," my father shouts.

"Don't do this. I'm happy with Theo. I know what you planned. I overheard Leo and Luca talking about it. Was I ever more than an asset to be traded?"

Leo curses.

Luca says nothing.

A muscle in my father's jaw twitches.

"I wasn't alone when I overheard them either. There were other witnesses. Everyone in this clubhouse knows."

At this, my father casts a sideways glance at Leo, who blanches. I guess the power my father has is happily exerted against his own sons too.

Suddenly, his mood shifts. "You're talking about things you don't understand yet, *Puparu*. This is not how Viscusos do things. In front of strangers. Enemies. Just come home with us, and we can talk about this."

I hate the soft tone to his voice, as if I'm a child throwing a tantrum who can be placated with an ice cream.

"That sounds like an admission," I say. "And, no, I'm not coming home."

"You forget who we are, Sophia. I can have a warrant to search this clubhouse and rescue you within the hour. I'll have a witness statement from your doctor at the center saying you are mentally unstable within the same. That this man kidnapped you under pretenses to gain leverage over my family. You're vulnerable. Not thinking straight."

"You can't do that," I shout. "It's not..."

Fair.

The word hits me hard. Nothing about this has ever been fair. I'm permanently injured, for life. "Do you know more of what happened the day I crashed than you are saying?" I ask him.

"No one knows anything," he replies.

I look into the face I had come to trust and love in my own way. I see no evidence that he is lying, but there is so much I've missed. "I don't think I can trust you."

"Yet you trust him? A biker?"

I look up to Theo, and a very real truth settles in my gut. "I do. And I'll fight everything you try to do to take me away from here."

"You ready to let me step in?" Theo asks.

I nod, grateful that he gave me the opportunity to speak with them first.

"Anything else you need to say to my wife will be said through me," Theo says. "First, if you think for a second everything you just threatened to do wasn't recorded by one of our cameras, you're a fool. Go get your judge, and we'll hand over the tape. Second, in the hour it takes you to get the warrant, we'll get the conservatorship destroyed. You think you got contacts? Well, I swear to God, ours go deeper. And third, you step foot on our land, we'll defend it."

Niro and Catalina step in front of me, their hands on the weapons in their holsters, and I'm eternally grateful. I guess up until this moment, I always felt there had been the tiniest sliver of a window for there to have been a mistake or misunderstanding.

But no.

I don't have a family. I'll face a legal battle to try to reclaim what was mine. And I have no support system in place...for life or for ongoing medical treatment.

Hell, I don't even know if I have any kind of medical coverage. I know Theo said he has lots of money, but I can't bring myself to ask for any of it. He saved me. He shouldn't have to fund me too.

I thought I felt lost when I first woke up in the hospital and couldn't remember any facet of my identity. Then, as friends began to extricate themselves from my life, I thought that was as alone as I was going to feel.

But in this moment, I know this is the bottom.

I've never felt more alone.

And yet...

Maybe this is where I meet myself. Maybe this was what Niro was talking about.

"Soph." It's Alessio; he's left my father's side. While the bikers are focused on my father, Alessio is focused on me.

I go to walk toward him, but Niro puts his hand out to stop me. "Don't go too close, sweetheart."

"What?" I ask my brother.

"You would have wanted this," he says. "I knew you better than anyone else in this family. You knew this was your destiny. You embraced it. You felt pride that you could do something for the family like this. I don't know why you got in the car, but it wasn't because of the prospect of marriage."

His words seem sincere. "I find it hard to accept that."

He runs his hand over his jaw. "I'm sure you do. Just as I find it hard to accept that you really want this. It's going to come back to you in a flood of memories why you shouldn't be here. And when it does, I want you to call me. I'll come get you."

"So you can get me on an airplane to Sicily?"

"When it comes back to you, you'll want to go."

I look over to Theo, who is calmly watching my father rant about getting me back, about lawyering up, about suing the Outlaws.

"I doubt it," I reply.

"It was something else that made you run that day. You never ran, Sophia. Not once. Not even when our enemies broke into our house. You always fought. You were as ruthless as the rest of us. More accurate an aim than any of our brothers. Whatever you learned that day scared you enough to flee. It must have been serious. And I'm determined to find out what it is for the sake of our family."

I shake my head. "I have no answers for you. But this isn't the way you get them. And assuming everything you say is true... Who's to say that what I heard wasn't connected to the wedding? Who I was marrying?"

He glances in the direction of our father, then lowers his voice to a whisper. "I know it wasn't. You said something to me that morning. Call me, Soph. There's more I have to tell you that Papà doesn't—"

"Back the fuck away from the gate," Theo says as he comes to stand by my side. He's staring my brother down, but I put my palm to his chest.

"It's okay, Switch," I say. "I'm done here."

He looks down at me. "Switch, huh?"

"I think the circumstance calls for it. I want to go back inside. Alessio, if you really care for me, you need to persuade Papà to drop this. To leave me alone and let me heal. Accept I'm married. Otherwise, you don't really care for me at all."

We turn to walk back inside, but my brother's voice echoes through the lot. "Think about what I said, Sophia. You know I'm right."

21

SWITCH

As soon as we get through the doors, I tug Sophia close and hold her tight against me. Her body shakes in my arms. I never intended to let her leave without me, to let her out of my sight even. But in situations like that, you have to be prepared for the unexpected.

"You okay?" I whisper.

"Not really, but yes. A lot just happened."

I cup both her cheeks. "Did it ever. We need a plan. To get you out from beneath that guardianship. The club has a lawyer...at least, they used to. I assume they still do. Wait, no. We move and I find us a lawyer. I have a place in mind we can go and be safe."

"I need to stop for a minute and get my head around what's just happened. Everything is moving too fast."

And then Sophia laughs uncontrollably. Distress is written on her face.

"Fuck, I had a handle on this." She gasps.

"BAT," I say, gripping her wrists. "Do it with me?"

"When you focus on me like this, I find it hard to breathe," she admits.

I can't help but smile. "Kinda like sweet words from your mouth, Sparrow. Now breathe with me."

She takes in a deep breath, and I nod. "Now adjust."

Sophia rolls her shoulders back and stands a little straighter.

"Good girl. Now think."

"It's harder to control when I'm under stress."

"Makes sense. My words disappear when I am. We'll go somewhere you can rest. I promise."

The brothers start to peel back into the clubhouse.

"What just happened?" Rae asks King. "What was that Sophia said about a contentious vote?"

"Club business, Duchess."

Rae takes one look at Sophia. "It's not club business when it affects one of the old ladies. It becomes all our business."

King sighs. "Sophia's family came to take her back."

"My family organized an arranged marriage," Sophia says. "I'm not a hundred percent sure, but I feel like my accident and my injuries were sustained trying to escape it."

Iris looks at Spark, her face like thunder. "Were you one of the ones going to vote against backing Theo up when he saved his wife from an arranged marriage?"

"Little chick. It's not as simple as—"

"Don't 'little chick' me right now."

King puts his hands up. "We're not doing this."

Vi looks to Bates. "Was it you?"

Bates grimaces. "They're the fucking Sicilian Cosa Nostra, before you give me shit. The best interest of the club is not pissing them off."

"I understand," Vi says sweetly. Too sweetly. "You had to put your own safety ahead of your brother and his wife who needed your help."

"That's not what I said." Bates rubs a hand across his jaw.

"Fuck me," says King. "We need to stop. We don't discuss club business like this."

"Given I was taken against my will, you better not have voted against," Briar says to Saint. "Or you will be sleeping in the spare room you just finished painting."

Saint tugs on the end of Briar's braid. "I was a yes before King even asked for the vote."

Briar wraps her arms around his waist. "And there's the man I fell in love with."

"King?" Rae says.

"If you're gonna yell at me in Shakespeare, Duchess, just get it over with," King says.

Rae steps right into our president's space. "Shakespeare would turn in his grave if I wasted any of his words on you today."

Gwen steps forward. "I propose a vote. If our men won't take care of Theo and Sophia—"

"Babe, I voted for," Clutch offers.

She glances his way. "Yes, but what kind of vice president can't convince his men to follow in his direction?"

"Ouch," Niro offers. "For the record, I helped the two of them escape."

King glares at Niro. "Do we have to tell them fucking everything? This is a fucking MC. Women don't get a say or a vote."

Cat coughs. "No?"

King rolls his eyes. "Don't be pedantic. We voted *for* in the end."

"*In the end* is doing a lot of heavy lifting in that sentence. I'll talk to *you* later," Gwen says, glaring at her brother. "Anyway. If our men won't take care of Theo and Sophia, we'll show them that we will. All in favor."

The hand of every single old lady goes into the air.

"Motion carried," Rae says.

King shakes his head. "Doesn't work like that, Duchess."

"Thanks to Niro, we can shoot as well as you," Vi says. "We've learned surveillance. There are enough of us to form a rotation."

Niro rubs his hands together and whoops. "Fuck me. I formed a rebellion." He crosses the floor to stand with the women. "There are more pussies on that side of the room than there are on this."

Rae glances to him. "Too far."

"Really?"

Briar nods. "We don't use that word in that context. Linking a word used to show weakness to vaginas is sexist."

Sophia laughs, then puts her hands to her lips, her body shaking. "Sorry. Can't help it. My brain doesn't filter things the same way."

"It's okay. We got you, sweetheart," Niro says as he winks at her.

I pull her close to me and feel the shudder of her breath. She really does need a minute.

Perhaps we both do.

"Anyway," Niro continues. "I'm still on the right side of history where we protect our brother, no matter what the cost," Niro says as he looks to Spark. "You married into the fucking Irish mob. You should be on our side automatically."

It's such a juvenile thing to say, but he says it with such passion, I feel every word.

"And what side is that?" Spark asks. "The dead-man-walking club?"

Niro shakes his head. "The 'men who made women they should have left alone their old ladies' club. Clutch fucked his best friend and president's sister. You married into the Irish mob. King kidnapped Rae. *Kidnapped.* And I know what you all thought of me wanting to keep Catalina."

"You didn't keep me. I stayed," Catalina says with a soft smile.

He turns to face her, the anger leaving immediately, and he kisses her sweetly. "Can we agree it was both?"

"Compromise? Geez, you have come a long fucking way," Saint says.

Niro flips the bird at him.

"Makes me feel like the normal one in the group, marrying the first woman I ever fell in love with, knowing she was the only one for me without bringing threat of death or destruction to the club," Bates says.

"Hey," Halo says. "Speak for yourself."

Bates raises an eye. "Did you forget you met her because your fucked-up brother tried to wipe out your family?"

Halo huffs good-humoredly. "You know what I mean. And Vi arrived here because some goons went looking for you."

Vi shoulder checks Bates. "Don't you be saying sweet things when I'm still mad at you."

Niro turns to face me. "You got to unite us, Theo. It's what you do best. When we're at odds. You ever notice how we just keep talking at each other instead of closing shit out? That was your skill. You point out the fucking obvious and stop us rambling in circles."

I realize everyone is looking at me. Brothers. Old ladies. Prospects.

I take a deep breath, trying to recall anything from the

last ten years that might come to me. But nothing does. And maybe that's the story.

"I don't know why I ended up injured like this, but from what I've heard from all of you, it's because I acted first and thought...well, never. It didn't occur to me in that instant to consider how this would affect me. Only how it would affect Halo. And Ari. And Lola. And while I can't remember everything about the last ten years, certain things are coming back to me. And every single one of them, we're in it together, no matter what we were facing. Even if it was wrong." I tuck Sophia beneath my arm, taking her weight as she leans against me. "All you have to do is decide what kind of person you want to be. And if it takes you longer than two seconds to decide, you aren't the people I thought you were." I look to the old ladies. "And you all are beyond my estimation."

Niro grins. "This feels like when a minor league team beats the major league team."

"Are we the minors?" Gwen asks.

Niro chuckles. "Given their behavior"—he tips his head in the direction of our brothers—"right now you're the A-Team."

Sophia leans a little heavier against me. She fidgets, which tells me the left side of her body aches.

"Thanks for all this," I say, pointing to the decorations. "But you'll understand why we don't much feel like staying to celebrate."

I start to lead us back to our room, my mind whirring with what we do next. My gut tells me it starts with moving closer to my parents. We can't fly after a traumatic brain injury without doctors signing off, and I can barely drive. But I know if I tell my dad, he'll set off with his truck and one of my brothers, and they'll drive through the night to come get us.

We'll go to my house, get supplies, and head off in my truck. Between Sophia and me, we can head towards them. My brother can take over driving. Ryan didn't want to join the club, too law abiding, but that doesn't mean he can't throw down if he needs to.

"Wait," King says. "I fucked up. Hard thing to admit in front of a clubhouse full of old ladies and prospects, but Sophia was right. Was standing outside wondering how we would've reacted if the Irish had come for Iris in full force once Spark had declared for her. Or if Saint had unleashed the power of the ATF or FBI on the club to get Rae back. Brotherhood first or we're just fucking cowards. But it means one thing, Switch. You're all in with the club. You had your out to leave, but I won't honor it after this."

A rebellion brews within me. A part of me wants to tell King where he can shove his offer. That we'll be better off on our own. That the club doesn't deserve the two of us. But I've had such a prolonged connection with the club that I have to believe I would want to stay. I doubt I was the kind of man who hung around when things did not align with what I wanted out of life.

Maybe that's something I know for sure.

I believe in who I was...who I am...as a man enough to know that leaving would not be what I want either.

I squeeze Sophia's hand. "Then it's done."

A smile grows on King's face, and he steps towards me as an explosion rips through the front of the club. The wall of heat and sound smashes into me, taking Sophia and I to the ground.

My ears ring. I can barely hear voices through the high-pitched whirring screaming inside my eardrums.

I immediately roll so that Sophia is behind me. A weapon slides across the floor before stopping in front of me. Catalina winks and crawls beneath the height of the remaining wall, just as bullets begin to pepper into the clubhouse.

Niro joins her, and they begin to fire shots out onto the lot.

"Get the women out back," King shouts to me, and I nod.

"Can you crawl?" I ask Sophia.

"If the other option is dying, yes."

"Go behind the bar. There's an entry on the other side. Stay as low to the ground as you can. Go." Sophia does as I say, and I reach for Rae as King sends her my way. "Follow Sophia."

"I know what to do," she says with measured confidence.

Spark is stuck near the entry to church, his whole body wrapped around Iris. Her service dog, Mac, howls. Looking around, I flip the thick wooden table with all the boxes of party food on it and drag it across the room.

"Spark," I shout. "Hand her to me."

At first, I don't think he heard me, but then I realize he's paralyzed by...PTSD. Fuck, it comes to me with certainty. Spark was injured in a bombing where everyone else on patrol with him was killed.

"You're crushing...me," Iris manages to say, but Spark just tightens his grip and holds her down in front of him.

Even though it feels like every muscle in my arm is tearing apart, I grab both of them and tug.

Bullets hit the front of the table. I glance up and see Halo jump over the bar and then crawl his way to provide cover for Briar and Gwen to escape down the rear corridor. Clutch is already up front with King, firing back.

But I heave Spark and Iris behind the table. Mac follows.

"Spark," I say, "you're gonna hurt Iris."

He looks up at me. I've seen that kind of fear in a man before. I don't know where, but I have.

In another time and place, there may be a more measured approach, but I do the only thing I can think of.

I slap him. "Spark, I need you to come back to us, brother."

He shakes his head, then takes in what is going on around us. "Iris," he says.

"I'm safe." She places her hand on his cheek. "But we need to move."

With burning muscles that feel like they are being shredded in my weak arm, I grip the top edge of the table and shunt it across the floor, feeling the force of every bullet. Bates uses our movement to duck low with Vi and get her to the other side of the bar, and the two of them disappear into a room. When they re-emerge, it's with Ari, Lola, and their own daughter, Avery, who is crying in Bates's arms. Vi covers her baby bump protectively with her hands.

But it's Sophia I'm looking for.

"Let's get them all into the medical room," Bates says.

When I get there, I see Sophia sitting with Briar. She has her arm around the young woman, who's in obvious distress.

"You okay?" I ask.

"Just another day in paradise," she says with a soft smile.

I like that she isn't falling apart, that she's offering comfort. I don't have much in the way of weapons on me, so I tug my switchblade out of my cut pocket and hand it to her. "If anyone other than one of us makes their way in here, you use it…"

She takes the blade, holds the safe handle, and flips the bite handle and blade around her hand in a maneuver called a butterfly. It's fast, and her hand moves as if she's done it a thousand times before.

She huffs and looks up at me. "I wonder what Dr. Polunin would say about this little bit of procedural memory?"

"Don't give a fuck, but for now, I'm going to be really glad you remember how to use it, and we can try and figure the fuck out why when this is over."

And with that, I return to the front of the building.

22

SOPHIA

Theo is in the medical room, patching up those who need it. I saw the moment training overtook everything else. He needs help threading the needle but is steady enough to stitch. He's calling out what needs to happen before he knows why.

Dressing versus stitches.

Who needs x-rays he can't provide in the clubhouse.

And I haven't seen Spark and Iris since Theo calmly took them and Mac to Spark's room and settled them inside. The rest of us, he told to leave them the fuck alone.

I did what I could to settle the women while the rest of the club took care of my family. My emotions are volatile. Shifting. They are my family. *Were* my family. But the mental image that galvanized me into action was, if at the end of all this, there were a line of dead bodies in the club-house lot, I'd rather they were my family than Theo and the women who voted so resolutely to stand by mine and Theo's side.

My family knew where I stood. What they were

attempting was a kidnapping. And I'm sure they are aware of what a motorcycle club stands for.

After fifteen minutes, silence fell. Bullets stopped. And, eventually, King called it clear.

The clubhouse was in disarray. The front wall decimated. Three bodies, none of them my immediate family, lay face down on the asphalt outside.

Conversation muted as everyone processed what had just happened.

Avery clung to Niro like a limpet and sobbed so hard that Niro was in tears trying to comfort her. Spark and Iris never reappeared. Ari held Lola while Halo held her.

"Those motherfuckers," Clutch muttered.

King looked around. "Let's shore this shit up. Can't leave bodies out there like that. Bates, figure out how to get them out of here. Clutch, Niro, figure out how to make the front of the building safe. The rest of you, let's clean up what we can."

And then people got to work.

I tried to help in the bar, but I couldn't sweep, and bending down to pick things up is still a center of gravity issue.

So, I dragged a stool to the sink and began washing up all the glasses and dishes people bring in after Briar has scraped them off.

She's stuck to me like glue since we were in the medical room together.

"How are you so calm?" Briar asks.

I shrug as I dip the glass I'm about to clean into the soapy water. "I wish I knew."

Which isn't completely true. Two things came together today.

I clearly know my way around a switchblade. I could flip

and spin that sucker in a way that proved it wasn't my first time holding one. And then there was something my brother said.

It was something else that made you run that day. You never ran, Sophia. Not once. Not even when our enemies broke into our house. You always fought. You were as ruthless as the rest of us. More accurate an aim than any of our brothers. If what you learned scared you enough to flee, then it was serious. And I'm determined to find out what it is for the sake of our family.

I never ran.

Did my heart race when the explosion went off? Of course. Anybody's would.

But was I terrified?

No.

If muscle memory kicked in over fear, then I've been through things like this before.

Not even when our enemies broke into our house. You always fought.

"We're dividing up," Rae says as she joins us by the sink. "We can't stay in lockdown here tonight. Without a front wall or heat, we'll freeze. King wants us in as few houses as possible tonight. I've got Bates, Niro, and Vex with their families all going to stay with Halo. We're suggesting King, Saint, Spark, Clutch, and Switch all stay together. It's a lot to ask, but you think Theo would be happy to have us at his house, given it's the biggest?"

"He hasn't been home since the accident, beyond the garage to get his bike. I can go ask him."

"Please," Rae says. "He apparently always wanted a big house for lots of his family to be able to stay at one time. King and I can bring a spare mattress from home if we need it."

I wipe my hands on a cloth and head to the medical

room. Saint is sitting on the medical bed, his feet on the floor, as Theo wraps a bandage tightly around his upper arm. "If it doesn't stop bleeding, we might need to stitch it."

I see a laptop open with a video paused of a wound getting stitched. "Research?" I ask.

Theo snaps off the medical gloves he's wearing. "Of a fashion."

Saint chuckles. "Didn't seem to need it though. Training just kicked in." He stands and slaps Theo on the shoulder. "Thanks, brother."

The door clicks shut, and Theo tugs me into his arms, kissing me deeply. It's the first normal thing to happen in a while, and I allow myself to sink into it.

A child's sobs filter through the open window. "Look what they did to our bike, Uncle Colton."

Theo pouts his bottom lip as we continue to listen.

"It's okay, Ave. We'll get another."

"But I like that one."

"Then we'll ask all your uncles to help us fix that one. Will just mean we can't ride it for a while."

"I can pay for it with my panda-bag money."

There's a soft chuckle. "Don't worry, Ave. I'll make them pay."

You'd have to be an adult to understand the nuance in his last statement.

Their voices fade away, and doors slam.

"Her panda-bag money?"

Theo shakes his head. "No idea. Pretty fucking cute she offered to help fix a bike that likely costs a small fortune. How are you, Sparrow?"

"Surprisingly okay."

He kisses me again. "Almost had a heart attack when that explosion went off, worrying that they'd get to you. Vex has the video. Your dad ordered one of his more junior men to launch a grenade or some shit. Alessio was furious once the shooting started. Ordered everyone back into their cars and got the fuck out of there."

"I wish I knew what the truth is."

"So, we'll make our own truth." He tucks my hair back behind my ear. "You're not wearing your eye patch."

"At some point tonight, it no longer felt important. It's just a prosthetic eye."

"Close your eyes."

I do as he says, and he presses a gentle kiss to my injured lid. The gesture makes me feel squishy inside.

"We're staying together," I say, my eyes still closed. "King has asked if Clutch, Spark, Saint, King, and their families can stay at your house because you have more bedrooms."

He tucks a curl of hair behind my ear and kisses my other eyelid. "I have no idea if that's true."

Finally, I open them again. "Rae said it was because you wanted a place where your whole family was able to come stay, but...if it's too much...you know, going home tonight, we can say no."

Theo shakes his head. "I'd hate to make wounded people sleep on the floor if I have the space to help them all out. It was a pretty big house."

"Then we'll do what we have to do to make everyone comfortable."

"We will, will we?"

I wrap my arms around his waist. "I guess this is our first hosting event as a couple."

Theo chuckles. "Hosting event? I'm not even sure there's food in the house."

"Well, I saved a whole bunch of the food prepped for the party. We'll just split it with the other house."

It takes another hour to organize transportation. And at least an hour again for King and Clutch to stop cursing their bikes getting shot up while trying to organize a split lockdown and security for the exterior of the club.

Then another thirty minutes to get everyone settled into the rooms before I meet Theo in the den.

He's looking at photographs that line the wall.

I dip beneath his arm and tuck up against his side. He taps a frame. "That was Sturgis Motorcycle Rally, the year before I enlisted. I was still a wet-behind-the-ears prospect. Halo had patched in already. But look how fucking young we were."

"Look how much hair you had. And how wavy it was."

He runs his hand over his short hair. "Meh. It's more unruly when it gets too long."

"Is it weird, being back here?" I ask.

Theo nods. "It's like I'm wearing a skin that isn't mine."

"I felt the same way when I went to my apartment for visits. Nothing fit. Not the clothes. Nothing. I even took two well-thumbed books off the shelf that my brother assured me were favorites, and I hated reading them."

He looks up at other photographs on the wall. "There are so many pictures of me and Vex doing shit together. I guess I've been keeping everyone at arm's length."

"It's hard, isn't it? My friends stopped coming over. They were ready to just continue with our friendships, and I wasn't even sure if I wanted to build one with them. Maybe my family interfered with that."

Theo kisses the top of my head. "I'm gonna make more of an effort to hang out with him. He clearly meant a lot to me."

"That's a good idea. Maybe he can become a friend of

mine too. I look forward to getting to know him better. And the old ladies. I really like them too."

"We should take them all down. Start again with new pictures of things we can actually remember."

"Especially that one," I say, pointing to a picture of a shirtless Theo with two topless women, one under each arm, by a campfire.

"Given I don't remember who they are or why I hung this on my wall, I think you can cut me some slack."

"Or cut the two of them. Turns out I'm handy with a blade."

"Yeah. Think we can conclude you weren't a passive observer in the family business."

"It feels like a leap to say that, but I think you might be right. I keep thinking about what Alessio said. About how I never ran. How I always fought. It bothers me."

Theo takes my hand and leads me upstairs. I'm tired. My limp is more pronounced. "Lean on me, Sparrow," he encourages, and I do.

Once in his bedroom, he sits me on the edge of the bed. "What bothers you about what your brother said?"

"Let's imagine I'm a completely different me. For what they are saying to be true, a few other things must be true too. I had to have been utterly complicit. I had to be a Mafia princess willing to do whatever for the success of her family and somewhat mercenary to marry a stranger for money and power. I must have been so shallow."

Theo slips the hoodie I changed into over my head. The soft T-shirt of his follows. "You believe that?"

"My family showed me photos. I clearly loved the life-style. Champagne. Private jets. Summers in Sicily. I don't look like I'm hating life in any of them."

"That doesn't mean you didn't want something more."

He helps me stand and slides my leggings and panties down my legs. "Go brush your teeth," he says.

I do, and Theo follows me once he's naked. "Guess I must have liked the idea of there being someone else here with me," he says, touching the marble vanity with two sinks.

We open and close drawers and cupboards and rustle up a spare toothbrush. "I would have shared yours."

Theo wrinkles his nose. "That might be taking our relationship a little too far."

I can't help but laugh. "We broke out of a brain-injury hospital, got married, argued with your club, argued with my family, got bombed, and are currently housing one half of the Iron Outlaws leadership team, yet sharing a toothbrush is your limit?"

Foam spills out of the side of Theo's mouth as he chuckles, then spits. "Fair. Brush and then finish your thoughts."

Theo rinses his own mouth, then rubs circles on the bottom of my back while I brush mine.

It's intimate.

Reassuring.

As soon as I'm done, he kisses me. "Toothpaste never tasted better," he says. "I'll give you another minute."

I appreciate the privacy to finish up, and then I go join him in bed. "So, this is our bed."

He flops back against the pillows. "Feels like I picked a good mattress."

"Better for sleeping with all those topless women?"

Theo tugs me to him and chuckles. "Jealousy looks good on you. Wait, switchblade—we're jumping all over the place with this conversation. You said you were thinking about what your brother said. About how you never ran and always fought. Tell me more about that."

I place my head on his chest, and his fingers drag lazily up and down my spine. "Just that. From the pictures I saw, I enjoyed the life. And from what my brother said, I was a willing participant in it. And there was something utterly familiar about holding the switchblade. So, if all those things were true and assuming I'm the old me who knew what I was doing, who was okay being married to this man, why on earth did I run so recklessly that it almost killed me?"

"I don't know, Sparrow. But I'll tell you this: You were interesting before. But you are even more interesting now."

I look up at Theo, and he wiggles down the bed so we are face-to-face.

"Yeah. Watching you flip my blade around gave me the fixings of a boner."

I laugh. "You're weird."

His lips find mine. They aren't especially gentle, and my entire body clenches in excitement. I slip my knee up over his thigh. "Nope, just happen to be falling for my wife a little more each day. I don't think that's a bad thing."

He's falling for me.

My heart skips a beat, and a band of excitement squeezes my chest.

My husband is falling for me.

But there is another feeling I must confess before I admit it to him.

"But what if I'm a bad person, Theo?" I say, voicing the fear I've been feeling since I spoke with my brother.

"What?" Theo cups my cheeks. "How are you a bad person?"

"I don't know. I feel like I had a morality reset. I came to in a hospital. I've watched movies and had therapy for over a hundred days straight to get here. Nature versus nurture. I became what I was because I grew up in a Cosa Nostra family. I may have done things that are hard to reconcile right now. What if I'm a bad person? What if my memory comes back and I've killed people and been involved in horrible things and—"

Theo's lips crush mine. His hands pull my body tight to his. I feel his cock swell between us, and even with the fears rattling through my body, his presence cuts through it all.

"I'm the medic for an outlaw motorcycle club. I'm a one-percenter. You don't get that patch for shits and giggles. It's a life I was born into because my father was an Outlaw before me. But it's a life I chose because I patched in when I didn't need to. And you were born into a life too. And I don't know whether you enjoyed it or had to make the best of it. But I'm never going to judge you for what you did then, Soph. This life requires a backbone. It requires making decisions the rest of the world won't make because of who we are and what we do. If anything, it reassures me that our lives will mesh together well."

"When you put it like that..."

"Plus, I'm starting to think it's all fated. How we met. Why we were both there at the same time. We both have brothers, both belong to an outside-the-law family. Heck, my road name is Switch, and today we found out you're handy with a switchblade. There're too many coincidences for it to be anything other than fate."

"Aren't you worried fate has us on a path of no return?"

Theo shakes his head. "If that's fate's plan, then we're going to have to tame it because I can't help but believe this leads to anything other than something real fucking good."

23

SWITCH

s the words come out of my mouth, I mean every one of them.

It *is* fate.

Kismet.

And where the heck do I know that word from?

"I mean it, Soph. You're meant to be here with me right now. We're supposed to be on this path together at this very moment."

"Is this optimism I'm hearing from you, Mr. Serious?"

I smile at her teasing. I love the way her eye sparkles with mischief. "Call it whatever you want. None of this could possibly be a mistake."

"What if life is more like those choose-your-own-adventure books they had in the speech therapy room? There are a million different outcomes based on the choices we make. What if the options become our fate based on our decisions?"

I run my knuckle down her cheek, then rub my thumb over her lush lower lip. "It's the exact same thing as fate. The river runs where it needs to, even if it has to wear down rocks over hundreds of years…it's still gonna run exactly where it wants. All those paths are just the water coming up against rocks and finding ways around them. Your destiny still takes you where it's meant to."

Sophia gently bites my thumb, and my cock twitches. "I like this poetic and sage and romantic side of you, tough guy. I peered around the end of the bar and saw you flip that table to save Spark and Iris. I think what we're learning about old me is that she would have greatly appreciated your courage and bravery and strength under fire. But current me likes this version of you."

"Then, as old me returns, I'll try to not forget to be this guy every now and again."

Sophia laughs, and I wrap my arms tightly around her until all our good bits line up. One brush of my lips against hers, and I'm sunk for her all over again. I roll her until she's on her back and I'm settled between her legs. Her hips tilt against mine, and it would take nothing to slide into her.

Bareback.

I don't remember having done it before, yet, somehow, I remember what *bareback* actually means.

But I also remember enough from the lectures Dad gave me when I was a kid that I should wrap it up unless I want to knock up the woman I'm with or catch something that would make my dick rot.

I'm sure it's not as simple as that.

"We should get tested," I say.

"Tested for what?"

"Sexually transmitted diseases. Then we don't have to use condoms."

"Wait. You can… eww." Her nose wrinkles. "Why did no

one fill in the blanks about sexually transmitted diseases for me?"

"Don't overthink this now. We can use condoms and be fine. Then we can go get tested, and if neither of us has anything contagious, we can go without."

"But then I'll get pregnant."

"Not if you go on birth control. You don't want kids?" I ask.

"I don't know what I want right now. I haven't thought that far ahead about kids. Have you?"

I think about my family. The rough-and-tumble nature of my brothers. "Yeah. I want kids. I want a family like I had growing up. One with siblings who fight and tease and would defend each other to the last. And parents who love each other fiercely, through thick and thin."

Sophia reaches up and pushes a lock of hair back off my forehead and then chuckles when it flops straight back down again. "I'm sure that's the kind of childhood I had. Not sure where I fit being the only girl, but I get the feeling we were close. So, if I had to put a stick in the ground, I'd say the odds are that I'd like kids someday. But I'd be happy getting to know myself first before I spent time getting to know children."

I kiss her softly, because for all she said the words in jest, there's an ache of sadness when she talks about getting to know herself.

"I know a way you can get to know yourself," I say, my lips dangerously close to her ear. She smells...soft. Sweet. Like a man could lose himself in her for a couple of hours or a lifetime.

"What's that?" Her hands come around me and stroke down my back. It tickles in a way my cock really appreciates.

I shuffle down the bed, planting kisses as I go: on the rise of her breast, her nipple, her ribs, the soft plane of her stomach. Using my thumbs, I part her pubic hair and lips so I can swipe her with my tongue.

The gasp she emits cranks my engine.

Her knees come up, her thighs by my ears.

"This. You either get to know yourself, me, or God. I'll let you choose."

She chuckles. "I choose you, Theo."

The words make me feel more than I'm probably supposed to. I fucking love the fact she chooses me.

Her pussy is soft and wet, and I eat it like a starved man. Nothing makes me feel stronger than when I make Sophia fall apart. When I see her color rise and hear her breath catch. I dig my fingertips into her hips, holding her still as her hands slide into my hair.

Her whole body stiffens as she grinds against my face. It's messy and loud and uninhibited.

I grind my cock into the mattress, aching for release, staving off the discomfort.

When she comes, it's a relief for us both.

Climbing up her body, I place kisses on her skin, savoring the softness of it. Clutch always talks about Gwen being his soft place to land. And I finally get what he means.

If I never get the rest of my memories back, it'll be enough to replace them with new memories of Sophia.

Kissing her lips is like coming home in all uses of the word.

She's mine now. I'll never let her family get their hands on her again. Won't let her be traded for power. Unlike Halo and Spark, I don't find I need to be in control. I want a queen. An equal.

I want my Sparrow.

I lift off her, my left arm shaking as I do, but I'm

learning to live with it. Sophia wriggles beneath me as I grab a condom from the drawer and then kneel to put it on.

"I know you're questioning yourself now, Soph. I know you wonder who you are, where your place in the world is. But I'm here. I'll be your constant. I'll be your anchor. I'll hold you in place until you figure out where you want to be. I promise."

"Theo," she says, her voice ripe with emotions I find hard to express.

So, I show her. I slide into her. My full length in one push. There's friction, but I keep going because nothing about her body language disagrees with my decision.

"Just desperately want you right now, really fucking bad."

I lean forward and kiss her. "Then take me." Still keeping her impaled, I grab my pillows and help Sophia lift her head so she can see what I see. "Look how fucking good we look together."

Her thick cream already coats my cock when I pull out. I gather some on my thumb and then offer it to her lips. "You ever taste yourself?" I ask.

Sophia shakes her head. "Not that I remember."

I smile at that. "You taste really fucking good." She opens her mouth, and I place my thumb inside, sliding my cock into her as she closes her mouth.

Two parts of me inside two parts of her.

My cock throbs.

Her tongue slides around my thumb, licking it clean. Then, more seductively, she licks my thumb like it's my cock.

"Fuck, Soph." My words are gruff. Layers of whiskey and need.

As I move my cock, she mirrors the action in the same

way with her tongue. Same pace. Same intensity. Same need.

"Bite," I encourage. The word comes out of nowhere. But something inside me craves the bite of pain to mingle with the pleasure.

She does, but it's gentle. And I feel the need for something...

"More."

With wide eyes, she does what I ask. She clamps my thumb in place and teases me with her tongue.

It feels unbelievably good. Stripping past everything that has already happened between us.

"Hold it there, no matter what I do."

I shallow my strokes. Pressing my cock upwards until she begins to moan. Her teeth remain clamped, but her mouth opens as she gasps.

Her eyes grow wide with need and panic.

"Stop biting, and I stop fucking you," I warn, even though I have no intention of stopping.

Her gasps turn into moans. Her abs tense, her body clenching as she lets go. A gush of liquid runs between us, coating my cock, spilling out onto the bedding. But I don't give a fuck. I fucking love it.

"Theo," she cries, letting go of my thumb.

I miss the sting of it, but my cock has a mind of its own. My lips clash with hers as I lie down over her and grip the cheeks of her ass.

"Bite my shoulder." The words are a command.

Sophia pulls me down to her and does as I say. It's like a switch flips inside me, and suddenly I'm fucking her.

Hard.

Possibly uncaring.

I don't have to tell her what it does to me.

She knows.

She sucks hard, likely bruising my skin, and it feels so painfully good. Intimate on a level I hadn't expected.

My cock aches, and the pain pushes my orgasm back. It's like a seesaw, teetering on the most intense line between the two. Clinging to a place where both exist together.

Everything disappears. Nothing comes into focus.

Boundaries blur.

She releases my skin as she comes a second time, sucking in air after she cries out my name. Then her teeth are back on me.

I thought I'd willingly bleed for Sophia. But does that mean I'd bleed at someone else's hands to save her? Or at her hands because I can't think of anything more sexually arousing?

While she doesn't break my skin in that way, I can't help wishing she would.

My blood running between the two of us is the hottest thing I can think of. Images of Sophia taking that switch-blade of hers and drawing a line across my chest. The thick liquid spreading as we fuck.

I want to instruct her how to do it. I want to see how deep I'll let her go before the pain blocks everything else out. Then I'll stitch myself and heal before letting her do it all over again.

The combination of the visual and the way her cunt is squeezing the ever-loving fuck out of me has me coming harder than I remember.

The world shimmers at the edges. Likely all that blood I was thinking about pulsing through my temples as I come deep inside Sophia.

My vision blurs a little. Probably to do with my head injury. But I ride out the last waves of pleasure before reaching between us to pull out and take care of the condom.

When I kneel up, Sophia gasps.

"Oh my God, I made such a mess of your shoulder. I'm so sorry."

I try to glance down but can't really see. Instead, I run my hand over the tender skin. It burns a little to the touch, which makes my spent cock twitch with life and makes me sigh.

"Guess I learned something about me," I say, taking her hands. "I fucking loved that you hurt me. Does that freak you out?"

Sophia struggles to her knees, and I offer my hands in assistance. It takes a second for her to maneuver her left leg beneath her, but she manages it. And I'm really fucking proud of her.

"No. I liked being told to bite you. But I don't want to hurt you."

She says the words, yet without thinking, she presses her fingers to the bite marks. They burn in response, and I close my eyes and sigh. There is something utterly peaceful about it. The way my brain settles, the way my soul sucks the heat in and warms me.

"You didn't. At least, not in the way you think of hurt and pain. You think you'd be open to doing more of that?"

She blushes a little, her cheeks pink. "As long as you tell me what to do. What you need. And that you tell me to stop if it hurts more than you need."

I tip her chin. "You really liked it?"

"It was hot, Theo. Yes. But I don't know..."

I touch my knuckle to her cheek. "Safe words work both ways. I'll say 'Harley' if it's too much. And I'll tell you expressly what I'd like so you never have to guess. I want that control, even in this."

"Okay. You'll tell me what you need. And we'll both use 'Harley' if it's more than we can do or take."

I lean closer and kiss her.

Hoping she realizes just how precious she's become to me.

24

SWITCH

I study myself and my wet hair in the mirror in my bedroom in the clubhouse. "You sure you know what you're doing?" I ask Vex as he brandishes the scissors.

"You can't be bothered to get a haircut, I'm gonna pin you down and give you one. It's all uneven. And what you don't remember is that I've cut your hair for the last four years."

"Fine. Cut."

"You normally take your shirt off so you don't get hair everywhere."

If I remove my shirt, Vex is going to see all the bruises and teeth marks Sophia left on my skin, and it's all I can do to not get another fucking erection thinking about them. We lay in the mess of the bed, wrapped around each other for another hour, feeling utterly connected after we'd talked.

And when Sophia finally got in the shower, I searched online for whether you could be a dominant and a masochist. Turns out you can.

Which means I've got shit to explore, because I can't remember where I was at on this journey, or if I even was on it, before the accident. I'm not ashamed of what we did. Knowing we're two consenting adults who had incredible sex, I don't feel bad. But something tells me this is private and...precious.

I don't want to have to explain it to anyone.

"Yeah. Well. Not today. Just cut the damn thing."

Vex chuckles. "I'm on it."

He begins to snip, and I see the hair fall. I can also tell this isn't Vex's first rodeo with the scissors. "So, you said you manage my investments?"

"Yeah. I do. You got quite the portfolio. Built it up to six million. You get paid a salary by the club as a medic, and you get your share of any take. You and I flip houses. Buy 'em cheap. We pay my brothers cash in hand to renovate them. Give them cash for supplies. Then we sell the property at a profit and take the cash back out before repeating the cycle. The profit goes to the investments we have."

It's a surprise to find out just how wealthy I am. "No shit."

"It's cool if you don't want to keep doing it."

Hair flutters down my face, making my nose itch. "Nah. If it's working that well, we should keep doing it. You'll have to tell me what my role is though."

"You found the property."

I huff at that. "That's wild. Sophia used to be in real estate."

"Must be fate," he says with a laugh. "Perhaps she can help you pick 'em."

He cuts away at my hair for a few more minutes in silence then says, "You and Sophia? Is it real?"

I look up and see he's watching me in the mirror. "What do you mean?"

"We've been friends a long time. And at this point, I

know you better than *you* know you. Sudden was not your M.O."

If I want to rebuild authentic relationships with my friends again, I'm going to have to start trusting them. And given Vex was my best friend, he seems the safest place to start. "It was intense 'like' at first."

"And now?"

I can't help but smile. "Last night we were talking about having kids."

"I'm happy for you, brother," he says.

When he's done cutting, he brushes what hair he can away. "You know Mom's going to want to meet her."

"The way you say that sounds ominous."

Vex laughs. "She cares about you. Hopefully it's not too much of an interrogation for Sophia."

I stand so I can bundle up the paper and hair on the floor.

"Can I ask you a question about what happened that night with Halo?"

Vex moves the chair out of my way. "I wasn't there at the beginning, but I'll tell you whatever I know."

"What's the deal with all the money people keep mentioning?"

"I hacked the Righteous Brotherhood, traced all their financial schemes, and emptied them. Got the club around eleven million. The Brotherhood wanted it back. The leader, Daryll West, Halo's half-brother, kept coming up here sniffing around because he had a connection to a woman up here, as well as Halo. Foster kids together. His time in care was messy. But we still have it and have started spending it."

"You really are a clever fucker, you know."

"Yeah, I am. You good?"

I glance in the mirror. "Yeah, I'm good. Thanks for this."

Once he's gone, I change into a hair-free Henley and put on my cut. It's soft, and the weight of it on my bruised shoulders feels familiar. As does the assortment of weapons on the vanity in front of me.

It's wild I've become such a wealthy man through becoming a biker.

My phone rings, and I glance down at the number. An area code I was waiting for.

"Doc," I say.

"Theo. It's Dr. Polunin. I'm so glad you called. Where are you and Sophia? Are you both well and safe?"

"On a scale of one to I'll-die-before-I-tell-anyone-your-secrets... where do you and I fall, Doc?"

"I fall on the Hippocratic oath."

"The what?"

"Ask any of your friends. It's the oath doctors take. The original text is somewhere along the lines of, 'And whatsoever I shall see or hear in the course of my profession...if it be what should not be published abroad, I will never divulge, holding such things to be holy secrets.' Does that put your mind at ease?"

I have no choice but to believe her. "Sophia's family was prepared to marry her off to some man she didn't want to marry. We think that's what she was driving away from before her accident. So, we left, and I married Sophia."

I hear a cough and splutter on the other end of the line. "When I picked up my coffee to take a quick sip, those were not the words I was expecting. Boredom, the need for a little freedom, some excitement. But marriage? You married Sophia? And escaping an arranged marriage?"

"That's what I said, Doc. I need you to see her."

There's a pause. "Theo. Her family closed out her account here. They came and emptied her room."

"I guessed they would. But I'll pay. I'll cover her bills. I'll even pay you cash in advance if you're worried about me not being good for the money."

Another pause. "Theo. What I do? It was never about the money. I'd come and see the two of you simply because I care about my patients. And, quite frankly, if what you say is true, I would help her do anything to escape her family. But, Theo, you need to know. On a medical scale of one to ten, I care about Sophia's somewhere around a three. Because she has been with us for a while. She's healed. She's done therapy and rehabilitation. Her injuries are as healed as they are likely to get. You, on the other hand, are a nine. You need the care we can provide significantly more than Sophia does."

I look at myself in the mirror. I see the narrowing of my eyes because the light in here seems too bright. Because I feel another headache coming on. "Fine. You can see us both, Doc."

"Then I have a deal for you, Theo. I will continue to see you both if you tell me exactly what happened to you the night you were injured. I will sign a nondisclosure if that makes you feel more comfortable."

I take a deep breath. "Done. I will bring both of us in one evening. Sophia's family can't be notified. If they are there when we get there, there will be bloodshed on your hands, Doc."

"Understood. I have no intention of ever communicating with them on Sophia's behalf again. If I am seeing you both for one night, I would like to have some of the others stay to see you. You will be seen by our staff for any CT or MRI required. I will book you in under pseudonyms. Of course, the staff will recognize you both immediately when you arrive, but I will, in real time, warn them that they are not to contact her family."

"If it helps, they are trying to enforce a guardianship agreement put in place to get Sophia back, saying I influenced her."

"I can very quickly write Sophia a letter to show I find her to be perfectly capable of making these decisions for herself now. I can have it to you within thirty minutes."

I let out a whoosh of air. "You're the best, Doc."

"Doctor Polunin. And, yes, I am."

I chuckle at that. "You don't really want me to call you 'Doctor Polunin,' do you?"

I hear her laughter. "It's lovely to hear from you, Theo. I will see you in four days. To be safe, it should be late."

"Midnight work for you, Doc?"

"Midnight. Promptly. At one second after, I will be walking to my car."

"We'll be there."

I hang up the phone, relief in my chest. I send a quick text to Sophia, knowing she is home with Catalina. All the women will be there soon, being dropped off by their men on the way to the clubhouse. The house will be well protected with prospects and everyone not holding key positions.

I tuck my various weapons into their holsters and hit the medical room on my way to the bar.

"You busy?" Spark asks as I complete an inventory I found on the computer in there. Never thought something so mundane as separating triangular, tubular, and roller bandages could be so satisfying. I tick off the amounts I need.

"Not doing anything that can't wait. What's up?"

Spark comes into the room and perches on the medical

bed, his feet out in front of him, his arms crossed. "I wanted to talk about what happened the other day."

I close the inventory list. "Yeah?"

"I thought I was over it. Thought I'd processed everything. But with the baby and Iris...guess I haven't."

Over the past couple of days, I've read up on PTSD. "PTSD recovery isn't linear. Retraumatization and setbacks are all par for the course. And the likelihood increases during stressful moments."

The look of anguish on his face tugs at me.

"I asked Vex to fill me in on everyone's history in the hospital," I continue. "I know what happened to you at Abbey Gate in Afghanistan. And about what happened to Iris. I've felt a fraction of that at the thought Sophia's family might take her away. So, I can't imagine how you felt going through the thought she might be taken from you permanently. And we were bombed. Right here, in a place where we are meant to be safe, while your woman, pregnant with your baby, was right there. Two minutes earlier, she'd have been sat by the window. If you draw a Venn diagram between your history, Iris's abduction, and the bomb, right in the middle is you and PTSD."

Spark blows out a deep breath. "So how do I fix it, brother?"

I feel helpless, wishing I could remember more of my training so I could provide better answers. Stalling for a moment, I sit next to him and mirror his body language.

Spark glances sideways at the scar that runs up the back of my skull. "Feel crap coming to you and burdening you with my stuff when you've got shit of your own going on."

I shake my head. "Don't. Sharing it is the most important thing. That's kinda how I realized there was something special with me and Soph. She held my hand when I practically collapsed on the floor after one of my..." I can't think of the word for what happened that day. Fits? Episodes, maybe? "Anyway, my point is, I don't know much for sure right now, but I'm pretty sure one way to get through shit is to share it. The club has lots of money right now, right?"

Spark rubs his face. "Yeah, money we liberated from the Righteous Brotherhood. Eleven million. Less now. Bet we've spent about a million developing the compound, paying off some of the older brothers to clean house."

"Then we use it. Soph and I need to finish our treatment. I've made an after-hours agreement with one of the docs I trust. Was going to ask King for some backup to travel there. Why don't you see the team there too? I mean, it's a brain-injury place, but the therapists are still therapists. They have all these cutting-edge solutions. Perhaps they have an approach that might help you."

Spark stands. "I did treatment once though. But when it came down to it, when her life was on the line, I froze. I fucking froze, brother. What kind of fucking one percenter am I if my first thought wasn't to pull my weapon and protect her? You had to protect both of us."

I stand and grip his biceps. "Don't fucking do that. You know what your first thought was? That you'd die for her. You wrapped yourself around her so that no part of her was exposed. That's the kind of one percenter you are. That's the kind of man you are. You would have died for her without a single fucking thought and never regretted it for a moment."

And then I realize I'm crying.

And I'm shouting.

I don't know why.

And I'm shaking Spark like he doesn't understand the first fucking thing I'm saying.

And then we're holding on to each other.

"Fuck," I curse.

"Yeah," Spark says.

We stand like that for a moment, and then I wipe my hand across my face.

"Sorry. Don't know what the fuck just happened," I say.

Sparks huffs. "Is this where I remind you that your first fucking thought when you were up at the cabin was to protect Halo, Lola, and Ari? That *you'd* fucking die for *them*? That you threw yourself into the path of danger because that's the kind of one percenter *you* are?"

"We were talking about you, though. Not me."

"Pretty sure all that shit you gave me at the beginning about trauma responses not being linear applies to you as much as it applies to me. You had a great fucking life, Switch. Now you've got a different life. Like me. You got a woman you clearly care about. And you gotta somehow figure out how to build a new life on a solid foundation even though it's built on the rubble of chaos."

We stand in silence for a moment, the air heavy between us as we process our thoughts.

"And another thing. I'm sorry," Spark says. "Should have immediately voted to back you. Too wrapped up in the idea of safety for Iris and the club that I forgot who I was for a second. Won't happen again."

I take a deep breath. Then another. "Perhaps we should do this together."

"I'm not fucking meditating," Spark says.

I laugh at that. "Maybe we just try everything once and get over it."

"Spark!" King's voice echoes down the hallway.

"Yo," Spark yells in return. "Medical." He glances back at me. "It's a deal, brother. We'll walk to the other side of this together."

I turn to the sink and splash cold water over my face, then run it back through my hair.

There's a knock on the door, and King walks in just as I'm drying my face. "Spark, you want to tell me why your uncle-in-law is outside waiting for the gates to be unlocked?"

"I'm not an oracle for Cillian. How the fuck should I know why he's here?"

King throws an arm over Spark's shoulder. "Let's go find out together."

When I get to the front of the lot, the only brothers are King, Spark, Vex, and Clutch.

Cillian is there with three other men.

"Who are they?" I whisper to Vex.

"His second in command, Callum, is in the navy suit," Vex replies quietly. "The redhead is Iris's brother, Thomas. And the third is Callum's younger brother. He's more of an enforcer."

"So, the rumors are true, then?" Cillian asks. He wears a black suit with a charcoal gray sweater beneath it. His shoes are polished to perfection. But his hands are rough, and there are scars on the knuckles, recent ones. The costume presents a polished gentleman, but the hands reveal the truth of a fighter who worked his way up the ranks. "That the front of ye building was blown up by the Sicilians?"

"Who knew the underground world was such a bunch of gossips?" King says.

Cillian looks over to Spark. "Son. You're lucky I'm not putting a bullet in ye for putting my niece and that baby at risk."

"I'm not your son," Spark says stoically, but given our conversation in the medical room, I squeeze his shoulder. It can't be easy hearing someone else accuse you of the very thing you fear you did.

"Sorry," Cillian says with a steely glint in his eye. "Nephew-in-law."

"No women were hurt," I reply.

"Looking at the front of ye building, I would say that was more good luck than any plan on your part. I've got a proposition for ye. I hope you'll hear me out."

King steps back, allowing the four of them to enter the lot. Once we're seated in the bar, King opens the floor. "Why are you here?"

"I want to know why the Sicilians think you are worth this kind of effort," he says.

Spark shakes his head. "Club business, Cillian."

Cillian eyes Spark. "Well, the enemy of mine enemy is my friend. And I'm feeling very familial today. So let me rephrase: The Sicilians are a fucking pain in my arse, trying to sweep the New York docks out from beneath me. Yesterday, they weren't there. My docks ran like clockwork. I need to know if their feud with you is a temporary thing, or something likely to take some heat off the docks for a while as they pursue the New Jersey side."

I look to King, but he doesn't even glance my way as he replies, "It's a one-time thing. In fact, we aren't retaliating, so they feel like we're even, in the hope they fuck off back to New York."

"That's a shame."

"Why?" I ask.

"Well, I came to ask for help. When your boy here"—he tips his head in Spark's direction—"stole my niece—"

"I didn't steal your fucking niece. She's a grown woman who made her choice. Don't talk about her like she's a phone I left lying around in my truck."

Cillian puts his hand out like you would to settle an annoying child.

Spark's hands turn into fists. "Fucking raise your hand like that to me in my own clubhouse, and I'll be raising mine right into your face."

"Settle," Cillian instructs, but I see he's saying it to Callum, who has eased his hand toward his holster. "I seem to recall you said you'd help us if we had problems at the docks. And I'm asking for that help now, because it's lapsed as of late."

"We're on hiatus," Clutch says. "Had too much heat, too much shit dealing with the Righteous Brotherhood. Had a brother in a coma."

"A fucking hiatus," Cillian says, laughing as if it was the funniest shit he ever heard. "If I'd known, I would have made a play for the Jersey side of the docks."

"And we'd have handed you your *arse*," Vex says, mocking Cillian's accent.

King bites back a smile. "If you've got a New York problem, it stays a New York problem. I'm not getting into a permanent fight with the Mafia or Cosa Nostra that will just drain our resources with little or no gain."

Cillian leans back in his chair. "You're scared of them."

King crosses his arms. "Not in the slightest. But what do we gain out of going to war with them? They don't want the Port Newark-Elizabeth Marine terminal, which is the only route we need kept open. So, they came here to shoot their mouth off a little. They did some damage to the building. We killed three of theirs, they injured a few of ours, but no one seriously. We could go after them in revenge. Plan a hit on Long Island or Little Italy or some shit to rough a few of them up. But what do we gain?"

Cillian slams the table. "You get your fucking pride. You

keep your reputation as fearless. Accepting all this"—he gestures to the work at the front of the building—"makes you look weak."

I huff. "I barely remember my own name right now, so I haven't got any memory of ever meeting you before. But I'm guessing that right there is why you've got problems with the Five Families. You think about every single individual battle. You've got to lose some to win the war. You keep them permanently pissed at you, they're going to want a piece of you so bad that they can taste it. Let shit go."

"Now I see why the Brotherhood kept coming back to take a piece of you." Callum grins. "You let them chip away to avoid a fight until you had no choice."

Niro and Bates walk into the bar and casually go stand either side of King, just behind him. They don't interrupt. Don't ask questions. Just flank our president without even speaking.

I like that loyalty.

Cillian stands. "I'm disappointed in you. Thought you Outlaws were supposed to stand for something, that we could share intel, but I can see when the fighting spirit has left. We'll see ourselves out."

Vex watches them leave. "Fuck him."

"Permission to step outside to demonstrate my fighting spirit on Cillian's face," Niro says.

"Permission denied," King says. "Sit your ass down. We aren't going to worry about everyone's favorite Irish mobster when we have weapons to pick up at the docks in two days."

25

SOPHIA

I made a decision in the aftermath of the explosion at the clubhouse.

I am who I am.

Some would say that's not a particularly revolutionary sentence, but in my mind it is. Because I've been chasing *her*. I've been looking for clues to piece the old me back together. As if the me I am now is just a stepping stone to normality. When in reality, she's not coming back. Even if I get my memory back, my old life isn't coming with it.

From now on, it's about how to make the best possible life I can for myself. It starts here and now.

I run a towel over my freshly showered hair as I glance into the pitiful state of my wardrobe.

Theo walks past me, naked, his inked shoulders and taut biceps making my tender pussy clench. There is no reason for it to be needing anything.

Last night, he fucked me hard with his hand over my mouth so we didn't make too much noise. This morning, he used his fingers to get me off in the shower before forcing me to my knees so he could come over my breasts. I say *forced*. With one hand on my shoulder, he applied downward pressure, but the other hand held tightly to my forearm to stabilize me as I went down.

He also commanded me to squeeze his balls very tightly. I felt a sense of power that I could make him come that hard with a dizzy feeling of subservience in doing what he needed. The combination is as heady as it is confusing.

The two sides of me and Theo.

Need and care.

I sigh when I look at my clothing options. The girls have been gathering at the clubhouse during the day. In the evening, we'd return to the two separate houses with the men and eat together. Vex had moved in too and was sleeping on an air mattress in Theo's den.

Arms wrap around me from behind. "What's got you sighing?" He places his lips to my neck.

"Honestly? My clothing choices. The girls are coming over tonight so we're all together while you go on your run, and I have no clothes that I love. Finding out the state of my finances is the second question I have for the lawyer this morning."

"Good job I love you in nothing, then," he says with a chuckle. He slides his hand between the folds of the towel but does nothing more stimulating than stroke my skin.

"Sadly, the rest of the old ladies don't have quite the same taste as you do. I believe in polite society, clothing is not optional. And all I have is brain-rehab chic. Soft clothes for the even softer brain."

Theo places a kiss to the side of my neck. "That's an easy problem to solve. I'm taking you shopping when we've finished with the lawyer."

I turn to face him. "I'm not letting you pay for unnecessary things like extra clothing. The fact I'm here, married, protected, and building an unexpected life is enough."

Theo smiles. I like him best when he does. His eyes crinkle at the corners, and he has the most perfect lips and teeth. "Pretty words, Sparrow. But I'm buying you clothes today. You can pick 'em. Or you can wear what I buy you. But you're getting new clothes, and I strongly recommend picking them yourself because I might have shit taste." He points to his closet. A thousand pairs of jeans in various stages of distress. Three pairs of boots that all look the same, three pairs of sneakers, and stacks of T-shirts. "See?" As he says the word, he tugs on the towel wrapped around my body, then slaps my butt.

"Hey."

Theo shrugs. "Babe. You're naked in my closet. You think I'm not going to take my chances to feel you up? Even if it's just a little slap."

This was the other thing I thought of as I huddled with Briar in the medical room. I have a man. A very attractive and attentive one who reassures me I'm beautiful most days in both his words and actions. It's time I believed it. Not just that Theo is a good man in saying them, but that deep down, at the most visceral level, I believe I'm beautiful as I am.

Even if my definition of beautiful didn't come anywhere close to the traditional standards.

I could own what I had.

When we get downstairs, Rae and King are already in the kitchen. "We made coffee. Hope you don't mind," Rae says.

"Fine with us," Theo says as if it's always been the two of us.

King glances up from his phone. "You headed to the

clubhouse? The builders are arriving to patch up the front wall."

"I've got a few errands. Need to take Sophia to meet the lawyer and to pick up a few things she needs, seeing we split the center so quickly."

Clutch walks bleary-eyed into the kitchen. He's shirtless, and I can see why Gwen might be the way she is with a man like that at home. But there's something about Theo's leaner, fitter frame that makes me blush.

"Morning," he says, his tone a rolling grumble, before pouring himself a cup of coffee.

It's amazing how at ease these people are in Theo's home.

"Take two escorts with you," King says. "Clutch, you free to take Switch and Sophia to the lawyers?"

"Yeah, Gwen's just getting ready for work. If we can go past the hotel on the way so I can drop her off, that would work," Clutch says. "I'll go tell her to get moving and get Vex to come with."

We finish up and travel to the lawyer's office in Theo's truck. There's a biting cold wind, the kind that churns up the sea into a dirty, sandy, foamy wash. Theo loaned me a thick leather jacket with a fleecy warm lining. It's way too big, but it's comforting.

Unlike the look on Theo's face when my lawyer says he needs a moment with me alone before Theo can join us.

"Sophia. So good to meet you," Al Huston says as he shakes my hand. Then he leads me to a sofa opposite two taller chairs. Despite being guided to the sofa, I take the chair. It'll be easier to get out of when this meeting is done.

Al sits opposite me, opening the button on his jacket as he sits before rearranging the glasses on his nose.

"You too. Thank you so much for fitting me in."

"I needed to have a word with you first for my own peace of mind." He runs a hand through his white-as-snow hair. He glances in the direction of the closed door. "You are absolutely here under your own volition?"

"Volition?"

"Your own choice."

I nod. "Oh. Yes. One hundred percent."

"Good. Good. I would have found you a discrete way out of the building if not. But I am glad you are here by your own making. And one last question before we let Switch join us. Are you married by your own choice too?"

I glance down at the ring that sits on my finger. "Absolutely. I'm happy to be married to Theo. And you should be grateful that I know how to keep the peace, *Al*, because I won't mention you doubting his character to Switch."

I use his road name deliberately and deliver the lines with a smile.

"Of course. Of course. We can invite Theo to join us." He hurries to the door and opens it wide for Theo to come in.

There are frown lines on his brow when he enters. "You okay, Sparrow?"

I smile. "Al was legally obligated to ensure I was here of my own accord and not under duress, but I explained we're very happy together."

Theo's shoulders drop, and he smiles before taking my hand and kissing over my ring. "Understatement of the fucking year, Sparrow. So, what's the deal?"

It takes about an hour for us to pull together a full plan with Huston's guidance. We make calls, get witness statements. Dr. Polunin is as good as her word and has already begun the process of getting statements from the relevant members of staff at the center. And we submit a legal request for return of access to all my financial accounts.

When we leave, everyone relaxes. "You don't like lawyers?" I ask.

Clutch shakes his head. "Generally, if a biker needs one, things have gone to shit."

"Back to the compound?" Vex asks.

"Need a detour," Theo says, and then explains.

The shopping is chaotic. I watch as Clutch continues to tease Switch by attempting to pick out lingerie for me.

"I'm happy for him," Vex says, handing me a small pile of highly practical yet stylish clothes. An ivory blouse, cashmere sweaters, and high-quality denim.

I smile at that. "You are?"

Vex looks down at me. "Yeah. He has such a close family, like me. It's unusual in the rest of the brothers. But I think that's what he's been searching for. The foundation of a family of his own."

Switch punches Clutch in the arm, and Clutch laughs loudly as other shoppers keep their distance. I see two security guards watching the two of them but doing nothing.

Vex places his arm casually over my shoulder. "I think you're the difference. I love you and him together, Soph."

Friendship is such a foreign concept. But as I navigate my way to making friends with people, I realize there is joy in it. "Thank you for being such a good friend to him, Vex. I think you've been the difference to him too."

And that's how several hours later, I'm standing in Theo's kitchen, with the rest of the old ladies, in soft slouchy pants and a champagne-colored cashmere sweater that is buttery soft against my skin that Vex chose.

"I hear my man was useless at shopping today," Gwen says as she joins us in the kitchen.

"He wasn't useless, in a scenario where I wanted to work

a pole. He picked out outfits that would have guaranteed epic tips."

Gwen chuckles. "Yeah. He likes it when the tits and ass are both hanging out. I save the things he buys me for alone time when we're at home."

"Remember that red thing he bought you for Christmas?" Iris asks with a chuckle.

Humorous exasperation etches Gwen's face as she grips my wrists. "It had cut-out hole access to all the good bits."

Rae throws her arm over Gwen's shoulders. "Men are simple, visual creatures. Lingerie does it for them. Especially when they can sneak access to your genitals."

Ari chuckles. "Genitals is such a weird word."

"Oh, God," Briar gasps. "I thought I was the only one who thought so."

I look down at the large kitchen counter and at the plethora of people and things in front of me.

"This is all amazing," I say finally. "Honestly."

"It was Catalina's idea," Rae says. "We each brought something we like to eat, something we like to drink, and something we like to read."

"I skipped the reading part and just brought a buffet of weapons," Catalina says.

I laugh as I take in the guns and knives of different sizes. There's a switchblade, and I reach for it before flipping it around as if it were made for my hand.

"Oh," Vi says. "Can you teach me to do that? Bates would lose his shit if I did that with one of his knives."

"Why would you deliberately make Bates flip his shit?" I ask.

"Oh, it's not that kind of losing his shit. It's the kind where she'd end up naked and pregnant"—Gwen glances at Vi's growing bump—"again. Or more pregnant. Whatever."

Catalina leans close. "Bates has a thing for knives and a thing for Vi."

"Oh," I say. Then: "*Oh!*"

Gwen laughs as Vi blushes. "Seriously, you are the worst keeper of secrets!"

Ari pats my hand. "You get used to her after a while. The group chat is outrageous."

Rae pulls out her phone. "We should add you. Then you'll get to know everyone's private business. What's your number?"

I recite it to Rae, who adds me, and then my phone screen lights up on the counter.

"I should have brought vomit bowls," Iris says, looking at the bottles. "If you're all gonna mix them, you're going to be hot messes."

There's gin courtesy of Gwen. Iris brought a hot chocolate mix with whipped cream. Briar brought a coffee-based liquor. Rae brought a chilled Pinot Grigio. Catalina brought tequila. Vi brought an herbal tea she likes. And Ari brought Wishniak black cherry soda.

"I was sitting here wondering how the fuck we were going to mix them," Gwen says.

Catalina rummages in her bag and presents lemon and salt. "Mine doesn't need mixing."

For food, there is an equally wide assortment.

Ari brought sour soothers. "I eat so many of them, they start to take the taste buds off the side of my tongue."

"I made the crumble from an old English recipe and rhubarb and apples I grew in the yard," Rae says. "I like gardening."

"I brought cheese...because who doesn't like cheese?" Gwen says. "Five different types, so you can pick what you like best."

Catalina grabs another bag. "Niro's cinnamon rolls."

The other women groan.

"Oh, let me have mine now," Iris says, reaching for the container. "I don't care what else any of you brought. In fact, I'm willing to trade. My share of the cheese for your cinnamon roll, Gwen."

"Um, let me think about that for a second. Nope."

"Niro bakes?" I ask.

Rae nods. "He's the best."

Then I remember the morning in the clubhouse and shake my head. "I knew that. He made me and Avery pancakes."

"Cupcakes," Vi says as she places her food on the counter. "They were meant to be pretty flowers, but Avery wanted to help."

I can't help but chuckle at the excessively rainbow-sprinkled globs of icing on each cupcake.

"I knew there would be no substantial food, hence the Irish stew." Iris glances to the pot bubbling away.

"We figured you might not remember trying some of these things, and you could decide if you liked them or not," Catalina says.

"That's really..." Tears sting a little, but I bite them back.

Ari places her hand on my back. "I've come to learn that this is really a group for the misfits. Except Rae, because she always has her shit together. And perhaps Gwen, who *pretends* like she has her shit together."

"Fake it till you make it, baby," Gwen says.

"And I don't always have my shit together, although bless you for thinking I do," Rae adds. "I find lipstick works when everything else fails."

"The things we've enjoyed reading are things like books from our book club and magazines," Briar says.

"I hate you for bringing mine and Bates's story," Vi says to Gwen as she winces. "I'm normally proud of my books."

"Hey, if the rest of us all know about all the ways Bates fucked you in your early relationship, it's only fair Sophia has to wash her eyes out with bleach too," Gwen replies.

I love that they've tried to do something unique for me, and the way they include me in their banter. I've been in a brain-rehabilitation unit, not living under a rock eating insects. I've eaten many of these things. I happen to love cheese and know that my stomach puffs up like a bowling ball if I eat too many pastries.

But they thought about me. And that's enough.

"I want to try something before it gets too dark," Catalina says, gathering the weapons. "I want to see how good Sophia is with all these."

Rae pats Catalina on the shoulder. "Wise to do it before anyone has had any alcohol."

We step out into Theo's yard. It's large and backs onto some woods. It's also handily set up for the makings of a target practice after Theo and Vex were out there letting off a few rounds this morning.

And I itch to get my fingers on those weapons, even though I can't remember why.

26

SWITCH

"Then we're all set," King says. "In two hours, we leave for the docks. Usual formation. Two vans. One decoy. The weapons will have been unloaded by the time we get there. Spark and Halo, the two of you finalize the route we're taking, and the rest of you get some food."

He slaps the table of polished wood, and the sound ricochets through my head. About ten minutes ago, Niro began to blur around the edges. The window behind him started to fucking sparkle so bright, I could barely look at it.

Saliva pools in my mouth as that metallic tang takes over again.

I take the opportunity to hustle to the medic room and grab a container of heavy-duty painkillers, the kind of illegal black-market meds you can't get over the counter, and pop two into my mouth before dipping my head to the faucet to suck in some water.

Sweat forms at my brow, and I grip the edge of the counter tightly.

"BAT," I mutter. "Fucking breathe."

I leave the water running and place my fingers beneath the flow until it is cold.

Then I grab two palmfuls and splash it over my face repeatedly.

"Fuck. Not now."

I grab two paper towels from the stack and dry myself off. Unable to do much else, I turn off the light, stumble to the medical bed, climb on, and close my eyes.

Everything narrows to the pulling at my temples. To the agony crashing through my skull. To the flashes of white light I still see behind my eyes in the darkness.

Swallowing over and over, I refuse to give in to the urge to be sick.

Mind over matter. That's all this is. I can will myself better.

Which is a fucking joke because I know I can't.

What's that famous saying? Healer, heal thyself.

If it were that simple, I would have been better months ago.

I don't know how Sophia has gotten herself to the frame of mind where she can accept being as she is, even as she works to improve. When we returned from shopping, she pushed us both to do our rehab exercises.

I feel the weight of my recovery.

Sleep feels like an impossible task, but I keep my eyes closed in the hope the meds and the dark will take the edge off.

Memories of Sophia talking to me while I was at the rehab center come to me, and I grab my phone out of my pocket.

Squinting, I dial her number, but I get her voicemail.

"Hey, it's Sophia. Sorry I'm not around to take your call, but if you leave a message, I'll get back to you soon."

I hang up.

Then dial again.

I don't expect her to answer, but just hearing her voice brings me calm.

This time, I leave a message. "Was just thinking of you. Hope you're having a good night with the girls, Sparrow."

This time when I close my eyes, I manage to fall asleep.

I'm not sure how much later it is when the door to the medical room bursts open, and the lights flick on, rousing me from the sleep of the dead.

"You good for tonight?" Vex asks when he sees me lying on the medical bed. He eyes the painkillers still out on the counter with the lid off.

Concern radiates from him.

As I rub my hand over my face, I realize that only the dregs of a headache remain. "I'm good."

I flex my fingers in and out. My hand felt tight during target practice. Maybe *tight* isn't quite the right word, but my fingers don't seem to have the mobility I expect from them. It felt the same when I tried to stitch Clutch's thigh.

But my fingers are the least of my problems.

"I'm fine."

Vex crosses his arms. "Man, you look anything but fine."

"So, I had a headache. I took care of it. I'm good."

"If at any point tonight you don't feel good, you get the fuck out of there. And I'm telling King you're riding in the van with me. Not on a bike."

"Fuck you. I'm going—"

"Nowhere. You're going nowhere if you can't safely ride. So don't be a prick and make me worry about your ass."

I shake my head.

"We'll tell King it makes sense for you to be available to

help people as we drive in the event of trouble or some shit. I don't know. I'll wing it and make something up."

"Fine."

Vex takes the painkillers and puts the lid on. He reaches up into the cupboard where two other containers sit. "I'm gonna take these as a precaution. You need one, you come get them from me."

I know what he's doing. The meds are strong. And the effect they have, powerful. "My gut says I should tell you I'm fine and to leave them. But, yeah, perhaps you should. Once every four hours. No more than eight a day."

Vex nods. "Got it."

"Now that we've gotten this out of the way, there's something you need to come see."

When we step out of the medical room, we see Halo and Bates.

"You guys should come see this too," Vex says.

"What should we see?" Halo asks.

The rest of the men are in the kitchen. "Perfect," Vex says. "I got something for us to bet on."

King glances at Vex. "We're leaving."

Vex chuckles. "Yeah. But I promise you're gonna want to see this."

He hurries to his cupboard off the back of the kitchen with the meds, then brings out his largest laptop. He recently told me it's an old beast of a thing that's cumbersome but he loves because it never crashes.

"So, I got an alert that there were people in Switch's yard and just checked in. You wanna place bets on whether your old lady is the best shot?"

When he turns the screen on, the video is paused as all the old ladies stand around the table Vex told me Niro built for me to place all my weapons on when I'm target shooting.

Niro laughs. "I feel like I have insider knowledge 'cause I work with them all on their target practice."

"You should know, Cat and Sophia did some test runs," Vex says. "I saw Sophia gesture to her eye then move her hands in and out from one another, so I'm guessing she has some depth perception issues. But from the trial runs, once she adjusted for her vision, she was sharp."

Clutch puts twenty bucks on the counter. "Gotta take Gwen even though I know she can't shoot for shit because I know one of you bastards will tell her I didn't bet on her if I don't."

"Is Vi throwing a switchblade around there?" Bates says, stepping up to the screen to look real close.

King nudges him out of the way. "Don't go getting a boner. We're not waiting to leave while you jerk off over it."

"Fuck," Spark mutters. "Might as well burn the twenty. We all know Cat's gonna take it. I'll take Iris for the exact same reason Clutch is taking Gwen."

Everyone puts their twenty down, as do I. I guess this is why Sophia didn't answer her phone.

"I hope they haven't been drinking," Saint says.

"Ari gets drunk at the smell of liquor. Glad I got a sitter for the whole night." Halo unfolds a twenty.

Vex presses Play, and we watch the shootout unfold. Catalina holds up three fingers, and it looks like she's teeing up rules. Gwen whispers something to Rae, who laughs, and I see King smile at his twin sister and old lady getting along.

He was always so obsessed with the idea of the club. What it stood for. Never thought I'd see him settled down, loyal to an old lady, but I like it.

Iris goes first and totally misses.

"Fuck," Spark curses. "I told her that stance of hers was gonna get her into trouble."

Niro grins. "You give her feedback like that in bed too?"

I can't help but laugh when Spark nails Niro's shoulder with his fist.

Rae goes next and punches the air when she manages one can with her three shots.

"Color me surprised, Duchess," King says. "Don't doubt her courage but figured her aim had just been lucky in the past."

Catalina makes sure the safety is on in between every round and takes the gun with her when she goes to line the cans back up.

Briar goes next and hits two.

"Atta girl," Saint says. "Gonna tell her she can get the bookshelves she wants in her little library for that."

Vi raises her arm too high, and Catalina lowers it. Whatever Vi says makes Catalina go stand behind Vi to help her aim.

"Our girls are hot," Niro says.

"That they are," Bates concurs.

"Together, they're even hotter," Vex says.

Both Bates and Niro look at him with the same glare, and I can't help but laugh. "Not up for fueling Vex's threesome fantasy?" I say.

"Fuck you," Niro says, but there's no menace in it.

With Catalina's help, Vi gets two. They high-five each other when they are done.

Gwen gets none and Clutch groans. "Made me feel better knowing she carries a gun. Now I'm terrified she can't shoot it."

"She normally does a lot better," Niro says.

"Thank fuck," Clutch says.

Ari goes next, and she's clearly squeamish about holding the gun, but with the encouragement of the other women, she picks it up and fires a bullet off into the woods.

"What kind of stance is that, frog boy?" Saint asks Halo.

"The kind of stance that fired the bullet that killed my half-brother. She can miss every single shot from today on, because she hit when it mattered." Halo looks to me. "Ari doesn't know that. Decided she'd been through enough and didn't want his death on her conscience."

"Would have made the same call," I say as Ari misses her other two shots.

"She's fucking cute holding that gun though," Halo says. "Might take her to the range so I can witness it up close."

Finally, it's Sophia's turn. I barely have time to lean forward before she hits all three cans without breaking a sweat.

Catalina looks at Sophia and says something, then throws her arm over her shoulder. I don't need to hear the words to know Catalina is suggesting she's found someone like her.

I glance at Niro, who winks like we have the special ones. A part of me thinks he's right. I married Sophia before I really knew anything about her because I knew I could protect her. I know what's currently in Sophia's heart. What she doesn't see is that in coming into herself, she has the potential to be formidable.

And, honestly, I love it.

In hindsight, having a woman like Ari or Briar or Iris might have been more than I was really ready for.

Catalina goes next and expectedly hits all three. Niro whoops loudly.

"Split pot," Vex declares, then divides the bills between me and Niro.

"Told you I should have just set fire to that twenty," Clutch grumbles.

King laughs. "I'm gonna tell my sister you said that."

"So, in summary, during a crisis, we should all hide behind Cat and Soph," Niro says, folding his cash.

I shove my cash in my pocket, knowing full well I intend to give it to Soph. After all, she earned it. "I'll drink to that."

"Let's get ready to ride," Halo says.

One by one, people leave the kitchen, Vex takes his laptop back into his tech cupboard. But King continues to stare at the spot where the laptop had been.

"I saw the way you looked at Sophia," King says, without looking up at me.

"Saw the way you smiled when your sister whispered something to your old lady. So?"

"She really means that much to you?"

"She does."

King nods. "I never gave much thought to what it would look like when we'd all settle down. But I remember when Mom was still here, and she and the other old ladies would hang out and do shit together. Made life easier for the men."

"Made it easier for them to cheat." I look around the kitchen. "I haven't seen many club girls of late."

King shakes his head. "There are some. But the ones who wanted the top patches are gone."

"Penny," I say, pulling the name out of the deepest recesses of my mind.

"Wondered if you might ask about her. I told her to stay the fuck away."

"Why?"

King laughs. "Because I was worried she'd try some entrapment-type shit on you while you had no memory. Didn't want her spinning some yarn that you had proposed the night before and now couldn't remember like some shitty rom-com."

I focus on pulling Penny into memory. She was a favorite of mine. But not more than a friend with benefits. "I remember her. Things are coming into focus more."

"Let's keep it that way. I put the club before a brother the other day. That wasn't right. I need to know you're fully back in before we leave tonight. Not one foot in, one foot out."

I look at King. "I'm in. I believe in the man I was before. He steered me here."

He squeezes my shoulder, and I follow him into the night.

27

———

SWITCH

The ride to the docks takes an hour. Halo had us weave off the highway and overshoot the Port Newark-Elizabeth Marine terminal. It's standard practice when we're doing a weapons pickup from the docks. Along with different days of the week and times of night.

Sticking to routine in our line of work is a recipe for disaster. Makes it easier for the FBI to track us, or worse, our enemies to ambush us.

I'd give anything to be on my bike tonight.

Clear sky.

Full moon.

Even though it's cold for mid-November.

Soon it will be too cold for these runs to be fun.

But as we approach our entrance into the docks, the skin on the back of my neck prickles.

I don't understand if this is true foreshadowing, if I really feel like something's off.

Or if I'm simply out of my depth, doing something I feel ill prepared for.

This is my first outing with the club since the accident. Loss of memory has taken away the value of experience. I feel like a plumber sent to do an electrician's work with the wrong toolbox.

"It's too quiet," Vex says.

Bike brake lights come on in front of us. Clutch and Halo pull up alongside King and discuss something. I see Saint looking up at the large dock building to our left.

The docks look deserted. But I can't recall what they previously looked like. "Isn't it always?"

"We pay a lot of people to turn the other way when we ride in. So, there's always someone. It hasn't been the same since Jasper Haven, our contact, was killed. Now we have this new guy. Dougie. Doogie. I don't remember. He reached out to the club. Checked out as Haven's brother-in-law. Said he knew about the extra money Haven made. But I don't trust the guy as far as I can throw him."

"You think he's bad."

Vex shakes his head. "Worse, I think he's too good. I feel like the very first time he's picked up by the cops, he'll confess the shit out of everything to avoid going down."

The bikes slowly begin to move again, and I take in the docks at night, with their tall cranes and lifting gear illuminated at the very top. The occasional muted light eases our path and reflects off the water.

We pull up near a container, and King quickly dismounts. There is a number-combination lock on it, and King enters the code quickly.

Vex reverses toward the container until we come to a stop. In the side mirror, I see Bates pull the container door open.

I jump out and unlock the rear doors to the van.

It strikes me that if any of this goes south, Vex and I will be the ones taking the fall. We'll be the ones in the van with a shit load of weapons. All the more reason for me to be vigilant. I look around, trying to make sense of what I'm seeing.

I reach for my gun, more to check it's there than seeing anything to point it at. It rests reassuringly in its holster.

Halo and Spark stand on either side of the shipping container, looking around the lot like I am, while Bates, Niro, Clutch, and King load the truck. I notice there is a difference between the way the veterans hold their weapons versus the rest. Our hold is active, ready to fire immediately.

Vex stays in the van, ready to drive if need be. For a heartbeat, I wonder if he'd drive off without me. But something tells me he'd no sooner leave me behind than chop off his own arm.

A rat scurries into the warehouse; its claws scratching on the concrete only amplify just how fucking quiet it is.

I look at the containers in the next storage bay over and see the slightest flash of light escape from the bottom of the doors. A second look shows the door is not locked, just pushed shut, but the light is long gone.

Waving, I grab Halo's attention and, using hand signals, gesture that I suspect there are people in the container. The silent message ripples through the brothers. The others hustle to get the weapons into the van.

Spark comes around to my side of the van as Halo disappears, only to reappear on the opposite side of the rogue container. With help from King, Saint is boosted on top of the container the weapons are in. He lies down on top and points his rifle toward the unbolted container door.

When the last of the weapons has been loaded, the others lean into where we are focused. "You sure you saw something?" King whispers when he comes to stand next to me.

Did I?

A flash of light.

An unlocked door.

Are my insecurities playing a part in what I'm seeing?

BAT.

The acronym comes out of nowhere. But I do what it suggests. I breathe, adjust, and think.

"I saw light."

And just as I utter the words, the doors are shoved wide open. Men dressed from head to toe in black pour out. Bullets are fired. I shove King to cover behind our shipping container's door.

Autopilot kicks in. Muscle memory. Somehow, I know exactly what to do without a single deliberate thought.

Opening fire, I take out the two men closest to me.

I'll deal with the knowledge I'm taking lives later. Because in this moment, it's more important that my life isn't one of the ones taken.

Halo takes out three before getting shot in the leg. He limps behind a different container, but the sound of bullets pinging off metal suggests he's been followed and is still being shot at.

But they underestimate what those few seconds of me seeing them gave us. Saint, on the roof of the container, begins to take them out one at a time. I run behind the hood of the van and provide cover as Bates, Niro, and Spark run behind me, aiming to come at our assailants from behind.

When they are safely across the lot, I head for Halo, coming up behind the asshole pointing a gun at him and pistol whipping him to the ground.

"Where are you shot?" I ask.

"Thigh." Halo grunts. "Feels like a through and through that missed bone."

I pull out my knife. Shift my warmer layers out of the way and cut a three-inch strip off the bottom of my shirt before tying it around Halo's thigh as a tourniquet.

"Motherfucker," he whispers.

"Sorry. I'll take a look when we get out of here."

But from the explosive sounds of gunshots hitting containers, we're taking more fire than we might be able to handle.

BAT.

Those three letters come to me again.

Breathe. We'll get out of here.

Adjust. I need more firepower.

Think.

"Swap weapons," I say to Halo as I switch my Glock for Halo's assault rifle.

The sound of gunfire increases.

I hear Bates yell Niro's name.

There are too many of them. We were ten. They must have twenty. Maybe even thirty. King is out of ammo but he's astraddle a guy, pulverizing his face with the handle of his gun.

I run to where Vex and Spark are taking heavy fire from four assailants on the other side of the lot, and I open fire indiscriminately. The volume is way too loud for us to have not attracted attention.

"We need to get out of here," I shout to Spark.

"Tell those motherfuckers that," he replies.

"They want the weapons," Vex says. "I have the keys to the van, but they could boost it."

We make our way slowly back to the van. I grab Halo, allowing him to put all his weight on me. But it's too much.

My left arm still doesn't function properly. My right is holding my weapon.

Seeing us struggle, Spark steps in and grabs Halo from me. "Provide cover. Go."

I hate the feeling of helplessness.

That I somehow wasn't enough this evening.

And that's an indulgent thought when we are still taking live fire.

We get Halo to the van and slump him in the back.

My ammo runs out about ten steps away. "Fuck," I curse.

Bates has his back to a container, his knives in his hands. He must be out of ammo too.

Saint climbs down from the top of the container but is met by two assailants.

We're losing ground.

We're out of time.

I can't believe Sophia and I survived what happened to us for me to die at the New Jersey docks.

Two vans screech around the corner, and more men join the fray, but then I hear the accent and breathe a sigh of relief. It's the fucking Irish.

I watch Cillian's men, on fresh legs and with surplus ammo, take over and finish the fight we started.

Vex offers King some ammo; he takes it and runs to back Bates up while Spark provides strategic cover.

"We need to get ready to get out of here," I tell Vex. "Halo. Give me your keys. I'll ride your bike back."

The Irish wrap up the rest of the men. At least, those who don't run when they realize they are outnumbered.

"Let's go," King shouts.

"You're welcome," Cillian says as he reaches us.

"I'll throw you a party in thanks once we get the fuck out of here," King says, glancing over his shoulder.

"That's what allies do," Cillian says. "We show up when the other is in trouble and help. We help you on your side of the dock, biker. And you help us on our side."

I think through everything that has happened. "Wait. Those men were Sicilian."

Cillian nods. "Indeed."

"How the fuck did they know we were here?" I ask.

King turns to me. "Your wife running her mouth?"

"Watch how you speak about my wife," I say. I don't need to ask her to know she wouldn't. I trust her. "She didn't."

"You have a Sicilian wife. Now I'm fucking intrigued," Cillian says.

I turn to face him. "My wife is none of your fucking business. But even if she had, how did *you* know to be here tonight?"

King steps up to Cillian. "I'd like to hear an answer to that."

Cillian's men step up behind Cillian, their weapons pointed in our direction. "Perhaps I heard something. Perhaps I thought I'd leave you to handle it alone, so you got a flavor of what I'm facing on the other side of this fucking water."

"You set us up, you motherfucking cunt," Clutch says.

Cillian grins. "Lesson learned about who your allies are, yeah?"

"We're not fucking friends," King says. "If we were, you would have told us what their plans were. Not waited until we were screwed."

Cillian reaches out and squeezes King's shoulder.

He shrugs it off angrily.

"I never said we were friends. I said we were allies. *Ni mhaireann solas na maiden don lá.* No morning sun lasts all day. Most relationships have lifespans. Many come to an end when they are no longer mutually beneficial. You either help me with the Italians, or I let them eat you."

Spark steps forward. "And what would you tell Iris if I'd been killed tonight? What would you tell our kid?"

Cillian looks up at the sky for a moment. "I'd tell him it was part of the life he was born into, whether he wanted it or not. And that's always been the difference between me and all of you. And that his father never understood that."

Spark lurches for Cillian, and we hear the sound of weapons being primed as both Clutch and I grab Spark around the waist and chest.

"Think about it," Cillian says, looking around at the dead bodies on the dock. "Then call me when you're ready to truly act like allies worthy of the fucking Irish."

28

SOPHIA

"I ate too much of that crumble," Iris says, rubbing her hand over her belly. She's settled in the corner of the sofa near the fire that smolders as it dies down. Theo left it built and ready to light for us, and it's added to the comfortable evening.

Ari hands Iris a cup of herbal tea. "I'm pretty sure that's the baby taking up so much room in there, not crumble."

Iris takes the cup. "Eight weeks. That's all I have left, and then Spark and I will have a baby."

Vi pats her own stomach. "You have the cute bump. I have the second-pregnancy spread."

"Which Bates can't keep his hands off." Gwen sits with the rest of the cheese board on her lap.

Rae sits on the floor, leaning against the sofa, and Briar lies on the floor, her head on Rae's lap.

"We should all sleep down here tonight," Gwen says. "Like a proper sleepover."

Briar chuckles. "You think we should have pillow fights?"

Rae shakes her head. "Absolutely not."

"Why not?" Ari grins. "It sounds like fun."

"Well, I'm sure *Daddy* Halo will play pillow fights with you when he picks you up tomorrow," Vi says.

Ari blushes. "You honestly don't want to know what Halo does to me."

"No. We don't," Catalina says as she shoulder checks her gently. "Could you imagine Colton's face if I called him 'Daddy'? He wouldn't let me out of bed for a week."

"Or King? I think he'd jump on me for sure," Rae says.

Briar chuckles. "Saint would just think I'm making fun of our age gap."

I love how easy these women are to be around. They have a genuinely kind and teasing relationship with each other. And they love their men in an unapologetic way.

"Thank you," I say. "For being so...welcoming."

Rae glances up at me. "You're one of us now."

"I just realized; you use your men's road names more than their real names. I only ever call Theo...'Theo.' Should I be calling him 'Switch' because I think I only used it a couple of times?"

"For me it depends on the context," Gwen says. "Like, around the clubhouse, he's Clutch. But at home, I'm more likely to call him 'Landon.'"

"It's easier to use their road names," Ari says. "It's how everyone else refers to them."

"And their names have just become an extension of their personalities," Catalina says. "Like, the concept of a birth name is pretty weird when you think about it. Your parents kinda guess what name might suit you. It's usually gendered too, forcing you into a box. With road names, at least they mean something."

Gwen laughs. "Yeah, but you haven't heard some of the

road names. Two weeks ago, Clutch met up with a friend from the Vegas chapter called Twinkle Toes."

"Hey, Cat," Briar says. "Why is Niro called 'Niro'?"

Catalina grins. "Because of a typo."

"What?" I ask.

"Shortly after Niro saved Camelot, he went into ADHD hyperfocus about Emperor Nero. Started quoting him about poisonous mushrooms and fiddling while Rome burned. Camelot chose his name and got the patch made without bothering to check the spelling."

"And he never pointed it out to Camelot?" Gwen asks.

Catalina shakes her head, a soft smile on her face. "He's worn a misspelled patch for as long as he's been with the club because he loved Camelot too much to embarrass him by pointing it out."

"That's Niro," Rae says.

"Isn't it?" Iris agrees.

The fire crackles, and the candles I've lit create a soft but tiring light. My eyes start to droop. "I may head to bed."

"Me, too," Vi says, climbing to her feet. "It's so lovely that Avery has friends. And really convenient for nights like this when I can get her a sleepover."

"I love having Lola, but I'm also really grateful she can sleep like the dead once I put her down for the night," Ari says, glancing upstairs where Lola is sleeping and Joules, the babysitter, is keeping watch. "It was thoughtful for Halo to get a sitter for tonight so I could just hang out with you all."

Briar stands and reaches for Iris's hand to help tug her out of her seat. "You get to sleep with me."

Iris chuckles. "We should tell the boys we're having a threesome. You, me, and the baby."

Briar grimaces. "Let's not do that. It sounds weird."

"I'll share with Rae," Gwen says. "And I'm totally telling

my brother that I'm sleeping with his old lady to squick him out."

"I'll take the sofa," Catalina says.

Slowly but surely, everyone pairs up and disappears to the bedrooms, and Catalina helps me with the last of the cleanup.

"I can't believe how much I drank tonight. It's a wonder I'm still walking...well, any more than I usually walk."

Catalina tuts. "Don't put yourself down like that. I got hurt and Niro came off his bike earlier this year. And you've met my husband. You've seen his face. The two of us, perhaps more than anyone else, have a...what's the word... fraction of what it's taken you to be here."

I set the dishwasher to run and close the door. "Thank you. But at some point, it's the past, right? I was thinking, I used to run the company's real estate portfolio. I'd need refreshers. But I find that things I've forgotten, I'm quick to pick up. Do you know who manages the Outlaws' portfolio?"

Catalina grins. "I'll ask Niro. He used to be the club secretary/treasurer. But I like the idea there might be another woman in the club who is more than just an old lady."

"You don't like being an old lady?"

"I love being Niro's wife and old lady. I love being the first female Outlaw crew member. But I want so much more. I'll be a brother one day. But what if there were a financial officer for the club who wasn't a man? Or if there were a female Vex?"

I shake my head. "I'm a Sicilian daughter. From a Cosa Nostra family. I was headed for an arranged marriage for power. In our worlds, women don't have the right to vote."

"Fair. But look at you and me. We're changing it, no?"

She gestures up and down my body. "You're in this situation because you are valuable. I've settled for crew because it's an official stake in the ground. I can't go backward to being nobody. But I can claw my way up to being a brother. By showing them I can do everything they can. I think you should do the same. We could do it together."

A ripple of excitement trickles through me. "We could?"

Catalina places her arms on my shoulders. "We could."

She glances past me, out the window over the sink to the back garden, then hurries to the light switch and flicks it off. "Call Theo. Tell him there's someone outside. I'll let the prospects on guard know."

"Don't go outside, Cat," I say, but it's too late.

Just as the door closes, the kitchen window shatters.

I drop to the ground as I hear more gunshots. My phone is on the kitchen island, and I reach up, staying low, and pat my hand over the surface. When I find it, I grab it, then crawl towards the stairs.

Theo has weapons in the closet near the bed, but stairs are my nemesis. I can't climb them quickly, but if I'm going to help Cat, I have to.

Gwen runs to the top of the stairs, a gun in hand. "Are you okay?"

"Yes, but Cat went outside." I begin my ascent. It's messy. My foot drags.

I pause to dial Theo. He doesn't answer on the first ring, so I call him again. This time, he answers.

"Sparrow, I can't talk right now. Just got back to the clubhouse with shit to clean up."

"We're under fire."

"Fuck. How bad?"

"I don't know. Bullet through the kitchen window. Cat

ran outside to help the prospects; I'm headed to get weapons from the bedroom."

"We gotta go," I hear Theo shout. "Be there in ten. Fuck, Sparrow. Be careful."

I climb the rest of the stairs and see Rae pushing Vi into the hallway. "You and Iris need to stay away from windows," Rae says firmly. "Stay in the hallway unless someone breaches the house."

"It's too dark outside," Gwen shouts from the bedroom. "I can't see who to shoot at."

"Catalina is out there," I say. "She went to alert the prospects. We need to cover her. There are weapons in our bedroom if you don't have your own."

Pain is a funny thing. It can creep up on you. Overwhelm you. Then dissipate and make you wonder if you imagined how truly horrible the whole thing was. You think you have no control over it, that it controls you.

And yet, the pain, like a hot poker through the fleshy part of my hips, reminds me that survival is a state of mind.

I find the weapons and hand them to Rae, Briar, and Ari.

"I don't know how to use it," Ari says.

"Hopefully you won't need to," Rae says. "Just remember the training Niro gave you. Hip-width stance. Aim for the torso."

I take a weapon and hurry to the rear window with Gwen, who is standing on the very edge of it, shielded by the wall and hidden by the drapes.

My phone rings. An unknown number. I just look at it.

"You should answer it," Gwen says. "It could be one of the prospects or something."

I stay down beneath the window and do as she says.

"Sophia. This can all end tonight," my father says. "Just

come to the front door. Luca and Leo are waiting to bring you home."

I'm an intelligent woman. I could be noble. Sacrifice myself for the greater good. But I know Theo and the club are on their way. What I need to do is stall. "Why would I come home? I've told you I don't trust you."

My father makes a sound. A humph. A sigh. I can't tell what. But something about it rubs me the wrong way. "Just come home. You don't belong there."

You don't belong there.

My father is not outside. He's doing his dirty work from a distance.

This all seems too implausible. I'm not that precious. My family still has power without this marriage. It's been months since I was supposed to marry this man. I'm already married to someone else.

There has to be something more at play here.

I just don't know what.

"Tell your men to back off. I won't talk to you while there are gunshots outside."

My father blows out a harsh puff of air. "You are coming home one way or another tonight."

"Why? I don't believe this is about an arranged marriage anymore."

There is a long pause, peppered with the sound of bullets outside. "You remembered?"

"What do I know?"

He hangs up the phone.

"What do I know?" I shout.

But my whispered words are drowned out by the roar of motorcycles.

29

SWITCH

"You okay?" I ask Catalina an hour later.

Sweat is on her brow, and her usually tan skin looks gray and pale. She's lucky it was a through and through to the fleshy part of her waist. I'm confident no major organs were hit, but I'll keep an eye on her.

"Okay, enough. Don't let him...do anything he'll...regret."

I check the drip I got in on the second attempt and add some pain relief. "Sleep, Cat. I'll make sure he's okay. I promise."

I close the door to the medical room and sprint across the lot to the shed where Luca and Leo and what's left of their men were taken.

When I push the door open and step inside, there's a dead man lying on the floor in front of me.

King has a blood-covered Niro's head in his grip, forehead to forehead. Saying something in hushed tones that the rest of us can't hear.

Because Catalina being shot has sent him spinning off into another universe.

What I wanted to do was be a part of this. To ensure the men who had attempted to take my wife got what they deserved. But my training kicked in. It was as the doctor had said, that part of my memory was like a muscle that remembered exactly what it was supposed to do.

The moment I saw Sophia was alive and unharmed and Catalina was in pain, nothing else was more important than making sure I could treat Cat, who had refused a trip to the hospital. She had been reluctant to go, not because she was worried about the cost or trying to explain to them what happened but because she had wanted to stay by Niro's side.

And I understood that desire to put other people first. It made me think that my need to be a medic was something more than a decision. It was a calling, something I had always been unable to resist.

I only hoped my wife would see it the same way, considering that I chose to care for our friend before I sought out revenge.

But now that I've done that, there's a rising compulsion to teach these fucks a lesson.

Leo and Luca are both suspended by their hands, which are tied to a beam that runs through the center of the shed. Luca is unconscious. Blood pours from a wound on the side of his head. It drips silently onto the concrete floor and forms a puddle by his feet.

Leo glares out of the one eye that remained open. "You may think you have gotten away with this, but you're going to die for it."

I walk straight up to the motherfucker and punch him in the stomach.

Hard.

Hard enough to rearrange his internal organs.

I jump back just in time as he pukes.

"She's your fucking sister. She's told you she doesn't want to come back to you. And yet you try to pull some shit on us at the docks as a distraction. Why the fuck can't you let this go?"

Leo huffs. "Like you don't have club rules and club politics. She's promised to another family."

I get close to him. "Yeah. Well, she's my fucking family now. And we have a rock-solid case to get your father's guardianship over her removed."

"And what? You gonna take it over and control her to control us?"

I shake my head. "Don't need manipulation to keep you fuckers in line. The fact you're in my clubhouse—" I look up at the ropes eating into his wrists "—tied to my beams, your brother unconscious and not receiving any medical help, proves that."

"Proves shit," Leo says.

Vex comes into the shed holding a phone he offers to King. "Their *famiglia* is on their way."

King is still focused on Niro. "Go to her." Those three words snap Niro out of whatever mist descended over him.

"Fuck, Cat," he mutters, as if he just woke up and remembered something important. "Where did you take her?"

"She's in the medical room getting some sleep," I say.

"She good?" he asks me hoarsely as he walks by.

"She will be." I look down at his hands. "Wash those cuts with the disinfectant I left on the sink."

"You sure you want to do this?" King asks me as he comes to stand by my side.

"I am. Don't want Sophia's immediate family's death on

my hands." I glance at the body on the floor. "The rest of them, do whatever you want."

Leo looks at me. "You think you can get away with—"

I pull my arm back and punch him hard, knocking him unconscious.

King throws his arm over my shoulder as we move out of earshot of the Sicilians. "Welcome back."

I give him side eye, and he chuckles.

One of the injured Sicilians tries to stand, and Spark kicks him down and places a boot on his chest. "I'm getting tired of this shit," he grumbles.

"So much for some time off," Clutch says.

"You think Cillian is right?" I ask.

"In what way?" King replies.

"That we need a show of force. It feels like people are starting to creep around our edges. The Brotherhood got a bigger piece of us than they should have."

"You remember that?" King asks.

I shake my head. "Not yet. But I've learned enough." I rub my hand over the scar on my skull. "Should go check with Sophia. She felt something was off. That this was nothing to do with the marriage, but perhaps her father."

"She wanted to marry him," Luca says hoarsely as he lifts his head. "That's why we keep coming. We know what she actually wanted. And it wouldn't be you. It wouldn't be this."

"Like fuck you do. She told you she doesn't want to be married to a stranger."

"No?" Luca says and holds my gaze. "'Cause she knows you so well?"

Deep down, I know exactly what he's saying, and it reverberates through me. I say nothing in return, but don't look away.

The motherfucker wants a stare down, I'll give him one.

Knowing they are defeated, the Sicilians settle while we wait for Vincenzo Viscuso to arrive. But we're disappointed about forty minutes later when it's Alessio Viscuso who arrives in a flashy-looking red sports car.

A second car pulls up alongside it, and two men in black suits get out first. Then Alessio pushes open his car door.

Tension crackles through the lot. While only three of us stand outside to greet them, I know Saint is positioned on the club roof. Clutch, Halo, and Vex remain with the tied-up hostages, and Bates remains locked in the medical room with Niro and Cat to stop Niro from coming for a piece of Alessio.

Two vans pull up opposite the curb. There appears to be only one driver in each, and while this could quite possibly be a Trojan horse, they'd be foolish to pull that shit when Clutch has two Viscuso brothers in his sight. We instructed any vans to remain parked down the road.

Also, per our request, he raises his hands as he walks toward King, Spark, and me.

"Are my brothers still alive?" he asks. While I have no sympathy for him or his family, I can place myself in his shoes if this were my brothers. It's the only reason I don't pull my weapon.

King nods. "They are." His words come out with little white puffs in the bitter night air. "Some of the others are not."

I want to tuck my hands into my pockets but keeping them free to grab my weapon should I need to is more important.

The look of relief on my brother-in-law's face as he absorbs the news is palpable.

"*Grazzi a tia*," he says, then rolls his eyes at our blank

faces. "Thanks to you. My father is old-school. And impulsive."

"If that's your pathetic way of apologizing for this fucking shit show…" Spark says.

Alessio glances at Spark but then turns back to King. "Can we talk? Man to man?"

"We've been clear with you," I say without waiting for King to respond. "Sophia is married to me. We're in the process of revoking the guardianship you have over her. You need to leave her alone."

Alessio rubs a hand over his face. "You are fortunate to not be so governed by the old ways. My father does not want to lose face. Sophia is promised to my father's best friend's son. One of the oldest families who can trace their entire genealogy to a single town in Sicily."

"So inbred then?" Spark asks and chuckles.

Alessio looks over to one of the vans on the street. "An illustration?" he says, then steps right into Spark's space. There is barely an inch between their chests. "You might think you have the upper hand here. Your lot. Your rules. Your space." A whirring sound starts. "But we no longer bring a gun to a pissing contest; we bring drones."

"Ballsy statement given you're the one truly standing in our lot," Spark says. He looks over Alessio's shoulder to the two men behind him.

"You'll still be dead before one of those fuckers takes me down," King says. "And we have cameras. If you think the men currently holding guns to your brothers' heads won't pull the trigger if they see anything happen to us, you're delusional."

Alessio smiles grimly. "The end of your life is not determined by where you are standing. If you think I wouldn't take at least one of you down with me before you attempted to kill me, you'd be mistaken. I'd prefer it wasn't my new *frati*. My sister can hold a mean grudge, and killing her husband would definitely set her off. But if it was either of you two"—he looks between King and Spark—"I think she'd be okay with it."

The crack of a bullet ricochets around the lot, and the drone drops to the floor. "Guess I'll take a sniper over a robot any day," King says.

The two men behind Alessio go for their weapons. Spark goes for his holstered gun, but King puts out his palm and stops him from moving forward.

Alessio takes a step back. "Besides, I have an offer. Marriage was supposed to create a partnership. It's our goal to manage the New York side of the docks. You wish to run the Jersey side. Perhaps we could work together."

I glance at Spark, who looks back my way, realizing at the same time as I do that he and I are married to women on opposite sides of this fight.

"I think what we need to do is discuss what the fuck happened tonight," King says. "There have been penalties delivered. You don't get to attack us while we're carrying out business on our side of the harbor, and then say, 'my bad', and offer a deal."

"Then discuss," Alessio says calmly.

"You tried to steal from us," King says. "If it weren't for Switch, we'd all be fucking fish bait in the harbor. But maybe I'm feeling generous. A wedding gift, of sorts."

"It depends on who you killed."

"Is that what people are to you?" I ask, thinking about Sophia. "Disposable assets to be swapped, shared, or disposed of, as long as the goal is the same? To come out on top."

Alessio steps up to me. "Perhaps your brain injury has led to you forgetting what this life is really about, *brother*."

"Fuck you."

King steps between us. "We'll bring your brothers, the men we hold, and the bodies and lay them out on the concrete. Once we have moved inside, you can come claim them."

"Was anyone of yours hurt?" Alessio asks.

"A woman," I reply. I can still feel the way Catalina gripped my wrist as she begged for pain relief I was trying to administer.

"My apologies. Perhaps we can consider this an even score. You keep Sophia. I take my brothers. And then we can work together."

"You're lucky we're letting you leave with your life," King says. "You'll owe us. I want payment. Repair of my property. And the agreement you will never come for our side of the docks."

"Fair," Alessio agrees.

"In that case, we'll bring your men around," King says.

Alessio looks to me. "I need a word with Switch. Man to man. Nothing to do with any of this. No weapons. You have my word he's not at risk."

I nod to King. "I'm good."

Alessio watches until Spark and King are a safe distance away. I'm on edge, because while my Spidey senses say Alessio is a man of his word, I wouldn't put it past him to pull a knife on me. But I'm reassured that Saint has me covered.

"What?" I ask.

"I want to see Sophia. I want to talk with her. Is she okay?"

I shake my head. "You ask me that after you just had a

fucking goon squad try to take out the men protecting her and her friends so you could get to her? I'm sure she's fucking great and having a party right now, knowing we beat the shit out of her brothers."

Alessio looks up and takes in a deep breath before exhaling it into the night sky. "My father puts too much trust in my younger brothers' skills."

"Let's just add that to his list of mistakes."

Alessio tips his head in the direction of the clubhouse. "Is she in there?"

"No."

"I want to meet with her. She isn't returning my calls. Can we arrange it, you and me? You choose the location, and I will meet you, alone. I only have your word for it that she is here voluntarily, and we have zero grounds to trust each other. I need to know that she wants to stay with you in a place where she can walk away with me if she wants to."

I huff at this. "Given tonight's activities and the bomb you threw at our building, you've proved that you would happily hurt her to get what you want."

Alessio curses and runs a hand through his dark hair. I can see the resemblance between Alessio and Sophia. Similar nose. Similar jaw. "She was never meant to get hurt."

"And yet you did it anyway. Here's the thing: Sophia is in charge of her own fate. I'm not going to conspire with you to set up a meeting. I"—I nearly say the word *love* but catch myself at the last second—"respect my wife too much to do anything that could undermine her trust in me. So, no. I won't. But I will tell her you are concerned about her. And that you asked after her. And that you think her brothers are a fucking goon squad. If that means anything at all to her after today, I'm sure she'll call you."

Alessio shoves his hands in his pockets as Vex and

Clutch drag Luca and Leo around the corner of the clubhouse.

"*Porca miseria!*" Alessio snaps. No idea what it means, but by the tone, he's pissed off. "Get them into the truck," he says to the two stooges standing by his shoulders. Then he reaches into his pocket.

Swiftly, I reach for my gun and aim it at Alessio.

"Steady, biker. Give Sophia this. I was unaware of what was going to happen tonight. And I think Sophia is the key to understanding why my father is so obsessed with getting her back."

It's a white envelope. When I take it from him, it feels as though there is a key inside. "What is it?"

"It's for the storage locker of her things. She might want to collect them."

As Alessio follows his brothers back to the van, I stand looking between him and the clubhouse, wondering where all this ends.

30

SOPHIA

I hold the letter from my brother and re-read the last line.

I promise, I won't let anything happen to you from tonight on. I'll make it stop.

Ale.

I'm guessing it's what I used to call Alessio. He addressed the letter to *Puparu*, and there is a smiley face drawn next to it. And there is something familiar about the paper, the scent, the writing. It's not memory. I can't remember ever seeing or smelling any of it before.

But there is something...compelling about it.

I pick the key up off the bed. It's cool, solid in my palm. A note tells me the location of a storage locker and the unit number where the key fits. There's also a black credit card with my name on it, but I have no idea whether the card is mine or an extension of Alessio's own accounts.

But it's the plea in the letter.

Call me.

We've all been through enough this year. You more than any of us. If you remembered, you'd know why.

Theo is in the shower. He said he'd give me time to read the letter, that he'd be there for me as a sounding board if I wanted to discuss it, but that he trusted my judgement if I felt clear on what I wanted to do.

I take a deep breath and call him.

"*Puparu*," Alessio says, and I hear keys dropped into a dish. "So, you called me. Are you well?"

"Very. Why did Luca and Leo come for me tonight?" I feel disproportionately calm given the events of the night. I'm angry, of course. But it's measured. I realize I'm deliberately not sharing with Alessio the real depth of my feelings.

"Because Papà is an idiot, as you'd remember. You and I...we...can I trust you like I used to, Soph?"

There is something about the way he says my name. There's a torn quality to it. Like he...misses me.

"We trusted each other?"

"You knew everything. All the things I couldn't say in front of our family. There are so many things I've wanted to talk to you about since the accident but decided not to unless you remembered on your own, to keep you from harm."

"What kinds of things?"

"I missed you," he says. "The you that you were. My confidant. You called me that morning. Before your accident. You told me that you were working on something that didn't make sense. That you were up to your neck in spreadsheets and numbers, but something didn't add up."

"I told you there was a problem?"

"You did. And now neither of us will know what it was unless we start from the beginning."

"Then yes. You can trust me," I say.

"You and I talked about what it would look like without Papà. How we'd organize differently. You always believed I could be one of the youngest underbosses in La Cosa Nostra history."

"And what was I going to be?"

Alessio sighs. "My invisible right hand. You know this life. It's cutthroat."

Word association kicks in. "A switchblade?"

Alessio laughs. "What about them?"

"I carried a switchblade."

"You remembered?"

There's so much hope in Alessio's tone that my heart hurts. "More muscle memory. I held one recently and suddenly knew what to do with it."

"You have a collection of them. Go to the locker and find them. You sure you don't recall anything from that day? Was Papà on to us? Did he know our plans? Is that why you ran?"

"I have no idea. But surely if he did, he would have said something to you by now."

"I've had a million theories with no proof to any of them. I wondered if perhaps Papà wasn't on to us like I initially thought. Then, I thought, maybe Papà was willing to keep you in that center for a reason. I wondered if it's because he thought you had repressed memories of what happened and he needed to know what you know, or if he was terrified of what you might know and had paid someone at the center to tell him if you ever remembered. I wondered if he was the center of it all."

I take a breath as I think through what Alessio just told me. "I have zero memories. But at some point, I need to start living in the present, on my own terms, instead of seeking something in the past. I don't know that I can be a participant in what you are planning, but you have my word I won't tell our father or brothers what that is."

"Are you happy with the biker?"

As he asks, Theo comes out of the bathroom in a puff of steam and a white towel that hugs his hips. He rubs his hair with a second towel as drips of water settle on his inked torso.

He's utterly delicious.

"Yes," I say loud enough for Theo to hear. "I'm very happy with the biker."

Theo stops rubbing his hair at that and smiles at me.

"I believe you."

"Good. Because next time anyone comes near me, I'll have a blade in hand."

"That's definitely more like the old you."

Theo tosses the hand towel back onto the sink and lets his bath towel drop to the floor. He's aroused, his cock thick and proud as he puts his palm around it and strokes himself.

I lick my lips. "I have to go."

I end the call and move the envelope and its contents onto the bedside table.

"Everything good?" he asks.

"I'll tell you about it later. Are we really alone?" I ask.

He studies me for a moment, as if trying to read how I feel about the call with my brother. Whatever he sees reassures him. "Fucking amazing, isn't it?" he asks.

As a result of the night's action and my family nursing their wounds, King felt it was safe for everyone to go home tonight.

"Heaven."

He lets go of his cock for a moment to fish something out of the jeans he'd tossed over the chair. I assume it's a condom, but I'm surprised when he tosses eighty dollars onto the bed. "That's yours."

I gather the twenties. "Why?"

"Three bullets. Three cans." He crawls onto the bed, reaches for my ankles, and tugs me down until I'm lying flat. His hands massage my thighs, nudging upwards before stopping just short of the hem of his T-shirt I borrowed.

"You saw that?"

Theo grins. "Vex has the outside of all our houses covered with security cameras. We all saw it."

I open my mouth in mock offense. "You were spying on us?"

He laughs. "We were betting on you. You were a risky pick, but I saw the way you handled that knife. Figured it couldn't be the only weapon you were used to using."

"What if we'd been naked?"

"In the backyard?"

"Perhaps it's a full moon. Perhaps I'm a witch."

Theo climbs over me and settles between my thighs, his cock pressed right up against my clit, which takes about two seconds to get very hungry. "You gonna cast a spell on me, Sparrow?"

"Do I need to?"

His lips whisper over my skin. Along my cheek, by my ear, down my neck. I wriggle to give him more room.

"No," he replies.

"Does it always feel this good, Theo? From what you remember."

"Sex?"

I place my hands on either side of his head and force him to look at me. "No. This. You and me. How good it feels to be a little reckless. To fall madly."

He places his lips on mine and kisses me. It's messy. Sloppy even. He licks my tongue. My teeth. Then bites my lip. I can't form a thought as I tumble into what he's doing to me.

"Never."

"I like that answer."

"So, you're falling madly?"

"I am. Are you?"

Theo looks away for a moment, then grins as he shakes his head. "Just thinking how happy my mom is going to be about all this. I mean, not that she knows it was fake, but that it's going to last."

"This doesn't feel like the right time to be thinking about your mom." I wiggle my hips to remind him that his cock is perfectly lined up against me.

He slides his hands beneath my butt and rolls his cock against my clit. It's raw and reckless, and I don't want him to stop, consequences be damned.

"Yes, Sparrow. I'm tumbling all the way into you."

Warmth blossoms in my heart. "Good."

"Good. Is it okay for me to make love to my wife now?"

"Make love, huh?"

"You have a problem with that?" he asks as he drags the tip of his nose behind my ear and nibbles on my neck. His lips are warm against my skin.

"Definitely not if you keep doing that to me." I grind my hips against him, eliciting a groan.

"Feel good?" Theo asks.

"Everything you do to me feels good."

He reaches between us and slides the hem of the T-shirt up over my stomach. "Good. It's meant to."

It's amazing how quickly he can take me from zero to so incredibly aroused. He slips the T-shirt over my head, and I'm not sure there is any better feeling than being naked with this man.

Suddenly, he shakes out his hand and winces.

"Aching?" I ask.

"Nothing I can't deal with," he says.

I wriggle up and push him down. "Maybe it's a sign you shouldn't be putting any weight into your hand right now."

He lies back on the bed, and I take his hand, stretching his palm by applying gentle pressure to his thumb and pinkie. Using the pads of my thumbs, I press deeply into the taut muscles.

"That's not the only muscle that hurts," he says and then groans. "You're so good at that."

"Want me to keep going?"

"Yes." He glances down at his cock. "And no."

I continue to massage his hand until I feel the cramp release and the frown disappears from Theo's brow.

When I place a kiss to his palm, he says, "For better or worse. Sickness and health, right?"

"One hundred percent."

He reaches for me and tugs me to sit on his lap. It doesn't go smoothly. I need help getting my foot over his hips, but once I'm there, I find I'm comfortable.

"You okay there?" he asks.

"Surprisingly, yes."

He threads his hand around the back of my neck and grips it firmly before tugging me down to his mouth.

I don't know what sorcery there is that lips kissing lips can make every part of me light up like the fireworks I watched from the roof track of the rehab center on the Fourth of July, but they do.

Every part of Theo makes me feel safe. And confident.

"You're beautiful, Soph. Don't know if I told you that before, but you are."

Beautiful.

"You almost make me believe it," I say quietly.

"I'll work on it until you do. Will you ride me, Soph? I

want to see you take what you want from me. I want to watch your pussy swallow my cock." He hands me a small knife. "And I want you to mark me with your initials."

I'm not certain how steady I'll be, but when he asks me like that, his voice all rough with need, there is no way I want to refuse. I take the knife from his hands.

"You're sure?"

"Most definitely."

He places his thumb on my clit and rubs slow circles as I grind on his cock. We need condoms, I know. I don't want to have kids when I'm still finding my own place in this world again. But I want Theo inside so badly, it hurts to breathe.

I reach over to the drawer I know he keeps the condoms in and grab one from the packet. Ripping it open, I shuffle back down Theo's thighs until I can hold his cock.

Biting down on my lip, I focus on the endeavor, remembering what I've seen Theo do.

Pinch the tip, roll it down.

"Fuck, your hands feel good," Theo says. He raises his arm and lays it over his eyes. "But I can't watch because then I'm going to come all over your fingers."

I chuckle. "There. Done. Do you need a minute?"

Theo groans and moves his arm. He grips my hips and tugs me up and over him. "No. What I need is you riding my cock like you can't get enough of me."

I reach between us and hold his cock to my opening. His thick edge nudges between my lips, the sensation is overwhelming. I can feel myself getting wetter.

"I can't get enough of you," I admit.

His eyes meet mine, and I slide slowly over him. An inch, then I lift. Two the next time. Three and four. Until I'm finally seated over him and both of us groan.

"I thought I'd feel self-conscious like this."

His fingers dig harder into my hips, encouraging me to grind against him with his cock deep inside me.

Theo is watching where we are joined. "Like what?"

"You know. So..." I gesture up and down my body. "I don't know. So obvious...available...like you can see every part of me."

31

SWITCH

"You know what I see, Sparrow?"

"What?"

I trail my gaze up her body painfully slowly. "I see the way our pubic hair is matted between us because of how wet you already are. And there is nothing hotter than a woman who is aroused by you, by what you do to her, by what you do to each other. I see the way your hips crease and flare, which does something for me. It's feminine. Lush. Soft and yet capable of surviving being manhandled by me. Gives me something to hold on to. Then I see that cute innie belly button and the heaviness of those lush tits that hang with wide tawny nipples that I love touching."

I reach up and tug on both of them. I roll the nubs of her nipples between my fingers and thumbs and feel the way she clenches around my cock.

Her cheeks go pink. "Theo."

"Don't be getting shy and embarrassed when I'm appreciating my wife's body."

When I say *wife*, she clenches again. I tug her down to

me, until our lips are so close, I can feel her warm breath against them.

"I love the way your soft skin is still naturally olive while my tan fades in winter. And yet I can still see mottled patches of red on your chest that tell me you are as aroused as I am."

I ease out and thrust up into her. Her iris, dark brown with flecks of gold around her pupil, goes wide.

She sucks in a breath and gasps.

It feels good. Too fucking good. But I still have more to say to this woman.

"I can see the edges of your scars where they wrap around your ribs and over your shoulder. And the scars on your face. And while my heart breaks for you that this happened to you, I see nothing but courage and bravery and a desire to survive. And thick lips that I love wrapped around my cock as much as I like listening to the words that fall from them."

I see tears glisten in her eyes. "Don't cry, precious. I see you. I really fucking see you. And I want to be the man who is there by your side as you step back into the obvious power you had. Whatever that looks like now."

A tear slips over her lashes, and I scoop it up with my thumb and suck it into my mouth.

"How were you hurt?" she asks, before kissing me tenderly. "Honestly."

I continue to thrust into her slowly as I debate for a moment whether telling her goes against club rules. And then I realize it doesn't matter to me whether it is or not. "Halo's half-brother was trying to kill him and Lola. He had us cornered. I don't remember the actual incident, but Halo told me I stepped between him and a man who was about to slam a large rock on his head. I took the brunt of the rock. Twice."

She slips her hand to my head, where the worst of my scars are. "You know what I see when I look at you?"

I thread my hand into her hair and tug tightly. "I'm fucking dying to know." I want nothing more than to know how she sees me.

"I see an incredibly loyal man. A man who puts the saving of a life over taking it, in a world where the latter is regarded more highly than the former. I see a man who cares deeply about other people. A man who would face his own death before he allowed a friend to be injured. A man who gave away his freedom to give me mine. I see a man who has accommodated my every need without question, who has found solutions to every problem we have come up against, and yet has never made me feel like we are less than partners when his peers view their partners as property."

I slide her hair back over her ear. "I'm still going to ask you to wear a property patch."

"And I'll wear it because I know you see me as so much more than that."

I pull her to me again and kiss her, but she pushes on my chest.

"Wait, I'm not finished."

I grin. "Well, you'd better get on with it because"—I thrust hard into her, balls deep so she can feel every inch of me—"there's something else I want to finish."

"Oh, well, I'll keep it brief. You're strong. I get hot just looking at your biceps. Your tattoos are the kind Vi writes about in her romance books. Your cock is magic, and I really like the things you do to me with it."

I can't help but laugh. "I'll keep all that in mind."

"But what I like best," she says, placing kisses along my

jaw. "Is this. The way we are. The way we talk to each other. The way we're falling in love with each other."

I thrust into her again "This okay?" I ask.

She nods. "Make love to me, Theo," she says.

"Mark my chest while I do."

Sophia flicks the blade open, and I hiss as she presses the tip of the blade to my pec. I feel every millimeter of progress. It's like a tattoo, maybe a fraction more painful. But, fuck, my wife is riding my cock as she slides the knife along my flesh.

Pleasure and pain combine as I fuck her.

Lazily.

Slowly.

Deep thrusts, pauses.

I feel her heat build.

I feel the knife dig a little deeper, feel the bloom of pain and blood. A letting of everything inside me. I feel the red-hot pinch as she carves the letter *S* into my chest.

The friction and tension burn as my breath catches.

I don't remember all the sex I had in the past decade, but I'd put money on it that none of it felt like this. If it had, I wouldn't have let that person go. I tug her to me.

"Please," she begs. "It feels so good."

"Yeah. I feel it too." And I change nothing. Because something tells me that when a woman is telling you something feels good, you should keep doing it as is.

I can feel my own orgasm start to build, but my eyes are firmly fixed on Sophia. The way her eyelids are wide open. The way her mouth forms an O, like she can't believe how intense it all feels.

The cuts on my chest throb.

A shiver runs down my spine; my balls tighten.

"I need you to come soon, Sparrow, or I'll be finishing you off with my mouth."

Sophia's back arches, but she presses her fingertips to her initial on my chest. Her fingers slide in the blood as my wounds burn.

"Theo," she cries, and I feel her cunt spasm, choking my own orgasm from me.

I come in achingly powerful waves that bring clarity: I already love my wife. As I reach for her and tug her down to me, drenched in the scent of her, the intensity of it all hits me.

My life took this unexpected detour. But without it, I wouldn't have met Sophia.

Without it, I wouldn't be me.

I once overheard Rae talking to Briar about this concept that in every minute, you have the chance to become a completely different person. That you can change the direction of your life. Change your outlook. Even change your surroundings and your job to align with the new vision you have for yourself.

I'm Theo. I'm Switch. I'm an Outlaw. I'm a medic. I'm a son and brother. And I'm a husband in love with his wife. And I can live my life however the fuck I want.

Losing my memories has no impact on the decisions I make today about how I show up in the world. Knowing how many lives I saved or took doesn't need to impact the choices I make in this moment.

"I get to wake up tomorrow, with you here in my bed, in my arms, and it's the best fucking decision I ever made." I kiss her neck and she shivers.

"What if I run away tonight?" she asks.

I roll the two of us over. "Do I need to tie you to my bed so you don't?" I take my weight in my arms so I can look at her, grateful that my hand no longer cramps. I don't miss the way her pussy clenches.

Sophia blushes. "It's not a bad idea."

I reach between us and ease my cock out of her before tugging her down next to me, too blown away by the sex we just had to deal with the condom straightaway. "Next time, I'm going to get some handcuffs and secure you to the bed with them."

Sophia rolls onto her side. "What else should we try?" she asks.

"You trying to get me hard again?" I turn my head to face her.

She runs a finger down my face. "Maybe. I don't know. I'm curious. Every position is new to me. I watched this show while I was at the center. Some billionaire guy basically sex trafficked this girl and then they had this 'I hate you I love you' kind of relationship with super-hot sex in it. It was the first time I masturbated...well, probably not the first time, but you know, since the whole...well. Anyway..."

I feel my cock stir and slip off the old condom before it becomes tight on my cock again. "Like I said, are you trying to get me hard again? You can't be telling me you watched chick porn and touched yourself, because that's something I'd pay to see."

She glances over at the side table. "Well, you did give me eighty dollars already tonight. You should get your money's worth."

I groan as I rub a hand over my face. "I think I just died and went to heaven."

Sophia laughs. "You know what I mean...I feel like I'm having a second sexual awakening."

My cock thoroughly engages in the conversation. "Then

it will be my pleasure to be the warm body you take that sexual awakening out on. What do you want to try?"

She taps a finger over her lips. "Well, maybe with something beneath my hips, you could take me from behind."

I picture it and try to think what we could use. Pillows. Sofa cushions. "Over the edge of the bed. The mattress would take most of your body weight so your legs wouldn't have to."

Sophia slides her hand down to my cock and strokes it gently. I twitch in her hand. "That's a good idea."

"What else?"

"Maybe we could get a book of positions and try them all."

"You want a copy of the Kama Sutra; I'll get you one. You can pick a page number and we'll give it the old college try."

"It's a bit cold now, but outside in summer sometime. Maybe on your bike, if that's even possible."

"Dear God, I'm likely going to die, but what a way to go." I roll onto my side to face Sophia. Her cheeks are pink, and she looks happy.

Really fucking happy.

And I realize I am too.

32

SOPHIA

"I fucking hate New York," Niro complains as we survey the large industrial building now acting as a storage facility.

"It's going to be a warren of corridors and shit lighting," Theo says beside me. He pulls me close to his side, his hand tangled in a fistful of my hair. We've been this way since we had sex the previous day. An intimacy you simply can't fake. "I don't want you lifting things and hurting yourself."

"I'll carry things because I don't like feeling limited. But" —I turn and kiss his cheek—"I will gratefully accept your help in carrying anything heavy."

"Good enough," he says. "I like this side of you."

"What side of me?"

"The forthright Sophia." He squeezes my hand.

Spark, Vex, Bates, and Niro flanked us on the ride. We're making a quick stop here just to see how much stuff I have and see if there is anything I need in the short term. Then we're headed on to the rehab center to meet with Dr. Polunin and her team.

Theo and I came in his truck, and I'm relieved. While he

didn't make a big deal about it, he had a headache, a dizzy spell of sorts, in the shower earlier. He promised that if it wasn't gone before we left, he'd let someone else drive.

From the smile on his face a moment ago, I can tell it's passed.

"Little Sophia," says a rotund man in a tight-fitting polo shirt as he approaches us. "Alessio said you might be around." He tugs me into a grip so tight, I'm suddenly uncomfortable and reach my arms out to my side instead of wrapping them around him.

"Hands off my wife," Theo says, and I hear Niro chuckle.

I push the man away and glance over at Niro, who tips his head at Theo, mouths *my wife* and starts making smooching faces.

It softens the quick flare of temper I had at being manhandled.

"Apologies. Old family friend. Would normally hug the girl. Think of her like a niece." He looks down at me. "You still can't remember shit?"

Theo steps up next to me and nudges me ever so slightly behind him, placing himself between me and the stranger.

"And you are?" I ask.

"Paul Russo. Or as you used to call me, Uncle Paulie. You don't remember that, huh?"

I shake my head. "Don't remember shit."

Paulie glances at Theo. "You married a biker, Sophia. 'Course you can't remember shit. Wouldn't have married one if you could." He laughs at his own joke like he's on a TV special.

"We're here for her belongings," Theo says. "Locker—"

"224. Yeah, I know. Helped the movers when they brought her stuff."

"Movers brought my stuff? Not my family?" I ask. I

suppose it makes sense given my family is wealthy, but I find I care that they let strangers see and touch my things. It feels like a further invasion of...me. Of my privacy.

Paulie laughs. "Can you see any of the Viscusos wrinkling their suits? Yeah, movers did it. Said your place was a right state when they did it too. Would have pictured you for a neat freak."

I reach my hand for Theo. I *was* a neat freak. The last time I visited my apartment, everything was neat as a pin. I took photographs so I could learn the layout of my belongings.

"I'd like to see my things," I say.

Once Paulie has shown us to a large unit, he tries to hang around.

"We can take it from here," Bates says, blocking my view of Paulie.

When he disappears, I turn to Theo. "The last time I went to my apartment, it was spotless. There wasn't a thing out of place. I was a neat freak."

"You think someone went through your stuff?" Theo says.

"I'm not sure what I think, just that the mess doesn't sound like me. I just..." I glance over my shoulder to see where the others are standing. I know Niro could hear me if I speak normally, and I don't trust him with this information. I drop my voice to a whisper. "The call with Alessio. Maybe my father does know that I knew something. Do you think I could have had the evidence in my apartment?"

"We don't have time for a full search," Bates says.

I didn't hear him come up behind me. "That was a private conversation."

Bates looks at me indifferently. "It affects one of us, it affects all of us. You dragging my brother into some internal shit in La Cosa Nostra could have implications for the club. Now isn't the time for secrets."

"You're right," I admit. "I'm sorry."

Spark looks at his watch. "We have two hours. We can search through as much stuff as we can."

Theo leads us into the large storage area, and I take in my belongings. They are all out of order from how they were in my apartment. Kitchen appliances mingle with books from my living room. Clothes sit on rails covered in clear plastic.

"I don't know where to start."

"If there's possibly evidence in here that might lead you to better understand what's going on in your family and how at risk you are, we should go through it with a fine-tooth comb. It's unlikely anything is going to obviously trigger a memory," Theo says.

"Please be gentle with my things." I take a deep breath to bite down on the overwhelming feeling of panic enveloping me. "I have no idea what's important or not, but I'd hate to break or ruin things I might want to keep."

"Do we have any clue what we're looking for?" Vex asks.

"I have a feeling it's some information about Cosa Nostra business or my father. I have no clue what form it will take, but I'd look out for reports, paperwork, a laptop, maybe."

We spend the next two hours rearranging the storage space. We go one item at a time. Opening books. Digging in pockets of clothes. Poking through jewelry to see if we find any mysterious keys to a security box.

Anything.

It turns up nothing.

I start a small pile near the door of things to take to Theo's. Winter clothes. Cashmere sweaters. Some thick-soled boots and a long champagne-colored parka.

"Maybe they found what they were looking for," Niro says. "If all your stuff was already searched."

"Anything is possible," I say. "But it strikes me that if my father had found out that Alessio and I knew something, say my father was stealing from the family for example, he—"

"Your father was stealing from the Cosa Nostra?" Spark asks.

I shake my head. "No. Well, maybe. Like, if you think it through, I held a position with financial responsibility regarding real estate. My brother told me I was looking into some financial data and was up to my neck in spreadsheets. Doesn't it make sense it was financial irregularity? Oh, but, please, you can't mention it outside of this room."

Theo squeezes my hand. "You can trust every man here."

Niro laughs. "It's like you don't even know me."

Spark throws his arm over Niro's shoulders. "Don't put yourself down. You're doing so much better."

"Can you tell that to Rae?" Niro asks.

"You tell her," Vex says.

I sit down on the now cleared sofa that had been covered with boxes. "I would have thought it would have been in here somewhere."

Theo crouches down in front of me. "It might still be. When we move your stuff into my place, we can go through it all again. But for now, we have somewhere we are meant to be. We need to go see Dr. Polunin. So, we need to shift the sofa so we can get back out through the door."

Playfully, Niro, Spark, Vex, and Bates pick the sofa up with me on it. I laugh as I fall back against it.

"Wait," Bates says. He moves his hand along the sofa. "There's a fucking switch."

They put the sofa down, and Bates drops to his knees.

When he clicks the switch, I hear a thud, and a panel falls out of the back of the sofa.

"Secret panel. That's some James Bond shit, Sophia," Niro says.

My hip bothers me, and I press my palm into it to relieve the tension as I walk around the back to see what is in there.

The shelves start at the bottom of the base of the sofa and stop at sofa cushion height. There's a series of identical notebooks. Five in total.

And a laptop.

I pull one of the notebooks off the shelf. They look like detailed journals that dance between business and pleasure. The handwriting is definitely mine, even if I don't remember writing what I'm reading. There are also copies of financial ledgers.

"I saw a gym bag, an empty one, earlier. Let me see if I can find it again," Spark says.

"My phone," I say suddenly. "When I got my belongings back from the crash, they gave me all I had on me that day that was salvageable. My shoes, my driver's license, and my phone. It was dead. Had a shattered screen. I assumed it wouldn't work anymore. Vex, could you take a look at that to see if there is anything on it?"

Vex nods. "That's easy. Where is it?"

"I left it at the clubhouse in the drawer next to the bed."

Theo unwinds a key to the room from his keychain. "Feel free to grab it when you get back."

Spark hands Theo the bag and begins to slide the books into it. I give him the one from my hand, but I'm anxious to read them first before the club. Before Theo. I need a minute to digest my life before they do.

Once everything is packed up, including the clothes I piled in the corner, we leave.

"King'll want to know what we found," Spark says as he carries the bag with all my clothing.

Theo carries the one with the journals and laptop in it. "And we'll tell him, once we know if there is anything important here."

Once we're in Theo's truck, I say, "Promise me you won't let them take the laptop and journals before we've had a chance to look at them first."

"I like the way you used the word 'we', Sparrow. We won't let them take it. I promise."

33

SWITCH

"Theo," Dr. Polunin says with obvious relief as I greet her by the back entrance to the rehabilitation unit. "I'm very relieved to see you." She glances at my wife. "And you, too, Sophia. I've had momentary envy over your escapades. While I would never advocate escaping rehabilitation, I have to believe you feel the adventure worth it."

"Doc," I say. "Thank you for seeing us so late."

"I think you should call me 'Katarina.' I feel everything about this is unusual, so formality at this point seems trivial."

"You and I both know I'm sticking with Doc. This is Spark. If you think I'm reluctant to be here, Spark might be even worse."

Doc eyes him carefully. "Ah. I'm very pleased to see you, but I am not calling you 'Spark.' I need a first name at least."

"Tyler, ma'am."

"I love it when he speaks all respectful," Niro says.

Vex puts his head down to hide the smile.

"As it's midnight, all the doors around the facility are

locked to the outside. I have a schedule for each of you. I hand-picked a small team. Sophia, Lori has stayed to see you for physio, which I'm sure will make you both happy. And then you can follow up with Raheel for massage therapy. You know the way?"

"I remember." She starts off down the hallway.

"Soph. Wait," I say. "Niro will come with you."

"I will?" he asks.

I nod. "Yeah. I need someone I know will die trying to keep her safe. She took out three cans and can flip a switchblade. She's more like Cat than she is anyone else. Women like that are rare, and I know you can handle it."

Niro salutes. "I got it."

"I will be meeting with you first, Theo," Doc says. "I have scans arranged too."

Bates squeezes my shoulder, then reaches for his Glock. "Vex and I will split up and do a perimeter check."

Doc glances at him. "In my facility, you will put the gun away unless it is an absolute desperate last measure. I try to keep people alive in here, not kill them."

It reminds me of something Sophia said, and I smile.

"With respect, I'm trying to do the exact same thing," Bates says. He doesn't put his weapon away. He does concede to lower it though.

Vex and Bates begin to check the exits.

"Tyler, Theo told me a little about your situation. With that information, I asked Dr. Curran if he would see you. He's a veteran, purple heart. Retrained as a psychologist upon retiring from the military on medical grounds. I feel like he will be the perfect fit for you."

A tall Black man with the walk of an officer appears. He's Spark's size, and I see my brother's shoulders sag in relief.

"Walking to the other side together," I remind him.

Spark nods, but heads towards Dr. Curran.

"So, it's just you and me, Doc," I say.

"Yes, Theo. There are very few people I would stay awake until midnight for, but you happen to be one of them," she says. She unlocks the door to her office and gestures me inside. "I would prefer, in the event of future visits, that you and your...friends...come unarmed."

I take a seat on the beige chair. "You really need some color in here, Doc."

"It's restful."

"It's bland."

"I'm glad to see you are having fewer challenges with your speech. And I noticed you didn't respond to my comment about the weapons."

"That's because they'll be armed next time."

"Next time, I will not let you into the building if you have them with you. That is my boundary. Your friends can keep you safe from the outside."

"You're a tough negotiator, Doc."

She smiles at that. "I feel like the terms under which we are meeting mean I do not need to maintain my usual polished veneer. So, how have you been feeling, Theo?"

"Like I got bashed in the head by a rock. Twice."

Doc leans forward on her desk and rests her chin on her hands. "So, we're finally going to get honest."

I hand the envelope of cash I grabbed from our club secretary before we left to her. "I feel like this buys a lot of confidentiality."

She looks at it but doesn't reach for it. "It most certainly does. Are you still having headaches?"

I place it down on her desk. "Yeah. The worst fucking kind that nearly take me out each time. And when I get any kind of stress, my speech difficulties come back."

"Then let's see what we can do for you to pick up where we left off."

By the end of the evening, it's almost three in the morning. Thankfully, I see Raheel last and at Doc's instruction, he pulverizes every last kink out of my body. It's so far from a relaxing massage that I've felt better after taking on Clutch in a fistfight. Taut muscles everywhere are stretched and brutally encouraged to relax. Knuckles hit pressure and pain points.

And when I stand, I feel so disorientated for a second that I reach out to the medical bed I just lay on to regain my center of gravity.

"You okay?" Raheel asks, handing me a bottle of water that came from Tahiti or someplace.

"It can't be good for the environment to take this water from that far away, fly it here, and fucking bottle it in plastic," I say.

Raheel laughs. "I say the same thing every day. Even researched water in cans. Something about rich people not wanting canned water. But just drink it. That was a lot of muscle-release work. You're gonna feel sore and lightheaded for a while. But given I didn't know when we'd next be seeing you, I had to make it count."

I roll my neck from left to right. "You certainly did. My head doesn't even feel like it's properly attached to my neck right now."

"That's because your splenius capitis and splenius cervicis were rock solid. They're thick straps of muscle in the back of your neck. So were the rectus wapitis anterior and lateralis. We've loosened everything up. It might help with the headaches. Apply heat to them. Did Lori give you some stretches?"

"Feel utterly ridiculous doing them. I mean...chair stretches. What the fuck kind of exercise is that?"

Raheel shakes his head. "I know the kind of man you are, wearing that cut, but that won't make you any tougher than the next person who walks in here injured. You start where you are, Theo. My aunt lives out in Avon-by-the-Sea... about ten minutes past Asbury Park. I go see her every other weekend because she has no kids of her own. If you like, I can pop in and see both you and Sophia when I'm visiting. An hour treatment for you both every other week won't solve all your problems, but it might help some of them."

I shake Raheel's hand. "I'd like that. Cash in hand?"

Raheel laughs. "Yeah. That works. It'll be my off time from here anyway. My safety is guaranteed, yeah? I've watched enough outlaw gang movies. People like me aren't safe in many rooms filled with white men."

I crack the bottle of water open and take a sip. "Your safety is guaranteed. I promise it. And you might want to check your stereotypes."

"Please tell me you aren't 'not all white men-ing' me."

"Fair. You can see us at my house. Don't even need to step foot in our clubhouse. But if you ever want a walk on the wild side, you can come as my guest sometime."

"Your house will be fine. My idea of walking on the wild side is not wearing matching socks."

That makes me laugh. "Thanks, Raheel. For doing this. It's appreciated."

"Anytime. I need to get some sleep. I'm on shift at nine. You know your way back to Doctor Polunin's office, yeah?"

I nod, grab Sophia's bag, and head down the corridor. I pass the family meeting room and step inside. Spark is sitting on the sofa, his back to me. He's texting someone, and my guess is it's Iris, even though it's late.

"Let her get some sleep," I say.

"She is. I just had some shit I needed to get off my chest before we left."

I sit down next to him. "Feeling better?"

"Define 'better.' I feel like I just got sucked into a blender at high speed, then poured back into a mold of my body."

"That's pretty graphic."

"I've been pureed."

I laugh at that. "I feel like I just did ten rounds with Clutch."

"Clutch is a pussy who cheats," Spark says. "Last time I fought him, he started fucking pinching my nipples."

We sit in silence for a minute.

"Trouble keeps coming for our club, and it always affects the women. Not sure I know what I'd do if anything happened to Iris. Told Curran I'd probably take one of my weapons and put a bullet through my brain if anything ever happened to her. Not even sure if there's a fucking afterlife, but on the off chance there is, I'd kill myself to follow her."

I throw my arm over his shoulder. "What did Curran say to that?"

"Told me to put down a tarp and call the cops just before I do it so only a professional team has to deal with the cleanup, then write it into my will that I owed those first responders ten grand each so they could get therapy to deal with having to clean up after my dead ass."

I turn and look at him. "For real?"

Spark laughs. "It's cool. I got his point. He's a good guy. I'm going to have a call with him weekly."

"Good. Takes balls to confront your shit, man. I'm proud of you."

"Yeah. Well. I got a baby on the way who's gonna look up

to me one day. Want to be the best fucking example I can be for them."

Those words really tug at my heart. I feel them as a man. As a son. And as a man who hopes he can convince the woman he loves to have kids with him one day.

I slap his back gently. "You've got this. I'm gonna go find Sophia, and then we can leave."

I see Vex in the hallway. "Just grabbing Soph and then we can go."

I approach Dr. Polunin's office. In the quiet of the night, without all the usual hive of activity, I can hear their conversation. I know I shouldn't listen in, but I'm only fucking human.

"...you think I was wrong to marry him?" Sophia asks.

"I have no opinion on that, Sophia. What I worry about is you both making permanent decisions that affect your long-term future while in a stressful period of your life."

"I was injured, fleeing a situation I believe was linked to me being married off to my father's best friend's son to secure the long-term success of my family. If you know who Theo is, then you also know who I am. You must have looked up my family."

I smile at that. I like this evolving feisty streak of Sophia's. There are glimpses of the Mafia princess her brother Alessio seems to think she was. It's not even memory. It's who she is.

"But...I hear you. I've fallen for Theo so quickly that I worry about what the future holds. I know who I am. I see who he is. He's recovered from his injuries far better than I have. There may come a time when my limitations bother him or hold him back. I know the path for us is far from smooth. It might even be treacherous. I'm falling in love with my husband while simultaneously preparing myself for the fact there may come a time when he decides I'm not the person for him."

34

SWITCH

I lie in bed, Sophia fast asleep in my arms, thinking about what I overheard last night.

I'm falling in love with my husband while simultaneously preparing myself for the fact there may come a time when he decides I'm not the person for him.

And I come to one conclusion.

We rushed everything.

And because we married to avoid her being married to someone else, and for me to help my mom fight her cancer, Sophia is always going to wonder what my real motives are.

So, we need to go back to the beginning.

I need to date my wife.

I need to romance her.

I need to show her in actions how much she's coming to mean to me.

And perhaps in doing that, we'll fall all the way in love to a place where we feel comfortable telling each other.

I slip my arm from beneath her, grab my phone from the side table, and pad downstairs. It's cold in the house, and I adjust the thermostat so it's warm when Sophia wakes.

Once I have a cup of coffee in my hand, I sit on the sofa and open the group text.

Me: *Brothers. I want to spoil my wife. She's been through shit and it's time I started building a life with her instead of bouncing from one issue to the next. I need ideas. What should I do? Where should I take her? What should I buy her? What works for your old ladies?*

Given it's only six thirty in the morning, I don't expect a lot of answers.

So, I send another message to my mom.

Me: *Just checking in to see how you are doing. I hope the nausea has stopped and that you managed to keep some food down. I'm thinking Soph and I might fly down to see you soon if you are up to it and the doc says it's okay for us to fly and for you to have visitors. Love you.*

After trading my phone for my coffee cup, I take a sip and lean back against the sofa.

Halo told me it was an incredible feeling, creating a house, and then it becoming a family home, like his did for him, Ari, and Lola...the opposite of what he envisioned. I look around the large kitchen made for catering for lots of people and the sectional sofa that can easily sit eight. I don't know what I envisioned this house becoming, but I hope it becomes home to a large family with Sophia.

Even if it means I have to get used to La Cosa Nostra as in-laws.

My phone vibrates on the table, and I pick it up. Surprisingly, my whole muscle chain from my shoulder to my arm feels so much looser. Raheel has good hands, and I find myself wondering if I shouldn't just pay the guy to come here every week.

Niro: *Fight sex, weapons, and baked goods. Doesn't matter*

what's going on with Cat...bad mood, period shit, whatever. One of those three things will solve it.

I laugh at Niro's reply.

Me: *How very on brand! Why you up so early?*

Niro: *Baked goods. I was an asshole yesterday. Life went a little off-kilter. Cat understands, but making baked goods this morning shows I do too.*

I think about what Niro just said. It's in the showing. I need to show Sophia that we're tight. I can't simply tell her with words and it be enough.

Me: *If those baked goods include cinnamon rolls, can you make a couple extra and I'll ride over and pick 'em up?*

Niro: *Done. I'll message you.*

Halo: *Sex toys. Nothing says I love you like multiple Os.*

Niro: *Guess we all know why Halo's awake.*

Halo: *One day you'll have a one-year-old and realize you gotta fit fucking in around feeding and going to baby yoga.*

King: *You go to baby yoga?*

Halo: *Fuck no. But Ari does. And I can't fuck her if she's with twenty other moms at the corner of Memorial and Sunset.*

Me: *Weapons and sex toys weren't what I had in mind.*

Vex: *Maybe they should be. Haven't met a woman yet who hasn't been relieved at the sight of a vibrator. They all secretly fucking love 'em.*

Vibrators aren't a bad idea given our conversation on a previous night. If she wants to try everything, I could get some additional supplies. I love the idea that someday soon I could fuck her ass if she's down with us trying.

King: *Rae loves that restaurant on Emory and Bangs. Won't let you in with your cut or any visible colors. I'd beat the crap out of the owner for that alone, but Rae loves their raw shit.*

Clutch: *Take her to a fancy shoe shop and tell her she can buy ten pairs of shoes. Not gonna tell you what Gwen did in return seeing King's in the chat.*

King replies with a row of vomiting emojis.

Clutch: *Seeing you asked so nicely... Told her she had to fuck me once in every pair. Winner, winner, chicken dinner.*

King: *I DID NOT FUCKING ASK.*

Spark: *Why the fuck is the chat going off at this time in the morning? You assholes woke Iris.*

Niro: *You really don't know the answer to that? Like, can't you read?*

Spark: *Fuck you.*

Niro: *Wow. Someone's a grouch this morning. Does someone need a hug?*

Bates: *Vi loves sentimental shit. Got her a bracelet with mine, her, and Avery's initials as charms on it. Took her up to my uncle's cottage where we'd been before. Shit like that. Memory type shit.*

Saint: *Picnics.*

Clutch: *Picnics? Who the fuck are you? Martha Stewart?*

Niro adds a row of laughing emojis.

So does Bates.

Saint: *Fuck you all. Briar fucking loves when I grab some food, wrap her up in one of my thick riding jackets, and ride down the coast. Thermos of coffee. Talk about important shit or nothing at all. Then ride back with her on the back of my bike. Leaves her feeling some kind of way when we get home. Never feel closer to her than those days. Costs fuck all but a bit of time and effort.*

King: *Gotta agree with that one.*

Niro: *Rare I get Cat to agree to be a backpack rather than take her own bike... but when I do ... yeah. I feel that.*

Spark: *If you're all turning into sentimental pussies, I'm going back to sleep with my old lady. Night, motherfuckers.*

Niro: *Technically it's morning, motherfuckers.*

Halo: *Find things that relax her mind. Ari likes puzzles and journalling and shit. Speaking of which, Ari's just walked back into the bedroom. Gotta go, fellas.*

The chat fizzles out, and I'm sipping my coffee when my phone vibrates with an incoming video chat.

"Hey, Teddy Bear," Mom says.

She looks tired. Dark circles sit beneath her eyes. But Dad reassures me that everyone on her medical team is incredibly optimistic about her treatment. She's on the deck at the back of the house in a blanket, and the pre-dawn sky is dark blue with slashes of purple and orange.

"What are you doing awake?" I ask.

She takes in a deep breath and looks up at the sky. "I've got a new appreciation for the sunrise these days."

I hear the unspoken words. That life is short and precious and can be taken away in a heartbeat. That the sunrise is a sign you made it through another night and live to fight another day.

"I love you, Mom," I say, trying to choke down the emotion I feel.

"And I love you, sweetheart. How's Sophia?"

"She's good. Her family don't particularly like the fact I'm an Outlaw." I gloss over the reason why.

She huffs. "Lord knows why they wouldn't love you. A veteran. A medic. A good man. Tell them I didn't raise you all these years for them to turn up their nose at the sight of a little leather."

I chuckle. "Always the momma bear."

She raises an eyebrow at me. "Would you expect anything less? I can't wait to meet her in person. You think she'd be okay with me messaging her? Just to get to know her a little."

The idea of the two most important women in my life loving each other warms me inside. "I think she'd like that."

There's a comfortable moment of silence between us. I sip my coffee while Mom looks up at the sky.

"Hey, Mom," I say. "Can I ask you something?"

"Anything."

"I rushed things with Sophia."

She immediately looks concerned. "You're regretting it?"

I shake my head. "No. God, no. I'm not regretting it. But I am regretting that I haven't put more of an effort into, you know…"

Her face softens. "You want to woo your wife?"

"Yeah. I do. What should I do?"

"You wanna know what your father's first words to me were?"

I place my coffee cup on the table. "I'm not sure. Do I?"

She chuckles. "He said I'd look great riding his face but would look even better on the back of his bike."

I can't help but laugh. "Dad. Always the charmer."

"From that day until now, he's always made me feel good about myself. Not once has he put me down, made me feel less, or called me names in an argument. He's made me feel like his equal in a world where women are called property. Sure, he's bought me expensive things, but it's the flowers he brings me every Friday and the way he's not missed a single medical appointment with me that show me just how much he cares for me. Woo her by showing her you'll be there for her in every way that matters, Theo. Because that's what love is."

Tears fill her eyes, but she's no longer looking at me. She's smiling at someone. The phone suddenly shifts angle. Mom squeals with laughter. And when the video settles, she's sitting on Dad's lap.

He kisses her cheek. "Love you too, sweetheart."

"Theo wanted to know how to woo his wife," Mom says. "What advice would you give him?"

"First, I would have said find a girl who makes it easy to love her." Dad glances at Mom, even though she's looking at me. "And then don't forget you're a husband first. Carry the heavy shit. Fix the broken things. Make the money. Give her the easiest life you possibly can."

Mom chuckles. "You know you still didn't clear the gutters yet?"

Dad rolls his eyes. "I'll get to it when the sun's up. Just... make sure she knows she's safe with you. That you aren't going to let the world hurt her. That *you* aren't going to hurt her either."

I think about Sophia. "I'm starting to think she's more than capable of taking care of herself."

Mom smiles. "Well, that's when she's going to need you most. If an adult woman is that capable of taking care of herself, it's usually because she's never had anyone else she can turn to. Show her what it means to be able to fully trust another human being, Theo. Show her what it means to love and trust another person with your whole heart."

I think about Sophia in that context. Growing up in a life like this one. Straddling the law. Constant jockeying in power struggles. The risk of being kidnapped or becoming collateral. It takes a toll.

"I'll do that," I commit. "Thanks for being the best fucking role models of what it means to love someone for life."

Mom blows me a kiss. Dad nods.

"We'll speak to you later," Dad says. "Got some shit I'd like to say and do with your mom now."

"That's more information than I needed. Love you."

I hang up the phone, feeling better for speaking to them both.

And Operation Woo My Wife begins ninety minutes later when she makes it to the kitchen in one of my hoodies.

"Are those Niro's cinnamon rolls?" she asks, looking at the two monster rolls on the platter, thick with his cream cheese icing.

"Yup. And coffee. Went to an Italian cafe down on the shore and grabbed you a double espresso."

"God, you are the best husband." She steps up onto her toes and kisses me. "Thank you."

"You're welcome. I also made some plans, so sit, eat and drink, while I tell you them."

"I was hoping to make a start on the journals and the laptop," she says.

"Shit. Yeah. Got caught up making plans. They can wait if you want."

Sophia looks at me, a smear of cream cheese icing on her lip. I rub it off with the pad of my thumb, then press it into her mouth. Her tongue swirls around it, and now I'm sitting here with the fixings of a boner.

"What were the plans?"

I managed to get ahold of Bruiser, a club hangaround who runs a bike shop fifteen minutes away. "Step one, getting you your own leathers and boots. Step two, checking in on Vex that he got your smashed phone. Step three, riding south down the shore for as long as we feel like going. Step four, picnic if it's dry, lunch somewhere if it's not. Step five, stop at a sex shop I know on the way home so we can start working our way through our list of things to try when we get home. Step six, dinner before I have to go out tonight. But we can do it another day."

Sophia takes another bite of her cinnamon roll, then

shakes her head. "If we can condense things a little, I can look at them this afternoon."

"Fucking perfect."

Step one goes smoothly, and while I thought Sophia looked good in Catalina's leathers...she looks even better in her own. And she has fun picking out the boots and the helmet. She settles on a black one with silver lines on it.

"How do I look?" she asks.

"Utterly fuckable," I answer honestly.

Bruiser laughs as Sophia blushes.

We then go home and pick up the bike. I connect our helmets so we can talk to each other.

"You sure you feel up to this?" Sophia asks as I climb on and lean the bike toward her.

"Seeing Raheel and Lori really helped. And I don't have any sign of a headache. If I do, I promise I'll pull over and call for one of the guys to come bring us home. Put your hand on my shoulder and let me take as much weight as you need to."

I've backed the bike up to the step from the driveway to the path to the front door. Figured it would be easier for her to maneuver herself onto the bike with the extra height.

It takes us a minute. I lower the angle of the bike, putting my foot on the step and taking the weight of the bike in my arms. It helps Sophia get her leg over the seat. And finally, we're good to go.

"Ready?" I ask, pulling in the clutch before revving the engine.

Sophia laughs and we get underway.

God, it feels good to be out. Saint's idea was perfect. I take the long way to the clubhouse, but it's still not long enough. There are bikes parked outside, and I pull up next to Vex's.

The clubhouse stinks when I open the door. Bikers lay strewn on sofas; girls lie on bikers. And I remember a night...the chapter from Bethlehem was with us. I slept with Penny. Ended up hungover for two days after.

Penny.

Fuck.

She had a sweet side but wasn't always a kind person. The sex was on fire, but I didn't love her.

I haven't seen her since I came back, and that's probably for the best. Not because Sophia should feel threatened, but because I suddenly remember her being cruel to Vi. I'm glad she isn't around to put Sophia through that.

Sophia's hand slides up my arm. "You okay?" she asks me quietly.

"Yeah. Just thinking I actually don't miss this. Well, the drinking and telling stories and hanging out with brothers part? Maybe. But the women and sleeping on sofas got old. And now I have you at home. Yeah. Think I'll always prefer to be back with you when I can be."

"That's actually really sweet."

We make our way into the kitchen, and I knock on Vex's office door. "What's up, brother?" I say when I find him with his head down behind his monitors.

When he looks up at me, I can see the concern in his face immediately. "Was just about to call you."

He hands Sophia a brand-new phone. "Don't ask me how I was able to do this. It took all night."

Sophia takes it from him. "But I don't need a new phone."

"It's got all the stuff from your old phone on it," Vex says. "That way you can get rid of the phone you have now given we don't even know whose name the contract is in."

Sophia looks to me, and I nod. "Thank you, brother. Was her data still on it?"

Vex glances at me while Sophia looks at her phone. "Yes. There's an unsent message, a video, to Alessio. I saved it to the device."

Sophia's brow furrows. "You went through my messages?"

"Of course I went through your messages. Went through everything you have on there," Vex says without apology. "We're an MC, not a mall repair shop. Needed to know what kind of risk you put us in."

"And?" I ask.

"You need to watch it, but you should sit down first," Vex says.

Sophia ignores the advice and presses Play on the video. "Ale. Answer your damn phone. I'm being followed. Chased."

The video footage is chaotic. Seeing Sophia without her facial injuries is a shock. Seeing the fear in my girl's eyes has my gut in turmoil.

"Dad knows I'm on to him," she continues. "Those spreadsheets I was talking about earlier? Dad's been syphoning off money from the investors. It's a lot, Ale. Like, a hole so big, I don't think he's going to be able to close the gap. He told me to meet him for lunch at the house. And when I got there, he had two of those stooges from the Aglieri crew with him. Mickey Junior and Tony. I overheard him saying it was important to find out what I knew so they could follow through on making it look like I was at fault. I considered running for the front door, but Uncle Carmine was in the hallway, so I went to the bathroom and escaped through the window. Ale. I think Aglieri's men are following me. I don't know how I'm—"

The rest is hard to watch. The sound sickening. It was difficult enough seeing the extent of her injuries. Knowing how they happened was the stuff of nightmares.

There's a loud scream.

Crunching metal.

The phone flies through the interior of the car at such speed it's impossible to make sense of what we're seeing.

Then nothing.

"Oh, God. I think I'm going to be sick," Sophia says.

And while I take care of my wife, I make a vow that I'm going to kill her father.

35

SOPHIA

Alessio was right.

And with Vex's help, I found the most recent files I was looking at on my laptop before the accident. Which seem to show that for every contract my father had with his business partners, he skimmed fifteen percent off the top.

And there is an account, registered in Switzerland, in his name. There are photographs of a laptop screen and papers on a desk that I recognize as Papà's office from my visits to their home.

They were uploaded to the cloud some time on the Sunday before my accident.

Did I stumble across them, or had I gone snooping around his house for evidence? I'm not sure I'll ever know, but the ends are the same.

"Fuck," Theo mutters as he looks over my shoulder. I'm seated at the small table in his room at the clubhouse. I realize it's late, and I'm exhausted.

"That's one way of saying it," I reply.

"Your father knew." Theo's statement is undeniable.

"It makes sense, doesn't it? I mean, from the date stamp, it looks like these photographs were uploaded to the cloud the weekend before my accident." I lean back in my chair. "When I spoke to Alessio the night he gave you the key to my stuff, he told me how I called him the day of the accident. That I'd been working on something that was confusing me. Something to do with spreadsheets and numbers. It must have been this."

I reach for my phone and message Alessio.

Me: *Ale, were we at our parents' house the Sunday before my accident?*

Ale: *Should I be worried why you're messaging me at two in the morning about it?*

Me: *Just answer the question.*

Ale: *Yeah. Lunch after mass. What's going on, Sophia?*

Me: *I think I've found what made me run.*

My phone rings, and I don't need to look at it to know it's Alessio.

"Do I answer it?" I ask Theo.

"We're safe here in the clubhouse, so yes."

I answer the phone but put it on speaker so Theo can hear. "Alessio."

"You can't trust phone lines. They aren't secure."

"I found something though."

"Come see me tomorrow. I'll send you my address."

"No," Theo says. "Neutral ground. I'll send you the location. And you come alone."

"That's one hell of a guard dog you got, Puparu," Alessio says.

Theo grins at that. "I've been called worse, pizza boy. Send Sophia the time and I'll send you the place."

Alessio ends the call.

"Pizza boy?" I ask.

"Meh. Not my best insult. Niro would have done better. It was pizza or pasta. Urgh, I should have gone with 'dough boy.' And I'm proud of you, piecing all of this together." Theo pushes a lock of hair behind my ear. "Beauty and brains. Mighty powerful combination, Sparrow."

Despite the situation, I melt a little at his words. "I feel like someone hit the beauty and brains with a dimmer switch of late, but I'll take the compliment."

Theo kisses me. "Take it. I mean it. You're still badass. I'll need to take this to my club in the morning though. Tell 'em what we're doing. What we know. Since the vote, they've done nothing but support us. I'll fire a message to King to bring him up to speed, so he knows."

I think about what Theo is saying. "Can we talk to Alessio first? Make more sense of it all?"

"It's the talking to Alessio I'm nervous about. Not as much as I was, given this really incriminates your dad. But I'm smart enough to know that a guy who bragged about having drone cover is most definitely not going to show up tomorrow alone. It would be foolish to attempt to handle this on our own when we can have backup."

I shut down the laptop and tap the lid. "I suppose it would be foolish to take this with us too."

Theo nods. "We can ask Vex to make a copy of the drive. Maybe a virtual one and we give Alessio the link. Or put the data on a portable device or whatever."

I want to push back, but I can't identify why. Maybe it's because there's a deep-down part of me that knows I'm a Viscuso and I know the old me wouldn't have wanted an outlaw motorcycle club to know our business.

But I'm also now a Reavis. Theo's wife. Catalina's aspirational partner-in-crime to reform the club. I'm a friend to the old ladies.

"Okay. Let's talk to the club in the morning." I let out a sigh.

Theo rubs circles on my back. "You okay?"

"In a way, I'm relieved."

He crouches next to my chair. "In what way?"

"When I thought this was about the arranged marriage, it felt like my whole family thought so little of me. That I was an asset to be used and traded. But I think I understand why I might have been okay with it in the context of who I used to be. If I thought Papà was stealing money, being married to the godfather's son would have given the family some stability after Papà was found out. It feels like a balance sheet I would have been okay with."

Theo raises his eyebrow. "An arranged marriage is looking more appealing to you now?"

"God, no," I say, wrinkling my nose. "But it feels better to know I might have been okay with it than thinking my entire family was willing to hand me over like a sacrificial goat. And knowing the accident was most likely caused by me trying to escape my father than the clutches of strangers makes more sense too. It means my brothers weren't complicit. At least, not all of them."

"Leo and Luca have a lot to answer for." Theo takes my hand and helps me stand before pulling me close.

The scent of him, his comforting warmth and reassuring strength settle me. "But even then, they were doing what my father told them, operating on twenty percent of the story. And I find myself trusting Alessio."

Theo rubs his hands up and down my back. "I don't know that Alessio and I will ever be the best of friends, but my trust in him is growing too. We need to get some rest. You've been working all day and look exhausted."

"Oh no. We didn't get our day," I say. "I'm so sorry."

Theo drags his lips along the side of my neck. "There will be lots of other days."

"But we talked about playing with the pinwheel we were going to buy." I tilt my neck to give him more access.

I was intrigued by the Wartenberg pinwheel with its little spikes that looked like a cross between a pastry chef tool and a medieval torture implement. Theo was excited by thoughts of how it would feel pressed into his skin.

"That was fourteen hours ago, before all this came to light, and you stared at your laptop screen without a break."

"I ate the food you brought."

He smiles, his eyes so incredibly kind. "Because I forced you. You have quite the degree of focus."

"I was looking forward to focusing on your back with that wheel."

Theo kisses me soundly. "And I look forward to that at a time when I'm not worried about you falling asleep standing up. We'll get a pinwheel eventually. And it might do me good to have to wait for it."

"That sounds a little like you are dominating yourself."

He kisses the tip of my nose. "I've stopped trying to put a label on it. Just putting it all under the heading of Shit that Makes Me Feel Good."

"Well, for the record, you always make *me* feel good."

Theo slips his hand around the back of my neck and grabs a fistful of hair firmly. "I know. Which is why you're going to get naked while I send Alessio the details of the meet-up point. Go get ready for bed. We'll sleep here at the clubhouse tonight."

I do as he says. "Be nice."

"Can I have a little bit of fun with him first?"

"No," I say. As I reach the door to the bathroom, I pause

and turn. "We're not really a fake husband and wife anymore, are we?"

Theo grins. "No, Sparrow. We're not."

When I re-emerge, the text must have been sent as Theo is stripping his clothes.

I tug the sheets back and climb beneath them. "Do you remember when we slept here the first night? We barely knew each other."

Theo slips beneath the covers and rolls me onto my side before pulling me close. "We've come a long way."

"It's been fun getting to know you."

His hands roam my skin, the callouses on his palms tickling me. "You feel like letting me get to know you some more?" he asks.

His breath whispers across my ear, making me shiver. "Is that a euphemism for sex?"

Theo chuckles behind me. "If I need to speak more plainly, I'd really like to fuck you so we both sleep well."

I tilt my head, giving him room to plant more delicious kisses along my neck. "In that case, yes, please."

His hand dips between my legs. At first, he simply cups my pussy while he kisses and gently bites along my shoulder. I can't help but roll my hips against his palm. It feels so good.

It feels even better a moment later when he slides one of his fingers into me, then drags the wet digit out over my clit, before repeating the action all over again.

Theo rubs his cock along the crease of my ass. He's hard. Thick and heavy.

I reach behind me and scratch my nails over his hip. His gasp of breath tells me he likes it. Theo grabs my wrist and forces my nails harder into his skin. His cock twitches between us.

Creating an urgency, a need in someone else is heady. That this strong biker forgets himself when pleasure and pain combine at my hands amazes me. And for reasons I don't understand, I enjoy it. Not because I enjoy hurting him, but because he does.

"Soph." He grunts as I follow his lead and dig in harder.

Theo slips another finger inside me, pushing them in up to his knuckles. I visualize his tattooed fingers sliding deep inside me.

Suddenly, he removes his fingers, and my back is cool for a moment as I hear the bedside table drawer open then slam shut. There's a moment while he puts the condom on, then his palm strokes over my ass before slapping it.

"I really need to fuck you, Soph."

He pushes me onto my front, then slides two pillows from the bed beneath my hips. On instinct, I open my legs, and it takes less than a second for Theo to ruthlessly enter me.

"Fuck," he cries out as I moan. "This okay?"

I mentally check my body. My hips are supported by the pillow. It feels a little strange being face down in the mattress this way. But my clit aches with a fury that only Theo can ease.

"Yes," I gasp.

Theo grips my hips and begins to pump furiously into me. My whole body vibrates with need. It's overwhelming, borderline too much.

Not pain, but the all-consuming need for release.

Theo lowers himself down, his chest brushing my back. He kisses my neck, then bites my earlobe gently. I catch sight of him in the mirror above the desk, his hips hammering into me. There are long, red scratches along his hip and thigh. And I can't explain what seeing him like this does to me.

Seeing just how much he wants me.

How much he wants what we are when we come together like this.

His hands find mine and grip them over my head.

I can't respond. He has me pinned down in every way that matters.

My orgasm slams into me, blinding me for a moment with flashes of light and a pure out of body pleasure that I can't begin to describe.

"Theo," I cry out as I come harder than I thought possible.

"Fuck, yeah, Soph," he says. "I feel it. I fucking feel it."

"Then come for me, Theo. I want to hear you come too."

"Soph," he barks as he loses his rhythm. I feel his cock twitch inside me as he does. His strokes shudder then slow. "Jesus. Every time it just gets better."

I agree. "It does. I hope it always feels like this."

Theo gently reaches between us and pulls out of me. Before he deals with the condom, he helps me lift my hips and removes the pillows. When I roll onto my back, he kisses me softly.

"I didn't hurt you, did I?" he asks.

I shake my head. "No. Far from it. Did I hurt you? I mean, more than you wanted?"

Theo smiles. "Definitely not. I don't think you could ever hurt me, Soph."

And I hold on to that eight hours later when we meet Theo's club brothers in the large room he refers to as church.

Bizarrely, it's not that I feel bad about what we're going to tell them. Theo told me it makes me interesting that things like this don't turn me into a quivering wreck. Instead, I pull my shoulders back, take a deep breath, and hold Theo's hand as we enter the room.

"You causing mischief again, sweetheart?" Niro asks as Theo pulls out his chair for me to sit on.

"If we keep having old ladies coming in here to explain why their presence is causing chaos, we're going to have to get a spare chair for this fucking table," King says, winking at me.

Clutch chuckles. "Life would be boring without them."

Theo stands behind me, his hand on my shoulder. "Tell 'em, Sparrow."

"Thanks to Vex, we were able to find evidence on my phone and laptop that suggests I was trying to evade my father when my accident happened. That I'd found evidence at my father's home. I called my brother that morning to say I was up to my neck in figuring something out."

"Why are you telling us all this?" Clutch asks.

Theo squeezes my shoulder. "We're meeting with one of her brothers this morning to hand over the information."

Spark leans forward. "Why are we handing it over? Feels like we should let the Cosa Nostra tear themselves apart."

"You don't have to be a Mafia expert to know what happens when a family is suspected of stealing from the *famiglia*. I can't let all my brothers, and by extension, me, go down for something they aren't involved in. If I give this to Alessio, he can clean house. I had faith in him, before, when I remembered."

Bates rubs his hand over his chin. "So, you're saying, if we ignore this, and some mob boss finds out, that they might come for you seeing you were part of their organization, and by association force our hand to look out for you?"

I shake my head. "I don't know exactly what I'm saying. I may be spinning conspiracy theories. But I do know my father intended to make it look like his thefts were my fault. And I need to get ahead of that by giving this proof to my brother."

King looks to Theo. "What's your take on all this?"

"If you park club business, I think Alessio is good on his word. And I'd rather nip Cosa Nostra business in the bud before it comes for my wife."

"So, what do you need from us, Switch?" Halo asks.

"Don't fancy heading uptown to meet Alessio without backup. I told him to come alone, but we all know the chances of that happening are slim. And while I believe he isn't gonna fuck with Soph, I'd like backup to make sure it doesn't happen."

"How do we explain this to the Irish?" Saint asks.

King's brow furrows. "We don't. Cillian fucked us over." He glances in my direction. "And this isn't the time nor place to discuss it. We go because Switch asked for our help. We are going solely with the goal of getting Switch and Sophia there and back in one piece. I do not want a war with the Sicilians, but I'm inclined to believe Sophia and Switch that Alessio is trustworthy. All in favor?"

I blow out a breath of relief when all the hands rise without discussion.

"Gimme the address," Halo says. "I'll set the route."

"Catalina's gonna be pissed she can't ride with us," Niro says. "But I'm in the mood for evening the score."

"Killing is a last resort," King says.

Niro huffs. "Well, you're no fun."

"We need pictures of your family if you have any. I want to know who all the key players are. Your brothers, your parents, any members of the crews you might be aware of," Spark says.

"I only have my family, and you've met them already, but I can happily show you photographs as a refresher," I say. "In hindsight, I think my father wanted to keep me far away from the family business because he knew I knew, and he didn't want me to do anything to jog my memory. But if I could ask one thing? Don't hurt my brothers."

King stands. "That will depend on whether they try to hurt you or us. If they succeed, I'll kill them myself."

36

SWITCH

When we pull into the lot of the derelict manufacturing plant, Alessio is already there.

There are no signs of drones or other vehicles. At least, no obvious ones.

But I'm hopeful that Alessio just set the tone for this meeting by showing up as instructed.

"Biker," he says when I flip the lid on my helmet.

"Mobster," I say, leaning the bike so Sophia can get off.

Vex appears and holds out an arm to help her stabilize herself. I debated long and hard about bringing the truck, but as Bates pointed out, our exit would be faster on the bikes.

Alessio rubs a hand over his face. "I love your definition of 'come alone.'" He tips his head in the direction of the bikers behind me.

"I like to think it's insurance."

"Can you two stop bickering?" Sophia says. She walks closer to Alessio, and in spite of the urge to hold her back, I let her go to him. "Hey, Ale."

"Hey, Puparu." There's emotion in the way he says it.

And the next thing, they're hugging.

And while I'm watching, Vex shoulder checks me. "You didn't think to stop her from going over there?"

I shake my head as they say something to each other I can't hear. "No. He's not gonna hurt her."

Vex glances at me. "How do you know?"

"Call it a sixth sense."

Alessio throws his hand over Sophia's shoulder and leads her back to me. When he's standing in front of me, he offers me his hand. "Welcome to the family," he says.

I take it and shake it.

I glance back at my brothers, who are standing in an arc behind me. "Wish I could say the same."

Alessio laughs. "Fair. So, tell me what you know."

I let Sophia lead, telling Alessio what she found. About the spreadsheets and the double accounts and the syphoning of money off the top of every project. Vex loaned us a laptop that is cleaned of everything except the files and evidence. There is also an email address specifically for her and Alessio to communicate that Vex has worked his magic on to make sure Sophia will never be tracked when using it.

She explains that she doesn't know what it all means, that she can't remember compiling it all, and can't necessarily confirm all her sources.

But it's enough.

Alessio blows out a breath, then looks up at the sky. "*Sulu pa morti un c'è rimediu.*"

"What does that mean?" I ask.

"Only for death is there no remedy."

"What are you going to do?" Sophia asks.

"I'm going to speak with our brothers. You are welcome to join, but only alone. I'll share this information, and we will vote."

Sophia rolls her eyes. "You men and your votes."

"It's the only way," Alessio and I say at the exact same time.

A measure of respect passes between us.

"We need to get ahead of this before—"

The first bullet hits the dust by my feet. The second pings off my bike. The third slices through the hem of Alessio's suit jacket.

It's rapid fire, but before the fourth shot is fired, I've dragged Sophia behind Alessio's car. "Theo," she cries as she lands on the ground.

"Stay down, Sparrow. Until we know where the shots are coming from."

Halo pulls his weapon on Alessio and drags him by the collar behind a low wall. "You fucking betrayed us, motherfucker."

"It's not me. I swear," Alessio says, pulling his own but aiming it toward one of the buildings. "Don't know who the hell this is."

"They're aiming for Sophia and Alessio," Clutch shouts. "Can we draw fire?"

Vex drops down next to me behind the car as one of the car windows is blown out. "We need to get Sophia out of here."

Sophia clutches the laptop to her chest. "I'm okay. Do what you need to."

I climb to my knees and peer over the hood of the car as a bullet bounces off it, missing my face by inches.

I feel the heat and air of it as it blows past me.

Spark and Saint close in on the building under the cover of Bates and Niro to commence a cordon-and-kick search. Vex and I add additional firepower as four men come around the side of the building. I take down one; Alessio takes down another. As we provide cover, King and Clutch take out the remaining two.

A handful of shots are fired inside, and then Spark shouts, "Clear!"

Alessio sprints to the four downed men, and I follow him. One of the assailants is injured. I can't tell whether it's a fatal wound.

It sure as hell doesn't help that Alessio kicks him in the gut, making him groan. "Who the fuck sent you, and how did you know I was here?"

The guy opens his eyes and attempts to stare Alessio down.

Alessio responds by shoving the muzzle of his gun into the guy's mouth. "I'll find out who the fuck you are. I'll go to your house. I'll kill anyone I find there. And then I'll find your mom's house and kill her too. Now. Who. The fuck. Sent you?"

The guy almost chokes until Alessio removes the gun. "Your father."

"Fuck," Alessio says before putting the gun to the guy's head and pulling the trigger.

The sound of the last bullet ricochets through the air.

The bullet fest is over.

Vex has helped Sophia to her feet.

Alessio takes a deep breath and turns to Sophia. "Our father's done."

Sophia comes to my side, wincing as she walks. "You have my vote," she says to Alessio.

Clutch squeezes Alessio's shoulder, and I remember something about his father getting shanked in prison.

Alessio faces King. "What would it take for you to help me make it happen?"

King blows out a breath. "We aren't a hit squad."

"Yeah. But this solves both our problems. Because if anything happens to my sister while she's on your watch, I'll kill each and every one of you."

I huff. "Wow, you really know how to ask for a favor."

Alessio shrugs. "It's obvious I can't ask any of our men yet as I'm not sure who is on my father's payroll."

"Technically, they are all on your father's payroll," Niro says.

Alessio glances at Niro and rolls his eyes. "You always this pedantic?"

"Just getting started," he replies. "Are you always this much of a cunt when you're alone with a bunch of bikers who have no time for you at all?"

"That doesn't mean I haven't left clear, time-delayed information for my right-hand man to let him know where I went, who I was meeting with, and what we found. Anything happens to me, you won't survive the wrath of the five families."

"What do we get if we assist?" I ask.

"Beyond my sister?" Alessio asks. "And the promise to never come for your side of the docks?"

"Touché," Bates says.

"The next time you need an army-sized backup for something, we'll answer," Alessio says.

"You have the authority to authorize that?" Clutch asks.

Alessio stands tall. "I have over a thousand soldiers at my command as a captain. But if this works, tomorrow I'll be the boss of our family. Don Viscuso. Then there won't be anything I can't authorize. But back to the issue at hand. The easiest way to fix the problem we all have is to get rid of my father."

"Where does he live?" King says.

"Brooklyn. But it's a busy neighborhood. His brownstone

is a fortress. We need to get him out of there in a believable way."

"You need bait," Sophia says. "You need me."

"No fucking way are you being bait to get your father," I say.

"Why not?" Sophia looks up at me with defiant eyes and a level of bravery that amazes me.

"Because I won't let you get hurt."

"I call him. Tell him what happened here. That I'm confused. That Alessio is dead, and I'm scared. That I need him to come and get me."

"Still no."

"It could work," Alessio says. "He'll have to think on his feet and move fast. He might bring cleanup with him. But we could be ready. In position."

Saint looks up to the buildings. "Plenty of good spots to set up. If Soph could get him to say on the call how long it will take to get here, we'd know what we are working with."

I think through what they are saying, and the thought of Sophia caught up in the crossfire makes me feel so ill, I want to throw up. "She makes contact with him, and then I get her out of here."

Spark nods. "I'd make the same call."

"But if Papà arrives and doesn't see me, will he even get out of the car?" Sophia asks.

"Sophia," I warn. "We're not staying."

Not wanting a fight in front of my club, I take her hand and lead her away from the group a little. "Soph. We've done everything backwards. We married before we fell in love. I met you when you were already injured. I can't stand here and watch it happen in the present."

"You love me?" she asks.

"Off topic. We're talking about why you can't stay here if your dad comes."

"For the record, I love you."

"Your timing is terrible," I say.

"Maybe. But it's always the right time to tell someone you love them, right?"

I cup her cheeks and kiss her with all I have. "Yes, I fucking love you, Soph. Which is why I can't let you stand out here as bait."

"I'll be safe."

"How do you know that?"

"Because I have you. Because I know you aren't going to let anything happen to me, are you, Switch?"

The use of my road name catches me off guard. Not in a bad way. Something settles.

I glance back at my brothers, knowing they'll back whatever decision I feel is right today.

I take in the chaos of this life. That I'm here. That the air threatens snow. That blood pumps throughout my veins.

And I take in the warmth of my wife's cheeks, the affirmation of life as I run my thumb over the scar that crosses her cheek. The fact I'm fucking loved.

"My road name sounds good coming from your lips," I say before planting another kiss on them.

"Help me. Theo. Help me take back what happened to me. Help me be a part of its resolution. I just...I need to be a part of how this ends."

I take in a deep breath. When she looks at me like this, her eyes pleading with me, resolute in her faith in me, I can't say no.

"I'll help you end this. I'd scorch the earth for you if I had to."

"Then we'll do this how we've done everything else. Together."

Which is how I find myself passing Sophia a cigarette five minutes later.

"You sure this is going to work?" Halo asks.

I take a draw on the cigarette because fuck knows I need the nicotine, then blow the smoke away from Sophia before handing it to her. "Yeah. She needs to look distressed. I let her try one once and she coughed and spluttered like she was dying."

"I did not look like I was dying," Sophia says. Niro applied some dirt to her face and clothes to make it look like she's been through some shit.

"Sparrow, your eyes streamed for a good five minutes."

"Because these cancer sticks are poisonous. When we're done here, you need to stop."

Halo chuckles. "You should ask King about his Stop Smoking stickers."

"Fuck you," King says, dragging one of the dead bodies to Alessio's car.

Clutch is clearing off a ledge so he can rest his gun on it, pointing towards the lot. "One gold star for not smoking that day was a blow job. Went all the way up to twenty points for—"

"You say another fucking word and you'll be the dead body sitting in this car," King says.

Sophia takes the cigarette from my hand, steps up onto her toes, and places her lips close to my ear. I grab her arms to steady her. "What if you could write your own pain chart?" Her words are breathy against my ear. "Like, one point and I dig my nails in real hard, and ten points mean I'll stitch your skin whether it needs it or not."

"Jesus, Sparrow," I say as my cock hardens in my jeans.

"Always willing to help." The smile on her face tells me she knows what she just did to me.

I reach into my pocket, grab my half-finished pack of smokes, and toss them to Halo. "I'm quitting smoking."

"Of course you fucking are," Halo says as he catches them. "Not sure I ever want to know what you're gonna redeem your points for."

"I'm going to need to bleach my ears out," Alessio says. "There are some things a brother isn't meant to know about his little sister."

Sophia grins. "Maybe you shouldn't be listening in on private conversations."

King slaps Alessio's back. "That fucker is engaged to mine." He points to Clutch. "And I know exactly what you mean."

"You ready?" I ask Sophia.

"I am."

I settle everyone around us, and Sophia takes two long, spluttery, coughing inhales on the cigarette before she hands it back to me, then huddles into the corner of the old building.

Tears stream from her eyes. The coughing fit brought color to her cheeks. The dirt Niro applied to her face becomes tearstained.

"Papà," she says when he answers the video call. "Please. Can you come get me?" She pauses and pretends to look around, terrified.

I can't catch everything he says in response. As planned, Niro lets off two rounds of bullets into the air outside, and Sophia winces as she jumps.

"Something happened. We were attacked. Men. I don't know who. Alessio is dead. Theo abandoned me."

She swipes at her eyes and sobs. "Please, Papà. I don't know who else to trust."

When she finally tells him where we are, I breathe a sigh of relief.

The moment she ends the video call, I rush to her. "I'm proud of you."

"You okay, Puparu?" Alessio asks.

Sophia nods and I help her to her feet before using the sleeve of my Henley to wipe her eyes.

"Puparu? What does that mean?" I ask.

Alessio checks his phone. "It means 'puppeteer,' because even from when she was little, she's been able to pull everyone's strings. How long until he's here?"

"Forty minutes," Sophia says.

And it's the longest forty minutes of my life. We construct a place for Sophia to wait, and a concealed spot right next to it for me to hide in made from abandoned crates and lumber. There is the tiniest sliver in its construction that allows me to see a little.

Alessio lies on the ground by his car as if dead. The guy had cooly swiped some blood from the guy he shot through the head and wiped it over his own shirt to give the appearance of a lethal wound.

Got to admire the man's balls and commitment.

When Vincenzo Viscuso arrives, it's with three other vehicles. But I'm grateful that when they exit, there are only seven people that I can see.

It's almost suffocating, remaining hidden the way I am. Reminds me of all the time in hospital, being squeezed into tubes while doctors tried to figure out what had happened to me.

Sophia steps forward. "Papà," she says.

She isn't meant to move. I know Halo and Saint have the

area covered from an upper floor of the building. And, I see Bates, Niro, and Vex shifting behind the vehicles, preventing an exit. King, Clutch, and Spark are behind my position.

"Sophia," he says. "What the fuck happened here?"

She moves closer to him.

"Sophia," I hiss. But she ignores me.

"A lesson," she says coldly.

Vincenzo walks closer to his daughter, and I'm ready to burst out of my hiding place. Given we don't want a war with the Sicilians if this goes to shit or if Alessio goes back on his word, I remain out of sight.

I've often wondered what I felt the night I got injured. Was I scared? Did I know I would get hurt and did it anyway? Did I think I was safe and then get caught off guard?

But if it was anything like this, then it was a gut-level belief that what I was about to do was the right thing.

Because when I see Vincenzo's arm lift a fraction of an inch, I know he's going for a weapon. And I'm running before he even has time to acknowledge my presence.

Alessio jumps to his feet and throws a garrote around his father's neck.

My brothers take out Vincenzo's men until he's the only one standing. With my gun raised, I reach Sophia's side.

I don't have a clear shot because there's every chance a through and through would happen, taking out Alessio, who stands behind him.

"What happened that morning?" Sophia asks.

"The two of you will never survive this," Vincenzo shouts as sweat beads on his forehead.

"We'll take our chances," Alessio says, tightening the wire around his father's neck until he's squirming, trying to get his fingers beneath it to make some room to breathe.

His face gets redder and redder.

My brothers emerge, creating a circle around us, their weapons drawn.

"You're dying today," Sophia says calmly. "There will be no priest to hear your confession, no one to act 'in persona Christi.' So, tell me."

Vincenzo's shoulders drop. "You know what I did."

"Why? Why try to get me to Sicily to marry a stranger? Why set this up? Why any of it?"

"Because it all got out of hand," Vincenzo says finally. "It was getting harder to hide the missing amounts. I knew if you were married to Don Consolo's son, it would be harder for him to kill me or ex-communicate the rest of you from the family. But you wouldn't let it drop. You came to me with spreadsheets you said made no sense. You thought someone else in the family was stealing first, and I could tell the day you realized it was me. I saw the security footage of you in my office after mass. I tried to stop you from running that morning, but you stole one of the cars on the driveway. I chased after you, but..."

"It was you in that car? Not one of Aglieri's men?" Sophia asks.

"There were two cars close to the house on the driveway. They'd both left their keys in 'em so Carmine could take a look at them. You remember how he was good with cars."

"Thanks to you, I don't remember shit," Sophia says.

Her father shakes his head, showing no remorse. "They were closer to the bathroom window. You just grabbed one and took off. When Carmine told me what he saw, I took the other. I followed you until..."

"You just left her?" Alessio asks with fury. "You saw her fucking accident happen and left?"

Sophia laughs. I can see the panic in her eyes. Alessio

loosens the hold of Viscuso for a moment, worry etched across his features.

"Soph?" I warn and pull her to me as she breathes, then stands up straight.

BAT.

"They estimate I was stuck in the wreck for several hours before I was found. That maybe if I'd received medical help sooner, the injuries wouldn't have been as severe."

"Should have stayed and made sure you were dead," her father says.

Sophia shakes in my arms, and I do the only thing I know will comfort her. I reach into my cut pocket for my switchblade and offer it to her. "I can do it for you, or you can do it yourself, Sparrow."

She takes it from me and as she walks to her father, she flicks the blade open and closed.

Vincenzo starts to fight harder against Alessio's hold, struggling to break free, even as he recognizes his fate.

"Sophia. No. Wait."

And when she reaches him, she stabs it straight through her father's eye.

EPILOGUE ONE
SWITCH

"Wait," Sophia says as I try to tug her down onto the rug in our family room where the fireplace roars and the lights on the Christmas tree sparkle.

"I've been a patient man. You wouldn't let me fuck you because you were too excited for all the presents. But most of them are unwrapped now, and I can't wait any longer."

My wife's laughter, when it's genuine and at the right moment, might be the sweetest sound I ever heard.

"I have one last present for you, and I know you're going to love it," Sophia says before disappearing out the room.

Wrapping paper litters the floor, and unwrapped gifts are stacked on the sofa and table.

It's been a busy month. We made a trip to Florida for Mom to finally meet Sophia, and they got on like a house on fire. And Sophia persuaded King that we should buy the abandoned lot we met her father on. Convinced him of the potential of a professional long-term industrial storage site. Then there was the utterly unsuccessful attempt to contact Cillian.

He's cut off all communication with Iris too.

When Sophia returns, she has a large board and a tool-box. "We doing some handiwork?" I ask as I stroke my cock through my gray joggers.

"I was thinking about something we talked about the day he died."

Sophia no longer talks about her father by name. He's not Papà nor Vincenzo. He's been relegated to *he* or *him*. There was no funeral. Alessio took care of the disposal of his body. And Sophia never asked any more questions about him.

I thought an MC was capable of some questionable shit, but even those closest to Vincenzo, like his wife, moved on without hysterics.

We went for dinner at Alessio's last night. Her brothers were all there. We ate *sfincione* and *falsomagro* and *anelletti al forno*, and I survived an evening with my wife's five brothers and mother. And no one mentioned Vincenzo.

"What was that, Sparrow?"

"The sticker chart for quitting smoking. We jokingly discussed it, but then never made it. So, here it is to help you quit."

I've *tried* to quit. It's been hit-and-miss. We went to Bethlehem to take some weapons to our brothers there, and too much alcohol led to smoking again.

"So," she says. Before I can say anything, she turns the board around. "With your permission, I thought I could help."

I climb to my knees and gesture with two fingers for her to bring it to me. As she gets closer, I can see her cheeks are blushing. In blocky letters it says, "QUIT SMOKING LADDER."

It has ten boxes, each with a day over it. The dates seem to be by week and go from January to March.

"In the toolbox are ten…things…that can inflict pain. And I thought that, well, if you went a week without smoking, you could pick one of the things out of the box and tell me to use it on you."

My whole body vibrates, wanting to know what's in the box.

"Every week, I get to pick one?"

"Only if you didn't smoke. If you did, we wipe all the marks off and start again. The goal is for you to get to ten weeks in a row without smoking."

She glances down at my joggers, which, quite frankly, are doing nothing to hide the raging boner I have.

"Open the toolbox and show me what you got me. Tell me what it does and how it hurts."

My voice sounds like it dropped an octave.

"Wait," I add. "Lose the pajamas first."

Sophia bites down on her lower lip and shimmies out of the pajama pants, then opens the buttons on the pajama top, leaving it just open enough that I can see her pussy but not her tits.

"Stay like that, because you look really fucking hot," I tell her.

She kneels close to me. So close, our knees almost touch. I want to reach out and nudge the pajama top off her shoulders. Or grab her hand by the wrist and put it on my cock for some relief.

The metal clasps make a rattling sound as she opens them, and I imagine getting used to the sound on a Saturday night, waiting for whatever is going to come out from within it.

"It starts small. This is a bead picker." It looks like a fat, lumpy pencil. But as she pushes the top, four claws come out. "It's used in jewelry making to pick beads up, but I thought..." She leans forward, pushes the four claws into my pec, and then releases the pusher, allowing the claws to pinch and scrape my skin as they close. It's the tiniest bite of pain. But then she does it quickly, over and over again in the same spot until I suck in a breath.

I tug her forward and crush her lips to mine, sinking my hand into her hair, pulling it firmly in the way I know she loves. Finally, she shoves at my chest.

"Do you want to see the rest?"

"Fucking yes!"

She pulls out a small crop. Like, leather. The kind that can slice skin. I take her wrist and lead her so the crop runs over the head of my cock. Even with the soft fabric between us, I can feel the rigidity of the crop. It'll hurt.

"Is this okay?" Sophia asks, her voice breathy.

I love the way she sounds when she's turned on.

"More than okay."

Sophia makes her way through all ten of them, leaving a scalpel till last. She runs her fingers over the scarification tattoo design I have on my chest. "This is for week ten. Niro is teaching me how to do this so that I can do it for you. I'm not the world's greatest artist, so it will only be a simple design. But by the time you get to week ten, I'll be ready."

"Your initials," I say immediately. "SCV."

"Then that's what I'll practice. But I'm thinking it should be SCR, right?"

My last fucking name. "Perfect."

She squeals as I tug her so she's sitting over me. I wiggle my sweats down over my hips, and then ease her down on my cock, making us both gasp.

"Fuck, you feel so good."

We got tested, and Sophia went on birth control. Kids are a thing she's decided she wants, but after consultation with her doctors and an honest discussion where we agreed we just want to enjoy being a couple for a while, we decided it was best to wait. And to be honest, I love the way we are right now. The two of us are creating the best fucking life we can.

"You'll do it while riding me like this. I want you to fuck my cock while you hurt by body."

Sophia tips her head back as she rides me. I grip her hips and thrust up into her.

Being so deep in her pussy is the best it's ever been. And I can say that with certainty as significant chunks of my memory have returned over the past month. So has my understanding of my relationship with pain.

Shockingly, I ended up talking to Doc about it. And Doc showed how fucking cool she is by helping me understand it.

There's no trauma I'm trying to escape.

No deep reason of why I like it.

I just do.

Like a good fucking orgasm, I love those ten seconds your world shakes from pain.

Even better if the two things happen together.

And Soph...she just rolls with it. No, more than that, she enjoys it.

We have a delicate balance. A power exchange that only works for the two of us. I tell her to hurt me, and she loves doing it to me. She's no sadist; it's the joy that comes from doing exactly what I tell her. We can't really explain it to anyone else.

And the dynamic never slips outside of sex.

I reach for Sophia and pull her down to me so I can kiss her. "Thank you. For all of this. For knowing me. For taking me for what I am and embracing it with me."

She smiles. "Thank you for marrying me even before we really knew each other."

I'm so into fucking her that I almost forget. "I have one last gift for you." I flail my hand beneath the sofa where I tucked it last night. "Here."

She sits up and takes it, the gesture impaling her so fully on my cock there is no space between us.

The wrapping is a total hack job because, quite frankly, my left hand is never going to be quite the same again. Brain function, nerve damage... Who knows why I struggle to bring my fingers and thumb together? Physical therapy has helped. But if all I'm left with is an inability to wrap gifts and a preference for clothes without buttons, then I'm doing okay.

It takes Sophia all of two seconds to shake the cut I got for her free of the paper.

"Sparrow," she says softly as she takes in her name patch. Then she turns it around and her smile grows. "Property of Switch."

"Check the pocket."

She does as I say and pulls out a small box. When she opens it, her jaw drops as she sees the wedding ring I put in it. "You got an engagement ring that we used at the wedding. So, this is your wedding ring. Inscribed with Theo and Sophia. The cut is who we are to the world. Switch and his Sparrow. But the ring is who we are to each other. Theo and Sophia."

I take it from the box and slide it on her finger as she hasn't put her engagement ring on yet for the day.

"I love you," she says.

"Good. Because I love you too. Now finish fucking me, because you're the only thing I really wanted for Christmas."

EPILOGUE TWO
VEX

"Uncle Vex?"

I look down at Avery, my brother Bates's little girl. "What's up, sweet cheeks?"

She climbs up onto the barstool next to me, ignoring the New Year's Eve party swirling around us.

The clubhouse is full, the rock music is loud, and the single brothers have been put on notice by Niro that if he sees any of them doing anything above PG-grade shit with club girls in front of Avery, he'll slit their throats.

"What are invest-i-ments?"

I grin. "Investments?"

"Yeah. Those."

"It's when you take a hundred bucks and use it to buy into something, like a company. And if the company does well, they give you more than a hundred bucks back."

Her eyes narrow. "How much more?"

I shrug. "That's the problem. You don't know. They might even make a loss. So, they only give you ninety of your hundred bucks back."

Her mouth opens and little lines form across her nose. "They steal your money?"

"No. It's like, they used that hundred bucks to make more money and it didn't quite work, so they can't give you it all back. Or, sometimes, it works so well, they give you lots of money back. Why you asking?"

"I overheard Uncle Switch tell Uncle Clutch that you are really good at making him money."

She's not wrong. Neither is Switch. I'm a goddamn genius. Plus, I write and run a little code to trade foreign currencies off against one another. "That's fair. I am."

At this, she grins and shrugs her panda backpack off her shoulders. "Is there a hundred bucks in here?"

We all know what the panda backpack holds. Every time Niro swears around her, he pays her five bucks. At one point she was saving for a dog. Don't know what the fuck happened to that, but I heard Bates's old lady, Vi, is allergic.

And Avery never lets anyone look inside her backpack. Bates is worried it's going to need its own security detail eventually because of how much cash is stuffed into it.

"You want me to count it for you?" I glance around to see where Bates and Vi are and find them dancing together, but Bates's eyes are on his daughter.

"She okay?" I can't hear him over the music, but I catch his drift.

I nod. "I got her."

Bates grins and looks back at Vi, causing a ripple of envy to pass through me.

"Okay," I say, grabbing a cloth that sits on top of the bar. "Lesson one about money. You gotta respect it and be grateful for it." I wipe the bar top down until it is dry.

"I said thank you to Uncle Colton for the money."

"Good girl. Now, open panda up."

When she does, fives spill out all over the bar top. Some are crumpled, some folded, all are bent. "Ave," I say. "Girl. We gotta take better care of the notes than this. Let's unfold them all and lay them flat, yeah?"

Avery kneels up on the stool. "I have so much money, Uncle Vex."

"I can see." I mean, there might even be a grand here. Maybe more. "What are you going to do with it?"

"I'm gonna buy my own bike and start my own clubhouse where boys aren't allowed and only girls make the rules."

Her answer makes me chuckle. "You're gonna need a bit more than this."

She turns and points secretively to my brother, Niro. "Do you think Uncle Colton is gonna stop swearing anytime soon?"

"Definitely not."

She claps her hands with glee. "I know."

"Girl, you are gonna be a troublemaker when you are older."

I glance up to the mirror that frames the bottles behind the bar and can see club life playing out behind me.

Voices raise, women hug, couples kiss.

Blah. Blah. Blah.

If my life were a movie, this would be a montage. Beer spilling in slow motion. Happy faces. A room full of hope and potential for the next three hundred and sixty-five days.

Another three hundred and sixty-five days of...

I draw a blank.

I've got no New Year's resolutions. Don't even know what I'm going to do tomorrow or beyond. My life plays out no more than a few hours in front of me. I'll turn and hug my best friend Switch, I'll message my mom, I'll drink a few more beers, then I'll find a club girl to take back to my room for some...

What? Fun?

I glance back down at the growing piles of notes as we straighten and unfurl them. This is more fun.

"You know, if I invest this for you, it means you'll have to give all these notes over to me. And we'll have to get you a little book called a ledger, where we write down how much you gave me, and I write down where it's all gone to be invested."

Avery bites on her lip for a second. "It won't be in your office?"

I shake my head. "It will be in a safe place though." I'm not gonna explain to a kid how internet banking or trading platforms work. Not when I've already got too much whiskey sloshing through my system.

"I trust you, Uncle Vex."

When it's all unfolded, we put them into piles of twenty notes. "So, if each pile is one hundred dollars, how many piles do you have?"

Avery taps the top of them. "Nineteen."

"So, what's nineteen times one hundred?"

Avery laughs. "I can't count that big, silly."

"It's nineteen hundred dollars which is a lot of money. Bet I can double it for you."

Her jaw drops wide open. "You can do that?"

The way she looks at me like I'm a superhero says I'll do even better or pay her the difference myself. "Sure thing, kid. What kind of things do you like so I can decide good investments for you?"

Avery drums her fingers on the top of the bar. "I like Daddy's motorbike. And princess movies, but only if the princess fights. I like Uncle Colton's pancakes. And

Mommy's face when she wears makeup, and sometimes she lets me wear lipstick. And Mac, Auntie Iris's service dog that I'm not allowed to touch. And I liked when we went on an airplane to Mexico for Uncle Colton's wedding, and I got all this money that had different coins. Oh, and I want my ears pierced, but Daddy said no, then even Uncle Colton said no. And if Uncle Colton says no, it must be a really bad idea, because usually he says yes to whatever I say."

I smile at the innocence of her answers. "Okay, I got a plan then. Let's invest in a diamond for princess sparkle and possible future diamond earrings. We could invest in currency, because that's what all the coins and notes are called. And I'll see where airlines and bike and cosmetic manufacturers sit on a price-to-earning ratio and see if we can find one of each."

She climbs up onto her knees, cups her hand to my ear and whispers, "I only understood the diamonds."

I put my hand around her waist so she doesn't fall off the stool. "I'm gonna invest in the things you like. Diamonds. Money. Airplanes. Makeup. And bikes."

Avery grins at that. "Yes. Make me enough to buy a clubhouse."

"I'll do my best."

She zips up her empty panda backpack and drops down off her stool. "I love you, Uncle Vex."

But she runs off before I have time to reply. "Yeah, love you too, sweet cheeks."

Everyone turns their attention to the flatscreen TV. There's a scramble as people find the one they want to be standing next to when the ball drops. Quickly, I stack the notes and shove them in my pockets.

"Ten," everyone calls out.

Bates lifts Avery into his arms and sandwiches her between him and his pregnant old lady.

"Nine."

Avery stretches out her hand behind her father's head so she can reach Niro, who has his arm around Cat. He holds her hand.

"Eight."

King wraps his arms around Rae's back, pulling her closer.

"Seven."

Halo lifts Ari into his arms and she wraps her legs around him, kissing him as if the ball already dropped. A baby monitor hangs off the back pocket of his jeans.

"Six."

Clutch thrusts a champagne glass into Gwen's hand as she laughs.

"Five."

Spark places his hands on Iris's very pregnant stomach, and whispers something that makes her place her hand over his heart.

"Four."

Saint fists his hands in Briar's hair and studies his woman intently.

"Three."

Catalina slides her hand into the back pocket of Niro's jeans.

"Two."

Switch cups Sophia's cheeks and kisses her like a starved man.

"One."

I'm all alone on this fucking stool wishing I was anywhere other than here.

"Happy New Year," Clutch booms and the clubhouse explodes around me.

More hugging. More backslapping. More shouts of making this year special.

"Happy New Year," Switch shouts in my ear as he finally lets go of Sophia and pulls me into a hug. "Let's make it a fucking good one, yeah?"

I admire his optimism. The last twelve months were rough on him and his woman. "To better things," I say.

I hug Sophia and kiss her unscarred cheek. "Happy New Year, sweetheart."

She grins. "Thank you. Do you have any resolutions?"

"Meh. Not really," I say. "You?"

Switch leans against the bar. "She's got a color-coded list."

"But the biggest one is I want to ask the club to let me build a real estate portfolio for them," Sophia says. "Plus, it's an easy way to wash cash."

"I like the way you think," I say. "I'd be interested in hearing more."

"Good," she says. "Because I have a whole presentation that—"

"It's New Year's Eve, Sparrow," Switch says. "Well, New Year's Day now. It's a party. No presentation talk tonight."

She looks up at Switch. "You're no fun." She looks back to me. "I suppose he doesn't want me to tell you I was talking about you yesterday morning either."

"You were?"

"My brother is having some issues with someone trying to hack into their system."

I love the way she says it so nonchalant. Like her brother isn't Alessio Viscuso, head of the New York Cosa Nostra.

"Pretty sure you shouldn't be telling me that," I say.

Switch pulls Sophia back against him and nuzzles the back of her ear. "I said no work, babe."

Sophia grins and ignores him. "I told him I'd ask you if you'd come take a look at it for him. It appears his tech team aren't as capable as you are, and I think that might piss him off a little."

"Pretty certain my president might have an issue with me helping out another criminal enterprise, but I'll run it by him," I say.

Sophia places her hand on my arm. "Thank you. I'll make sure he owes you for it."

And there's the natural shrewd businesswoman. Sophia may have lost her memory, but she knows at a visceral level how this game is played.

The noise of the clubhouse starts to bug me.

I'm grateful my club is happy, but I retreat to my office in the back of the kitchen.

I've been asked many times why I set up here in the old pantry, and they all think I'm just a nerd who wanted a cubby.

But the truth is so much more than that.

First, no wall is an exterior wall. If anything happens to the exterior, like when the Italians fucking bazookaed us, nothing will happen to my set up.

Second, if by some miracle someone manages to break into the clubhouse, they'll start with the offices on the other side of the club. Church, maybe. The treasurer and club secretary offices. By then, I'll have been notified through all the alerts I set up, and help will already be on the way before they have the time to find all my computers.

And third, it's fucking quiet most of the time. But when it's not, I hear the wildest shit. People forget I'm in here.

I know Ari and Halo have secretly started treatment at a

fancy clinic in New York to see if they can't find a way to have kids together, but it looks like their chances are slim from the early findings and I heard Halo hold and reassure Ari he was going to love her whether they had biological kids together or not.

I heard Rae ask King what it would feel like if he wasn't president of the Iron Outlaws. And for a sweet ten minutes, they pretended he wasn't before the reality sunk in that he was. He said he'd go into the carpentry and construction business with Niro because his dad would have liked the idea of the two of them looking out for each other. And Rae told him she'd love him no matter what he did, because any life would be better with him in it.

Clutch was devastated one night because Gwen safe-worded on him, and I heard Switch pick him up and put him back together, reminding me all over again why Clutch is a good man and why Switch is my best friend.

Still puzzling over why the fuck Gwen's safe word is flounder, though.

And I know Niro sees Avery as a do-over for his little sister who was murdered. One very drunken night, I over-heard him telling Bates that he wonders why hanging out with his sister when she was young was such a chore, because having Avery in his life is such a blessing. And he's angry that Bates has, in Niro's words, one point seven babies and Niro has none. The man is so fucking in love with his wife, that he's putting what he wants on hold so she can have what she wants. Freedom. A crack at becoming a brother. Something more than being an old lady. But that man needs babies of his own like a biker needs the road. Through the crack in the door, I saw Bates hug the shit out of his best friend.

Observing is what I do.

Through the security feeds to everyone's home and the trackers on their phones and vehicles, I keep watch.

It's how I keep everyone safe.

I flip my screen to the cameras around my folks' place. The lights of a flickering TV tell me they stayed up to watch the ball drop. No sign of a party though.

But there is a strange car lingering outside Mrs. Moray's drive.

I zoom in on the plate, my heart skipping a beat as I think through the possibilities.

Mrs. Moray only has one child.

A daughter.

Callie.

And once upon a time, she was my very best friend.

Our parents were friends. Mom knew her mom through church. We used to hang out on the front porch at night. As we grew older, we'd hack shit together. Once, we hacked our high school and changed our grades. Then we started doing petty shit. Stealing small amounts from big companies. Nobody paid attention. Two hundred bucks here. Five hundred bucks there. Suddenly we had some cash in our pockets. Until she went too far.

The pentagon.

The police.

Then she stole shit from me. Hacked *my* account to teach me a fucking lesson.

And while I was trying to figure out where we went wrong, she started to fuck with the kind of people you *really* don't fuck with.

She planned to hack the Outlaws.

She'd heard they made good money and was intent on taking a piece.

I might not have been able to protect her from the rest of

the world, or even from herself, but I knew I could protect her from the MC. So, I made a deal with Camelot.

I'd protect the club, to protect her. If she never stole from them, they wouldn't kill her for fucking them over.

Becoming an Outlaw wasn't something I thought I wanted. But I didn't know I'd find a home here.

The last time I saw her, well over a decade ago, she told me she'd kill me if she ever saw me again.

I run the plate. It's registered as a fleet vehicle for a company that does private rides from the airport. But just as I'm about to follow the trail to see where it leads, a tall woman dressed in black with a long ponytail steps out of the car.

And even in the shadows of night, Calista Moray has never looked better.

She checks something on her phone, then gets back into the car without stepping foot on her mom's driveway.

As I see the taillights moving away, I think back to what Sophia just told me.

About the Italians and how they're being hacked.

"Fuck, Callie," I mutter. "If that's you, I don't know how the hell I'm gonna save you this time."

I KNOW, I KNOW …
IT'S FINALLY VEX!!!

Read on for how to claim BONUS CONTENT.

I'm so incredibly grateful to you all for taking the time to read Switch and Sophia's story. What a whirlwind it was to write (and was by far the longest Outlaw book to date!). I hope you loved them as much a I do. It was quite the undertaking and as always involved lots of my favourite RESEARCH!

And, yes, it's obvious now that Vex is the last and final book in this original New Jersey Chapter series. And, GAH, it's hard to let them go. You've heard how Vex joined the Iron Outlaws from everyone except Vex. But only he knows the real truth. At least, he thinks he does. But when his former best friend and fellow hacker returns to New Jersey over a decade later, they're forced to piece the full story of their lives together and it won't unravel how he or the Iron Outlaws expect.

You can pre-order Vex's story now.

And, yes, I did mention bonus content featuring Switch and Sophia. If you remember early in their relationship, Sophia told Switch she think's she a forest girl now … and Switch decides to test the theory!

You can access it by signing up for my newsletter here https://newsletter.scarlettcole.com/thefateswetame. Don't forget to double opt in or you won't receive it. Be warned … as always, it's utterly NSFW. (You'll need to sign up again to get it if you are already on my list.)

ACKNOWLEDGEMENTS

I'm so grateful to all of you for taking the time to read Switch and Sophia's story and would love you forever if you would take a minute to rate or review or share it if you loved it. The series has only been possible because of how generous you've all been with your love for these boys. I had no idea when I started we'd make it all way to nine.

Thanks to my amazingly talented team:

Manu, Nicole, and Virginia for making the story shine.

Letitia, Wander, and Brandon for the incredible cover.

Dani and Josh for their marketing and advertising wizardry.

To my Passionistas for just being the very best place on the inter web!

Thanks to Rachel Hamilton. The Bates to my Niro. You really are a rockstar, but still need to learn how to share my heroes.

And thank you T, F, & L ... you support what I do with infinitely more energy than I deserve. I love you all.

ABOUT THE AUTHOR

Scarlett Cole is a contemporary romance author that calls both Toronto, Canada and Manchester, England home. A born city dweller, she periodically quashes the urge to live in the country by hiking up a mountain to remind herself that living away from people would terrify the pants off her.

She believes everybody deserves their love story to be told and loves her heroes on the rough and rugged side...and usually tall (because she married one of those 6ft 6" men you read about in romance books!). She's an A-type personality and Scorpio star sign, so good luck getting her to do anything she doesn't want to.

When she isn't writing, she's happy to talk about hot men and expensive shoes while drinking a cold gin and tonic. Don't bring up olives. As far as Scarlett is concerned, they are the devil's food. As long as you don't bring up olives, she's happy to hear from you any time.

ALSO BY SCARLETT COLE

Iron Outlaws MC Series

The Sins We Hide

The Games We Play

The Lies We Tell

The Bonds We Break

The Vows We Keep

The Loves We Lost

The Souls We Claim

The Fates We Tame

The Deals We Make

Excess All Areas / Sad Fridays Series

One Day Like This

Next Time I Fall

How Good It Was

Love You Like That

Let Me Love You

Love Distilled Series

Love In Numbers

Love In Moments

Love In Secrets

Preload Series

Jordan Reclaimed

Elliott Redeemed

Nikan Rebuilt

Lennon Reborn

The Sweetest Gift

Second Circle Tattoos Series

The Strongest Steel

The Fractured Heart

The Purest Hook

The Darkest Link

The Greatest Risk (Novella)

Love Over Duty Series

Under Fire

Final Siege

Deep Cover

Made in the USA
Monee, IL
09 December 2024

73012608R00213